IR

CODE OF CONDUCT

BRAD THOR

CODE OF CONDUCT

**SIMON &
SCHUSTER**

London · New York · Sydney · Toronto · New Delhi

A CBS COMPANY

First published in the US by Atria, an imprint of Simon & Schuster, Inc, 2015
First published in Great Britain by Simon & Schuster UK Ltd, 2015
A CBS COMPANY

1 3 5 7 9 10 8 6 4 2

Simon & Schuster UK Ltd
1st Floor
222 Gray's Inn Road
London WC1X 8HB

www.simonandschuster.co.uk

Simon & Schuster Australia, Sydney
Simon & Schuster India, New Delhi

A CIP catalogue record for this book
is available from the British Library

Hardback ISBN: 978-1-47115-189-7
Trade Paperback ISBN: 978-1-47115-190-3
eBook ISBN: 978-1-47115-192-7

Printed and bound by CPI Group (UK) Ltd, Croydon, CR0 4YY

For my outstanding literary agent, Heide Lange.
What a ride! Thank you for every magnificent second.

"If you must break the law, do it to seize power."

—Julius Caesar

PROLOGUE

When word leaked that the President had been taken to the Bethesda Naval Hospital for observation, panic set in. If the President of the United States wasn't safe from the virus, no one was.

Scot Harvath swerved around the car in front of him and sped through the intersection as the light changed. The traffic was worsening. Quarantine rumors had sent people rushing to stores to stock up.

"We don't need to do this," the woman sitting next to him said.

What she meant was that *he* didn't need to do this. He could leave too. He didn't have to stay behind in D.C.

"I've already talked to Jon and his wife," he replied. "You'll be safe there."

"What about you?"

"I'll be okay. I'll join you as soon as I can."

He was lying. It was a white lie, meant to make her feel better, but it was a lie nonetheless. They were already talking about shutting down air traffic. That's why he needed to get her out tonight.

"What if we're overreacting?" she asked.

"We're not."

Lara knew he was right. She had seen the projections. Even the "best case" numbers were devastating. The cities would be the hardest hit. Hospitals were already at surge capacity, and were being overrun by otherwise healthy people who had convinced themselves they were showing one or more of the symptoms. It was beginning to make it impossible for real emergencies like heart attack and acute asthma sufferers to be seen. And it was only going to get worse.

Cities, towns, and villages from coast to coast scrambled to figure out how they would continue to deliver essential services, much less deal with the staggering number of bodies if the death toll reached even half of what was being predicted. In a word, they *couldn't*.

As they succumbed to the virus, or stayed home to protect their own families, fewer and fewer first responders would be available. Soon, 911 call centers would go down. After that, water treatment facilities and power plants. Hospitals, pharmacies, and grocery stores would have all long ceased operating—the majority of them looted and burned to the ground. Chaos and anarchy would reign.

The only people who might hope to survive were those who had exercised some degree of caution and had prepared in advance. But even then, there was still no guarantee. Riding in the wake of Death and his pale horse was another force that would prove just as devastating—those who planned to take advantage of the chaos.

Suddenly, two blue-and-white Department of Homeland Security Suburbans spun around the corner and came racing toward them, their lights and sirens blaring.

Harvath jerked his wheel hard to the right to get out of their way. Even then, he came within inches of being hit before the DHS vehicles swerved back into their lane.

Lara turned in her seat as they sped past. "Jesus!" she exclaimed. "Did you see that? They almost hit us."

The chaos had officially started.

Before he could respond, his cell phone rang. "Good," he said, after listening to the voice on the other end. "We're ten minutes away."

Disconnecting the call, he pressed harder on the accelerator and told her, "The plane just landed. Everything will be ready by the time we get there."

Nearing the private aviation section of Reagan International, there was a sea of limousines and black Town Cars. He wasn't the only one who had seen the writing on the wall. Those who could get out were getting out now.

Not wanting to get tied up in the parking lot, he pulled to the side of the road near the entrance and hopped out to get Lara's bag.

Opening the rear of his Tahoe, he plugged his combination into one of the drawers of his TruckVault and pulled it open.

"I already have my duty weapon," Lara said. "Plus, my credentials and extra ammo."

She was always armed. He knew that. Removing a small, hard-sided Pelican Case, he handed it to her. "Just in case," he said.

Lara popped the latches and flipped open the lid. "Sat phone?" she asked.

Harvath nodded. "If this gets worse, the cell phone network won't stay up for long."

"Is my cell even going to work up there?"

"Once you leave Anchorage, you might as well turn it off until you get to the lodge. There's no cell service there, but you can make calls over their WiFi."

Removing the battery cover, he showed her where he had taped the number for the sat phone he kept in his bug-out bag. If everything failed, the sat phones would be their fallback.

Closing up the Tahoe, he picked up her bag and walked with her to the Signature Flight Support building. Inside, it was pandemonium.

Wealthy families jostled with corporate executives to speed the departure of their jets. There were mountains of luggage and from what he overheard, a vast array of destinations—Jackson Hole, Eleuthera, Costa Rica, Kauai—likely second or third home locations where they hoped to ride out the storm.

Harvath spotted their copilot who took Lara's bag and the Pelican Case and walked them out to the jet.

Harvath didn't want a long goodbye. He wanted them in the air as quickly as possible.

Wrapping his arms around her, he kissed her. It felt detached, distant. His mind had already left the airport. It was on to the dangerous assignment that lay in front of him.

"It's still not too late," she said.

It was and she knew it.

"You need to get going," he replied, giving her one more kiss as he broke off their hug.

"See me onto the plane."

It was too loud on the tarmac to hear the chime, but he felt his phone vibrate in his pocket. Pulling it out, he read the message. Now he really needed to go.

"I can't," he said, kissing her one last time. "Let me know when you get there."

With that, he turned and walked back to the Signature Flight Support building.

• • •

As soon as he was inside, he called the person who had texted him. "Are you positive about this?" he asked.

"One hundred percent," the voice on the other end responded.

"How long do I have?"

"Could be hours. Could be days. What are you going to do?"

"What would you do?" Harvath asked.

"Get my affairs in order and hope it's painless."

CHAPTER 1

The heavy truck rolled through the early morning darkness. Mist clung to the damp jungle road.

Scot Harvath pulled out his phone and watched the video again. How many times had he seen it now? *A hundred? Two hundred?*

It was shaky and parts were out of focus. A team in biohazard suits could be seen going into a small medical clinic. Moments later, there were muzzle flashes and gunfire. Then nothing.

The footage had been emailed to CARE International, the U.S.-based charitable organization that had helped establish the clinic. The video quickly made its way to CARE's founder, businessman cum philanthropist, Ben Beaman.

Over the next several hours, Beaman tried to contact the Matumaini Clinic in eastern Congo. No one replied. Finally, he hit the panic button and reached out to the most senior person he knew at the State Department. But with no Americans at the clinic at the time, there was little the State Department could do. It was "outside their mission," as his contact informed him. The man offered to make some calls on his behalf, but told Beaman not to get his hopes up.

Beaman saw CARE as a family. An attack on one of them was an attack on all of them. He made no distinction whether the person was from Kinshasa or Kansas City. If the State Department wouldn't help, he'd have to look elsewhere.

But where? Even if he knew someone there, the FBI and CIA were just as likely to say no. Some tiny African clinic in the middle of nowhere was outside everyone's "mission." But there had to be someone who could help him.

Which had gotten him thinking.

When one of his doctors had been kidnapped from the CARE hospital in Afghanistan, a particularly resourceful man had been hired to fly over and get her back. That was the kind of help he needed.

It took Beaman several phone calls to track Scot Harvath down. He was working for a private intelligence company that didn't advertise. They didn't need to.

The majority of the Carlton Group's work had previously been via black contracts through the Department of Defense. Now, though, they were finding themselves repeatedly tasked on covert operations by the White House and the Central Intelligence Agency.

There had been a rough patch when the Carlton Group had no choice but to take anything that came their way, but that was in the past. They seldom took private assignments anymore. When they did, there had to be a compelling reason.

Similar to Doctors Without Borders, CARE went where few dared and even fewer wanted to go. From Mumbai to Mogadishu, they had set up shop in some of the worst poverty-stricken backwaters of the third world.

While there, CARE's western volunteers not only treated locals but helped local medical personnel improve their skills. They were good people who did good things for those in desperate need. The organization was also one that was no stranger to violence.

Over the years, their facilities and personnel had experienced a handful of attacks. They took security seriously, but there was only so much they could afford to do. They wanted to use as much of their money as possible helping people. That was their *mission*.

They had been planning to open two more clinics in Congo, but Beaman had put a temporary stop to those. Until they knew what had happened at the Matumaini Clinic, they weren't moving on anything.

While the U.S. Government didn't like to use NGOs for covert operations, the Carlton Group's founder had a different view. He had a couple of relationships already, but nothing like CARE. Getting them into his back pocket could be invaluable.

Even better, Beaman had offered to pay the Carlton Group a significant premium. It was a dangerous assignment and Beaman appreciated the risks. He only had one stipulation. He wanted Scot Harvath leading the operation.

Right out of the gate, they had a problem. Technically, Harvath wasn't available.

He had been working at a furious tempo and had just come off of a hellacious operation in Syria. Everything at home had been put on hold, and that included his relationship.

She lived in Boston and Harvath lived outside D.C., near Alexandria. The distance made things difficult enough. What was making it almost impossible, though, was how many times Harvath had rescheduled with her or had left the country entirely without giving her any notice at all. She had asked him to put one week on the books, then set it in stone, wrap it in bulletproof Kevlar, and bury it under fifty feet of concrete.

Harvath picked one, went to Carlton, and had him sprinkle holy water on the dates. The deal was done.

They would take in New England's fall colors. She pulled strings at work to have the same week off. She rented the perfect cottage on the water and convinced the Realtor to take delivery of two cases of their favorite wine. It would be a great surprise.

They would stop at her favorite general store on the way and stock up on supplies. Once they arrived at the cottage, the wine would be there and they wouldn't have to leave for anything. The master bedroom had enormous windows and they could watch the colors peak from there. It was exactly what they needed.

When Reed Carlton, or the "Old Man" as Harvath referred to him, called, he got right to the point. "You've got a meeting in the office tomorrow morning. Be here by seven-thirty. Wear a suit."

Obviously, somebody important was coming in, but Carlton hadn't offered up any details. *Typical.* The old spymaster never revealed more than he wanted anyone to know.

Harvath didn't mind. He was used to it by now. He was also already half checked out, looking forward to a week away up in New England.

The next morning, the five-foot-ten Harvath showed up at the Carlton Group's offices in Reston, Virginia, coffee in hand, wearing a coal gray Ralph Lauren suit, white shirt, and a dark blue tie. With only cardio for his workouts overseas, he had dropped about ten pounds from his already fit frame.

His blue eyes stood out against his tan skin, and his sandy brown hair appeared lighter. In the mirror that morning, he had looked more like a beach-going Southern California college student, than a U.S. Navy SEAL turned covert counterterrorism operative.

The Old Man was already in the conference room with their guest. Harvath stepped in and was introduced to Ben Beaman, the Director of CARE International.

After Harvath asked how the doctor he had rescued in Afghanistan was doing, Carlton invited everyone to take their seats and then steered the conversation to the matter at hand.

Beaman had brought his laptop and ran both men through a quick PowerPoint about the Matumaini Clinic. The slides included pictures of the facility, its staff, and the people they served, mostly families with children.

The clinic's name came from the Swahili word for *hope*. It was deep in the jungle near the border with Uganda—the only medical facility for over two hundred kilometers. It boasted fifteen beds, an exam room that doubled as a laboratory, and a small dispensary.

Beaman's final slide contained the video of the attack. He pushed the *play* button and the three men watched.

When it was over, Beaman closed his laptop and sat back in his chair. "That's all we know," he had said.

The Old Man activated a flat screen beyond the conference table. On it, he explained, was recent satellite footage he had acquired.

When he clicked a small wireless device, the image was magnified, coming to rest on a small clearing that had been hacked out of the dense jungle. In the center was Beaman's clinic.

There was no sign of anyone anywhere near it.

Carlton held up his index finger as if to say, "There's something else," and then drew their attention back to the screen.

Manipulating the wireless device, he refocused the image, northwest of the clinic. There, they could see what looked like a long, scorched trench at the base of a hill. Tendrils of black smoke curled into the air from it.

"Any idea what that is?" the Old Man asked.

Beaman shook his head.

"Looks like a burn pit," Harvath replied. "A big one."

Carlton nodded. "I agree. Any thoughts on *what* they were burning?"

"I don't think it was trash."

Beaman looked from one man to the other, and the volume of his voice dropped. "Do you think they were burning *bodies*?"

The Old Man switched off the satellite footage. "It could be anything."

"But what if it *is* bodies?" he replied. "What if those are women and children? Our staff and patients?" He shifted his gaze to Harvath and asked, "If it's not trash, what is it?"

Harvath had been to more war-ravaged areas than he cared to remember. He had seen things beyond horrible. The worth of a culture, in his opinion, could be boiled down to one thing—how well that culture took care of its weakest members, particularly its women and children.

The satellite image of the burn pit brought back a flood of memories, none of them pleasant, none of them things he wanted to remember. Something about it, though, was odd. He tried to put his finger on it and when he couldn't, he relegated it to the back of his mind.

"Mr. Carlton is right," Harvath conceded. "It could be anything."

For a moment, Beaman didn't know how to respond. "But we all agree, it probably *wasn't* trash."

Harvath looked to the Old Man, then back at Beaman, and nodded.

An uncomfortable silence fell over the conference room. Finally, Beaman broke it. "Mr. Harvath, I want to find out what happened. Scratch that," he said, correcting himself. "I *have* to find out what happened. I owe it to those people, to *all* of my people. If this had happened to a team you were responsible for, I don't doubt that you'd feel the same way."

Harvath began to understand where this was headed. Beaman wanted him to lead the operation.

If their places were reversed, of course Harvath would want to know what had happened to his team. But this wasn't about a team of his. This was about Beaman's people, and there was a lot more to this story. It wasn't as simple as flying over and figuring out what had happened.

Congo was the world's *deadliest* conflict zone. Five and a half million dead in less than twenty years. Invasions from neighboring countries, wars, political instability—it was like a match factory, if match factories also stored buckets of gasoline and hung lit sparklers from the ceiling. Calling it unstable was too generous by half.

The danger and instability of the region were just two of the many problems Harvath saw with this situation. There was also a host of un-answered questions. No one even knew who had sent the video to CARE and worse still, no one could explain why the gunmen entering the clinic had been wearing biohazard suits.

According to Beaman, Matumaini was a small family medicine clinic. They didn't treat highly communicable illnesses. They didn't have the ca-pacity. The furthest they went was performing minor surgeries. If some-thing exotic or unusual walked in their door, they knew to call for help.

But as far as Beaman, or anyone at CARE knew, no such call had gone out.

Harvath didn't like it any of it. He hated loose ends. There were too many things stacked one upon another that didn't make sense.

Beaman was also running out of time. The longer it took to get a team over to Congo, the colder the trail would become. If something wasn't done soon, they might never know what happened and who was responsible.

Once again, a rush of unpleasant images moved across the screen of his mind's eye. The scenes of families were the hardest to stomach. He had witnessed what monsters could do. He knew what monsters con-tinued to do when not stopped. In this case, the monsters embodied an amplified evil. They had preyed not only on the sick and infirm, but also upon those who had helped to care for them.

His mind then drifted to his trip to New England, but only as an after-thought. He had already decided what he was going to do. What he told himself he *had* to do. The Carlton Group didn't have anyone else who could take on this kind of assignment with so little advance warning.

If he didn't agree to take charge, it wouldn't get done. The State

Department had passed, and Beaman was right, the FBI and CIA weren't going to help him either. Harvath was CARE's only hope.

It would be an absolute ballbuster of an assignment, and he would have to figure out a lot of it on the fly, but he knew he could do it. Just like he knew he could convince Lara that he had no choice but to postpone their trip to New England. He would find leaves for her someplace else, someplace even better. It would all work out.

And with his decision made, he had jumped in with both feet. Logistics, equipment, funds, support . . . it was chaos, but he relished the challenge because chaos was the arena in which he excelled. The Old Man had left him with one final directive. "Get in and get the hell out as fast as you can."

Within twenty-four hours, he was on the ground in the Democratic Republic of Congo. Twelve hours later, he had assembled his team and they were on their way north to the Matumaini Clinic.

Exiting out of the video player, he took another look at his text message screen before returning the phone to his pocket and powering down the tiny Iridium cube he used to access the satellite network. He had texted Lara when he had touched down to let her know that he had arrived safely. She had not responded and Harvath tried to put it out of his mind. He needed to get his head in the game.

If everything went according to plan, they would be in and out. At least that's what he had told himself. He had also told himself that he'd be able to sway Lara about cancelling, or as he had put it, *rescheduling* their trip. That had not gone over well with her at all.

But Scot Harvath had a bad habit of telling himself things he knew weren't true.

CHAPTER 2

Harvath's security team was made up of four Brits—all former SAS members. They had been with a private contracting company in Kenya called Ridgeback. There was too much money and too much action in Congo, though, so they left to form their own venture.

They called their four-man company Extremis. Harvath had never met any of them before, but they had come highly recommended. He had linked up with Patrick Asher and Mike Michaelson in Lubumbashi, where they loaded their gear onto the plane CARE had arranged for them.

Asher, or "Ash" as his men referred to him, was the team leader. He was in his early forties and reminded Harvath in a way of the Old Man. He was cordial, but all business. No jokes, no small talk, just straight to the point. His graying hair and dark eyes gave him an added air of intensity.

Michaelson, on the other hand, was different. Known by his teammates as "Mick," he was a short, muscular man in his thirties with a shaved head, and a neck like a tree trunk. Everything amused him. Within the first ten minutes of their having met, he had slapped Harvath on the back at least three times.

After loading their equipment, they flew north to Bunia, the provincial capital of Ituri. Waiting for them, were the other two members of the team, Simon Bruce and Evan "Eddie" Edwards.

On the flight up, Mick had referred to Simon and Eddie as the "Brute Squad." Meeting them, Harvath understood why.

They were large men, both in their thirties, well over six feet tall and half a block wide. Unlike their clean-shaven compatriots from Lubumbashi, they sported facial hair. But not just any kind of facial hair.

Simon had the biggest, reddest beard Harvath had ever seen. He looked like a lumberjack on steroids. Eddie sported a meticulous, jet-black Van Dyke that made him look like he had just stepped out of a Captain Morgan ad. Congo was already living up to its Wild, Wild West reputation.

Accompanying Simon and Eddie was their fixer, a skinny, young Congolese man they had nicknamed "Jambo," which meant hello in Swahili. Because his real name was practically impossible for anyone to pronounce and because of the manic enthusiasm with which he greeted people, the Jambo nickname had stuck.

Two white Toyota Land Cruisers stood idling on the tarmac. One was outfitted for carrying passengers, the other for hauling cargo. Both had been tricked out with off-road packages that included lift kits, snorkels, winches, and mud tires.

Like the fixer Ash had paid off in Lubumbashi, Jambo had made sure no Bunia airport personnel would interfere with them while they offloaded their gear into the vehicles.

As the team transferred everything over, Harvath handed Ash the car door magnets Beaman had provided. They proclaimed, in black and red letters on a white background, that the vehicles were on official humanitarian business from CARE International. They even included little red crosses.

There were stickers as well that showed AK-47s with Xs through them, and these were placed in the vehicle windows as well. Once the gear was packed inside, tied down to the roof racks, and ready to roll, they left the airport and headed into the capital.

Jambo had secured rooms for them at the best place in town, the two-star Bunia Hotel.

To its credit, it had high walls, a secure gate, beer, and a pool table. By eastern Congo standards, it was the height of luxury. The kitchen even turned out halfway decent Chinese and Indian food, something Harvath hadn't expected.

Even though the hotel's motor court was enclosed, Jambo had hired two of his relatives to spend the night with the vehicles.

After checking in and moving the most sensitive of their gear to their rooms, the team reconvened in the lobby. Their first round of beers had just been served when the final member of the operation walked into the lobby.

She was a tall blonde in a tight green T-shirt and even tighter gray REI hiking pants. A pair of Oakley sunglasses hung around her neck and dangled between her breasts. Her arms were buff and she sported a healthy tan. Freckles formed an imperfect bridge over a perfect nose. Her eyes, even in the half-light of the lobby, were a piercing gimlet-green.

Unshouldering her pack, she had dropped it next to the pool table and introduced herself around to the team. Brash and unafraid, right from the jump.

Before becoming a physician, Dr. Jessica Decker had been a war correspondent. She knew all too well what men were capable of doing to each other. Having seen enough suffering, particularly in Congo, she had decided she wanted to do more than just write about it. That's why she left journalism and had gone into medical school.

She had been working with CARE for less than a year when she was asked to open the Matumaini Clinic on their behalf. She went on to carry out three subsequent missions there. She knew the area and its people better than anyone else.

She was in the middle of opening one of CARE's two new clinics—a facility outside Kinshasa—when everything was put on hold.

Beaman had thought she could be helpful in the current situation and the Old Man had agreed. It had been two to one, and Harvath was overruled. Decker, Carlton had decided, wouldn't only be coming along, but she could also be part of their cover.

Not even Ash and his team knew the full extent of what was going on. As far as they knew, they had been hired to accompany a load of medical supplies and two members of CARE International to a clinic in the Ituri Province. It was dangerous territory and the middleman for CARE claimed they had been robbed twice before en route. CARE wanted to make sure that didn't happen again.

Ash had guaranteed that his team would do everything they could to make sure that didn't happen. He felt relatively confident this would be a sure thing. Then Harvath had stepped off the plane in Lubumbashi.

The American had "operator" written all over him. Ash could tell right away that there was more to this assignment than he and his team had been told. Quietly, he passed the word to each of his men to be on their guard. When the woman arrived, the complication factor escalated.

She was incredibly attractive, too attractive for Congo—a rough place where people prized commodities above all else and would pay or do anything to get what they wanted. She didn't belong here, yet she had walked in like she owned the place. Already she was playing with them.

The shirt that showed off her chest, the tight pants that hugged her ass, the careful application of makeup—just enough to make it look like she wasn't wearing any makeup at all—it all came together and spelled trouble. Ash was beginning to wonder if taking this assignment had been a mistake.

Harvath didn't know what to think of Jessica Decker either. The woman who entered the hotel was certainly not what he had expected. Beaman had forwarded a CARE newsletter to him with a bland photo taken in the field. It certainly hadn't prepared him for what she looked like in real life. Not that it would have mattered, much. The fact that she was here was just a reminder that he didn't have a say in the matter.

After introducing herself around, she had walked over to the bar to order. Harvath fought the urge to watch her, and he watched the security team instead. Ash's men looked like a pack of wild dogs ready to go to war over a pork chop.

There weren't a lot of western women in Congo and certainly not many, if any at all, who looked like Jessica Decker.

If Harvath knew that, she had to too, which meant she knew exactly what she was doing. That was fine by him. Some SEALs were notorious for their extracurricular adventures overseas. Why should it be any different for a woman? He knew all too well how hard it could be to maintain a relationship when you spent so much time away from home.

Whatever she did with her personal time was her business. As long as it didn't become a distraction, Harvath planned to ignore the whole issue.

They ate a good meal, played some more pool, and established a rendezvous time for the morning. Harvath was the first to excuse himself.

He had several emails to respond to, and wanted to take a shower before turning in.

He bought two bottles of Primus beer at the bar to go, said goodnight to everyone, and returned to his room.

When Harvath walked into the motor court at four a.m. that Thursday morning, Ash and his men were already there loading and inspecting the vehicles. It was cool, only in the low 50s, and had rained heavily during the night. The dirt road outside the hotel had already turned to red mud.

As Harvath placed his bag inside the Land Cruiser, designated as *LC1*, Dr. Decker appeared beside him. Reaching out, he accepted her pack and placed it inside as well. She smiled and thanking him added, "Is there any coffee anywhere?"

"Coffee, coffee. Yes, yes," said Jambo as he stepped out of the hotel with two large thermoses. "Breakfast too," he stated, nodding toward a staffer following behind with a hot tray of eggs, rice, and cheese wrapped in naan bread, nuked in the microwave and then wrapped in foil for the ride. Harvath helped himself to two.

After the vehicle inspections were complete and all the equipment loaded, Ash give the order to mount up. Once the gates were opened, they splashed out into the road and headed north.

Of the hundred thousand miles of mapped roads in Congo, less than two percent were actually paved. Of those paved roads, only half were in good condition. In short, travelling anywhere in Congo was an incredible pain in the ass. That went double once you got outside any of its larger towns. The few grass airstrips that existed required constant maintenance, and almost all of those that had been carved from the jungles had been abandoned over the years. Missionaries came and left. Nature always reclaimed what was rightfully hers.

In a poverty-stricken country of seventy million, with a landmass the size of the American Midwest, everyone was on the make. This was especially true in the lawless eastern part of Congo, where various rebel factions controlled almost everything. With the average wage about a dollar a day and an AK-47 selling for fifty dollars, locals got creative fast. That "creativity" only added to the stress of traversing Congo by car.

Ash radioed the Brute Squad in the Land Cruiser behind them carrying Jambo and the cargo, "LC1 to LC2. Tollbooth coming up. Fifty meters. Everybody stay calm."

All it took was a log, a rope, or a long enough piece of chain and anyone could establish a "tollbooth" in this part of the country. They were normally staffed by rebel forces, crooked police, or legit military looking to augment their meager incomes. Some of the impromptu tollbooths were said to pull in $700,000 or more a year. It was a racket, to be sure, and the men who ran them ruled the roads with an iron fist.

In order to make sure that no one assaulted these setups, or tried to blow through without paying, they hid ambush teams farther up the road. Depending on the terrain, sometimes the team was one hundred meters ahead; sometimes it was a couple of miles. It was the perfect insurance policy. You might make it past the tollbooth without paying, but you had no idea where the ambush team would be. Not only would the ambush team take your life, they would also use your corpse and that of your fellow passengers as an advertisement to others who might think they could avoid paying their fair share.

Ash had briefed Harvath and Dr. Decker about his position on the tolls as they rolled out of Bunia. While he hated paying off thugs, a hundred dollars for two vehicles was just the cost of doing business in Congo.

Despite the coffee and piss-poor roads, Jessica Decker had spent most of the ride sleeping on her rolled up fleece, pressed against the window. It was a skill likely developed from having experienced multiple war zones and learning to grab sleep whenever you could get it. The key was in knowing when to wake up. As the vehicles came to a stop, she did exactly that.

"What's going on?" she asked.

"Toll," Mick said from the front seat. "Don't worry. Go back to sleep."

Ash mumbled something under his breath.

"What is it?" Harvath asked.

"Looks like Congolese regulars," he said. "We'll drop a few bills into the collection plate and be on our way."

As the men up front rolled down their windows, Harvath hoped they were right. But there was something about this setup, something he couldn't put his finger on, that gave him a very bad feeling.

CHAPTER 3

The first soldier who approached their Land Cruiser appeared nervous, distraught. He clutched his AK-47 in both hands. *"Médecins?"* he asked, gesturing with his weapon. *Doctors?* French was the official language of the Democratic Republic of Congo.

"Oui," Harvath answered from behind Asher. *"Médecins."* His grade school had been run by an order of French nuns. Next to sports, French had been one of the few things he had excelled at.

"Allez," the soldier ordered, grabbing the handle and jerking open Harvath's door. *"Descendez."* *Get out.*

"Everyone stays in the vehicles," Asher commanded.

"No," the soldier said in broken English. "Doctor now."

Before anyone could react, Jessica Decker had opened her door and was stepping out.

"Stop," Harvath ordered her, but it was too late.

"I'm the doctor," Decker stated.

The soldier looked back at Harvath. *"Vous n'êtes pas le médecin?"* *You're not the doctor?*

"Moi, je suis—"

Decker interrupted Harvath. "I told you," she said, as she grabbed a medical kit from her pack, "I'm the doctor."

The soldier slammed Harvath's door shut and started walking around to the other side.

"Dr. Decker, I want you back in this vehicle right *now*," Ash instructed through Mick's window.

Ash and Mick were both wearing "bone phones," earpieces connected to radios hidden under their shirts that transmitted speech through bone conduction technology. Eddie and Simon must have asked for a situation report because Harvath heard Mick say, "Figuring that out now. Stand by."

"Someone needs a doctor," Decker stated with an air of haughtiness. "That's what I do."

"And what I do is keep people safe," Ash replied. "Whoever this someone is, they can wait five more minutes while we negotiate this. You're not going anywhere."

"These are soldiers from the Congolese army."

"We don't know that. Now get back in the vehicle."

Decker ignored him and walked forward.

He was about to reiterate his order when he heard the door behind him open up and Harvath stepped out.

Immediately, the other soldiers raised their weapons.

The lead soldier spun and angrily pointed his AK at Harvath. "*Que faites-vous?*" he demanded. *What are you doing?*

"Everybody relax," Decker said as she put her hands out, appealing for calm. She glared at Harvath. *It was a good question. What the hell was he doing?* From inside the Land Cruisers, the Brits were thinking the same thing.

"*Je suis l'assistant du médecin,*" Harvath stated, donning a headlamp he had retrieved from his bag. *I am the doctor's assistant.* He turned the lamp on and swung his head from side to side—blinding several of the soldiers with its intense glare. They threw their arms up to shield their eyes and cursed at him.

"*Si nous avons besoin de l'assistant d'un médecin, nous vous appellerons.*" If we need a doctor's assistant, the lead soldier barked, we'll call you. "*Retournez dans votre véhicule.*" Get back in your vehicle.

With that, the man grabbed Jessica Decker by the arm and steered her toward the jungle.

Facing a row of angry men with AK-47s, Harvath did the only thing he could do at the moment. Reluctantly, he climbed back into the Land Cruiser.

"She's insane," Ash stated.

Harvath had already developed his own opinion about Decker, but now wasn't the time to discuss it. "Look at their shoes," he said.

The SAS men did as he suggested.

"None of their boots match. Two of them are wearing tennis shoes."

Ash cursed under his breath. "The uniforms may be from the Congolese army, but these guys definitely aren't."

"So who are they?" Mick wondered.

Harvath nodded at the two rebels closest to them. "Both of them, as well as the guy Dr. Decker just walked off with have the same tattoo. Looks like a cobra."

"Shit," Ash replied. "Rebels. FRPI."

There were so many rebel groups in Congo, it was hard to tell the players without a scorecard. Harvath had uploaded a list of them to his phone before leaving and had tried to study up as much as he could on the flight over.

"Free Republic of—" he attempted before Mick interrupted him.

"Front for Patriotic Resistance of Ituri," he said, looking at the uniformed men. "Based out of Bunia. I've never heard any reports of them being along this road, much less posing as Congolese regulars. They must be desperate for cash."

They were desperate for something, Harvath thought. "How bad is this group?"

"The FRPI? Pretty bad. Rape, mass murder, drugs. You name it. But the tattoo is the problem. These guys are a unit of shock troops. Kind of like a republican guard. They do everything from protecting high-ranking FRPI leadership, to terrorizing civilians."

"Which probably explains why they're out here with an injured patient and not back at the hospital in Bunia. This is not going to end well."

"We don't know that," Mick offered.

"Listen, these rebels just hit the jackpot. They not only now have a doctor, they have a very attractive *female* doctor. They're not going to give her back. That goes double if whoever needs the medical care is a high-ranking rebel with a price on his head."

"What if you're wrong?" Mick asked with his eyes focused on the rebels.

"What if I'm not?" said Harvath.

"Then they're going to want to get rid of us," Ash stated.

"We're already outgunned. All they'd have to do is bury our bodies and torch the trucks. Wouldn't be the first time it had happened in Congo, right?"

"No, particularly not where the FRPI is concerned."

"So the longer we sit here," Harvath continued. "The worse our odds get. At some point soon, an order is going to come over that radio and they're going to open fire on us. We need to get off the X right now. What kind of weapons do we have?"

"*Torch the trucks. Get off the X. What kind of weapons do we have . . .* Who the hell are you?" Mick demanded as he turned around to face him.

"I'm the client."

Ash studied Harvath in the rearview mirror, and Harvath met his gaze. Alpha dogs always recognized another Alpha when they saw one. He was no ordinary client. They had known that from the moment they first met him.

Harvath couldn't keep them completely in the dark. If they were going to get out of this alive, they were going to have to work together. He would have to give them something.

"CARE sent me to assess the situation," he said. "They want to open two more facilities in Congo."

"What kind of assessment?"

"Security."

"And your background?"

"SEAL Team Two and then DEVGRU."

Ash continued to hold Harvath's gaze. Finally, he said, "You look it."

Harvath didn't know what the remark was supposed to mean. Before he could reply, Ash said, "We've got two Glock 17s up front with us and there's a shotgun under your seat."

"Can I get to it without flipping it up?"

"No. Besides, it's too loud. There's no telling how many more of them are up the road or out in the jungle. It would just draw them in."

"And the Glocks won't?" Harvath asked.

Ash nodded to Mick, who pointed over Harvath's shoulder and said,

"There's a box of car parts behind you. Inside are two inline fuel filters. They've been modified with a thread adaptor to screw onto the Glocks."

Homemade suppressors. *Smart.*

"What else do you have?"

"The Brute Squad have Glocks, as well as rifles," Ash replied.

"What kind of rifles?"

"AKs, like our friends outside."

"Can you slip me your Glocks without them noticing?"

Mick turned his shaved head back around and focused on the soldiers. Slowly, he began to work his pistol between the seat and the center console. Ash then did the same.

Careful not to draw any attention, Harvath reached behind his seat and felt for the box of car parts. Once he found it, he removed the two filters. He also grabbed the extra medical bag.

"What are you thinking?" Ash asked.

Harvath began screwing the makeshift suppressors onto each of the Glocks. "See the third soldier on the left?" he said. "The one with the dirty bandage around his left hand? That dressing probably hasn't been changed in a while, if at all. I think that's our best chance to get me close to them."

"And?"

"I get him into your headlights to examine his hand. If I can, I enlist two of his comrades to help, give them stuff to hold and keep them busy. When I give you the signal, you flip on your high beams, I pull one of the Glocks, and we go hot. Anything driver's side is mine."

"And Mick takes out the rest."

Harvath nodded.

"What about the others? We have no idea how many more are out there."

"We'll jump off that bridge when we come to it."

Ash thought about it for a second. "What do you want to use for your signal?"

Harvath slid Mick's pistol back to him. Removing some items from the medical bag, so he could stash the remaining suppressed Glock, he took out a penlight. Cupping his hand around it to hide the beam, he checked to make sure it worked.

"When you see me pull out the penlight, watch for two quick flashes. Once that happens, wait ten seconds and then hit your high beams and come out firing."

"That's it?"

"That's it," said Harvath.

Ash quietly radioed the plan to the Brute Squad. Once they had acknowledged, he looked at Harvath in the rearview mirror and nodded.

It was time to roll.

CHAPTER 4

The moment Harvath popped the Land Cruiser's door open and climbed out, the soldiers began shouting at him to get back in. Keeping a smile on his face, he ignored their commands. Instead, he moved toward them.

The medical bag was slung over one shoulder and in his arms he cradled an assortment of supplies. Nodding toward the soldier with the bandaged hand, he offered to change his dressing in exchange for being allowed to step off the road and relieve himself afterward.

One soldier in particular raised his rifle as if he was about to strike Harvath, but the man with the bandaged hand told him to stop. He needed his dressing changed, badly.

Harvath stepped into the beams cast by the Land Cruiser's headlights and motioned the man to him. Once he was there, Harvath convinced two more to join him and assist. Slinging their rifles, they accepted the supplies and did what Harvath asked.

Even lightly touching the man's bandaged hand caused him to wince. He was in considerable pain. Harvath could see that the wound was oozing. It was infected.

As he carefully unwound the bandage, he asked the young man how he had been injured. The soldier, who couldn't have been more than nineteen or twenty, explained that his hand had slipped while using his machete. Congolese rebels could be horrific butchers. Harvath didn't want to know the details.

The wound was a week old, and another soldier had dressed it for him. The bandage hadn't been changed. As soon as Harvath had it unwound, the stench alone told him the man's hand was a lost cause.

"Is it very bad?" the young soldier asked in French.

Holding the man by the wrist, Harvath rotated the hand from side to side. "We need more light," he said, moving the soldier farther away from the group. Gesturing with his head, he encouraged the other two to move with them. They did.

Once he had them where he needed them, he pretended to examine the wound once more and then told the man's compatriots what he needed them to do. Explaining that they had limited disinfectant, he told one man he would need to pour it over the top of the wound while the other man held a clean dressing underneath to catch the liquid as it poured down. They would then wring the bandage out over the wound to give it a second cleansing.

As men who led lives of unfathomable paucity, reusing the liquid made complete sense to them. In order to keep their attention focused on the wound and off of him, Harvath further instructed them to watch for any indication that the discharge was changing color.

Harvath had his patient, as well as his two assistants, squat down so they could all work better via the Land Cruiser's headlights.

One of the men became agitated when he saw him reach into his medical bag and demanded to know what he was doing. Harvath held out then penlight and showed it to him. Satisfied, the rebel returned his focus to his colleague's wound.

Taking one last look around and fixing everyone's position in his mind, Harvath instructed the man with the disinfectant to very slowly start pouring it over the wound and reminded the man holding the dressing underneath to make sure he caught every last drop.

Standing up straight, he moved the penlight to his left hand and held it where Ash and Mick would be the only ones able to see it. Then, sliding his right hand into the medical bag, he wrapped it around the butt of his weapon and took a deep breath. Exhaling, he depressed the light's tail cap, giving out two quick flashes as he began to count backward from ten.

When the Land Cruiser's high beams kicked on, Harvath already had the suppressed Glock free of the bag and his finger applying pressure to its trigger.

The three rebels next to him were stacked almost like a totem pole, with one head on top of another. Harvath started with the man who was pouring the disinfectant and worked his way down. Three headshots in less than two seconds.

Before the bodies had even crumpled to the ground, Harvath had his weapon up and trained on the remaining soldiers. Mick, though, had been just as deadly. All of his shots had found their marks.

Nevertheless, Harvath moved over to them to make sure they were dead. They were. The Brits joined him and quickly helped secure the scene.

After stripping the dead rebels of their weapons, ammunition, and sole radio, which they gave to an amazingly unperturbed Jambo to monitor, they tossed the bodies in the jungle on the opposite side of the road. Life in Africa, and especially Congo, was exceedingly cheap.

"How do you want to handle Dr. Decker?" Ash asked.

Harvath had never wanted her along in the first place. After what she had done, part of him wanted to leave her here, but he couldn't do that. He knew he was going to have to be the one to get her out.

He also knew that Murphy, of the eponymous law, loved Africa more than any other country in the world. If it could go wrong, it would go wrong, especially in Africa. That went double for Congo.

Looking at the weapons they had taken off of the dead soldiers, two options popped into Harvath's mind. A cigar roll or a picket fence.

In the cigar roll, he'd stagger Ash and his men along a route between the road and wherever Jessica Decker was. Once he had her, and they were making their escape, the shooters would give them cover and then join them in their retreat, "rolling" the cigar as they worked backward toward the vehicles. But that was one of the spots where Mr. Murphy would be waiting with the vehicles.

They needed to keep the Land Cruisers running and ready to go. There was no telling how many rebels they might have on their tail as they tore through the jungle. It would be a death sentence to arrive at the road and discover that something had happened to their only means of ultimate escape. They couldn't risk leaving the vehicles.

Judging by the little he knew about Ash, the Brit wouldn't like Harvath's plan. Ash was a good man, a soldier. He'd want to go into the jungle too, but Harvath couldn't ask him to do that. It wasn't right. Not with how much had already been kept from him and his team.

Harvath decided to go with the picket.

CHAPTER 5

A sh looked at Harvath in disbelief. "That's got to be the dumbest thing I have ever heard. Four blokes from the Regiment—*four*—and you want us to mind the car park? Are you out of your tree?"

"It's a SEAL thing," Harvath responded. "Don't take it personally."

"The hell it is. You have no idea what's waiting for you in there. If it goes pear-shaped, you're going to need backup."

"Give me a radio," he replied. "If anything happens, I'll call you."

"Sure you will, Superman," Ash said as he walked away to get a radio. "Bloody Americans."

Even though Ash didn't like it, the picket was the right way to do this, and he knew it.

Harvath walked over and checked on Simon and Eddie. It was amazing how fast they moved. He could almost sense a rivalry between the two as they fieldstripped the dead rebels' AK-47s, wiped everything down, and rapidly reassembled them. Lives depended on those weapons working, specifically the lives of Scot Harvath and Jessica Decker.

Mick duct-taped magazines together so that all Harvath would have to do was spin a spent mag upside down in order to reinsert a fresh one. He knew, though, that if Harvath needed a second mag for any of these weapons, it was because he was in more trouble than a second mag was likely to ever help him get out of.

"Here's your radio," Ash said, handing it to him. "Don't be afraid to use it."

"I won't," Harvath replied as he worked the bone microphone into his ear.

After a quick commo check, Harvath pocketed a stack of loaded Glock mags and shouldered six AK-47s. It was a rough load, but he had humped worse. It would get lighter as he got closer to Decker. Better to have it and not need it, than to need it and not have it.

"You'll want these too," Ash remarked as he gave him a handful of mini chemical light sticks.

Harvath thanked him, and without another word, turned and headed off in the direction Dr. Decker had been led into the jungle.

The great thing about the British SAS was that they viewed war the same way the American Special Operations community did. You didn't win by thinking inside the box and following someone else's rules. You turned the box upside down and made your own rules, no matter what the enemy threw at you.

Just as they had found a way to suppress their Glocks, they had also found a way to lay their hands on a pair of night vision goggles.

As Harvath picked his way through the jungle's total darkness with them, he was thankful for the team's ingenuity. Using a flashlight would have been like taking out a billboard telling the bad guys he was coming and when he was going to be there. With what he had planned, he preferred that they not have any advance notice. Surprise was one of the things he needed to keep on his side.

Though it wasn't raining, it might as well have been. Everything was damp and drops of water continued to roll off the heavy tree canopy high above. The rain forests of the Congo Basin contained so much water that they caused their own weather system, and were known as the "Lungs of Africa."

Harvath had operated in plenty of jungles, and he had never liked any of them. He hated humidity. He preferred the high desert. High altitude and cold were his favorites. Jungles were just plain dangerous. You not only had to worry about bad guys but everything else lurking out there that wanted to eat you too.

Then there was the orchestra of noise. One sound layered upon the next. There was so much of it, it was hard to think, much less listen for any indication of danger. You had no way of knowing if what you had heard was five yards away, or five inches. That went double in the dark.

The path Dr. "Do Gooder" and the lead soldier had taken was pretty well trampled and easy to follow. As Harvath positioned his first AK and marked its hiding spot with one of the mini chemlights, his mind was taken up by how pissed off he was at Decker.

She had placed her ideology over her instincts. Harvath, who was all instinct, had seen her type before. It never ended well for them. And in a conflict zone, it all too often ended very badly for the people around them. He had no intention of letting that happen here.

As he worked his way deeper into the jungle, he continued to hide rifles and leave chemlights along the way. What he wouldn't have given for a ruck full of Claymores, but it was much better than nothing.

The problem with spacing out the rifles was that he had no idea how far in he would have to go. It was all based on his gut.

As he was about to place the last one, he began to hear voices.

Every muscle in his body tensed and he stood absolutely still, his ears straining to not only discern what they were saying but also to determine how far away they were, and if they were moving in his direction.

Quietly, he stepped off the path and crouched down. His suppressed Glock was pulled in tight to his chest, his finger on the trigger, ready to fire.

Seconds felt like minutes. Drops of water thudded onto him as well as on the broad leaves of the plants all around him. It sounded like rain hitting a canvas awning. It made it difficult to hear anything else.

As best he could tell, there were two voices, both men, and they were coming closer. He slowly began to apply pressure to his trigger.

By the time they were close enough to be intelligible, they were almost on top of him. Whatever language they were speaking, he didn't recognize it.

They were walking in single file and appeared to be alone. There was no one else on the path.

Harvath discharged his weapon and a muffled spit accompanied each of the two rounds as they ripped through moist air and found their targets.

The lifeless bodies collapsed onto the wet vegetation, each with a dime-sized hole near the bridge of their nose. Any sound made by the clatter of their equipment was gobbled up by the cacophony of the jungle.

Stripping them of their weapons, he then dragged them far enough off the path that they wouldn't be noticed until daylight, which unfortunately was fast approaching.

Stepping back onto the path, he pushed on. Soon enough, he found what he was looking for.

The sentry was forty meters out. He dispatched him the same way he had the others and moved the body. There were no other defenses he could see between him and the small encampment.

Circling around to the west, he counted three canvas tents. There were no fires. It was a "cold" camp. They obviously didn't want to attract any notice.

For several moments, he did nothing but listen, trying to figure out which of the tents Decker might be in. The drops began falling harder and he realized that it was now raining. From somewhere, there was a rumble of thunder. If he was lucky, the storm might hold back the daylight and help keep the rebels in their tents.

There was no logic to picking which one to check first. She could have been in any one of them. He decided to work from right to left.

Just as he was about to step out of the bush, something caught his eye. *Trip wire.*

Backing away, he traced it to its source. It was a crude, but deadly antipersonnel device that had been fashioned by running a length of paracord to the pin of a hand grenade, which itself had been secured to a tree trunk.

Without any chemlights left, there was no way to mark it. Carefully, he stepped over the cord and slipped into the camp.

The rain was coming down hard enough to mask the sound of his movement even to his own ears. He could only imagine it sounded twice as loud for anyone inside the tents.

He approached the first one and listened as the rain beat upon the canvas. He couldn't hear anything.

Creeping around to the front, he parted the fly and peered inside. There were six soldiers, all asleep, their AKs propped up next to them. Two of his worst fears had been confirmed.

The first was that they had encountered something bigger than just a handful of rebels extorting money from passing motorists. The second was what he had said back on the road—that whoever the patient was, he appeared to be someone who couldn't go to a regular hospital.

The next tent contained supplies. There was a smattering of heavier weapons, what looked like an RPG crate, some ammunition, food, and water.

With two tents down, he only had one to go. Already, he was mentally composing his evacuation route out of the camp, back to the path, and down to the road. He and Decker would need to be extra cautious as they slipped out of the camp, making sure they didn't hit any trip wires along the way.

Coming up to the third tent, he stopped once more and listened, but the pounding rain made it impossible to hear anything else.

He took a deep breath and, readying his weapon, pulled back the fly. Two men inside were lacing up their boots while another two were sleeping. The men lacing up their boots looked up immediately.

Shooting with night vision goggles on was extremely difficult, especially when you had to move fast.

Harvath's first shot went low and through the man's throat. After drilling his colleague in the head, he came back and finished him, along with the other two who still lay sleeping.

There was no sign of Jessica Decker or the rebel who had led her away from the road.

CHAPTER 6

here the hell was she? Harvath tried to think as he dissolved back into the trees and inserted a fresh magazine into his weapon. If the soldier hadn't brought her to the campsite, where else would he have taken her? Deeper into the jungle? But why? To rape her? To kill her?

That couldn't be it. They needed a doctor and had been prepared to take him, until Decker had upended everything. So where were they? Where was the patient? Why weren't they in the camp?

He racked his brain. Why wouldn't you keep someone who was wounded in the camp? Why create a whole separate position that needed to be reinforced and protected? Was the patient in such agony that he prevented his comrades from sleeping? Was that why he had been separated off? Or was it something else?

Why would you need to give someone his or her own space? *To isolate them?*

A chill swept over him. He wanted to blame the rain, but he knew better. All this time, he had figured the patient was suffering from wounds sustained in combat. But what if that wasn't it at all? *What if he was sick?*

That thought sent another chill down Harvath's spine. Sick in Congo could mean a lot of things, none of it good. He needed to find Decker, and they needed to get the hell out of here.

Retracing his steps, he stepped back over the trip wire and circled the camp in a counterclockwise motion. Had he not been on the lookout for more trip wires, he never would have noticed a narrow path that had been trampled farther back into the jungle. He took it and moved as quickly, quietly, and carefully as he could. Less than two minutes later, he found it. *The isolation ward.*

A lone tent had been set up in a small clearing recently hacked out of the bush. Light spilled from inside. As he neared, he could hear voices. He could also hear vomiting.

One word kept going through his mind. It started with *f* and rhymed with *truck.* He didn't want to get any closer than he already was, but he had no choice. Decker had put all of them in a terrible position.

Raising his night vision goggles, he gave his eyes a moment to adjust. In a perfect world, he would have picked a safe spot, set the back of the tent on fire, and waited to shoot anyone other than Decker who ran out. But it wasn't a perfect world and he couldn't afford to alert the other rebels.

He thought about using a snake, but he didn't have the time, and he especially didn't have the desire, to go catch one. He could only imagine the field day Murphy would have with that one. This was one of those things he would just have to do the hard way.

Moving to the front of the tent, Harvath tightened his grip on his weapon and reached for the flap.

But no sooner had he begun to pull it back, than a hand reached out and grabbed hold of his wrist.

Harvath drove his arm down, pulling the figure off balance. As the man's head came into view, Harvath saw that he was wearing a piece of cloth fashioned into a makeshift surgical mask. Leveling his pistol, he shot him in the head and pushed the man into the tent.

Instantly, his mind took in the entire scene. A second similarly masked rebel was reaching for his rifle. A third couldn't get to his rifle, but had picked up a machete. Harvath shot them both and kept advancing on his objective.

Standing above a cot, holding an IV bag over the ill patient—a man with a long scar across his forehead—was a fourth rebel. He was a large man who didn't show an ounce of fear. Instead, he shot Harvath *I'm going to kill you* eyes and looked ready to shout the alarm.

Harvath double-tapped him with two rounds to the chest and followed with another to the head, dropping him where he stood. The rebel who had taken Decker into the jungle was nowhere to be seen.

The doctor, though, sat at the back of the tent. A gag had been placed around her mouth and her hands and feet had been bound.

Because he was a believer in keeping radio traffic minimal, Harvath had given the Brits a handful of code words he would use during his search. Unless there was an absolute emergency, they had agreed not to distract his op by hailing him. Harvath now recited the word that would tell them that he had located and retrieved Dr. Decker. "Omaha," he said over his bone mic.

Ash sent back two squelch clicks indicating he had received the message.

Holding his index finger to his lips, Harvath bent down and loosened her gag. He then untied her hands and feet.

"Can you move?" he whispered.

Decker nodded.

"Good," he replied, helping her up. "Where's the man who brought you here?"

"I don't know. He asked me some questions about medical supplies and what we had in the trucks, then he left."

Harvath quickly radioed the team and told them to be on guard. Pointing at the man on the cot, he said, "Who's he?"

"Their commander."

"What's wrong with him?"

"Without a lab test, I can't be sure. It could be anything. It could be the flu. It could even be yellow fever."

"Will he survive without a hospital?"

"Maybe. But without a proper diagnosis, I can't say either way."

Harvath picked up Decker's medical bag and handed it to her. "Follow right behind me. Step exactly where I step and do exactly what I say. Don't make a sound. Do you understand?"

Once again, she nodded.

Turning off the lanterns, he flipped his NVGs back down. Once his eyes were focused on the ghostly green image, he led Decker to the front of the tent.

He parted the flaps and took several moments to scan the area. When he was convinced it was safe, he waved her forward and had her step out into the rain.

As she did, Harvath turned and shot the rebel commander twice in the head. *No loose ends.*

He inserted a fresh magazine and led Decker back the way he had come, keeping a very careful lookout for trip wires.

There was also the issue of at least seven, and possibly more, heavily armed rebel soldiers remaining.

The six back in the encampment, if still sleeping, were of no importance to him. It was the seventh rebel, the one who had controlled the toll stop and had led Decker away that he was concerned with. He was a huge loose end and could be a big problem for CARE now and in the future. If they let him live, the FRPI rebels wouldn't stop until they had exacted their revenge.

They were nearly even with the encampment when Harvath's earpiece crackled to life.

"The rebels know you're there," Ash radioed. "You need to get the hell out of there."

Harvath was about to ask how the Brits knew, but then remembered that Jambo was monitoring the communications.

"Turn the vehicles around and move them half a click back," Harvath said. "If anybody wants to get to you, they'll be forced to come straight down the road."

"That goes for you too," Ash reminded him.

"Maybe not," said Harvath. "Hurry up. We'll get there as soon as we can."

Signing off, he picked up the pace. As they neared the antipersonnel trap he had seen earlier, he slowed back down. Because he hadn't been able to mark its position, it took him a few moments to find it. Once he did, he held the pin in place while Decker clipped the cord that functioned as the trip wire.

He thought about tossing the grenade into the tent that acted as the rebels' supply depot, but as quickly as the idea had entered his mind, he dismissed it. There was no telling how many rebels were converging on them. He only had one grenade. He would need to make it count.

Skirting the encampment, he could see the previously sleeping rebels pouring out of their tent. He had the thickness of the jungle and the darkness on his side, so he stopped just long enough to take two shots. Both rounds found their marks and two more rebels lay dead.

By the time their comrades noticed, Harvath and Decker were already on the move. That didn't stop the soldiers from firing wildly into the jungle where they thought their attackers had been.

It was chaos, which was the state Harvath wanted to put the enemy in. The more confused, the more unsure, the more stressed they were, the better it was for him. People who were off balance had trouble thinking and usually screwed up.

It was why, in his SEAL training, he had been deprived of sleep and stressed to the breaking point. Never allow failure to become an option. Adapt and overcome.

When they finally stepped out of the underbrush and rejoined the path that led to the road, Harvath could hear the rebels coming. He and Decker didn't have a big enough lead. They needed to open up a wider gap.

At the first chemlight marker, he told Decker to keep going. Snatching up one of the AK-47s he had cached, he turned and fired in the rebels' direction.

When he had emptied the first of the duct-taped magazines, he flipped it, and inserted the fresh one. He laid rounds right up the path again, and then swung the weapon from side to side, hoping to spray anyone who had tried to jump out of the way. Once he had run the weapon dry, he took off after Decker.

The move bought them an additional twenty seconds of a head start. He did the same thing at the next secreted AK-47 and the one after that, never knowing if he had succeeded in taking out any of the men giving him chase. Run the weapon dry and move. Run the next weapon dry and move. That was his picket line.

While the dense jungle provided concealment, the path didn't offer much in the way of cover. As they neared the last AK-47, Harvath had a decision to make.

They would be about fifty meters from the road. It would be incredibly slow going trying to move parallel through the jungle until they reached the Land Cruisers and could safely pop out. Should they make a break for it together and try to run up the road, or should Harvath make his stand here while Decker made a break for it alone?

By his count, he had two fully loaded Glock mags, in addition to what was already in his weapon, plus the two mags that would be with the AK-47. He also had the hand grenade. But that would only work if he could bottle the soldiers up. If they were spread throughout the jungle, it would be far less effective.

And where there was one grenade, there were going to be more. Once they began to close in on him, what would stop them from using them? If the coast was clear, he decided he'd take his chances with Decker on the road. They could always cut back into the jungle if they had to. He would use the last AK to buy them a few more precious seconds.

As they got to the last marker, their lungs heaving for air, he lunged for the weapon, but it was gone.

CHAPTER 7

Before Harvath could warn Decker to stop, the man had grabbed her. It was the same Congolese rebel who had escorted her into the jungle in the first place. He stood behind her, his left arm wrapped around her throat. His right hand held the pistol-style grip of his AK-47. His finger was curled around the trigger. The muzzle of the weapon was pressed into her back. The other AK-47 hung from the man's shoulder.

Harvath thought about his options. None of them were good. He didn't have a clean shot. The only thing he could do was save himself. The word that rhymed with *truck* popped back into his mind as he raised his Glock.

"Drop your gun!" the rebel ordered. "Drop your gun! I kill the woman! I kill her!"

Decker's face was twisted in a mask of fear. Her eyes riveted on Harvath, silently imploring him not to let her die.

"If you kill her, I *am* going to kill you. Do you understand me?"

"Drop your gun! I kill her! I kill her *now!*" the soldier yelled.

Harvath adjusted his weapon, trying to get the best sight picture possible. "I am going to count to ten. If you do not let her go, I am going to kill *you*."

"Please," Decker cried.

"Stop moving," Harvath warned her.

"I kill her!"

Harvath ignored him. "One. Two. Thr—"

Mick's suppressed round entered the rebel's skull just behind his left ear. It was like throwing a circuit breaker. Instant blackout. The man was dead before his body hit the ground.

Decker, who hadn't seen the Brit step out of the shadows behind her and take the shot, had no idea what had happened. All she knew was that the man had been there, his body pressed hard against hers, and then he was gone.

When she turned and saw the man standing there, wearing night vision goggles and the same voice-activated bone microphone in his ear as Harvath, she put it together. Even if she had known what to say, she wasn't able to speak. Shock was quickly overtaking her.

Bullets from the rebels approaching from up the path were now popping and zinging all around them. Vegetation was being shredded.

"Time to move," Harvath ordered.

Mick handed him the soldier's AK-47 and kept the one with the duct-taped double magazine. "You go," he shouted. "I'll lay down suppression."

Harvath flashed him the thumbs-up and got Decker moving as fast as he could back to the road.

Five meters before the path ended, he knocked her to the ground and covered her body with his.

The booming of a heavy, crew-served weapon was discernable even above the AK fire happening behind them. It sounded like a .50-caliber machine gun, and it was coming from out on the road.

At first, Harvath thought that the rebels had called in the weapon to shoot at him. Then he heard Ash and the Brute Squad over the radio report that they were pinned down and taking serious fire from it.

Rolling off of Decker, he held the AK-47 up and asked, "Do you know how to use this?"

She stared blankly at him for a moment before nodding.

"Good." He helped her sit up, her back against a tree, facing the direction from which they had just come. "If you see anyone other than Mick come down that trail, you shoot them. Do you understand?"

When she nodded again, he double-checked to make sure a round was chambered, handed the weapon to her, and took off for the road.

The shooting from the fifty cal was coming in short bursts with long pauses in between. It sounded like the gunner was trying to conserve ammo, or was having some sort of trouble. Whether it was a mechanical issue, or he couldn't pinpoint his targets, Harvath didn't care. He planned on using the pauses to his advantage.

At the end of the path, he looked out toward the road and saw it—an improvised fighting vehicle, more commonly referred to as a "technical." This one was a shitty, camouflage-green pickup truck with a .50-caliber mounted in the bed and spare fuel cans on the tailgate. Two other rebels stood in back with the gunner and there were two more in the cab. They were parked in about the same spot LC1 had been when the rebels had originally stopped them.

The gunner let loose with another barrage of fire and Harvath could immediately see why they were stationary and not advancing on the Land Cruisers.

At this range, their weapon was not only highly accurate and deadly, but it put them outside the reach of anything Ash and his men could unleash back in their direction. It was a very one-sided fight. Harvath intended to change that.

Crouching down, he made ready. As soon as they began firing again, he sprang and ran toward the road.

There were few things in life where "close enough" could be deemed a success. One was horseshoes. Another was hand grenades. Pulling the pin, Harvath sent his in a high, soaring arc. He would have been happy to have had it land anywhere near the truck. This one, though, was perfect and landed right in the bed.

It landed with a clank and then *failed* to detonate. This time, Harvath didn't just think the word that rhymed with *truck,* he said it.

All three rebels standing in the bed turned in unison, two of them with AK-47s in their hands. The first thing they noticed was Harvath standing in the middle of the road. They then looked down at their feet and saw the grenade. *That* was when it finally detonated.

The entire truck, along with its rebel occupants and cases of ammunition, exploded in a massive fireball.

Pieces and parts were sent in every direction. Before some of them had even landed, Harvath could hear Ash and the Brute Squad cheering over the radio.

As the rain sizzled on the flaming wreckage, Harvath ran back into the jungle for Decker. Mick was already there with her. Only three remaining rebels had come down the path, and he had killed them.

He offered to accompany Harvath back to the encampment to see if there were any more, but Harvath waved him off. They had killed everyone who had seen the truck and the name of the organization. There was no point in pushing their luck any further. The best course of action would be to put distance between them and what had happened. Lots of it.

Helping Decker to her feet, Harvath slung the AK over his shoulder and walked with her back to the road. Mick followed, keeping an eye on their six, just to make sure no one snuck up on them from behind.

When the time was right, Harvath was going to have it out with Decker. But right now, he just wanted to get in the Land Cruiser and get going. They were all exhausted and soaked to the bone. He would have given a month's salary for a hot shower, a few bottles of beer, and a bed.

But those modest luxuries were still hours away. And hours could feel like a lifetime in a place like Congo, especially when the most dangerous part of the assignment was still in front of them.

CHAPTER 8

Pierre Damien sat on the terrace of his luxury Quai du Mont-Blanc apartment and took in the view. The lake was particularly beautiful at this time of year. In a matter of moments, the sky could shift from sapphire blue to steel gray. Where the lake emptied into the Rhône, one of the city's most famous landmarks, the Jet d'Eau blasted a massive column of water nearly five hundred feet into the air. It was forceful, phallic. It represented the virility he felt, even in his sixties.

Life had been good to him. The world had been good to him. And he intended to return the favor.

Swathed in a silk Gucci bathrobe and leather slippers, he sipped espresso as he pondered which of the five newspapers laid out on the delicate table to pick up first. *They can wait*, he decided. There was something about this morning that he couldn't put his finger on. Something he wanted to savor just a little bit longer.

Closing his eyes, he felt the cool wind that was moving in over the lake. He heard the traffic down below, smelled the faint hint of a cigarette from some unseen neighbor on some unseen terrace who had stepped outside to partake in a smoke.

The odor offended him. Not simply because of its pungency, but because of the intrusion it represented. He despised smoking. It was a filthy, selfish habit that intruded, uninvited, into the lives of everyone else. Smokers tossed their discarded butts onto sidewalks and into streets with impunity as if society had bestowed upon them some special dispensation that elevated them to a unique class allowed to litter at will. *Disgusting*.

He opened his eyes, prepared to be in one of his moods, and was stopped cold by the vision standing at the open French doors onto the terrace. "You cannot come out here like that," he said with a grin.

The young woman wrapped the sheet tighter around her naked body. "Why not?"

"Neighbors, board members, paparazzi with long lenses."

"Then you come back inside," she replied, returning his grin with one of her own.

"I'll need another espresso."

Ignoring his warning, she stepped fully out onto the terrace and crossed over to him.

He was a handsome man. Toned, with intelligent eyes and impeccable taste. She had slept with men a third of his age that didn't have his stamina. Lacing her fingers into his thick, gray hair, she bent forward and pressed her lips against his. She lingered, her kiss communicating her invitation.

"I can't," he said. "Put on a robe and join me. Jeffery will serve us breakfast out here."

"I don't want breakfast," she said, smiling. "I want you."

He smiled back. "I have to leave in a half hour. Ring Jeffery. Eat breakfast with me."

She had always felt uncomfortable around Jeffery, but feigning a pout, she disentangled herself from Pierre and went inside to do as he had asked.

As she walked away, Damien watched her. The sway of her hips. The curve of her body. The spill of long chestnut hair over the impossibly white sheet. She was a stunning woman. Had he not been the one to pursue her, he might have even said she was too good to be true. Yes, life had been incredibly good to him.

She returned wearing a robe, her allure only intensified by the décolletage it revealed. For a moment, he was tempted to cancel his morning and return to bed with her. Then Jeffery materialized with their breakfast and reality once again asserted itself.

He scanned the papers, nibbled on a bit of toast and a soft-boiled egg before kissing her on the forehead and heading inside to get dressed. He knew that if he had allowed their lips to meet again, he would have been powerless to break away from her.

When he stepped out of the lobby, his black Mercedes sedan was waiting. His security team divided between it and a follow car. Mornings in Geneva were always the same.

As the vehicles pulled away, she leaned against the cold iron railing and watched. When the motorcade reached the next block, her phone chimed. Without even looking at the message, she knew who it was from.

Glancing at the other buildings, she tried to imagine where he was. She hadn't asked. Not that he would have told her. That wasn't how the spy game worked. Everything was kept compartmentalized—like bulkheads on a ship.

She pulled the phone from her robe pocket. He wanted to see her. Now, before she went to work. He followed up the first text with an address. She knew it. It was on the way to her office. They had met there before.

Deleting both messages, she returned inside and took a shower. She chose her clothes carefully as she toweled off. Bentzi liked blue.

Leaving the apartment, she conducted a surveillance detection route, or SDR, just as she had been trained. She took her time and made sure no one was following her.

She had made a daily habit of varying her route to work. It didn't matter if she was leaving from Pierre's, which was more and more the case, or from her little apartment near the University in the Plainpalais neighborhood. If anyone ever desired to set an ambush for her, they would have been hard-pressed to pick the right spot.

The tram would have been the quickest way to her rendezvous, but instead she had decided to walk. She was forestalling the inevitable.

The Café de la Gare was a 1900s style Parisian brasserie in the diminutive Hotel Montbrillant. It was located on a quiet street corner overlooking the rear entrance of the train station.

Sitting in the back of the café, beneath its stained glass ceiling, pretending to read a newspaper as he watched patrons come and go was her handler, Ben Zion "Bentzi" Mordechai.

Mordechai was a completely unremarkable man. Not tall, not short, not handsome, not unattractive. He just *was*. That was his gift. That, and an amazingly cunning mind.

His only memorable feature, if it could be considered such, was his hands. He had been captured once and tortured, each of his fingers broken. His hands were slightly deformed. If the weather was just so, and he was run-down or dehydrated, his fingers would twist in a painful knot resembling the roots of a gnarled tree. Today, thankfully, was not one of those days.

Setting his newspaper down on the table, he smiled and rose as she approached. "Lenka," he said, using her nickname as he kissed her on both cheeks. "Did you wear blue for me?"

"No," she lied. "It was the only clean dress I had left at Pierre's."

He knew her too well. She was lying to him, but he kept his smile and let it go. Calling the waiter over, he motioned for her to sit and they ordered. She only wanted coffee. He ordered traditional Swiss muesli and a carafe of still water.

"No problems getting here?" he asked once the waiter had departed.

"None," she replied. "I hope you haven't been waiting long."

She knew he had been, but again, he let it go. "You know why I asked to see you."

"Because you missed me," she said, playfully grabbing his forearm, "and you wanted to see me."

"Stop it," Mordechai replied as he removed her hand. "I've actually seen *too* much of you lately."

He was disappointed in her and the rebuke stung.

"The problem, Helena," he continued, addressing her by her first name, "is that I haven't heard anything from you."

"I'm this close," she stated, holding up her thumb and forefinger. "I just need more time."

"Your time is up. We're recalling you to Tel Aviv."

The young woman was stunned. "*Recalling* me?" she repeated. "You can't be serious."

"Do I not look serious?"

"Are you jealous, Bentzi? Is that what this is all about?"

"Don't."

"Don't what?"

"This is not a game, Helena," he snapped.

"Who says it is?"

"Keeping me waiting, the blue dress, the flirtatious hand on my arm. I know you."

She began to wilt under his harsh gaze. "You don't know anything," she replied, sitting back in her chair, trying to create some distance.

"I found you. I trained you. I *know* you."

"My God, you *are* jealous. How is that possible? *You* sent me to Pierre. *You* told me to do whatever I had to do. We both know what that was code for."

"It doesn't change the facts. You have had more than enough time. We're pulling you."

"Now I know you're lying to me. You're not going to scrap this operation. It's too important."

"I didn't say we were scrapping the operation," Mordechai replied, once the waiter had set their order down and walked away. "I said we're pulling you."

"And then what? The next operative you put in, you think she'll somehow magically have more luck?"

The Israeli took a deep breath and nodded. "If she doesn't fall in love with her mark, then yes."

The accusation cut her to the quick and she couldn't let it go unanswered. "That is outrageous."

"Is it?" Mordechai asked as he set a tablet on the table and encouraged her to swipe through the photographs.

Of course they had been following her. What was surprising was that she had been under surveillance even when she wasn't with Pierre.

"All these prove that I have done everything you asked."

"If you had done *everything*," he said, "we wouldn't be having this conversation."

"Damn it, Bentzi, this isn't fair."

"We don't do *fair*. Is it fair that the Arabs have oil and we have rock? Is it fair that we are the only nation on the face of the earth that has to fight, *and* win, every single day just in order to survive? Is any of that fair?"

"Are you questioning my dedication to Israel now?"

Mordechai cut her off. "Don't toy with me, Helena. You and I both know where your loyalty lies. I have never had a problem with that. So long as you followed orders."

"Which is exactly what I am doing now," she insisted.

"It's out of my hands."

"Please, Bentzi. I have never let you down before."

"That's why this is so difficult."

"But it doesn't have to be. Don't you see?"

Mordechai studied her. "I'm not sure what I see."

"*Oy.* Now with the guilt?"

He normally found her use of Yiddish amusing. There were times she could come off as just as Jewish as anyone at the Mossad, but that was the chameleon in her. It was an act, just as this was.

"I'll double my efforts. I can do this. Trust me. I'll work even harder."

"Go back to your apartment," he told her. "Call in sick. Nothing too specific. If Damien contacts you, tell him you're having menstrual issues."

She made a face. "That's not very alluring."

"Exactly."

"I still think—"

Mordechai held up his hand, silencing her. "You go back to your apartment and you stay away from Pierre Damien. You don't call him. You don't go over to his place. You don't so much as bump into him in the street. Those are your orders. Do you understand?"

Helena didn't respond.

Mordechai repeated himself.

Finally, she nodded.

"Good. I will contact you as soon as we have your extraction figured out," he said, sliding his tablet into his bag. He then removed a couple of notes from his pocket, stood, and placed them on the table.

"You're not going to eat?" she asked.

"I'll be in touch," Mordechai replied as he turned and walked out of the café.

CHAPTER 9

There had been a hint of something in her voice. *Was it melancholy?* Ben Mordechai wasn't sure and tried to sort it out as he walked. Helena had never been what anyone would consider "stable." While she hid her problems well, she was an emotional and psychological basket case. Had Mordechai gone through what she had suffered, he probably would have been too.

Hers was but one story among thousands in Eastern Europe. Young girls who had been tricked into the sex trade. Rings of professional traffickers lured them away from their villages. They were promised jobs as nannies with nice families in England or France. While they waited in a neighboring country for their alleged visas to be processed, they were raped, beaten, and hooked on drugs.

Their passports were withheld from them, and they were told horror stories about what would happen to their families back home if they went to the authorities. There were always families back home. The traffickers rarely picked the girls unless they had a substantial piece of leverage they could use on them.

Once broken, the girls were shipped to countries around the world. Helena wound up in Israel.

It was a national stain few Israelis would dare admit. The record, though, spoke for itself. When it got too bad to be ignored, the government would take action, but soon enough its blind eye would return.

Helena was held in the southern West Bank settlement of Kiryat Arba.

There she and the other girls were forced to perform sex acts with twelve to fifteen men a day. Some were Jews. Some were Palestinians. Many were businessmen from Tel Aviv whom her pimps had inveigled.

If she failed to do what she was told, she was beaten. If she failed to please the customers, she was beaten. If she was too ill to perform, she was beaten *and* starved.

On one occasion, Helena took so sick she almost died. If it had not been for the other girls sharing their food and nursing her, she never would have made it.

When one girl, a woman Helena deeply cared for, did die—that was her breaking point. The girl had been beaten to death by one of the customers—a wealthy but very drunk businessman. The pimps should have returned the favor. At least there would have been some semblance of justice done. Instead, they got rid of her body and blackmailed the man. With the money, they brought in two more girls. They were very young. Helena could still remember what it was like to be young. She had had enough. That was the night she snapped.

Because of the constant threat of terrorism, many Israelis carried concealed weapons. They were not allowed to bring them into the brothel, but customers who were known, trusted, and had paid a premium were allowed to.

There was a special area with small, pistol-sized lockers where they could lock up their weapons. Many of them feigned using the lockers or bypassed them altogether. One such customer was a client of Helena's. He liked her, a lot. But it wasn't reciprocal.

He often drank before arriving and then had a couple of drinks more before heading upstairs. He was a mean man who liked to get rough. Some nights, he would show up with a garment bag and word would quickly reach Helena. Those nights never ended well. Not that any of her nights trapped in that nightmare ever did.

Inside the garment bag was the wedding dress of the man's wife. As far as the woman knew, it was safely in storage, waiting to be handed down to their eldest daughter. He made Helena wear it while he disparaged his wife in absentia for getting too fat to fit into it. He was a jeweler and completed his sick fantasy by placing a replica of his wife's wedding ring on Helena's finger.

The more he would talk about his wife, the angrier he would become. And as his anger increased, so too did the level of pain and abuse he heaped upon Helena—until the night she snapped.

As it always did, word spread when the jeweler arrived that he was not only downstairs but that he had brought the garment bag with him. By the time he made it upstairs, Helena was ready for him.

He was unsteady on his feet, his eyes glassy. More inebriated than normal. She could smell his putrid, alcohol-soaked breath halfway across the room.

Reaching into his jacket pocket, he pulled out the small velvet box and threw it at her, telling her to put the ring on.

She did as he asked and waited for him to hand her the garment bag to put on the dress. She had everything planned. The request didn't come.

Instead, the man unbuckled his trousers and told her to come kneel in front of him. When Helena asked him if he was sure he didn't want her to change, the man barked obscenities at her.

He was making too much noise. If her pimps heard him this angry, they would step in, blame her, and she would take a terrible beating. She hurried to comply in the hope it would get him to quiet down.

The string of invectives continued until she was on her knees in front of him. Only then did he stop shouting at her.

He was a disgusting ape of a man covered in coarse, curly dark hair. The mere thought of him was enough to repulse her. The mere thought of any of the men that visited the brothel was enough to repulse her. She refused to judge any of the women who sought to escape the horror of their lives through the drugs the pimps provided. She herself had freely used the drugs throughout. But not tonight. Tonight she was sober.

It made doing her "job" even more difficult, but it was amazing what the body could be coaxed into doing if the mind was set upon a compelling goal.

Kneeling there in front of the jeweler, Helena prepared. He wobbled momentarily, unsteady on his feet. She paused, wondering if the man was possibly about to pass out. *Mistake*.

Angry that she was taking so long, the jeweler slapped her in the side of her head. The blow was so severe, blood began to trickle from her left ear.

She looked up at him half in anger, half in shock. When she did, the man punched her right in the face.

There was the crack of cartilage as he broke her nose, accompanied by a spray of blood.

He pushed her over backward with such force that her head struck the floor and she began to black out. She struggled to maintain consciousness.

Stripping off the rest of his clothes, the man then threw himself on top of her. He landed with his full weight, knocking the air from her lungs. It felt like being crushed under a collapsed, stone wall.

His coarse, wiry hair chafed against her skin like rough wool. She could feel his pawing hand searching her body for where her legs met. As she fought to breathe, and the air finally returned to her lungs, she struggled to move out from underneath the man. As soon as she did, he dug his teeth into her breast.

She began to scream, but caught herself. Instead, she felt for her weapon. It wasn't much—an old razor blade taped to a toothbrush—but it was all she had.

Grabbing as much of his hair as she could, she pulled his head away from her chest and bent his neck backward, exposing his soft, fleshy throat. She didn't think twice about what she did next.

Cutting as hard and as deep as she could, she pulled the razor from his left ear all the way across to almost his other ear before the toothbrush broke from the amount of force she was applying. It didn't matter. The job was already done.

She let go of his hair and watched as his hands flew upward. He clutched desperately at his neck and throat. His eyes, which had been wide with surprise, were now white with fear.

Shoving him backward with every ounce of strength she possessed, she toppled him sideways and quickly moved to get away from him and the blood that was spurting from his fatal wound. Even if help could be summoned, there was no saving him. He was a dead man.

She had hidden extra clothing in the room. After quickly cleaning herself at the sink, she got dressed.

She went through his pockets and took his wallet, his watch, and jewelry. She took his cell phone though she didn't have a soul in the world she could call to come rescue her—it might have maps or access to other information she might need. She also took his gun.

She had no idea what caliber it was or what company had manufactured it. All she knew was that it was loaded, and that the man also travelled with a spare magazine. As best she could tell, she had somewhere around thirty rounds total. More than enough.

She had only fired a weapon a handful of times in her life. She had an older cousin who had been a soldier. Sometimes, when he was home visiting, he liked to get drunk and let the younger cousins fire his sidearm.

She had enough experience to know that she had to pull the slide all the way back in order to seat a round from the magazine into the chamber. The pistol was already chambered, though, and as she did that, the existing round was ejected.

It rolled somewhere, maybe under the bed. She didn't have the time to worry about it. If everything she was about to do hinged on one round, she was destined for defeat anyway.

Holding one small towel against her nose to help stanch the bleeding, she wrapped another towel over the pistol and exited the room.

The back door was locked and only led to a small courtyard anyway, surrounded by an eight-foot-high wall topped with barbed wire. The only way out was through the front door. The only way to the front door, though, was through the salon.

Helena had long ago given up on God. No matter how badly she begged Him to save her, He had never come to her rescue. She had resigned herself to having been abandoned. This night, though, felt different.

Now she prayed like she had never prayed before. She prayed all the way down the stairs and into the salon. She felt the eyes of clients and of the girls on her. They were saying things to each other, whispering at first as she passed with the bloody towel clamped to her face and blood trickling down her neck from her left ear.

It was a spectacle, but nothing those who worked at the brothel hadn't seen before. Girls were beaten up. It was part of the business.

What they hadn't seen before was one of the girls crossing the salon, walking up to the muscle at the door, pulling a semiautomatic pistol, and shooting him in the chest. Whispers turned to screams.

Helena stood frozen, unsure what to do. When the door to the office opened, something took over. Her arm came up and she watched, almost detached, as the pistol fired. The man fell dead, as did the man behind him as she fired again.

There was a rush behind her and she spun to see clients running to the lockers to get their guns. One after another, she shot them.

There were shouts from the back of the brothel as the last two pimps ran into the salon with their fully automatic rifles, convinced they were under some sort of terrorist assault. Helena changed magazines, hid the weapon behind her back, and waited for them.

When they saw her and her battered face, they immediately disqualified her as the threat. She nodded toward the lockers.

That was all the pimps needed. They charged in the direction she had indicated. As soon as they had passed, she shot both of them in the back of the head.

Her bloodlust not yet sated, she walked back into the salon. Four men cowered along the wall near the bar. She shot each of them before heading upstairs.

She could read which girl was in each room, and she knocked and called them to come out. She told them it was safe. Once all the doors were open and everyone was in the hallway, she separated the girls off, and shot each of the remaining men. Then without a word, she turned and walked back downstairs.

The door was ajar, and she could see the lights of the town. *Freedom.* But with no passport and no one to help her, what exactly was she escaping to? At the moment, it didn't matter. All that mattered was that she get out.

As she was stepping toward the door, her foot got caught between two of the bodies. Or so she had thought.

Looking down, she saw one of the pimps. Half of his lower jaw was missing and blood was pouring from a hole in his chest. Even so, he still had enough strength remaining to grab her around the ankle. In his other hand was the small pistol he kept in his pocket and had used in the past to pistol-whip unruly clients and even one or two of the girls.

Helena brought her weapon up to finish him off only to see that the slide was locked back and she was out of ammunition.

Jerking her ankle from the man's grasp, she stomped on his opposite wrist, causing him to let go of his gun. She picked up the pistol and pulled its trigger again and again, emptying the magazine into him.

She then left the brothel. The bloodbath was over. But everything else was just beginning.

CHAPTER 10

When Ben Mordechai found her, she was holed up in a cheap Jerusalem hotel near the Chapel of the Ascension. The jeweler's phone had acted like a beacon, leading his team right to her.

He had been with Shin Bet at that time, Israel's internal security service. And though he had seen the carnage at the brothel firsthand, and had been told by all the girls what had happened, he still couldn't believe it. It was incomprehensible to him that a single, untrained woman could kill that many men and walk away unharmed.

They were treating the murders as a terrorist attack. When they hit the hotel, they hit it at three in the morning and hit it hard. A bag was thrown over Helena's head and she was spirited away in a waiting van to an off-the-books safe house for interrogation.

Mordechai knew within three minutes that Helena had not been trained by some radical group and smuggled in to massacre Israeli citizens. She was not a terrorist. She was, though, a murderess and this presented its own special set of problems.

Killing the client who had regularly abused her could very likely be defended in court. Killing the pimps who kept her as a sex slave could also likely be defended in court. Killing every other male in the brothel, even in an uncontrolled fit of rage, would be much more difficult. Compounding the issue was the fact that two of the businessmen she had gunned down were somewhat prominent.

Helena was an incredibly sympathetic figure. With all of the evil Mordechai had seen in the world, her story moved even him. He wanted to help her, but there was only one possibility. He left her in the interrogation room to make some phone calls.

When he returned an hour later, he laid out his offer and told her he was sorry, but that she would have to decide right then and there. They didn't have the luxury of letting her sleep on it. If she was to be spared a trial, multiple wheels would have to be immediately set in motion.

She agreed to the offer.

As soon as Mordechai had left the room to relay her decision, she broke down. She was free from the horror of the abuse and the beatings and the starvation. But she had traded one form of bondage for another. Looking for some sliver of hope, she focused on the fact that her family would be taken care of. If that was the only good that came out of this, it was better than nothing.

She was taken from the safe house to a private hospital where she was treated for her injuries and allowed to rest.

Mordechai visited her daily. She had been checked into the hospital under what would become her code name, Yael. It meant "to ascend" in Hebrew. He had chosen it because of the chapel near where he had found her. It was also a figure from the Bible who saves the Jewish people by destroying an enemy general. From the beginning, Mordechai put much more faith in her than she did herself.

Once she was rested, she began a series of transformations. As Michelangelo could look upon a block of marble and see the statute inside, Mordechai could see the goddess beneath her Slavic features.

A team of plastic surgeons refined and sculpted her nose, her breasts, chin, lips, and cheekbones. In the process, they noted that she had suffered an array of facial fractures, undoubtedly at the hands of the men who had held and abused her during her perilous journey to where she was now.

He brought her family to come see her and put them all in a home near the sea for a week. The father, who was a raging anti-Semite, blamed the Jews for the entirety of his daughter's traumatic experience. He chose to ignore that his own fellow citizens had abducted her in his own home country.

On Mordechai's advice, she had not told her parents that she had been forced into the sex trade. While they might have suspected she had been used sexually, he recommended that she explain that she had been abducted and forced to work in a factory. When she misbehaved or displeased the slavers, she was beaten. Her enhanced appearance was due to the grace of the Israeli plastic surgeons responsible for her facial reconstruction. Neither parent asked about her breasts.

She told them that she had been too ashamed to come home. She needed to heal from the trauma, emotionally and physically. During that time, she had met Bentzi. He ran a human rights organization focused on stopping human trafficking. She had been offered a job with the organization and intended to remain in Israel.

Her father was beside himself. Her mother cried for the rest of the visit. Helena cried too. The lies were difficult to tell, but they were necessary and the more she repeated them, the less painful they became.

When her parents returned home to their village, her training began in earnest.

Helena learned fast and she learned well. When Ben Mordechai moved from Shin Bet to the Mossad, he took her with him. She was far too valuable an asset to ever turn over to someone else.

But now, as he approached the white Ford Transit van here in Geneva, he was questioning her value.

Before he could reach for the handle, the door was opened for him and he climbed inside.

Two young Mossad agents sat monitoring a bank of electronics. Next to them was a chesty redhead in her late fifties.

"You heard everything?" Mordechai asked as he removed the wireless transmitter and placed it on the counter.

She looked at her two young agents and said, "Go get some coffee."

When the men had exited the van, she pulled out a pack of cigarettes and offered one to Mordechai. He shook his head.

Lighting up, she took a deep drag and then exhaled the smoke toward a small vent in the roof. "I'd say we've got a serious problem."

Nava Itzik was an assistant director in the Mossad's Special Operations Division or "Metsada" as it was known. Under their dark umbrella fell some of the Jewish State's most dangerous assignments. In addition to paramilitary operations, sabotage, and psychological warfare, they were also charged with carrying out assassinations. When Nava Itzik found something to be a "serious problem," she usually brought some particularly nasty force to bear in order to get it out of Israel's way. That was what she was paid to do. And as her deputy, Mordechai was paid to do whatever she told him to.

"If I had seen this coming," he said. "I never would have put her on this job."

Nava took another drag on her cigarette. "I saw it coming," she replied as she blew another cloud toward the vent. "I know more about Pierre Damien than she does, and I'd still probably go to bed with him."

"But that was her assignment. She was supposed to sleep with him. What she wasn't supposed to do was *fall* for him."

"I think she fell for you first."

Mordechai was taken aback. "Me?"

"You rescued her. Took her away from that brothel. You gave her stability. Some hope."

"I didn't give her any choice."

"She chose to trust you."

"What she chose was to *not* go to prison," he corrected.

"You're emotionally unavailable, Bentzi. Any woman can see that. It makes you more attractive."

"Are you psychoanalyzing me or is this supposed to be some weird compliment?"

"Neither," Nava replied. "I'm just telling you the truth. No matter how well she shoots or fights, she's deeply insecure. We both know that."

"Everyone's insecure. If you don't have doubts, there's something wrong with you. She may be insecure, but she's a good person."

"The hooker with the heart of gold. Except she isn't really a hooker anymore. She's an asset. *Our* asset, and whatever let's-play-house, happily-ever-after fantasy she has created in her mind with Damien, it needs to come to an end. Right now. Israel can't afford fantasies."

"You think that is what this is all about? She sees Damien as her way out?"

"If you're going to reach for a parachute, why not one spun from platinum?"

Mordechai let that sink in for several moments.

"Of course, the other possibility," Nava suggested, "is that she is trying to make you jealous."

"Jealous of what?" he demanded. "There's nothing to be jealous about."

Nava put her hands out. "Okay, don't get angry."

"I'm not angry. I just want this all fixed. There isn't time to start over again. If she's not successful, we're through."

"You mean Israel is through."

"Israel, the United States, all of us."

Now it was Nava's turn to think. "Maybe there's another way to motivate her."

Mordechai didn't want to hear it. He cared for Helena. The fact that they were trying to figure out how to manipulate her bothered him. It bothered him even more because none of this should have ever happened. She had failed him and in doing so, he had in turn failed Nava. It was just one enormous cluster fuck.

"We need to slam a red-hot jolt of adrenaline right into her chest," Nava continued. "Something that'll keep her attention no matter what Damien says or does."

A million things ran through Mordechai's mind, and none of them were good. No matter what depraved routes his brain was travelling, it was guaranteed Nava's were worse. Much worse.

"What are you thinking?" he asked. "Carrot or stick? Do you want to grab someone from her family?"

She shook her head. "If we did that, we'd lose her forever. I have a better idea."

As Nava crushed out her cigarette and lit another, she explained what she was thinking.

Mordechai sat there, stunned—not knowing if he could follow through. It was one of the worst things he had ever been asked to do.

CHAPTER 11

Ash and his team had mapped out a series of guesthouses and ranger stations between Bunia and the Matumaini Clinic. Like a chain of islands in a vast and unstable ocean, they could provide anything from food and rest to communications equipment and sanctuary.

Because of their encounter with the FRPI rebels, they had decided to backtrack and take a new route. There was no telling what would have been waiting up ahead on the road they had been on. There had to have been more vehicles somewhere. It would have been impossible to move all of the rebels they had encountered in one pickup truck—even as heavily as they filled them with men and supplies in Congo.

Backtracking had cost them hours. By the time they reached the first ranger station, the rain had stopped, the sun was out, and it was almost time for lunch.

Jambo was the first one out of the vehicles, pumping the rangers' hands, smiling and wishing them well in Swahili. He spun a long tale about how the team had managed to get one of the trucks stuck on the way out of Bunia that morning and had spent hours before finally getting it free. They needed to rest and take showers. They had brought their own food and water, but would gladly pay the rangers for their hospitality, as well as for any beer the men might have. Happy to augment their income, the rangers gladly agreed and threw in lunch for free.

Harvath didn't like the idea of drinking in the middle of the day, but after what they had been through, they needed to take some of the edge off. And much like the phony "we're not carrying any guns" stickers in the Land Cruisers' windows, drinking beer in the middle of the day sent a message that they were not a threat and had nothing to hide. Harvath had ditched the CARE International door magnets hours ago. There was no telling if the word had gone out among the broader FRPI or not. The less his team advertised, the better.

There was one shower at the ranger station and the Brits politely offered it to Dr. Decker first. She hadn't said a word since they had escaped. She had leaned against the window the entire way, eyes closed, pretending to be asleep.

While they took turns using the shower, they kept an informal patrol, watching for anything unusual. Taking a break to rest and recharge didn't mean letting their guard down.

Because the rangers would have been upset to see them carrying weapons, the Brits kept their Glocks concealed beneath their shirts. Harvath was unarmed. He left the rear doors of LC1 unlocked and made sure nothing was sitting on the rear bench. If anything happened and he needed a weapon, he would either take one off one of the rangers, or make a run for the shotgun under the backseat.

He watched as the rangers prepared lunch. When Jambo explained how much they were charging for their beers, Harvath understood why they were throwing in lunch.

When a small plastic bag with "fresh" meat came out, Harvath asked Jambo what kind of meat it was. "Bush meat," he replied.

Harvath immediately shook his head. "No way."

"Why?"

Bush meat was the vehicle by which some of the worst diseases in Congo travelled. It was his op and he wasn't going to risk anyone getting sick. "Please tell the rangers thank you, but we're vegetarians."

Jambo looked at Harvath for a moment, trying to figure out how he was going to convincingly communicate this, but ultimately gave up and relayed the message to the rangers. Why anyone would waste good bush meat was beyond them, but they didn't care. It meant more food for them and the money was the same. The rangers' deal only got better.

By the time it was Harvath's turn to grab a shower, the hot water had run out. He washed quickly, using the soap he had brought, being careful not to let any of the water get in his mouth or nose. The last thing he wanted was to get sick.

The thought of it brought him back to the rebel camp and all of the men who had been masked up. Decker said she thought it was yellow fever. If she was right, he didn't have anything to worry about. It wasn't communicable, unless an infected mosquito bit you, and he had already had the vaccine. But what if it wasn't yellow fever? What if it was something more serious? He tried to shake the thought from his mind.

Everything in Congo seemed to be covered in a layer of clay-colored, red dust. Turning off the shower, he toweled off with the only "clean" towel that was left—a small, lime-green hand towel with characters from a popular American children's movie. Finding slices of western culture in the middle of a place like Congo always reminded him that the world was a lot smaller and interconnected than most people realized.

As dry as he was going to get, Harvath dressed in fresh clothes and joined the rest of the team for "lunch."

While Jambo had no problem eating the bush meat, the rest of the team picked at stewed cassava leaves and boiled vegetables.

When the meal was finished, the Brute Squad rested on the front porch, keeping one eye out for trouble while Ash and Mick gathered intel from the rangers about the area they were heading into.

Jambo offered to clear the table and as he took the stack of plates to the sink, Decker approached Harvath. "Can I talk to you for a moment?" she asked.

Harvath nodded and, picking up his beer, followed her outside.

They followed a rubble-strewn walkway to a clutter of lean-tos behind the station.

Once she was satisfied that they were fully out of earshot of the men on the porch, Decker laid into him, "Don't you ever pretend to be a doctor again. Do you understand me? I'm the doctor, and I am in charge here."

Had Decker been a man, Harvath would have been torn between laughing and knocking him out. But since Decker was a woman, and he

lived by the code that no man should ever strike a woman—even an as-
toundingly arrogant one—he chose the former.

She glared at him. "You're laughing? How *dare* you?"

It was time to put her in her place. "Dr. Decker, I am going to make
this very clear, so that there's no misunderstanding. This is not a medical
assignment. You are here to assist *me*. That means you do what I say, when
I say it. If I tell you not to do something, then you don't do it. Do we understand each other?"

Decker's glare had turned into a glower. "Your arrogance is astounding. Do you know that?"

"*My* arrogance?"

"Yes," she replied. "*Your* arrogance. It wasn't you who opened Matumaini Clinic. It wasn't you who poured sweat and blood into making it
happen. And it wasn't you who lost very good friends there to God knows
what. So, yes, your arrogance is astounding."

She was in shock. That was the only charitable explanation he could
think of. Their encounter with the rebels would have been traumatizing
for any civilian, even a doctor who had previously been a war correspondent. Add to that the fact that she had already shown up for duty worried
about the staff from the Matumaini Clinic, and you had a more than perfect recipe for psychological disaster.

"You've just been through a pretty intense—" Harvath began.

"Don't you dare patronize me," she spat.

"No one is patronizing you."

"The hell you aren't."

Harvath needed to shut this down. "Dr. Decker, I'm willing to cut you
a little slack after what happened, but—"

"But what?" she demanded, cutting him off again.

"Either you start pulling your act together, or I'm going to arrange to
send you back."

That seemed to get her attention.

Harvath watched her for a couple of seconds. He had known some
emotional women in his day, but he had always thought it was demeaning to blame everything on emotion. People and arguments were usually
more nuanced than that.

There was, though, some convoluted chip that Decker carried on her shoulder. He had no idea where it came from, and he didn't want to know. That was for her shrink or, God help him, her boyfriend to figure out.

All Harvath cared about was whether or not she'd take orders, and whether or not he could count on her to see the rest of this operation through. He didn't like manipulating people, but Decker had positioned herself in such a manner that he had no problem doing whatever he needed to do. But before that, he wanted to make a couple more things crystal clear.

"After everything that happened this morning, we're very lucky that nobody died."

She looked at him, her eyes smoldering with incredulity. "Nobody died? *Nobody?*"

Harvath corrected himself. "We're very lucky that none of us died."

"So *they* don't matter."

"The rebels?"

"Yes, the men back there that you killed, *murdered* in cold blood."

Good Lord, thought Harvath. "All of those men were armed combatants."

"Who you shot before they could even get a chance to shoot you!"

What the . . . This woman *was* nuts. "You know that's the idea, right? To shoot them before they can shoot me?"

In Harvath's short time on this earth he had heard some incredibly stupid and incredibly offensive things, but that one was very near the top of his list. "Do you think I enjoyed shooting those men?"

"I don't know," Decker replied. "You tell me. You sure seemed pretty good at it."

"I'm good at it, Dr. Decker, in the same way I'm sure you're good at what you do. Because that's my job."

She had a triumphant expression on her face, as if she had just caught him in the lie to end all lies. "Except my job is to *save* lives."

"Mine too."

"But—" she began.

"But I've still killed people?" he asked, interrupting her this time.

Decker nodded.

"I have, and I would do it again because some lives are more valuable than others."

Once more the look of triumph flashed across her face, but Harvath shut it right down.

"Not every life is worth saving, Dr. Decker. In fact, some aren't even worth fighting for."

"*All* lives matter," she countered.

"The life of a Hitler? A Stalin? A Mao? A bin Laden?"

"The men we encountered this morning were not a Hitler, a Stalin, or a Bin Laden," she replied.

"No, but they tied you up and gagged you just the same, right?"

Decker dismissed his question as if it were beneath her. Her ideology was more dangerous than Harvath had originally feared. Not only had she been willing to jump out of the Land Cruiser and go blindly into the jungle with anyone who asked, but she also appeared to lack the capability to feel any shame or responsibility for what had happened because of it.

He was about ready to write her off for good when she made an interesting admission and asked him a question very few had ever asked.

"I don't get you," she said.

"Why not?"

"I assume you're a spy, or a soldier, or something."

"Or something," Harvath admitted.

She looked at him long and hard, as if the answer to her next question would have to already be written on his face for her to believe it.

"Why do you do it?" she asked. "Any of it?"

It wasn't a funny question, but Harvath laughed again anyway.

"You wouldn't believe me," he said.

"Try me."

She had said *try me*, not *trust me*. There were many explanations Harvath could have given her for why he had chosen the path he was on.

One was his desire to please his deceased father who had seldom been there for him because the man was always away chasing his own adventures. Another had to do with a desire to push himself further and challenge himself more. Yet another had to do with the fact that he was just plain addicted to the lifestyle and thought so highly of his ability that he had come to believe that he was the only person who could get the hard assignments done.

There was another part to why he did what he did. It had started when he was much younger and lived next door to a developmentally impaired boy who was regularly picked on. He had inserted himself as the boy's protector, which resulted in him getting into a lot of fights. He got into a lot of trouble, but he also became a good fighter.

Though he wanted to believe that what he was doing was noble, and it was, there was also a certain degree of selfishness to it. The boys he fought with were usually bigger than he was and there was often more than one of them. Nevertheless, he beat them time and again until no one challenged or made fun of his "friend."

It wasn't until he was older that he realized the gusto with which he had punched out any kid who made fun of the developmentally impaired boy came from a deeper place inside himself. What he did for that boy is what he wished his father had been around to do for himself and his mother. He was protecting him.

He also came to realize that what he had voluntarily chosen to do for his neighbor, his Navy SEAL father had also voluntarily chosen to do for others. There would always be people who needed the protection of others. True nobility came in offering that protection freely. Once he came to fully accept that idea, his path in life became pretty clear.

Looking at Decker he said, "We talk a lot back home about the American Dream. Without someone willing to protect it, it can't exist."

"You're right," she replied. "I don't believe you."

So much for building rapport, Harvath thought. Not that he was surprised. He could tell that they had much different worldviews.

"Your belief in why I do what I do notwithstanding, I need to know whether or not I can count on you moving forward," he said.

"That depends."

"Sorry, I need a yes or no answer. No contingencies, no qualifiers. Either you agree to do what I say, or you're not going back out with us."

Decker was quiet for several moments. "I really thought those soldiers were Congolese military. I wouldn't have gone with them had I known they weren't."

Harvath didn't know what to make of her statement. It almost sounded like an apology. Regardless, it showed she was capable of insight, which went a big way toward fixing the problem.

"I'm not saying you can't help people. That's what you do. I understand that. But right now, our job is to figure out what happened to the people at the Matumaini Clinic. That needs to be our focus. Agreed?"

Whatever storm had been raging inside of Decker, it seemed to be receding. Her face had softened and her posture was less aggressive.

"Agreed," she said.

Harvath looked at his watch and computed how much daylight they had left. If Ash and his team were onboard, he wanted to push to make it to the clinic before nightfall.

The sooner he was out of Congo, the better.

CHAPTER 12

After negotiating for some extra fuel and water at the ranger station, the team headed out. Typical Congo, everything was fine until it wasn't.

They traversed two relatively shallow rivers, only to discover that they had built an inflated sense of confidence when it came to a third. It was much deeper and faster than the others. The water rose almost to the windows, and at one point, both Land Cruisers began being pushed downstream. As they started to rock and threatened to roll over, Ash passed the word to be ready to bail out.

Luckily, the heavy tires finally bit into the riverbed, found purchase, and moved them over and onto the opposite bank. They had made it through the worst of it. From that point forward, it would only be ruts, bumps, and mud.

Harvath turned his attention out his window. Before leaving the ranger station, he had checked his phone again. He was using it in conjunction with a satellite system that would allow him to send and receive text messages, as well as make phone calls, as long as he had a relatively unimpeded view of the sky. Lara had still not replied to any of his messages.

He didn't like the fact that he was thinking about her while he was on an assignment. He was supposed to compartmentalize these things. He had chastised other operatives in the field for making the same mistake. If your head wasn't a hundred percent in the game, you quickly became a trouble magnet.

This wasn't like him. He usually kept everything wired tight. Part of it was because he knew Lara was pissed at him and had every right to be. He had told her that he had taken this assignment because he had to. That much was true. He believed he was the best person to handle the job. But that would have been true of almost any assignment that the Carlton Group had been tasked with. Where he had lied to her was in telling her he had no choice.

Of course he had a choice. He could have said no. The thing was, he didn't want to say no. He wanted to take this assignment because he hadn't done something like it before. He relished the challenge. He also knew that the trip with Lara was about a lot more than watching the fall colors. She was ready to start having the talk. He hadn't realized how disinterested he was in having that talk until he arrived in Congo.

No matter what any woman said to the contrary, at some point he'd be forced to make a choice. He couldn't have a family and keep this career. He had grown up watching what that was like. It was rough on everyone.

But what Harvath did now was ten times different from what his father had done. His father had gone into hostile nations accompanied by his SEAL Team. Harvath, though, often went into hostile nations alone. He took bigger risks than his father and couldn't imagine how he would be able to keep on doing that with a family back at home.

For the longest time, he had wanted his own piece of the American Dream, but now he was no longer sure what that dream looked like. He didn't know how he could have his and protect everyone else's.

He was also concerned about the consequences of obtaining the American Dream. Would having a family back home cause him to dial down his risk-taking in the field? Might that get him or someone else killed? Or was it more than that? Was he afraid that no matter how many visions he had had to the contrary, this—what he was doing right now— was what he was really cut out for, and not family life?

It was an idea he had kept relegated to a very cold, dark corner of his mind. One that he never fed, hoping that by ignoring it, it would slip away and disappear. But it hadn't disappeared. In fact, it had only grown.

He slammed an iron gate down on his thoughts and focused on what lay ahead. Another potential run-in with Ash and his team was looming.

The Brits were going to want to accompany him right up to the clinic's front door. Harvath couldn't allow that, not with what he knew might be waiting for them. He hadn't brought enough equipment. Somehow, he would have to convince them to hang back.

• • •

The turnoff for the road to the Matumaini Clinic was so poorly marked that they drove right past it. It took six kilometers before Ash and Mick realized their error and the Land Cruisers doubled back. Without someone regularly chopping away at it, the jungle quickly swallowed up anything left unattended.

The Matumaini road was worse than anything they had previously seen. Halfway to the clinic, the road was sliced open by deep washout several feet wide. Ash had Simon and Eddie bring up the bridging ladders strapped to LC2.

As the men maneuvered the beams into place, Harvath pulled Ash aside. "I want to talk about the footprint we're going to have when we get to the clinic," he said.

Keeping one eye on the Brute Squad, Ash replied, "Fine. What do you have in mind?"

"I want to keep it light."

"How light?"

"Just me and Dr. Decker."

"You're the client and you can do whatever you want, but I have to tell you that I think it's a bad idea. We don't know what might be waiting there. A quick web search for *CARE International* is all the FRPI would need."

"That's assuming any of the rebels who saw the door magnets are still alive," stated Harvath.

"And that there was no radio transmission by them before we took them out."

"If I was stuck in one place, hiding a critically ill rebel commander, I wouldn't be putting out a lot of radio traffic."

"Neither would I," Ash agreed, "but it still needs to be considered. We could be walking into an ambush. Hell, a few more kilometers and we could be driving into one."

"Which is why I want you guys to hang back. We'll get the vehicles off the road, set up camp, and then Dr. Decker and I will go the rest of the way on foot and check it out."

"You want to go in tonight? In the dark?"

Harvath checked his watch again. By the time they found a place to camp and got the trucks out of sight, it would indeed be dark. "I think that's the best way."

"You don't need all of us to stay behind. Mick and I will go with you. If you run into trouble, you'll have two extra trigger-pullers with you. How's that sound?"

In any other situation, it would have sounded like a great plan, but Harvath and Decker needed to go in alone. "I appreciate it, but it's just going to be the two of us."

"Your call," Ash replied with a shake of his head.

Harvath thanked him and then steered the conversation to where they should set up camp. He pulled up the satellite images stored on his phone, careful not to reveal any pictures of the burn pit, and gave the Brit an idea of where he thought they could stash the Land Cruisers and make camp.

Once the Brute Squad had piloted both vehicles over the washout, the team remounted the ladders and they headed deeper into the jungle toward the Matumaini Clinic.

As they drove, Harvath made a mental list of the gear he would need. Most of it, particularly the "scary" stuff as Beaman had called it, had already been prepacked into two large backpacks. The amount of kit he and Decker would be humping in was far too much for just a reconnaissance. It was going to raise a few eyebrows with the Brits, but Harvath figured he could once again use the specter of the rebels to his advantage.

Ash and his men technically had no idea what was in the packs. All they had been told was that they were filled with medical supplies for the Matumaini Clinic. They had no reason to believe otherwise.

Harvath would explain that he and Decker planned to cache this load of supplies in the jungle, not far from the clinic. If the rebels were already there, the clinic staff could wait until the coast was clear and then go pick everything up. If the rebels weren't there, they would empty their packs, come back to get the Brits, and then deliver the rest via the vehicles to the clinic's front door.

He had no idea how well that would go down with Ash and his team, but as long as they did what he told them, that was all he cared about.

Two kilometers from the clinic, they left the road and drove several hundred meters into the bush. The jungle was alive, raucous with the calls of birds and all sorts of other animals.

Simon and Eddie set up camp, while Ash and Mick returned to the road to cover their tracks. It wasn't perfect, but unless someone knew exactly where to look for them, nobody was going to find them.

Jambo worked on getting dinner started. Like the rebels from that morning, theirs would be a cold camp, no campfire. Cooking smells could draw unwanted human as well as animal visitors.

Jambo used Jetboil stoves to heat water. When it reached boiling, he poured it into bags of freeze-dried camping food and zipped them shut to steam.

Harvath had brought food for himself and Decker from the United States. He hated the precooked rations used by the military known as MREs. While the acronym stood for *Meals Ready to Eat*, service members normally referred to them as *Meals Rejected by Everyone*. This was his op and he intended to eat what he wanted to eat.

Because of the stress assignments often created, and as he was trying to bulk back up, he had focused on high calorie meals. One of his favorites was biscuits and gravy. He told Jambo to make sure to boil him enough water for two bags. There was no telling how long he and Decker would be gone. Whatever they faced, he planned to do it on a full stomach.

For Decker, he had thrown in a bunch of meals from a new company doing gourmet camping meals such as all-natural, gluten-free mushroom risotto, as well as wild salmon marinara with penne. Something had told him she was going to be a high maintenance pain in the ass, and in his experience, nothing dragged an op down quicker than someone who wasn't eating properly. They not only didn't get the necessary amount of calories to function well, but they also complained incessantly about being hungry.

While his meal steamed, he pulled the two packs he wanted from the back of LC2 and hefted them for weight. Both were heavy. Decker would have to suck it up. He couldn't reveal what they contained and repack them here in front of everyone. She would have to wait. Once they were far enough away from the Brits, he'd work on lightening her load. Setting the packs off to the side, he covered each with a poncho. It felt like rain again.

Simon and Eddie strung jungle hammocks between a series of trees. Being up off the ground would protect the team from snakes and the tented tarps overhead would keep them dry.

Harvath threw a set of dry clothes into his hammock, along with his sleeping bag, and his CRKT Hook & Loop Tool. It had been beaten into him as a SEAL to clean his equipment immediately after an operation—that included his boots. The ingenious little Trip Felton tool had a pick that would be perfect for scraping off the pounds of mud he knew he'd be dragging back.

He gave the hammock lines a tug. The Brute Squad had done a good job. He looked forward to coming back, servicing his gear, and then climbing inside and going to sleep—the Matumaini reconnaissance far behind him.

Of course, that would assume that everything had gone well—something Harvath knew better than to expect, especially in Congo.

CHAPTER 13

The biggest impediment they faced in walking to the clinic, beyond the weight of their packs, was the amount of water they needed. It was imperative that they be well-hydrated before going in, but that was nothing compared to the amount of water they'd need on their way out.

Harvath had known this was going to be a problem, even before leaving the States, and had planned accordingly. They couldn't depend on the clinic's well. If it didn't work, it could result in a death sentence. Harvath had seen enough wells fail to know better than to tie his survival to one in Congo.

Following the narrow river upstream to where it snaked behind the clinic would take them out of their way and increase the likelihood that they would bump into locals, but it would keep them off the road where they might bump into rebels, and it would solve their water issue. It made complete and total sense, except to Dr. Decker.

"You can't do this," she admonished him, once she had figured out what he was doing.

"Watch me."

"You really are a selfish asshole. You know that?"

Harvath had to take a breath and remind himself again that a gentleman never strikes a lady.

"You've never had a well go bad before?" he asked as he finished rebalancing her pack and cinched its top down.

"That's not what I am talking about. I'm talking about you being willing to wash God-knows-what-we'll-find downriver. Do you know how many people you could end up killing?"

Harvath unzipped a compartment on his pack and unrolled four canvas buckets.

"If you want to set up shop farther away from the river, that's fine by me," he said, tossing two of the buckets to her. "But you're going to carry your own water. Mine too, since we're partners."

Decker shot him a disparaging look and chided him. "Don't you have any sense of moral obligation?"

"My moral obligation is simple. I figure out what happened at Matumaini and I make sure we get out of here alive. Anything beyond that is not my problem."

"How about we try to leave this place better than we found it?"

"Put it on a bumper sticker," he said, standing up and holding her pack out to her. "This should be more comfortable now."

Decker took it and almost felt guilty over how much he had lightened it. He had removed a good forty pounds. His act of kindness notwithstanding, she was still angry at his lack of concern over the lives of the locals.

But before she could say anything else, or even swing her pack onto her back, he had picked up his now considerably heavier rucksack, and was moving upstream.

He had an answer for everything—even when his answer was silence. It was infuriating. The real salt in the wound, though, had been the lecture he had given her as they walked away from camp. After warning her about not wanting a repeat of what had happened that morning, he had threatened to tie her to a tree and leave her for the pygmies if she didn't follow all of his instructions to the letter. He had said it with his boyish smile, but it failed to disarm her. She could see right through him.

Harvath obviously had a problem with women, especially smart, accomplished women. He was nothing more than a caveman—a handsome caveman—but a caveman nonetheless.

"Hey," she said, trotting to catch up as he moved along the river. "Are you this much fun with your wife?"

"Not married," he replied and kept moving.

"Imagine that," Decker quipped.

Harvath ignored her.

They walked on in silence for twenty more minutes, until he stopped and checked his GPS. He took a long look around and then motioned for Decker to follow him up the riverbank and into the jungle.

It was slow going. He used a machete he had borrowed from Jambo to help cut a path.

Several minutes later, he stopped and turned to look at her.

"Far enough from the river?" he asked.

Decker nodded, not knowing whether to be pleased with herself or not. The bottom line was that he had taken what she had said to heart.

"Good," he replied, taking off his pack. "I'm going to clear the rest of this brush. You start getting the water."

She dropped her pack near his and disappeared back down the path, the red LEDs of her headlamp lighting her way.

While she went to get the water, Harvath screwed the PVC poles together and hung the plastic sheeting. Next, he filled the canisters with the powder and set their lids next to them.

In the tens of thousands of hours that had gone into establishing the protocols, he was positive that no one had ever envisioned something this primitive.

The ground was soft and he used the machete to trench a berm. It would help prevent the runoff from going all the way downhill and into the river. It was an additional peace offering. Decker had been right. They needed to take all reasonable precautions. They needed to keep it out of the river.

If she bitched about it ending up in the groundwater, there was obviously no pleasing her and he would tie her to a tree and make good on his threat to leave her for the pygmies.

By the time Decker came back, he had finished clearing their staging area, had unrolled the enormous bladder, and had positioned it inside its multi-point sling.

He walked her through everything and, after helping her fill the first canister with water, told her what he wanted her to do if he wasn't back in an hour. She wasn't happy about being left alone.

Handing her the machete, Harvath made her repeat what he had told her. To the letter, she repeated his instructions.

She had expected him to leave her with a final admonition over what had happened that morning, but to his credit, he didn't. Instead, he smiled and told her everything would be okay. Then, flipping his night vision goggles back down, he walked into the jungle and was gone.

•   •   •

Based on his GPS reading at the river, and a review of the satellite imagery saved to his phone, Harvath had a good idea where the clinic was, along with the best way to approach. It took him less than ten minutes to find it.

When he did, he remained in the jungle. He didn't dare enter the clearing. In his mind, there was a bright red circle painted around the building. He wasn't going to cross that line without having taken every single precaution possible.

He low-crawled to the edge of the clearing, parted the vegetation, and peered through his goggles. There was no movement to be seen, but even more unusual was the fact that there wasn't a sound coming from anywhere. It was as if even the animals were avoiding this place. The quiet was unsettling. Harvath tried to shake it off.

Retreating into the jungle, he worked his way around the perimeter. There were no trucks, or vehicles of any sort. No light came from inside the clinic. It looked completely abandoned.

Arriving at the northwest corner of the clearing, he looked at his watch. He wanted to check out the burn pit too, but he'd be pushing it time-wise. He wasn't sure if Decker would honor his instructions or not, but if he wasn't back in an hour he had to expect that she'd be gone. And if she was gone, he would have to abandon the operation. While he hadn't liked the idea of bringing Decker along, he couldn't escape the fact that it was a two-person job. He wouldn't have been able to suit up without her. The reconnaissance, though, would be incomplete without checking the pit, so he decided to push it.

He could smell the pit long before he could see it. More appropriately, he could smell the accelerant that had been used. Jet fuel had a unique odor. But the nearest airport was hundreds of kilometers away. *How the hell had jet fuel ended up in the middle of the jungle?*

For the moment, that question would have to remain unanswered. Nearing the pit, he stopped and listened. When he didn't hear anything, he crept forward to take a look.

There was no sign of anyone, but someone had been there. And they had come through with heavy vehicles, one of which was on treads.

A bulldozer, Harvath thought to himself. Not a good sign. The only reason you brought in something that big was if you had something very large to unearth or to cover up. Though he had never held out much hope for the staff and patients of the Matumaini Clinic, he had held out some. The revelation that a bulldozer had likely been involved in the pit now dashed that hope.

It also raised his concern as to who had staged the alleged attack on the clinic. Hazmat suits, jet fuel, and earth-moving equipment spoke to a very high level of sophistication.

He wanted to examine more of the pit. There was still that question poking at the back of his mind from when he had seen the original satellite footage of it. Something hadn't made sense. *Was it the shape of the pit? The part where the heat was concentrated?*

Unfortunately, he was out of time. He needed to get back before Decker took off.

Retracing his steps, he moved as quickly and as quietly as he could.

CHAPTER 14

By the time he got back to Decker, she had completely filled the canisters and was almost done filling the bladder.

"What did you see?" she asked. "Is anyone at the clinic?"

He shook his head. "Everything's quiet." Pointing at her empty buckets, he added, "Want me to finish the bladder?"

"Thanks," she replied.

Taking Jambo's machete, he chopped off a tree branch about the diameter of a closet rod, notched it in two places at both ends and then, picking up his buckets, as well as Decker's, headed down to the river.

When he returned with the pole across his shoulders and two buckets on each side, Decker was drinking from one of the large, plastic water bottles they had brought in with them.

"You want some?" she asked, holding the bottle out to him.

"No, you finish it," he answered as he set the buckets of water down. "You're going to need it."

"So are you."

She was right. Now was as good as any time to get started. He pulled a bottle from his pack, twisted off the top, and guzzled over half of it. Then he turned his attention to the canvas sling that held the bladder.

A gallon of water weighed almost eight and a half pounds. While he figured they would only need ten to fifteen gallons apiece, he had spec'd a forty-gallon bladder, just in case. Not counting the powdered-chemicals he had added, the weight of which was negligible, the bladder clocked in at over three hundred pounds.

Once they were a "safe" distance away from the river, he had begun looking for a level piece of ground with a strong enough tree. That's how he had chosen where to stop.

Into each of the sling's heavy-duty grommets, he attached a carabiner, which itself was attached to a cable leading to a hoist ring. He removed a ratchet lever hoist, suspended it from the tree limb, and went to work lifting the bladder.

When he had it at the level he wanted, he moved the PVC frame underneath it, extended the hose and tried the nozzle. The water was cold, but it smelled clean and the pressure was excellent. He positioned the supplies they would need and then returned to the bottle of water sitting next to his pack.

As he was drinking, Decker tossed him a pair of surgical scrubs.

"Time to get dressed," she said.

He half expected her to either retreat down the path, or behind the opaque sheeting affixed to the makeshift PVC shower stall, but she didn't bother.

Instead, standing next to her own pack, Decker began to slowly get undressed. Apparently modesty wasn't one of her strong suits. Neither was subtlety.

Harvath didn't want to watch, but he couldn't help himself. The way in which she took off her clothes practically begged for a cover charge and a two drink minimum. He disliked everything about her, but when her mouth was shut and her clothes were dropping to the ground, she wasn't half bad.

The only reason he shifted his eyes away was because he didn't want to give her the satisfaction of knowing he was looking.

As he focused on getting himself undressed, he had to give her points for style. If he had been a woman travelling in the wilds of Congo, he doubted a thong and sexy bra would have been on his packing list.

Shaking his head, he continued to get undressed. She was a boatload of trouble and he figured she probably knew it. Her undoubtedly expensive lingerie was completely impractical and totally out of place in the middle of the jungle. She had to have known that too.

It was, of course, total theater, but in one of the crummiest places in the world, Jessica Decker had decided that the show must go on. He had to give her an A for effort. Any man who couldn't applaud, or at the very least appreciate her dedication to maintaining a modicum of sex appeal, didn't deserve to call himself a man.

While it didn't mean he had any intention of hanging an "Open For Business" sign on his hammock, he decided to sneak one more peek. When he did, he found that she was already looking at him, admiring his body.

Their eyes met. They were both completely naked and they held each other's gaze for several beats longer than they should have.

It was Harvath who eventually broke it off and looked away. That word that rhymed with *truck* leapt back into his mind.

It might have been a game to Decker, but he knew he had to be careful. Hanging off a skyscraper, only a fool whipped out his knife and starting sawing away at the rope. It was amazing, though, how foolish even the most resolute of men could be.

Thankfully, when he looked back over, Decker was nearly dressed. She made a show of pulling the top of her scrubs over her breasts before smoothing it down. She was trouble all right and she *definitely* knew it. Harvath, though, had enough other things to think about and shifted his mind to those.

Taking only the bare minimum of things they would need, he repacked Decker's ruck and covered it with one of their ponchos. He used the other poncho to cover a hole he had dug and needed to keep dry. There had been no rain since they had left the Brits back at camp. For the time being, Mother Nature seemed to be smiling on them, or at least unaware of their presence.

When Decker indicated that she was ready, Harvath struck off toward the clinic.

The idea was to get as close as possible before climbing into the stifling heat of their biohazard suits. At most, they would be good for a half hour—and even then it would feel like they had done an Ironman race in one hundred degree heat. Dehydration and heat stroke were very serious concerns, which was why they had been drinking water and would be watching the clock once they were suited up.

At the clinic's perimeter, Harvath took a long look around and then removed his night vision goggles and allowed Decker to take a look. His primary goal was to put her at ease. If she was at all nervous, the stress would erode the amount of time she could remain in her suit.

His secondary goal was to give her an opportunity to reacquaint herself with the property and see if she noticed anything out of place.

After a couple of minutes, she handed the goggles back to him.

"Does it look the way you remembered it?" he asked.

"Pretty much."

"Okay. Let's get suited up."

Unpacking his ruck, Harvath laid out their gear in stacks of *his* and *hers*. Though they had already examined the suits, gloves, hoods, and booties for punctures, tears, or any other vulnerability whatsoever, they went through each pile once more and then switched, checking each other's work.

Content that the suits had not been compromised they began climbing into their personal protective equipment, also known as PPE.

The process required multiple pairs of sterile gloves and each one had to be taped to your suit. The tape had to be applied in a very specific manner, so as not to "tent," which might provide an opening for a virus or other deadly pathogens to get in. This was one of the biggest reasons Harvath had been overruled and Decker was along for the assignment. A person not only needed help donning their PPE, but it was crucial to have help in doffing it. It simply wasn't possible to properly remove the suit on one's own.

Decker had been through extensive training and knew what she was doing. She stepped Harvath through what he needed to do as her partner.

When he asked about the multiple pairs of gloves, she explained that while they were a protection against the outermost level being punctured or torn, their primary raison d'être was to provide uncontaminated gloves beneath the outer gloves in order to help you get out of your suit.

The whole process, right down to getting out of your boots and slithering out of the suit was like the board game Operation. Touch the sides at any time and that was it. It came down to partnership and absolute trust.

While Decker may have pissed him off immeasurably with her behavior that morning, right now she radiated professionalism.

Taping the seams at his wrists and ankles, running her hands over the exterior of his suit—all of it was expert and clinical. However coquettish she may or may not have intended to be while getting into her scrubs, all of that was now gone. Jessica Decker was one hundred percent business.

They were going through the final stages of taping when Harvath heard her curse.

At first, he thought he had done something wrong. Then, he saw what had triggered the expletive.

A large raindrop had landed on her face panel. It was quickly followed by another and then another. Without any preamble, the clouds had opened up and the rain was now pounding down. *Congo.*

"We need to work fast," Decker shouted over the din, "but methodically. Don't screw up."

Harvath did as she instructed, taking great care to make sure his tape didn't tent. They were working beneath their headlamps, which had been wrapped around a tree limb. It was already less than optimal conditions. The rain only made it worse.

When he was done, Harvath flashed her the thumbs-up.

She examined her seams, then his. It was now that faith entered the equation. They had either done everything right, or they hadn't. Only time would tell.

Taking a step back, Decker moved out of the way so that Harvath could lead.

The suit was extremely uncomfortable. Because of its bulk, his range of motion was severely limited. He felt like the midwestern boy in *A Christmas Story*, whose mother had over-bundled him with umpteen layers against the severe winter walk to school.

The hood not only impacted his hearing, but it also narrowed his field of view. His peripheral vision was all but nonexistent.

Usually, they would have taken each other's vitals before suiting up, but they didn't have the luxury of allowing vitals to dictate go or no-go for this assignment.

After powering up a small IR video camera, Harvath stepped into the clearing and kept his head on a swivel as they walked toward the clinic.

He had told Decker to inform him right away if anything seemed out of place. Twice he looked back at her and twice she flashed him the thumbs-up.

From across the clearing, the clinic had somehow looked more formidable, more robust. The closer they came, the more shabby and run-down it became. He had thought that maybe it was a trick of the rain streaming down his faceplate, but it wasn't. Like everything else in Congo, even this American-funded medical clinic was woefully underwhelming.

There was a crappy, hand-painted wooden sign above the dilapidated covered entrance. Written in French and English it read: *CARE INTERNATIONAL: MATUMAINI MEDICAL CLINIC.*

Its ridiculously hopeful blue shutters were drawn flush against the chipped and peeling white façade. The faded front door was also closed.

Standing beneath the overhang, Harvath wiped the rain from his faceplate and then leaned in to study the door.

"What is it?" Decker asked.

With his finger, he pointed to a discolored inch-and-a-half-wide strip around the frame.

"Something was taped over this door at one point," he said. And then, examining the windows on either side added, "The windows were too. Stay here."

Before Decker could respond, he had already stepped out from under the overhang and into the rain to examine the rest of the structure.

She didn't like being left alone, especially not right at the front door. What if someone was inside? What if that someone came out? How would she protect herself? Decker willed herself to calm down.

This was her clinic. She used to be in charge here. There was nothing to worry about.

Staring out into the rain, she thought about all the people she had worked with here. They were good people, hard-working people, whose only sin was to have been born in Congo. Why someone would attack this clinic was beyond her. In fact, why someone would attack any clinic was beyond her. It was that kind of senselessness that had made her want to stop reporting tragedies and become part of making people's lives better. They had done that at the Matumaini Clinic and she hoped they would be able to do it again.

A rumble of thunder echoed from somewhere off in the distance. Decker took a step back and pressed herself against the wall. It was pitch black and the rain was coming down in sheets. She couldn't make out where the clinic grounds ended and the jungle began.

Nevertheless, someone was watching. She could feel it. She had sensed eyes on them from the moment they had stepped out of the jungle. She wished she still had the machete. Something wasn't right.

No sooner had that thought popped into her mind than she heard the sound of glass breaking from inside the clinic.

CHAPTER 15

L ying in the sill to Decker's left was a short piece of rebar used for propping open the window. She grabbed it. It wasn't much of a weapon, but it was something.

There was another noise from inside, followed by the groan of metal on metal and the scraping of wood against stone as the faded front door creaked and began to open.

She made ready to strike until she saw the outline of Harvath's hazmat suit as he stepped out of the clinic.

"What the hell are you doing? I thought you were checking the exterior of the building."

"I saw enough. Come inside."

Decker followed him. Parts of the interior were illuminated with an eerie, greenish glow. Harvath had brought along a box of his own full-sized chemlights and was snapping and tossing them into various corners as he went. They provided enough light to see by, but not so much that it would be noticed from outside.

"What was that crash I heard?" Decker asked.

"Nothing," Harvath replied. "I had to break a window to get in."

"Let me check the integrity of your suit."

"I'm fine." He was already overheating and not in a good mood.

"Let me check," Decker insisted.

Harvath complied and she pulled out her headlamp, activated the low-level red beam, and examined him from head to toe.

"You're good."

"Thanks," he said. "Now, come look at this."

He led her into the main ward. It was a graveyard of metal bedframes. All of the mattresses had been stripped away. There wasn't a sheet or blanket to be seen either.

"It's like a swarm of locusts came through here," Decker stated. "Even the mosquito netting and privacy dividers are gone."

All of the bedframes had been jumbled together in the center of the ward. Harvath pulled a large plastic bottle of liquid from his bag and began spraying it in different places around the room.

"What's that?" she asked.

"Luminol. It reacts with the iron in hemoglobin. If there's any blood in here, it'll start glowing blue."

Decker waited, but she didn't see anything. Neither did Harvath.

"There," she suddenly said, pointing to an area glowing in the corner. "And there. And there."

Harvath turned and looked at each occurrence, along with several others that were actively glowing.

"My God," Decker exclaimed. "There's blood everywhere!"

"Take it easy," replied Harvath, as he began spraying more luminol around the room. He even stood on one of the bedframes to spray several spots along the ceiling. All of them started to glow blue.

"How is that possible?" she asked. "It's like the whole ward was painted in blood."

"Not exactly," he said as he exited the ward and made his way through the clinic, randomly spraying walls, doors, floors, windows, and ceilings with the luminol.

"It's all glowing," he heard her shout as she trailed behind him. "Every single thing you're spraying."

She caught up with him in the small dispensary that also acted as the clinic's laboratory. Harvath was spraying the small, empty refrigerator. It all glowed blue.

"I don't understand," she said.

"There's only two other substances that can cause luminol to glow like this and I don't think it's the first one."

"What's the first one?"

Harvath got out an *S* and an *H* before catching himself and saying, "Excrement."

"And the second?" Decker asked.

"Bleach."

"Bleach?"

He nodded. "I think this entire place has been sanitized. Literally from top to bottom. I also think," he began, but his voice trailed off as something caught his eye.

"What is it?"

Harvath motioned for her to back out of the dispensary. He had been bending down near the tiny fridge and saw something beneath the cabinets on the adjacent wall.

There was a narrow strip of black, plastic trim along the top of the fridge that had begun to peel back on one side. Harvath helped it the rest of the way off.

Lying down on his stomach, he slid the piece of trim under the cabinets and coaxed out the item from underneath. Once he got it out, he held it up.

"What is it?" Decker repeated from the doorway. It looked like a giant mint the size of a hockey puck. It was chipped, and a large portion appeared to have been burned.

"No one ever used these when you were here?"

"I don't even know what it is."

Harvath sprayed it with luminol. Seconds later it started to glow.

"It's a bleach tablet," he said.

"Why would that be here?"

"Drop this in a pie plate and set it on top of a camping stove, and you can gasify it. The fumes go everywhere and will sanitize anything your liquid bleach missed."

"Then you're right. The clinic was sanitized. But by whom? And why? What were they sanitizing?"

Good questions, none of which Harvath wanted to waste time deciphering right now. His scrubs were soaked through and the sweat was rolling down his face into his eyes. He wanted to finish looking around and get the hell out of here.

Retreating to the front door, he reenacted what he had seen on the video. Though someone outside had filmed it, he could approximate where the shooters had been standing when they entered and had opened fire.

In his restrictive biohazard suit, Harvath pantomimed a tactical entry, stepping inside with a rifle and shooting.

If the shooters had been following the same protocols he was, they might have wanted a few modifications to their weapons. Wearing the layers of gloves, the more refined features of the weapons would be difficult to manipulate. Perhaps they had upgraded to larger trigger guards and beefier charging handles to accommodate their thicker, less dexterous fingers.

It was also possible that for such a quick, in-and-out assignment where no resistance would have been expected, the men had just made do with whatever weapons they normally carried or had access to. There was no way of knowing for sure.

What he was able to know for sure came from examining the wall directly opposite the front door.

Based on the furniture scattered nearby, it had been some sort of clerical or nurse's station, likely the place patients checked in and then were shown to a row of chairs where they would wait to see one of the clinic's medical staff.

He ran his hand up and down the entire wall.

"What do you see?" Decker asked him.

"It's not what I see," said Harvath. "But what I don't see. There are no bullet holes. At least not anymore. Look."

She bent down and studied the places he pointed to.

"Whoever this was," he continued, "they were absolute professionals. They did a full cleanup job. Right down to digging out the bullets and patching and painting the walls."

While Decker looked for any records of what might have been going on at the clinic, Harvath examined the walls and floor in the ward and found more evidence of the walls having been repaired.

He was convinced that whoever it was had come in, killed the staff, and then had murdered all of the patients. He didn't need to ask where their bodies had been taken. He already knew.

Decker rejoined him from the back of the clinic and shook her head.

"I can't find anything," she said.

"I'm not surprised," he replied. "Don't worry. We've seen enough. Let's get out of here."

Decker nodded and they exited the clinic. Harvath went first.

As was his habit, he took a long, slow look around before signaling that it was safe for her to join him. It was still raining and the moment they stepped out from under the overhang, the rain began streaking down their faceplates.

Neither of them cared. They were both bordering on heatstroke. All that mattered was getting out of the suits.

Reentering the jungle, they retraced their steps to where they had positioned the canisters. Harvath had already mixed the solution inside, but he picked up each one and gave it a good shake before pumping their handles up and down.

It was a maddening process to have to go through when you were this uncomfortable, but because their lives depended on it, they took extra precautions not to rush things. They had made it this far. It was only a little bit further. Now was not the time to be cutting any corners.

Decker reminded Harvath to take a deep breath. It was thick with humidity, but he did so anyway. She then lifted the wand attached to her canister and began spraying him down.

He lifted his arms in the air and turned in a slow circle. She stopped to pump the handle and then had him repeat the process. He did the same for her.

They did it again and again until they had both exhausted two full canisters of the solution. Then came the hard part—doffing the PPE.

All sorts of horrible diseases had infected untold numbers of medical workers over the years—not because their suits had failed, but because they had failed to properly remove those suits.

Next to visiting an outbreak, the next most dangerous step involved was slithering out of the suit. The doffing procedure required steely patience and total concentration. Slowly, carefully, Decker walked him through every step.

Their scrubs and everything else went into the hole he had previously dug and packed with tinder.

While Decker showered, he doused the pile of gear with some of the kerosene he'd asked the Brits to source for the clinic. As soon as the fire was burning good and hot, it was his turn to shower.

He stood under the water and used the soap and shampoo to clean himself from top to bottom. His PPE had held and he was confident they had followed all the doffing procedures correctly. He wasn't a hypochondriac and didn't need to scrub himself raw.

He allowed the lukewarm water to trickle over his neck and shoulders. He was glad the clinic part was over. They would have to go back and check the burn pit, but it was pro forma at this point and at least he wouldn't have to get back in one of those suits. It did indeed feel like he had competed in an Ironman race in one hundred degree heat.

He reached down for one of the water bottles mixed with Gatorade powder he had left on the edge of the shower, but it wasn't there.

Straightening up, he saw Decker. She was standing there, naked, just looking at him with the bottle of Gatorade in her hand. Then, she stepped into the shower.

CHAPTER 16

Harvath was exhausted. So was Decker. He wanted to take a closer look at the burn pit, but now wasn't the time. Not in the dark and the rain. It was time to get back to camp.

Shouldering their packs, they walked down to the river and returned the way they had come.

The rain made it difficult to talk, and it was probably for the best. Decker had already made going to the burn pit an issue. She wanted to go with him in the morning. Harvath had no idea what she had seen as a war correspondent, but he had strongly advised her against it. There were certain things that couldn't be unseen. Once they were seared into your mind, they stayed there forever.

The additional reason he felt she should sit it out was that she had personal relationships with the people missing from the clinic. Based on what little he had seen, he knew the pit was going to be brutal.

Decker, though, had her mind made up. No matter how hard he might try to dissuade her, she intended to join him. There was no use fighting her on it and he let the subject drop.

When they entered the camp, they found the Brits, along with Jambo, sitting beneath a tarp slung between two trees and one of the Land Cruisers.

"How'd it go?" Ash asked.

"Not well," Harvath replied. "We need to talk."

The Brit motioned to the other Land Cruiser.

Inside, Harvath pulled his poncho off and threw it on the backseat.

Ash handed him a towel and asked, "What happened?"

"Someone hit the clinic."

"Hit it how?"

"It looks like a team of shooters came in."

The Brit stared at him. "The rebels? FRPI?"

"Not unless they travel with sanitation teams."

"It was sanitized?"

Harvath nodded. "Right down to digging the slugs out of the wall and patching the holes."

"It was a professional hit then."

"That's what it looks like."

It didn't make any sense. "It's a charity clinic," Ash replied. "Why would anyone waste those kinds of resources on it?"

Harvath shrugged. "No idea."

"Bullshit."

"I'm serious."

"No, you're not," the Brit stated. "You've been holding out on us since you arrived. I don't believe for a second that you came to do some sort of assessment. You're here to compile an after action report."

Lying to people was part of Harvath's job, but he hated doing it. Ash was completely correct. Harvath had been holding out on him. It was just the way things had to be done. At this point, though, he needed the man's help more than he needed to keep any further secrets from him.

"Several days ago," said Harvath, "CARE International received a video. It showed four gunmen entering the Matumaini Clinic and opening fire."

"Who sent the video?"

"We don't know."

"Who took the video?"

"We don't know."

"When was it taken?"

"We don't know that either."

Ash narrowed his eyes in the semidarkness of the Land Cruiser and tried to read Harvath's face. "What *do* you know?"

"What I just told you."

"But you haven't told me anything except that there were four gunmen. What did they look like? Were they black? White? Purple? How were they dressed?"

Harvath removed his phone, powered it on, and showed him the footage.

"Those are bloody biohazard suits."

Harvath nodded and waited until Ash had watched the full clip.

"Play it again," the Brit said.

Harvath did as he requested. When the video was over, he took his phone back.

Ash was not happy. "You and Decker went into the clinic, didn't you?"

"Don't worry," Harvath said. "We wore protective gear."

"What do you mean *don't worry*? What the hell is going on here?"

"We don't know."

"You knew enough to bring protective gear with you," the Brit said, adding, "That's why you wanted us to wait here, isn't it."

Harvath nodded.

"And you never thought any of this was worth sharing?"

"I was under orders not to."

"The hell you were."

"I told you. We don't know what's going on here either," Harvath emphasized. "The last thing CARE wants is a scandal."

"*Scandal?* You've got a bloody international incident."

Try selling that to the U.S. State Department, Harvath thought to himself.

"Listen, mate, those shooters didn't go in kitted up like that just to freak out the natives. There was something bad inside that clinic that they were very afraid of."

"I agree."

"So what was going on there? What would cause an armed team in biohazard suits to just show up?"

"No one on our side knows. It's just a basic medical clinic, period. They don't treat highly communicable diseases."

"Apparently, somebody thought they did," replied Ash. "And it was somebody serious because, according to you, after the wet work was done, they sent in a mop-up team to sterilize the scene."

"So let's narrow that down," Harvath said.

"How do I know you're not carrying whatever was in that clinic?"

"Because I told you, we wore protective gear."

"You've told me a lot of things."

He was pissed. Harvath would have been too if their positions had been switched.

"We wore full biohazard suits and followed the strictest decon procedures."

"That's what was in the packs? Not medical supplies."

"Correct," Harvath replied.

Ash shook his head.

"About that wet work team—" Harvath continued, but Ash held his hand up, interrupting him.

"Our fee has just doubled. And if I find out you have held anything else back, I'm going to double it again."

"I'll have to call back to the States to get approval for that."

"This isn't a negotiation," Ash stated. "You hired us under false pretenses and watered down the scope. The fee is double, or we pack up and drive you back to Bunia right now. Which is it?"

Harvath didn't like having his balls busted, but the man was within his rights. He agreed to the increased fee. Then, he steered him back to his previous question. "Narrow down for me who might have sent in a wet work team and followed it up with cleaners."

"*Narrow* it down? It could have been any foreign intelligence service in the first world, or from the second for that matter. How do you narrow *that* down?"

"Let's start with how many of them are operating in Congo."

"If they're smart, all of them are. Congo's untapped mineral resources alone are valued at over twenty-four trillion dollars. That's more than the GDP of the U.S. and Europe combined."

"But what nations specifically would you be focused on?" Harvath asked.

Ash thought about it. "You've got everyone from the Australians to the Swiss running a mining operation here. That includes the Chinese and Japanese as well. Even the Moroccans have established a presence."

"But whose intelligence service would send out a wet work team?"

The Brit shook his head. "The question isn't who, but rather *why*? As in, why would any foreign intelligence service give two whits about some medical clinic in the middle of nowhere?"

His point was well taken. It was the same question Harvath had been asking himself since seeing the clinic. But perhaps it wasn't the question that was wrong. Maybe, it was how he was asking it.

"Let's back up and start again," Harvath stated. "*Why* would anyone send a wet work team into a medical clinic in the first place?"

"That seems fairly obvious," Ash replied. "To make sure that someone, or *something*, never got out of there. And based on how those shooters were suited up, I'll bet they were after someone who was infected."

Harvath concurred. "So let's assume for a minute that they were trying to contain something. Why not just quarantine the clinic? Why go in shooting?"

Ash paused again and thought about the question. Finally, he said, "Because whatever they have, it's *beyond* bad."

"Even if it were beyond bad," Harvath replied, "you quarantine the victims and make them as comfortable as possible. You don't kill them."

"So what's the answer then?"

"I don't know," he said as he reached up and ground his thumbs into his temples. This entire clusterfuck of an assignment was turning into one big headache.

After thinking about it some more, Ash attempted to come at it from another angle.

"Do you have any clue what they did with the bodies?"

Harvath nodded. "That's the next thing we need to discuss."

CHAPTER 17

By the time Decker was awake and out of her hammock, Harvath had already gone. He had taken Ash and Mick with him.

While Jambo and the Brute Squad broke down the camp, Harvath and the two other Brits proceeded to the pit on foot. They wanted to establish a perimeter before calling in the rest of the team.

The rain had stopped overnight and when the first pale streaks of dawn began to paint the sky, it looked as if it would be a halfway decent morning. Harvath wanted to take it as a good omen, but he knew better than to put his trust in that kind of thing. Rain or shine, this was still Congo.

Per Ash's request, they had given the clinic a healthy berth on their hike in. They had stopped to survey it at a distance from the jungle, but only for a moment, and then had pushed on.

As soon as they neared the pit, they could smell the jet fuel. While it wasn't as strong as it had been the night before for Harvath, it was still unmistakable.

They worked their way around the pit and conducted a preliminary reconnaissance in the semidarkness. None of them spoke. They all knew what this place was. You could feel it.

Ash sent Mick out to the road as a lookout and then called in the rest of the team.

The sun was just beginning to pierce the trees when the white Land Cruisers rolled up.

Decker stepped out of LC1 wrapped in a fleece and holding a coffee cup. Her hair was pulled back and tied in a ponytail. She arched her shoulders and lazily looked around as if she had just shown up for a 5K and was searching for the sign-in table.

Then, the odor of jet fuel found its way into her nose and her demeanor completely changed. Her eyes found Harvath's as he walked over to her.

"We'll have good light in about ten more minutes," he said. "You can still opt out of this. I'll have them move the vehicles back and one of the guys will stay with you."

Decker shook her head. "I want to do this. I have to."

Harvath wasn't going to fight with her. "Okay."

"What's that smell?" she asked.

"Jet fuel."

"Did they use it to burn the bodies?"

"Probably."

Closing her eyes, she leaned into him and placed her head against his shoulder. "Seeing death up close never gets any easier, does it?"

It was one of the first purely human glimpses he had seen of her. "No," he replied. "It doesn't."

He knew the Brits were watching, and he didn't care.

Like most pure moments, though, this one was fleeting. Decker straightened up, turned her back on him and walked around to the other side of the Land Cruiser to drink her coffee and watch the sunrise.

Harvath removed his Toughbook laptop, placed it on the backseat, and turned it on. He had already uploaded the video footage from the clinic and had composed a brief SITREP for the Old Man. Now that he had an unimpeded view of the sky, he wanted to transmit it back to the States.

Powering up his Iridium WiFi cube, he set it on the roof of the SUV and angled its antenna. While it searched for satellites, he also powered up his phone to see if he had received any texts.

Once the cube was connected, he watched for the message icon to light up on his phone. It didn't. Turning it off, he focused his mind on business.

He had broken the video up into pieces to make it easier to transmit. Pulling up the string of encrypted emails, he hit *send* and then grabbed his video camera. The sun was strong enough now to begin seeing the pit.

Finished with her coffee, Decker pulled a box of high-end surgical masks out of her bag and offered them around. Everyone accepted one of the disposable respirators, even Jambo and the Brute Squad who would be staying with the vehicles and securing the road. There was no telling what was in the pit or suspended in the atmosphere around it.

Harvath doubted anything could have survived a jet fuel–assisted fire, but he knew that the remaining smoke and ash could present a whole host of health problems and so fitted his mask over his mouth and nose.

Turning the video camera on, he documented the tire tracks and tread marks leading to and from the pit. While a lot of it was nothing more than puddles of red mud, there was enough there to show what type of equipment had come through.

When he had what he needed, he joined Decker and they walked with Ash and Mick out toward the pit.

It was a solemn procession. No one spoke. With the sun up, they could see the occasional wisp of smoke rising into the air in front of them. *But with all of the rain, how was that even possible?* The horrific answer became clear soon enough.

Like most of the terrain they had been through, the area surrounding the clinic was mostly sloped. The same could be said for where the staff disposed of their trash. It was a narrow, level strip at the base of a steep, nearby hill. But it was what had been done with the hill that turned their stomachs.

Even through their masks, the smell of jet fuel was now overpowering. Harvath took one look at everything and knew why.

A bulldozer had definitely been brought in, but not to bury bodies. It had been brought in to engineer a grisly crematorium.

A huge chunk had been ripped out of the bottom of the hill to create the oven. With Decker following behind, Harvath climbed to the top and let his nose be his guide. It didn't take long to find the empty fuel barrels hidden beneath a makeshift blind. Each one had been punctured with a small hole.

Several yards away he uncovered the air shaft and knew exactly what he was looking at. He also knew why the satellite image had looked off to him.

"What is all of this?" Decker asked as he recorded it.

"A giant rocket stove."

"What's a rocket stove?"

Harvath pointed to the shaft and then at the barrels. "Oxygen would have been sucked in from the base of the hill and drawn up through this shaft. Those punctured barrels of jet fuel would have continued to drip-feed the fire.

"The stronger the fire got, the more oxygen would have been sucked in. And the more oxygen that got sucked in, the hotter the fire would have raged. The temperature would have been amazing; total combustion of almost anything placed down there."

"Including bodies?"

"If they stacked them right."

Decker suddenly didn't feel so well.

Harvath noticed that her color was off. "Are you okay?" he asked.

"I'll be fine."

"You sure?"

She nodded. "It's the jet fuel. Can we walk back down?"

"Of course," he replied, offering her his arm.

Decker accepted it, but let go halfway when the trail became too narrow for them to walk side by side.

At the bottom, Ash and Mick were studying something at the edge of the pit.

As he saw the Americans approach, Ash raised his hand for them to stop.

"You don't want to see this," he warned.

"See what?" Decker replied, undeterred.

Mick turned and gently tried to block her, but she nudged him out of the way.

She took one look and came charging back past Harvath with her hand over her mask. Seconds later, she was in the brush vomiting.

"Are you okay?" he asked, but she waved him off.

He looked over at Ash who motioned for him to come see what they had found. Harvath knew it wasn't going to be good.

The men stepped aside as he joined them. On the ground at their feet were the skulls of three small children. Beyond was a jumble of bones, also small.

While any loss of innocent life was lamentable, the loss of children was doubly so.

Though he didn't want to, Harvath raised the video camera and recorded everything. There was one thing that still didn't make sense—the size of the pit. If you were just going to murder the people at the clinic, why did this have to be so big? It didn't make any sense.

He was taking close-up shots when Mick asked, "What happened to Dr. Decker?"

Harvath paused the camera and looked around. He didn't see her either.

"Maybe she went to get a fresh mask," said Ash. "Or a toothbrush."

She probably just needed a break, thought Harvath. This was hard for anyone to handle.

"I'll go look for her," he said, handing the camera to Mick.

"Don't go too far," Ash warned.

Stepping away from the pit, Harvath looked uphill toward where the fuel barrels were. He doubted she had gone back up there, but he climbed the hill just to make sure. There was no trace of her.

She must have gone back to the vehicles. Walking back down the trail, he got to the bottom and headed back toward the Land Cruisers.

But as he got closer and could see everybody but Decker, his internal alarm system started to go off.

When Jambo, Simon, and Eddie all confirmed that they hadn't seen her, he radioed Ash and Mick and made his concern official.

CHAPTER 18

Eddie and Simon were exceptional trackers. Starting from where Decker had last been seen, they worked the ground inch by inch until they had picked up her trail.

Decker appeared to have started back toward the vehicles, but then had diverted for some reason. They couldn't figure out why. Then, they came across another set of tracks. She appeared to be following someone.

Whoever it was, he was leading Decker due west, directly away from the pit. Harvath was pissed off at her all over again. *What was she doing?* He could not have been clearer with her. *Damn it.* She seemed determined to get all of them killed, including herself.

Walking off, though, was soon no longer the worst part. Two hundred meters into their hunt, Eddie picked up on a third set of tracks. Decker was being followed.

Ash signaled for them to split up. He took Simon and Mick into the jungle to flank, while Harvath and Eddie stayed on Decker's trail and closed the gap with whoever was following her.

Despite his size, Eddie moved with incredible speed. He ran with his lips pulled back, his jet-black Van Dyke highlighting two sharp canine teeth that made him look like some kind of giant vampire.

While Harvath was tripped up twice along the overgrown path, Eddie never once lost his footing. It was like watching an enormous jaguar tear through the jungle.

And then, out of nowhere, he put on the brakes, thrust his left hand behind him, and signaled for Harvath to stop.

Harvath did as he was ordered and waited while Eddie surveyed something in front of them. Finally, he waved Harvath up to join him.

Cradling the shotgun he had taken from LC1, Harvath crept up to where Eddie was on his stomach peering through the foliage.

Through a quick series of hand signals, the Brit relayed to Harvath what he had seen. He parted a cluster of ferns and rolled to his left so Harvath could peer through.

In the distance, was a small village. There couldn't have been more than ten, perhaps, thirteen individual huts, as well as a smattering of animal pens and some sort of communal pavilion.

"Which one?" Harvath whispered.

"The big one," Eddie replied. "Three o'clock."

He had a small monocular with him and he handed it to Harvath so he could surveil the village.

After the pavilion, the hut was the largest structure in town, which wasn't saying much. There were pens, but they were empty. There were no animals, no signs of life at all. No children, no smoke from cook fires, no nothing. It was a ghost town.

"Are you positive?" Harvath asked.

Eddie nodded.

"Can you lase it for Ash?"

The man nodded and hailing his boss over the radio, relayed everything to him. He then removed a black tube the size of a half-smoked cigarette and depressing its switch, painted the roof of the big hut with a tiny green laser. Ash radioed back and confirmed the target. Now, all they had to do was come up with a plan.

Harvath snapped a mental grid over the scene and surveyed the village one slice at a time. He was trying to figure out two things—first, *where was everyone?* and second, *was this a trap?*

What looked like heavy tire tracks on the edge of the village helped bring the picture quickly into focus.

Handing the monocular to Eddie, he showed him what to look for. Once the man had seen it, he radioed Harvath's plan to Ash, who agreed. Stepping out of the jungle, Harvath and Eddie cautiously made their way down to the village.

There was sparse cover and concealment, and they took turns moving and providing overwatch for each other. In any other situation, exposing themselves by running through so much open space would have been insane, but the circumstances offered no other alternative.

When they made it to the village, they pulled up at the first hut, flattened their backs against the wall, and took several heavy, but quiet gulps of air.

Once their breath had begun to return, they tried to listen beyond the thudding of their hearts and the blood rushing in and out of their ears. *Was there any sound coming from inside that hut?*

They waited and listened. After enough time had passed, Harvath directed Eddie to the hut's lone window on that wall as he made his way forward in anticipation of hitting the front door.

At the edge of the wall, Harvath flashed Eddie the five-second signal and then disappeared from view. Coiled tighter than a jack-in-the-box, Eddie began counting backward, ready to pop into the window.

Harvath slipped beneath the hut's front window and positioned himself outside the front door. As he mentally kept track of the countdown, he placed his hand against the door and applied a whisper of pressure. This was a village in the Ituri rain forest. It was amazing there were even doors. He didn't expect to find any locks.

When his countdown hit zero, he applied pressure against the door. Encountering no resistance, he swung it open wide and spun inside. At the same moment, Eddie and his AK-47 announced themselves via the window.

The hut, as they had expected, was empty.

Harvath did a quick reconnaissance, while Eddie extricated himself and took up a defensive position outside.

There was nothing at all to tell Harvath what had happened. Everything seemed to be normal. As best he could tell, the family in this hut had been living their lives the way they normally did until something had happened, and they had all disappeared. Seeing a doll lying in the corner, Harvath corrected himself. The people of this village hadn't disappeared. They had been cremated.

Death dripped from the thatched rooftops of this village. The sooner they could get Decker and get the hell out of here, the better he was going to feel.

Stepping back outside, he waved Eddie up to the next hut and let him clear it.

It was empty—as was the one after that, and the one after that. The only hut that appeared to have any life was the big one, and that was where Eddie had seen a man rushing a woman, who they all believed to be Jessica Decker, inside.

One hut away from the big one, Harvath and Eddie stopped and crouched down.

"I guess we now know why the burn pit was so large," the Brit said.

It didn't make any sense. "Why would they need to take out an entire village?"

"Maybe they were all infected."

Harvath hoped that wasn't true. Not that it made any difference. These people were all dead. Their children were dead. Those were the little skulls they had seen back at the pit. There might be even more, just waiting to be uncovered. The idea of going through that little lake of ash with a rake was more than Harvath could take.

He held up three fingers, counted down, and spun into the hut. It was empty. Just like he knew it would be. With this side of the village secure, they waited inside for Ash and Mick to come down and join them. Simon would remain out of sight in the jungle to provide overwatch.

Once the rest of the team arrived in the hut, Ash deferred to Harvath.

"She's your colleague," he said. "How do you want this to go down?"

It was a sign of respect. Technically, she was his colleague and he should be the one making the call as to her recovery.

Harvath gave Ash a nod. "Okay," he said. "Here's how we're going to do this."

•   •   •

The improvised flashbang grenade Harvath had fashioned created more *bang* than *flash*, but it did the trick. Before the occupants of the hut knew what was happening, the entry team was already inside.

Harvath moved to cover Decker while Ash and Mick took down the two tangos.

No sooner had Harvath gotten to her, than she began screaming.

"No!" she cried. "Stop!"

She fought to push Harvath out of the way and get around him.

He grabbed her wrist and tweaked it, just enough to get her attention.

"That hurts," she protested.

"Good," he replied. "Now back up."

It wasn't a request.

When she failed to move, he applied more pressure. The pain brought her up onto the balls of her feet, and he stepped her out of the hut, to allow Ash and Mick to finish securing the two inside.

"Don't hurt them," she ordered.

Harvath let her go.

"Who are they?"

"The son's deaf," she replied. "The father used to help at the clinic."

"Why did you wander off?"

"I spotted the boy and I wanted to see where he was going. I thought he could tell us something."

"You should have gotten me first."

"And what if I had lost him? What if he hadn't come back here?"

She had a point, but Harvath didn't feel like debating with her.

"I don't care what the situation is," he answered. "You don't go off by yourself. Now, why was the father following you?"

"Because he was worried."

"About the boy?"

"*About everything*," she exclaimed. "Look at this village. There's no one left. What do you think they filled that oven with?"

"Did he tell you that?"

Decker nodded.

"Does he know what happened?"

"He knows more than we do. *A lot* more."

CHAPTER 19

Helena was angry. She was angry with everyone—with Bentzi, with Damien, with her father for never finding her, never rescuing her after she was kidnapped. The one person she wasn't angry with was herself.

She had an excellent quality of life in Israel. She had an apartment and a car. She shopped pretty much wherever she wanted and went to the best clubs and restaurants. She made more money in two months than she would have back home in Eastern Europe in a year.

She had thought about modeling. In fact, she had been asked countless times by photographers to sit for them, but Bentzi had forbidden it. He claimed it wasn't good for her to have photos floating around out there. It made sense, but as was usually the case with Bentzi, there was what he called the "truth" and then there was reality.

Israel was everything to him. He would say or do anything to protect it. Bending or flat out breaking the truth was all just part of the job. *Whatever needs to be done.* It was his one and only directive. And he applied it without remorse.

After what he had experienced at the hands of the enemy, she couldn't blame him. But she wasn't the enemy.

He didn't want her modeling because he wanted to keep her dependent upon him, for *everything.* The schedule, the insane travel, the assignments—all of it conspired to keep her isolated. Even when she did meet men from the Mossad, it was always when they were in the field. And the ones she liked were never assigned to her team more than once.

And then there was the work. While the pay was better, she was still in the sex trade. Bentzi, for lack of a better word, was simply an over-educated, government-employed pimp. He paid her, housed her, picked out her clothes, and told her where to go and what to do. She wasn't a Mossad agent, she was a Mossad *asset* and she carried no delusions to the contrary.

She was nothing more than a tool—a tool that Bentzi, and on a grander scale, Israel, could use to secure things it wanted. Tools were hard, cold objects that waited to be picked up for a job. Once that job was through, they were hung up, put in a box, or cast aside.

Maybe some affection from Bentzi would have made a difference. She caught snatches of it from time to time. It was why she liked to drink with him.

If they were someplace he felt safe, like the house by the sea, some-times she could get him to go beyond a second drink. That's when the real Bentzi came out. Unfortunately, those times were too few and much too far in between. They weren't enough to nourish a person. She needed more and there was a very good chance that Bentzi didn't have more in him. The only way she was ever going to find what she needed was to get out.

But to get out, she needed a plan. Pierre Damien was it.

The fact that Bentzi believed she had fallen for him stunned her. She was a good actress, probably better than most, but she had never been able to fool him about anything. When she said she hadn't fallen for him, she had meant it.

Nevertheless, he had decided to recall her. It wasn't like Bentzi. Some jobs took longer than others. He knew that. She had never failed him be-fore. She wouldn't start now. She just needed more time.

This wasn't about Bentzi. It wasn't even about Israel. This was about her. If she had given him what he wanted, the assignment would already be over. She wasn't ready yet. There was still something she had to put in place. When it was done, she would gladly give Bentzi everything, and then she would disappear.

Sitting in her apartment, she understood the pressure he was under. And though she had not seen Bentzi's boss, Nava—she could sense that she was in Geneva. Bentzi always acted differently when she was around.

More than likely, Helena figured, it had been Nava who had pulled the plug on the assignment and had moved to have her recalled to Israel. That would explain a lot.

Most of all, it would explain the high-level of concern the Institute—as the Mossad was known—was expressing over Damien.

Before being inserted into the United Nations, Helena had been given a heavily redacted file on him. The product of a Canadian father and an American mother, Damien possessed dual citizenship and had made his initial fortune in oil and natural gas, eventually branching out into petrochemicals and pharmaceuticals. He had been married only once and had lost his wife to cancer. They never had children, and he never remarried. Business and philanthropy were his passions.

Up until his forties, Damien's philanthropy had helped fund research into illnesses, like the cancer that had taken his wife, and had provided money to hospitals and universities, which saw his name placed on the wings of several buildings. Then, something changed.

It started with a book—a small, scholarly treatise that cracked a mental door. That book led to others, which led to lectures and documentaries. Those led to a reexamination of who and what he was supporting through his generous donations. He had made his money by taking from the earth, but he had never given anything back. It was an epiphany packed with revelations, one of the greatest being that he had done the world a favor by never having children.

When interviewed by the media, Damien was always quite candid about his conversion, and his belief that the earth couldn't sustain its current rate of human growth. Even with technological advancements like fracking, crop management, and vaccine production, there were a finite amount of resources being divided up among an exploding population.

People were not only breeding like rabbits, but thanks to advances in sanitation and medicine, they were no longer dropping like flies as one researcher had put it. Left unchecked, it was a death sentence for the planet. Damien had committed himself to doing everything he could to make sure that didn't happen.

In one of the articles Helena had read, an interviewer had labeled Damien a Neo-Malthusian—someone who advocated for population control programs in order to preserve existing resources for current and future generations. Damien, as he always did when people tried to put labels on him, laughed it off. The Mossad didn't, because they knew what Damien really was.

In addition to being a supporter of overpopulation theory, he was a eugenicist who believed that favorable genetic qualities should be advanced while unfavorable traits should be limited, or discontinued altogether. He dreamt of an earth with a much reduced, "healthier" population.

That, in and of itself, would never have been enough to rise to the attention of Israeli intelligence. People were free to subscribe to any crackpot ideas they wanted. But what had piqued the Mossad's interest in Damien was his particular enmity toward the Jewish state and the considerable wealth he was applying against it.

Via multitudinous foundations and so-called "advocacy" organizations, he was waging a global public relations campaign bent on painting Israel as the source of all the Middle East's problems.

In the United States, he sent groups into American churches to poison congregations. On college campuses, his organizations recruited addle-brained university students to spread the message about "the real Israel." Then he funded similar propaganda organizations in Israel, targeting young Israelis and convincing them their nation was evil.

Was it anti-Semitism? the Mossad wondered. *Anti-Zionism? A combination of both?*

The more the Institute looked into Damien, the more astounding the extent of his efforts became.

The man seemed particularly committed to weakening Israel's relationship with the United States. Billboards and newspaper ads had been taken out exploiting low points in their relationship and highlighting events such as the spying of Jonathan Pollard.

He had established a legal foundation that paid American lawyers to go after U.S. Defense contractors with class-action lawsuits on behalf of Palestinians wounded and killed by U.S.-made weapons.

Prostitutes were paid to sleep with and then threaten to blackmail pro-Israel Members of Congress while on Congressional delegations to the Jewish state. Ultimately, the hookers would back off, claiming that they had been hired by the Mossad and couldn't go through with it.

And then there was the UN.

Over his adult life, Damien had been offered plumb international ambassadorships by three different Canadian Prime Ministers. Each of which he had declined. Despite his professed love of Canada, where he made his home, he had been too busy running his businesses to focus on running an embassy.

That changed, though, in his sixties when he stepped back from the businesses and spent more time focused on his philanthropy. When Damien was asked to serve Canada at the United Nations, and was told which position he would get, he accepted.

He already had a good relationship with the Secretary-General and was honored when the General Assembly voted to appoint him to be Under-Secretary-General of the United Nations Population Fund.

The Fund touted itself as the lead UN agency for delivering a world where every pregnancy was wanted, every birth was safe, and every young person's potential was fulfilled. They prided themselves on shrinking the size of families while simultaneously making them healthier. It was the perfect place for Damien.

As an Under-Secretary-General, he not only received diplomatic immunity, but he was also admitted to one of the most exclusive clubs in the world, Secretary-General's Senior Management Group, or SMG for short.

The fifty-member SMG acted as a quasi board of directors, advising the Secretary-General and helping to ensure the coherence and strategic direction of the entire United Nations organization.

The UN had always been a hotbed of anti-Zionism, but Damien was like a bellows when it came to fanning the flames. Whether it was his charisma, or the esteem that members held him in because of his vast fortune, he possessed tremendous sway. He never missed an opportunity to harm Israel.

He was also very anti-America.

Normally, this would have provided an opportunity for the Israelis and the Americans to work together. A foreign diplomat working behind the scenes to undermine the efforts and image of both countries cried out for a concerted effort. Though his tactics were different when it came to the United States, Damien was working even harder and pumping even more money into weakening it. The sticking point was his dual citizenship.

But because he held American citizenship, the United States was limited in what it could, and would, do to him.

Had Damien been palling around with terrorists in Yemen, they would have droned him. But America took its rights of free speech and free association very seriously. Damien was free to donate to whatever causes he wished. If no laws were being broken, American intelligence made it perfectly clear that it had no desire to begin an investigation. Israel was on its own when it came to Pierre Damien.

It was incredibly shortsighted on the Americans' part. While the Israelis respected the United States' views on its freedoms and founding documents, it was the height of negligence to allow those same freedoms and documents to provide cover for subversion. It was like Palestinian terrorists using hospitals and schools from which to launch rocket attacks. At some point you had to make a choice. Do you sit still and absorb the attacks? Or do you go in and eliminate the threat?

As far as Israel was concerned, there was too much at stake to just sit back. The threat needed to be eliminated. And so, they had decided to go after Damien and take him out.

But on the night they did, something happened that changed everything.

CHAPTER 20

The United Nations Secretary-General had planned a retreat for the full SMG to the picturesque Austrian village of Alpbach. That's where the Mossad had decided to take out Pierre Damien. Nava Itzik and her Metsada team were mobilized and tasked with the assignment. Ben Mordechai would carry out the hit.

Alpbach looked like it had been built by Hollywood set designers. Cradled in a narrow valley, surrounded by lush meadows, the flowerboxes of its wooden chalets exploded in riots of color. Soaring pines gave way to jagged mountain peaks. It was clear why it had been voted Austria's most beautiful village.

Though not given to such thoughts, Bentzi had found himself thinking that there was probably no more perfect place for a honeymoon. But he hadn't come to Austria for a honeymoon. He had come to kill Pierre Damien.

The Institute was very nervous about the assignment. Not only because their target was a diplomat who held dual American and Canadian citizenship but also because a previous Metsada team had botched the assassination of Mahmoud Al-Mabhouh, the cofounder of the military wing of Hamas.

Al-Mabhouh had been wanted for numerous offenses, including the killing of two Israeli soldiers, as well as the purchase of arms from Iran to be used in Gaza.

The Institute had tracked Al-Mabhouh from Damascus to the Al

Bustan Rotana hotel in Dubai. So had Jordanian Intelligence, which wanted to capture him and bring him back to Jordan to stand trial. Instead of taking a breath and figuring out how to handle the Jordanians, the Metsada rushed their operation. Almost immediately, mistakes started happening. It was amateur hour.

Though they succeeded in killing Al-Mabhouh, they didn't succeed in making it look like he had died of natural causes. It took ten days, but Dubai officials eventually ruled it a homicide and began piecing together what had happened. In the end, still images from CCTV cameras of twenty-six Mossad agents were released to the press, as well as the names and countries of origin on the passports used to enter the country.

Once the names were out there, it became evident that the Mossad had stolen the identities of Israelis who held dual citizenship in Great Britain, Ireland, France, Germany, and Australia. The Dubai authorities also arrested two Palestinian Fatah operatives who had been assisting the Mossad team.

It wasn't as bad as the botched CIA operation several years earlier to snatch radical Egyptian cleric Abu Omar off the streets of Milan, but it was an embarrassment nonetheless. The Institute wanted the smallest footprint possible and absolutely no mistakes. The message had been sent from the top—if you screw up, don't come home.

The Institute had done its homework. They knew Pierre Damien—his quirks and idiosyncrasies, habits and routines. They also knew diplomatic boondoggles, which was exactly what the SMG retreat to Austria was.

There was always a big night at these things and for theirs, they had rented out the best restaurant in town. That was when Nava wanted to strike. Bentzi had agreed. Damien would eat too much and drink too much, making him an easier target and his "accidental" death all the more believable.

The Under-Secretaries-General departed the chalet hotel in a convoy of vans and minibuses accompanied by their UN security teams.

The housekeeping staff had been instructed to begin their turndown as soon as the guests had left for dinner. Bentzi watched from outside.

Once Damien's room had been serviced, he exited his vehicle, threw on a small backpack, and approached the chalet.

It was overcast, and there were no streetlights in the village.

Bentzi avoided the small stay-behind team and worked his way around back. It wasn't a good night for his hands. He had difficulty climbing, and it took longer than it should have. When he finally reached Damien's third-floor balcony, his hands were in a lot of pain.

He always carried two pills in a small paper envelope just in case. Pausing, he popped both and then, after pulling on a pair of special latex gloves, went to work on the lock for the large glass door.

The suite resembled the pictures he had viewed on the hotel's web site. The walls were clad in knotty pine, the floors covered with a patterned carpet similar to the drapes. A feather duvet lay across the foot of the bed, and a row of thick pillows in perfectly pressed cases were staged along the headboard. The crisp, white sheets had been turned down and bottles of water had been left next to the bed along with a card forecasting tomorrow's weather. After checking the bathroom, Bentzi made his way into the sitting room.

There was a couch, a coffee table, two side chairs, and a dresser. In the corner was a vintage tile stove. Not far from it was a desk. What there wasn't, was a laptop.

The Institute wanted a copy of Damien's hard drive. Because the death was supposed to look like an accident and not a robbery, the computer needed to remain behind. Damien had left for the dinner empty-handed, so it had to be somewhere in the room.

Bentzi checked the front closet, and there, on a luggage stand, was Damien's suitcase.

It was a ubiquitous, soft-sided piece. It's main compartment had been zippered and locked shut. Removing a pen, Bentzi applied pressure to the teeth of the seam and easily opened the zippered area. Inside, was a locked hard-sided briefcase. Sliding it out, he took it over to the desk.

The locks were tricky and the pain in his hands only compounded their difficulty. He took a deep breath and willed himself to slow down. Damien and his colleagues would only just be getting into their salads by this point. Even so, Bentzi radioed his team surveilling the restaurant for a situation report.

Once word came back that the party was still on cocktails, Bentzi relaxed and focused back on the case.

The thin picks were a challenge for him to hold, much less manipulate with his crooked fingers. The job should have taken seconds, not minutes. Had Nava known the state his hands were in, she would have replaced him. But she didn't know, and Bentzi was determined to see his assignment through.

When he finally had the case open, he lifted the lid and looked inside. There were several file folders on top. Beneath those were Damien's laptop and an additional cell phone. He had been spotted using an Apple phone and this one appeared to be an Android. Bentzi took it out and set it next to the case on the desk. The laptop would take the longest, so he decided to work on it first.

Opening his backpack, he removed a small tool kit and extracted an electric screwdriver. Once he had found the right sized head, he flipped the computer over and removed the screws from the bottom.

With the cover off, he slid an incredibly sophisticated black box the size of a paperback from his pack and began attaching leads to different places inside the laptop. He then depressed a power button on the black box and began to copy the hard drive.

The device used to suck the data out of the cell phone was smaller, about the size of a hockey puck. After finding the right USB cable, he connected the two and powered up the phone.

As the electronics did their work, he opened the physical folders and sifted through the papers. The first two were spreadsheets with budgets— dry, boring data that appeared related to Damien's businesses. But the contents of the next folder stopped Ben Mordechai cold.

The cover page was innocuously labeled "Outcome Conference," yet what he found on the pages that followed was anything but innocuous.

It had been prepared for a subgroup of the SMG called the "Plenary Panel" or P2 for short. Bentzi had never heard of it. Members of the panel were neither identified by name, nor their country of origin, only by number—one through seven.

After acknowledging a string of recent setbacks, the document outlined P2's chilling goals:

1. Decrease current human population below five hundred million and keep it in perpetual balance with nature.
2. Guide reproduction wisely—improving fitness and diversity.
3. Unite humanity with a "living" new language.
4. Redistribute global wealth under the more acceptable term "global public goods."
5. Rebalance personal rights with "social duties."
6. Replace passion, faith, and tradition with reason.
7. Make clever use of new technologies to go around national governments and establish direct ties with citizens.
8. Rebrand global governance as equitable, efficient, and the logical next step in human evolution.
9. Discredit, delegitimize, and dismantle the idea of the nation state/national sovereignty.
10. Prepare a mechanism to neutralize any challenges to United Nations' authority.

Ben Mordechai couldn't believe what he was reading. It was a blueprint for revolution. If Che Guevara was right and revolution wasn't an apple that fell when it was ripe, but rather was made to fall, then it looked like the Plenary Panel was shaking the entire global tree.

They identified the biggest obstacles to achieving their goals as the United States and Israel. With the two nations overwhelmed and laid low by a massive event, the panel was confident that no one would stand in the United Nations' way.

Damien's focus on weakening both countries began to make more sense. What wasn't clear, though, was what this massive event was intended to be and when it would take place.

In the margins were Damien's handwritten notes. There was a three-letter designator, *A-H-F*, followed by words like *pathogenicity*, *absolute risk*, and *dose response*.

Mordechai had more questions than answers. *Did the notes refer to a chemical attack? Biological? Something else entirely? When was it set to take place, what was Damien's role, and who were the other members of the panel?*

The only thing Mordechai knew for sure was that they couldn't kill Damien. Not now. Not with so many unanswered questions.

After photographing all of the documents with his phone, he reassembled the laptop and put everything in the room back the way he had found it. Then, he radioed the team that they had to abort.

Nava was livid. The Institute was going to be furious. She demanded to know why. Mordechai told her to trust him and then broke off communication as he slipped out of the hotel the same way he had come in.

He no longer cared about the pain in his hands. All he cared about was the information that he had discovered in Damien's room. The idea that a cabal within the United Nations hierarchy was planning a coup involving something so catastrophic that Israel and the United States would be too overwhelmed to respond was almost unimaginable. *Almost.*

He had seen enough to know that anything was possible, especially when it came to those who sought power. Around the world, the majority of countries were ruled either by dictatorships or some form of Democratic Socialism. In those nations, power resided in the state. Only a handful of countries were truly free, with power residing in the hands of individual citizens. Any attempt to seat some sort of global system of government would have to sideline Israel and the United States first, or it would never succeed.

In his notes about dealing with the United States, Damien had scribbled two letters—*MC. Were they initials? Roman numerals?* He was anxious to have minds back at the Mossad unpack everything and begin connecting the dots.

While Nava had been angry about Mordechai pulling the plug on her operation, when he showed her the documents, she eventually conceded that it had been the right thing to do.

Once they were back in Tel Aviv and had turned over all the materials to the Institute, all they could do was wait.

Their biggest expectation was for what would be pulled off Damien's hard drive and cell phone. Both turned out to be a bust. He was using a new form of encryption that they had never encountered before. Without his passwords, there was no telling how long it would take to crack. And even if they could crack it, there was no telling what they would find and if it would be in time. That was why Mordechai had decided to activate Helena.

With her background working for a human trafficking NGO, it didn't take much to align her with a program at the United Nations in Geneva. She used her Eastern European passport. There was nothing in her file or the apartment that had been set up for her to connect her to Israel.

The fact that she was not a UN employee, but rather working on a co-UN/NGO trafficking program, was especially important. Damien wouldn't have wanted to run afoul of the UN's code of ethics regarding dating subordinates. It happened all the time, but he took his role as Under-Secretary-General seriously. He didn't need a scandal hovering over him. Not with everything he had planned.

All Bentzi had to do was to "dangle" Helena. Damien's dick would take over and do the rest.

He was well-known for the attractive women he dated. His relationships were like monsoon season, steamy and short. He showered his girlfriends with gifts and expensive trips and as soon as he grew bored, he was on to the next.

He liked the ambiance of the bar at La Réserve Genève hotel. The views were exceptional, they had an excellent selection of whiskeys, vodkas, and cognacs, and their sushi chef was top-notch. The fact that it was close to his apartment was icing on the cake.

Bentzi parked Helena in a provocative but stylish cocktail dress at La Réserve Genève and let nature take its course.

Damien wasn't shy. He made a beeline right for her, and she played him like a pro. They had one drink together before she announced that she had to leave. He offered her a ride home. She declined. He asked if he might have her phone number. She said no. He offered her his personal card with his cell phone number written on the back. She placed it on the table and didn't bother to pick it back up.

The only personal information she had revealed was that she was temporarily assigned to a human trafficking project at the UN.

The next day, there were flowers on her desk. Inside the envelope was the card Damien had handed her and which she had left on the table the night before. She gave the flowers to one of her colleagues.

The cat and mouse game continued on with Helena playing disinterested and hard to get. It drove Damien wild. He wasn't used to women saying no to him.

He kept "coincidentally" bumping into her. His unsettling manservant-cum-assistant, Jeffery, had been following her. She had spotted him each time, but had never let on. Finally, she gave in and agreed to dinner.

To his credit, he didn't overdo it. He picked a small, local restaurant with exceptional food. He was a gentleman and very charming.

For their second date, he asked her what kind of food was her favorite. She said Italian. He flew her to Rome in his private jet, and she ate the best meal of her life.

After their third date, she began sleeping with him. It was the best sex Pierre Damien had ever had.

Bentzi had given her one task—to capture the man's passwords so that they could access his hard drive and cell phone.

To do that, she had been issued what looked like a wall charger for her cell phone, but what in reality was a covert keystroke logger. It had the ability to sniff, decrypt, log, and report all keystrokes within its immediate vicinity. It even had a small, rechargeable internal battery that allowed it to work even after being unplugged. All she had to do was to position it near Damien when he was logging onto his devices.

As she had explained multiple times to Bentzi, that was a lot harder than it sounded. Damien never used his laptop around her and the only phone she ever saw him use was his iPhone, which he unlocked with his fingerprint. Eventually, she assured him, she would get the passwords. It would just take time. But then everything changed.

Bentzi had told her she was being recalled and told her to go back to her apartment, wait for his call, and not have any contact with Damien other than to feign illness. How Bentzi thought he would ever be able to get anyone closer to Damien was beyond her. He was going to toss it all away, toss his precious Israel to the wolves. It was beyond insane.

Then her phone had rung. It was Bentzi. He wanted to make her an offer, or more appropriately, he wanted to offer her an *incentive*.

"Go ahead," she had said.

Gripping the phone, she listened as the Mossad agent laid it all out. Her first reaction was panic. He had used a name they had agreed never to speak of. Like Damien previously showing up every time she went out, she didn't believe this was a coincidence either. Bentzi was either lying to her, or had been lying to her all along.

"How do I know I can trust you?" she asked.

It was one of the biggest enticements he could have ever placed in front of her. The Israeli known as "Enoch" ran the trafficking ring that had kidnapped her back home and had forced her into the sex trade. She wanted to exact her revenge on him almost as badly as she wanted out of her life with the Mossad. *Almost.*

Offering up Enoch was an act of desperation. Bentzi knew he couldn't pull off his operation without her. Whatever Damien was planning, it was already in motion. If it was as devastating as the Mossad feared, they needed to get to the bottom of it, now.

She, on the other hand, didn't care what happened to Israel. She didn't care what happened to the United States either. If everything went according to her plan, she would be so far away from both, anything could happen, and it wouldn't matter. All she cared about was getting out.

But if she could figuratively run over Enoch and drag his corpse through the parking lot as she made her exit, it would close several disturbing chapters in her life and allow her to move on from a very troubling part of her past.

Bentzi knew she had been dragging her feet, he just didn't know why. After threatening to recall her to Tel Aviv, he was now offering her an incentive to stay and finish the job. Typical Mossad—stick first, then carrot.

She was going to have to push things, which meant there was a good chance she might screw up and walk away with nothing. But it was too good an opportunity to pass up.

Taking a deep breath, she opened her lingerie drawer and said into the phone, "Deal."

CHAPTER 21

Harvath never took his eyes from the man or his deaf son. Speaking to Jambo, he said, "Ask him again."

The translator did, and Harvath studied the man's face for any indication that he was lying. He was looking for microexpressions, sometimes referred to as *tells*. They were subconscious facial cues that indicated that a person was under duress because they were lying or had intent to do some other type of harm. So far he didn't see any.

When the man replied, Jambo translated. Harvath didn't see any signs that the man was lying. In fact, everything about him suggested he was telling the truth.

"Ask him about the video," Harvath said. "Who filmed it?"

Jambo posed the question and then listened to the man's response. Finally, he turned to Harvath and said, "He took the video."

"*He* did?"

Jambo nodded.

"With what?"

Jambo asked the man and then replied, "With his cell phone."

Harvath didn't believe him. There was no reception anywhere near this village. "Tell him I want to see his phone," he said.

Jambo bobbed his head up and down as the man spoke and then turned back to Harvath. "He doesn't have it anymore."

"Where is it?"

"He hid it in one of their trucks. The men who killed everyone in the clinic and then killed everyone in the village."

"Why?"

"He was worried he would be killed too," said Jambo. "There is no cellular service here. He pressed *send* and then hid the phone in a truck. He assumed that eventually the truck would pass into an area with reception and the message would be sent."

Smart. Harvath had to give the man credit. There was something, though, that was bothering him. "How did he know where to send it? How did he know that email address?"

Decker cleared her throat, and all eyes turned to her as she looked at Harvath. "Didn't you see all the signs in the clinic?" she asked. "The banners?"

Harvath had seen lots of things, but he had been focused on figuring out what had happened. "What signs?"

"The ones advertising CARE International's support of the clinic. Each of them has CARE's web address, as well as an email for more information. That's the address the video was sent to."

Harvath turned his attention back to the villager and said to Jambo, "Tell him I want to know about the trucks."

Jambo asked him, and the man rattled off a short description. There were no distinctive colors or markings. They appeared to be commercial, not military. Nothing special.

"How about the men themselves?"

"*Mzungu,*" the villager replied.

"What's *mzungu*?" Harvath asked.

"It's Swahili for *white people,*" said Decker.

"*White* people?"

She nodded.

Harvath asked Jambo, "Were they military?"

Seconds later he replied, "Apparently they carried rifles, but they were not wearing uniforms."

"How about their hair? Long? Short? Any beards? Mustaches? Tattoos? Anything at all that stood out?"

Jambo asked the man and then said, "They acted military. One man gave orders and the others followed. They all had short hair. No beards, no mustaches. No tattoos."

"How many were there?"

"He says somewhere between eight to twelve."

About the size of a military squad, Harvath thought. "What language were they speaking?"

Jambo translated the question and then said, "He's not sure. He didn't recognize it. He says maybe German. Or Russian."

"Would he recognize any of them if he saw them again?"

Jambo asked the man, and then nodded.

Harvath stepped outside, retrieved a pen and a piece of paper, and walked back into the dwelling.

"Tell him I need his cell phone number," he said, handing the pen and paper to Jambo.

Once he had it, he left Decker with Jambo to ask more questions and stepped back outside.

Positioning his Iridium system, he fired up his phone, waited until he had a strong signal and then placed his call.

When the man on the other end picked up, he apologized for waking him and then said, "I need you to locate a phone for me. It was tossed into a truck in Congo several days ago. The battery is probably dead, but I want to know all the other towers it touched. I also want a list of phones that touched those same towers at the same time, as well as where those phones are now."

"How soon do you need it?" the man asked.

"Right away," Harvath replied. Ending the call, he stepped back inside to join Decker. Jambo was in the middle of translating the villager's tale.

His name was Leonce, and he talked about a stranger who had shown up at the Matumaini Clinic, sick with a high fever. No one knew how he had gotten there. He lost consciousness soon after coming in. He had no ID, no money, nothing.

They placed him in a bed, started an IV, and began trying to figure out who he was and what was wrong with him.

He regained consciousness twice, but only briefly. Both times he screamed to be protected and begged the clinic staff not to "send him back." They were never able to figure out what he was talking about. A nurse said she thought he might be Muslim, a very minority community in Congo, as it sounded at one point as if he had moaned the word for the Muslim god, "Allah."

Per their protocols, they contacted the Health Ministry hotline in Kinshasa. The rather blasé bureaucrat told them it was probably nothing, but to take full protective measures.

An hour later, the clinic received a call from the World Health Organization representative in Kinshasa telling them to prep blood and tissue samples and deliver them to the airport in Bunia for transport. The rep also asked to be emailed pictures of the patient.

The clinic had one very small, very old, and very unreliable car. Leonce offered to make the trip to Bunia. When the clinic staff agreed, Leonce invited his son, the deaf boy named Pepsy, to come with him.

The staff took great pains to make sure the samples were completely airtight and properly packaged. Leonce was given money for fuel. Any food or lodging would be his responsibility. They had already given him all the petty cash they had.

Leonce had been to Bunia many times and knew the route well. He had a relative there, and he and Pepsy would spend the night before returning the next morning.

With their package safely on the backseat, Leonce ground the gears of the little car, he and Pepsy waved out their open windows to the staff, and they began their journey.

Their problems began almost immediately.

First came the rain. It was so heavy, it sounded like rocks being poured onto the roof of the car. Each enormous drop landed with a great splash.

Leonce activated the wipers. They swung to the left. They swung to the right. Then, they stopped. He and his son had to try to use their shirts to keep the windshield clear, but the rain was so bad, that they could barely see the road. Then they hit a roadblock.

"Roadblock?" Harvath asked.

"It would be more appropriate to designate it a toll," Jambo clarified. "Bandits set them up to extort money from motorists."

Ash and Mick, who had been listening to the interrogation, shot Harvath a look.

"Does Leonce know who these bandits were?" Harvath asked.

Jambo nodded. "FRPI. The Front for the—"

"Patriotic Resistance of Ituri," Harvath said, finishing the translator's sentence for him. "What happened?"

"They demanded that Mr. Leonce pay their toll. He had very little money with him. When they tried to take his package from the backseat, he struggled with them. One of the rebels struck him in the stomach with the butt of his rifle."

"And then what happened?"

"They wanted to know why Mr. Leonce was so protective of the package. They thought maybe he was transporting drugs. They moved his car to the side of the road and took him and his boy to see their commander."

Harvath looked at Decker. He could tell that she was thinking the same thing he was.

"Then what?"

"The commander did not believe Mr. Leonce. He opened the package and dumped out its contents. He says one of the vials broke."

"Ask him to describe the commander."

Jambo did and replied, "Medium height, medium build. Thirty-five with a thick scar across his forehead."

"Shit," Decker exclaimed.

Harvath couldn't have put it better himself. "So much for yellow fever," he said to her.

"We still don't know enough," she replied, composing herself.

"I know enough," he stated, turning back to Jambo. "Keep going."

"Mr. Leonce and his son were allowed to leave. They repacked the box and drove to Bunia. The plane they were supposed to meet had already taken off, so they had to wait until the following day for the next one.

"The car gave them trouble on the way back. They had no money for repairs, so they left it with a mechanic in a village several kilometers away and walked back. When they arrived at their village, they saw their animals being slaughtered and thrown into the back of a truck. None of the other villagers were anywhere to be seen.

"They ran through the jungle toward the clinic. They could hear gunshots from the area where they burn the trash. When they got to the edge of the clearing, they ducked down and watched as a group of four men put on protective suits.

"It was then that Mr. Leonce thought to film what he saw. The men walked into the clinic and began shooting. The rest of the story you already know."

"And Mr. Leonce and his son have been in hiding ever since?" Harvath asked.

Jambo nodded.

Harvath was about to say something else when his phone chimed.

CHAPTER 22

Even though his digital guru, Nicholas, was groggy and angry from having been awakened at such an ungodly hour back in the States, he had made quick work of the assignment Harvath had given him.

With his laptop balanced on the hood of LC1, Harvath scrolled through the satellite images. Nicholas had highlighted all the cell towers that Leonce's phone had shaken hands with.

The pictures drew a path back to Bunia.

"That's not good," Ash said over Harvath's shoulder.

He didn't bother turning to look at him. "What do you see?"

The Brit reached over, put his finger on a cluster of buildings near a cell tower on Harvath's screen, and said, "MONUSCO HQ."

"Let me guess," Harvath replied. "That's Swahili for *rebel central*."

"Worse. United Nations Stabilization Mission in the Democratic Republic of the Congo. MONUSCO is the acronym for the official name in French. You could probably pronounce it, but I don't *parlez* le frog."

The historical animosity between the French and the Brits always made him laugh. "Why is it worse than *rebel central*?"

"You ever work with a UN stabilization force?" Ash asked.

Harvath shook his head.

"Then trust me. As the old saying goes, you can't spell unprofessional, unethical, or unaccountable without the UN. The cholera outbreak the old blue helmets caused in Haiti? Over ten thousand dead, and it has spread to the Dominican Republic and Cuba. The rapes and sex crimes they have committed in Mali and everywhere else? The stories of their depravity and brutality are legion.

"Their entire 'military,' if you can call it that, is shot through with corruption and rampant lack of accountability. They even allowed two of their own unarmed military observers in Bunia to get slaughtered years ago because none of their fellow UN troops wanted to risk a rescue operation. They're pathetic."

UN troops were indeed known for a lack of honor and discipline. Harvath was familiar with the horror stories surrounding their deployments. He could think of no greater nightmare than to have his country reliant upon the UN to provide "peace" and "stability." He'd rather take his chances combatting whatever was causing the war and instability in the first place.

A fish rots from the head down and any organization that boasted a human rights council, yet accepted human-rights violators like China, Cuba, Russia, Saudi Arabia, and even slavery-infested Mauritania as members couldn't be taken seriously, much less be expected to police and field an effective and honorable military. In short, Harvath didn't have much use for the UN.

"What about this?" Harvath asked, advancing to another image.

"Downtown Bunia," said Ash. "About three clicks from the hotel we stayed at."

Harvath pushed a button and the red dots representing cell towers dimmed, and a cluster of green dots became visible.

"What do those represent?" Ash asked.

"Opportunity," Harvath replied.

•   •   •

Decker felt certain about one thing. If Leonce and his son were not already exhibiting symptoms of whatever illness they were looking at, they likely weren't going to.

Her emphasis on the word *likely* didn't put Harvath or the security team at ease. None of the men were willing to roll their personal dice on her assessment. She had signed on to be a doctor and willingly commune with the sick of Africa, they hadn't.

After Harvath gave her a wad of bills, Jambo drove Decker to the village where Leonce had left the clinic's vehicle. The repairs had been minimal, and the car was already waiting. She and Jambo returned twenty minutes later. In an act of solidarity, she would be driving back to Bunia with Leonce and his son while the rest of the team rode in the Land Cruisers.

Decker didn't have to worry about the harrowing river crossings they had conducted on their way in. Her little vehicle would never make it. They had to go far out of their way and cut back toward Bunia. All the while, Harvath and the security team were keeping their eyes peeled for roadblocks. None of them had any desire to bump up against the FRPI again.

Their trek was long, but thankfully uneventful. When they arrived at the Bunia Hotel, it was well after dark. After checking in, they unloaded all of their gear and secured it in their rooms. Ever eager to spread money around the family, Jambo had offered to ring up his relatives and have them come back and babysit the trucks, but Ash had said it wasn't necessary. Harvath, though, thought he might have another use for them.

Those green dots on his laptop earlier corresponded to six cell phones Nicholas had traced to a walled, concrete structure on the other side of town. It reminded Harvath of a poor man's version of the Bin Laden compound in Abbottabad.

He wanted to do a drive-by and Ash had agreed to go with him. They brought Jambo just in case.

When the hotel security guard opened the gates, Ash put the Land Cruiser in gear and pulled out into evening traffic.

Motorbikes carrying passengers, known as *boda-boda*, weaved in and out between cars, while bicycle riders piloting *black mambas*, so named because they left trails in the dust that resembled those of the deadly snake, grabbed onto trucks and other vehicles to hitch free rides. Harvath and Ash kept their Glocks under their thighs, hidden from sight.

The GPS system on Harvath's phone guided them toward their target. Along the streets, small, ramshackle shops sold everything from cheap Chinese televisions to cooking pots.

Harvath had long held that with its incredible resources, Africa should be the most powerful continent on the planet. But because of its tribalism and terrible governments, it was relegated to permanent third world status. Seeing it firsthand always made him appreciate even more what he had back at home.

Thinking of back home, he checked his phone again. Lara still hadn't texted him back. It was for the best. He didn't have time to get involved in any additional drama. His time with Decker in the jungle shower had been bad enough.

Decker hadn't liked being rebuffed, but that was her problem. He had tried to make it clear that he wasn't interested. She had persisted anyway, sensing that there may have been some sort of opening with him. She had been wrong.

When she had stepped into the shower and had tried to press herself up against him, that's when he steered her back out and told her in no uncertain terms what the situation was.

He couldn't have been the first man to say no to her, but watching the Brits continue to drool all over her, he wondered if maybe he was. Not that it mattered to him. He had something much better waiting for him at home—provided he could salvage it.

His fidelity seemed to turn Decker on even more. That, or she saw it as a challenge. In either case, he was glad to not have to ride to Bunia with her and was equally pleased to be away from the hotel and not have to deal with her there.

Nearing the compound, he tried to put Lara, Decker, and everything else out of his mind.

They would only get one look tonight and as their Land Cruiser rolled slowly by, he took in everything—the wall heights, window and door placement, the lighting, security measures, adjacent buildings, as well as all of the nearby businesses.

"I vote no," Ash stated as they kept on going.

Harvath looked at him. "No to what?"

"No to everything you're thinking right now."

"How do you know what I'm thinking?"

"The same way I knew yesterday morning that you wouldn't radio us even if it did go tits up out in the jungle."

"Technically, you said to call only if it went *pear-shaped*," Harvath replied.

"Are you taking the piss now? Is that what this is?"

"No, but that's a good idea. Pull over."

"I didn't say take *a* piss," Ash clarified. "I said taking *the* piss. It means—"

"I know what it means," said Harvath. "And yes, I'm pulling your chain, but I still want you to pull over. Up there by that bar. Pardon me, by that *pub*."

"I know what a bar is, you nonce."

Harvath smiled. "Just taking the piss again. Don't worry."

"Something tells me I'm going to have plenty to worry about soon enough," Ash replied as he pulled off the road and put the Land Cruiser in park.

From the backseat, Jambo looked out his window at the bar and asked, "Are we going in for a beer?"

"Ash and I are," said Harvath. "You're going for a walk."

CHAPTER 23

With his earbuds in, Jambo had pretended to be face-timing on his iPhone as he strolled the neighborhood and shot video. When they had reviewed it back at the hotel, Harvath and Ash were able to identify several places for static surveillance, plus launching pads if they needed to go dynamic. Harvath had no plans to attempt to breach the compound. However this went down, he wanted it to go down outside.

The next morning, they used Jambo and three of his relatives as cutouts to temporarily secure two second-storey apartments and access to a handful of rooftops ringing the target compound.

Even in a backwater like Congo, cell phone technology would allow Harvath and the team to feed images back to the Bunia Hotel. If Leonce and his son recognized any of the men, Decker would reply with a text.

With that said, there were limits to how clear a picture a camera phone would take. Harvath hadn't come equipped for a surveillance assignment with long lenses and spotting scopes. They would have to make do with what they had.

Ash and the team had binoculars, but they didn't have anti-flare lenses, so they were restricted to the apartments and forbidden from roof duty.

The team was operating under the assumption that they were dealing with active or former military personnel. From the little Jambo had been able to ascertain mingling in the market and throughout the neighborhood, the house they were surveilling was known by locals as the "white house." It wasn't a reference to the building in Washington, D.C., but rather to this structure's occupants—all of whom were said to be white men. The team decided they would use the same name.

No one knew who the occupants of the "white house" were. Though sometimes seen on foot, they usually came and went in nondescript SUVs. They all wore sunglasses and had short haircuts. That was the extent of the description people in the neighborhood were able to provide. It was enough for Harvath.

They sat on the "white house" for thirty-two humid hours before the package Harvath had requested from Nicholas arrived. Ash sent Jambo to the airport with bribe money to pick it up and make sure nothing happened to it.

"What is it?" Mick asked as Harvath opened the box and lifted the item out.

"It's a predator."

"As in the drone?"

Harvath shook his head. "No. This technology preys on human weakness."

"What?"

"Give me your cell phone."

Mick handed it over.

"Now give me your Glock."

"Why?"

Harvath motioned for him to hand it over, and Mick complied.

Turning the weapon in his hand, Harvath prepared to strike the face of the phone with the butt of the weapon when Mick intervened.

"Whoa, whoa, whoa," he said.

Harvath smiled. "Exactly." Handing them back, he stated, "That's what I'm counting on."

• • •

Included in the delivery from the Carlton Group was additional surveillance equipment, which they parceled out among their observation posts, along with tiny, wireless cameras for the rooftops.

Leonce had already identified two of the suspects, but as better imagery came rolling in, Harvath fed the pictures back to the hotel and Leonce grew more emphatic that they were on to the right group of men. Harvath agreed.

They were pros. The men did everything right when they entered or exited the compound. This was not some JV team. Their heads were on swivels and they took their time. Nothing was rushed. Everything was smooth and by the book.

In addition to sending the pictures back to the hotel, Harvath had also been funneling all of the camera phone imagery back to his office in Virginia. So far, there hadn't been any hits via facial recognition.

That didn't necessarily mean anything. The men wore sunglasses and baseball caps. With such poor resolution, it was tough to tag the appropriate markers. Now that the new cameras had arrived, Harvath was confident they'd know who the men were soon enough.

Back at the Carlton Group offices, Nicholas had been tracing the calls from their cell phones, the majority of which were going to South Africa. There was one phone inside the house, though, that Nicholas couldn't crack or trace. It was heavily encrypted and not like anything he had ever seen before.

He warned Harvath about it and told him that if he did end up hitting the house, to make sure he bagged all of the phones. Nicholas couldn't tell him what specifically to look for because he didn't know himself.

"Just bring me all the phones, and I'll sort it out," is what he had said.

Harvath, though, hadn't changed his mind. He still had no intention of taking the house down. There was no telling how many men were inside, how well armed they were, and what kind of resources they could muster if they got into a firefight. The last thing Harvath and his team needed were Armored Personnel Carriers full of UN troops rolling down the street and banging away at them.

The United Nations spent over $1.5 billion a year keeping twenty thousand troops in the Democratic Republic of Congo. It was their largest and most expensive area of focus. The UN had divided the DRC into six sectors, and Bunia was the seat of Sector Six.

Other than their phones pinging off a cell tower near the

MONUSCO HQ, there was nothing to connect the men inside the "white house" to the United Nations. What was interesting, though, was that of all the countries who had sent troops to be part of the MONUSCO stabilization force, only four others had sent as many or more than South Africa.

Harvath was willing to bet that a high prevalence of South African troops in the UN stabilization force and calls back-and-forth from the target house to South Africa weren't a coincidence.

What they needed was to identify not only when the "black phone," as Nicholas had dubbed it, was moving, but also who specifically was carrying it.

The phone had already left the compound once and returned, but had done so at night in a two-vehicle convoy carrying eight men. Harvath and his team had watched the needle and the haystack roll right past them, but hadn't been able to learn much about either. It was one of the reasons Harvath hated surveillance work. It could not only be mind-numbingly boring, but incredibly frustrating. And, if you were working with the wrong people, tensions could quickly mount.

To their credit, Ash and his SAS crew were thorough professionals. Nobody in their right mind enjoyed surveillance, but the Brits approached it with a sense of humor. Making fun of different people and things they saw happening down on the street, as well as directing jibes at each other, helped pass the time.

Jambo was an excellent cook, and they supplemented his meals with Chinese and Indian takeout from the hotel. With two long lenses, as well as IR cameras that could capture much better nighttime imagery, they recorded as much as they could and beamed it all back to the United States for analysis.

As they did, Nicholas's facial recognition and data mining programs began to return hits. The men were not South African military. They were former South African military. Recces—former Special Forces from the 5 Special Forces Regiment based in Phalaborwa in northern Limpopo Province.

Just because they were no longer active military didn't mean they weren't currently working for some other part of the South African government, like its intelligence division. But if that were the case, why would they have been involved in wiping out a charitable medical clinic and the adjacent village?

Harvath felt far more certain that the men were mercenaries of some sort, contractors. That of course, brought up all sorts of questions—most importantly who had hired them and what had they been hired to do? In order to get that answer, he was going to have to have a little talk with their head man. But before that could happen, they were going to have to ID him.

Twelve hours later, the gates opened and they got a clear view of one of the SUVs leaving. There were only two occupants—a driver in his forties and a passenger somewhere in his sixties. Nicholas confirmed that the black phone was in the vehicle and on the move. Harvath sent him the pictures they had taken.

An hour later, Nicholas called back. He had identified their target.

"The older man is your guy. His name is Jan Hendrik," he said as he transmitted the man's service record to Harvath's computer. "All of the men we have ID'd so far served under him. Hendrik was their commanding officer."

"What else do we know?"

"Nothing. I can't find anything. No credit card bills, no parking tickets. They're ghosts."

Harvath scrolled through several of the photos on his laptop. These guys might be good at covering their tracks, but they were still men and men made mistakes, even the best of them. Especially when the right pressure was applied.

Pulling up satellite footage of the neighborhood, Harvath gestured Ash over and began to lay out his plan.

CHAPTER 24

The jammer Nicholas had sent had been born out of necessity in Iraq. U.S. troops used much larger versions to help disrupt cell phone and other wireless transmissions as their vehicles were rolled. This, in turn, made it incredibly difficult for the enemy to remotely detonate roadside bombs.

On one of his ops in Syria, Harvath had used a similar device to part a terrorist from the civilians he was hiding behind so that he could take him out. He was hoping to conduct a similar operation here. The problem, though, was that his current target was much more sophisticated and there were several additional layers of difficulty.

Putting a bag over someone's head was always more dangerous and more complicated than laying up on a rooftop and putting a bullet between their eyes. Harvath would know. He had done both, many times.

The unknown element was buy-in from Asher and his men. While their SAS motto was *Who Dares Wins*, Harvath had taken them far beyond their agreed-to scope-of-work. Escorting a doctor and a civilian representative from a medical charity was one thing, but snatching a former South African Special Forces operator off the streets of Bunia was something entirely different.

Harvath figured he had one thing going for him. If Ash and his team hadn't been interested, they would have already taken off. Technically, they had completed their assignment. Harvath and Decker had been returned to Bunia safe and sound. They had fulfilled the terms of their contract—*and then some.*

Now, everything came down to what they wanted. And even more importantly, what they *needed*.

Harvath understood the men all too well. There was a reason they had become contractors instead of fishing guides or boat builders—and it went beyond them being good at what they did. Harvath probably could up and go to Wall Street at any time and make a killing, but that wasn't what he wanted, it wasn't what he needed.

He needed this. He needed the action. That was why he kept coming back. He was pretty good at it, and it still scared the hell out of him time and time again. But it was exhilarating. It was a rush he couldn't get anywhere else. He craved it like a drug. And like a drug, he would put it before everything else, even a trip to see the leaves turn colors with someone he professed was very important to him.

A common joke among operators was "don't be *that* guy." It meant don't be the guy who does something stupid and screws up. But it was also a warning to never do anything you'd regret. Harvath knew that if he got out of the business, he would regret it. He also knew that there was nothing more lamentable than a former action guy who pined for his gun fighting days. Harvath never wanted to be "that guy."

And so, he had stayed hard, and he had stayed in. He risked being shot, stabbed, and blown to pieces, all because he loved giving Death the finger as he sped on by.

Was it immature? Maybe. But the fact was that he was better when he was out here. At home he drank and recharged, ate and worked out, all the while looking forward to not knowing where the next assignment was going to take him. And all the while saying he wanted a family if he could just find the right person.

But he had found the right people, repeatedly—incredible women who would have done anything for him—and yet it hadn't worked out.

It wasn't about the women. It was obviously about him. He wanted his cake and to eat it too. It wasn't impossible. Other people balanced dangerous, high-speed careers with family. Why not him?

It was a question he hadn't been able to answer. At least not until a naked Jessica Decker had tried to climb in the shower with him. That had crystalized it. *He was loyal.*

Loyalty meant honoring the promises you made to other people—

whether it was an oath of service or the rules of your relationship. But there was something more to it than that, especially when it came to relationships. It meant that you didn't just think about yourself. You had to think about that other person. That's what Decker had helped him realize. That was what his problem was.

He was successful because he pushed everything right to the razor's edge. He *liked* pushing it to that edge. The harder the mission, the more he enjoyed it. It came partly from who he was and how he was raised. His father had taught him to push and keep pushing. It was the SEAL in him. When Harvath became a SEAL himself, they took him to a completely new level.

The only easy day was yesterday, Failure is not an option, and *Never Quit* were SEAL mottos that had become a part of him. They were so deeply burned into who he was that they impacted every decision he made.

But how could he look at a woman and say, *As much as I love you, my job will always come first?* Didn't that mean failure when it came to that relationship? Was it selfish? Was it immature? Unfair?

But as frank and as honest as he thought he was being with himself, there was something else tapping at the back of his mind. This was not the time to be trying to get to the truth, but he was closer to it than he had ever felt before.

Jesus, he thought, *this job is like a drug*. It fought like crazy to keep you hooked. It also provided great moments of euphoria, along with some amazing moments of clarity.

Instead of slamming the iron door of his mind shut, as was his practice, he decided to leave it open and focus his mind elsewhere. Maybe the answer he was looking for would come, maybe it wouldn't. As long as the job got done, that was what mattered for the moment.

• • •

The remaining items Harvath needed were not small, but with the help of a stack of currency, Jambo and his relatives had taken care of them in the blink of an eye. Mick had gone along with them to do the assessment and had given it his approval. With the final pieces in place, they were ready for their operation to go dynamic.

As Harvath powered up the jammer, Ash shook his head in disbelief.

"Bloody amazing technology," he said. "I never would have thought to use it like this."

"Any job's easy if you've got the correct tool, right?"

"But you're sawing boards with a hammer, mate. It's brilliant."

Harvath smiled and turned his attention back to the jammer. He had been right about Ash and his team. If the money was right, they were happy to be on board, especially with the action factor so high. Harvath had provided more excitement in the last couple of days than they had seen in the last couple of years. It had been a long time since they had played cowboys and Indians.

If the truth be told, they would have stuck with Harvath even if there was no money left to be made. What had happened at the clinic and to those villagers was horrific. It was an affront to their sense of honor. If they could help settle that score, they were one hundred percent on board and wouldn't quit until every last person responsible had been brought to justice. It was about doing what was right. Like Harvath, they believed in standing up for those who couldn't stand up for themselves.

With the jammer ready to go, Harvath hailed Nicholas and got ready for their first test. He would operate it remotely from the United States. When the time came, Harvath would need to be on the street, not up in the apartment pressing buttons.

"Okay," he said. "Whenever you're ready."

"Roger that," Nicholas said over his earpiece. "Stand by."

Mick looked at the jammer and said, "It's that accurate? You can focus on a single phone? It doesn't simply shut down the entire block?"

"Let's watch," Harvath replied.

Several lights on the jammer changed colors as Nicholas manipulated its levels from back in the United States. There was a slight lag in what he could see from the camera feed, but not so much that it would make a difference.

There was an art to this and Harvath had been very specific about what he wanted. If he drove the black phone straight into the dirt, Hendrik might become suspicious. It was better that everyone in the house experience some signal drop at first. It was Congo after all. Shit happened.

The Brute Squad was the first to notice movement inside the house.

"I've got someone at the window," Eddie said over the radio. "Second floor, northwest corner. Looks like he has his phone in his hand and is trying to find a better signal."

"Make sure to keep taking pictures," Harvath replied.

"Roger that."

Cell phones had gone beyond being simple electronic devices. They had actually become part of people. Harvath was convinced that every time a person's phone chimed, that a little blast of dopamine was released into the brain. It was like watching monkeys press on a bar for food. People were constantly looking at them, just in case a text or an email had come in. Take their phone away from them, even if only for a few moments, and they started to go into withdrawal.

"We've got movement in the courtyard," Ash said.

Mick joined him at the window.

"Oh, look at this guy," he laughed. "He's spinning around like he's got one foot nailed to the ground. Raise the phone higher you twat! That's it. Up over your head. Now jump up and down on your left leg and see if that helps your signal, you tosser."

Harvath smiled and asked in the room and over the radio, "Any sign of Hendrik yet?"

"We've got activity at the door on the west side," Eddie replied.

"What do you see?"

"Stand by. Nothing yet."

"Roger that," Harvath replied. "Standing by."

They all watched their respective areas of responsibility. Harvath was glued to the remote rooftop cameras.

"Okay, got him," Eddie finally said. "It's our guy. It's Hendrik."

"You're positive?"

"Yes. It's him."

With that confirmation, Harvath instructed Nicholas to slowly bring the signal strength back up to normal.

"Cracking!" Mick exclaimed as he turned away from the window and flashed Harvath the thumbs-up. "Time to have fun?"

Harvath nodded. "Roger that. Time to have fun."

CHAPTER 25

Asher knew his men better than Harvath, so once the plan was firmed up he decided who would take what role. With Jambo driving the van he had borrowed, Harvath and Asher would do the snatch. Mick would drive one of the Land Cruisers as a follow car, and Simon and Eddie would take sniper positions on two different rooftops. One of Jambo's cousins would sit in LC2 with the engine running a block away, ready to pick up the Brute Squad once they had pulled back. If everything went well, the job would be over in fifteen minutes.

They all knew, though, that if something could go wrong, it would go wrong, so they developed a set of contingencies and after checking their weapons and equipment, sanitized the apartments. They wouldn't be coming back. Mick would take the jammer with him in LC1 and run it off a converter. It was designed to be mobile, and Nicholas could still control it remotely from back in the United States.

Starting from several blocks over, they drove back and forth to the new safe house Jambo's relatives had arranged. It was just outside of town and remote enough that no one would know they were there. They familiarized themselves with the roads—using a different route each time—until they felt they had everything as figured out as they could.

The key was to pull this off as quietly as possible. Hendrik's men were going to turn Bunia upside down to find their boss. And if they had any pull whatsoever with MONUSCO, there would be thousands of soldiers helping them beat the bushes. Everything would come down to timing and staying as far beneath the radar as possible.

With one last radio check, Harvath and Ash climbed into the van, slid the door shut, and instructed Jambo to move out.

As they drove toward their target, Harvath kept in touch with Nicholas and Mick, while Ash fed him situation reports from Simon and Eddie who were watching the "white house" from their rooftop perches.

Once they arrived on their mark and had the van where they wanted it, Harvath stepped out and said to Nicholas, "Start throttling him down. Slowly."

"Roger," Nicholas replied.

Looking at Ash, he said, "Ready?"

The Brit nodded and he and Harvath took their places around the corner. Regardless of which door Hendrik exited, Nicholas could play Hot or Cold by increasing or decreasing the cell signal based on which direction the man moved. As long as he continued on the path they wanted, his signal would continue to get warmer. They didn't need him to go far. When he turned the corner, Harvath and Ash would throw a bag over his head toss him in the van and speed away.

"I've got movement," Eddie said over the radio. "West door, same as before."

"Can you ID who it is?" Harvath asked.

"Negative. Stand by."

Everyone held their breath. They tensed, coiled like springs ready to jump. Seconds passed.

"Got him," Eddie finally said. "It's definitely Hendrik."

"Roger that," replied Harvath. "Lead him to us."

"Will do," said Eddie as he then communicated over his cell phone with Nicholas, so he could manipulate the jammer accordingly.

Everything was going smoothly. Hendrik was nearing the corner when Simon's voice came over the radio.

"You've got company," he said. "A woman and two children just stepped out of a building half a block down. Headed in your direction."

Jambo, who was monitoring the radio from inside the van, didn't need to be told what to do. Harvath had placed his relatives at different positions nearby, and Jambo was already on his cell phone relaying instructions.

Moments later, Simon said, "You're all clear."

Harvath hoped that would be the extent of any interference.

Eddie began a countdown of how many feet Hendrik was from turning the corner. "Four feet out," he radioed. "Three feet now. Two," but then he suddenly stopped.

Once again, everyone held their breath.

"He's holding one of the phones up."

Come on, Harvath said to himself. *You're almost there. Just a couple more feet.*

Back in the United States, Nicholas boosted the signal and then dropped it. It was the push Hendrik needed, and he stepped around the corner. As he did, Harvath and Asher were waiting.

Ash landed the first blow. It was a punch to the gut that caused Hendrik to double over. Harvath brought his fist down between the man's shoulder blades, knocking the wind from his lungs and sending him the rest of the way to the ground.

As Ash placed the bag over his head, Harvath zip-tied his hands behind his back. By the time he looked up to see where the van was, Jambo had already pulled up and had the sliding door open.

Harvath and Ash picked Hendrik up by his arms and chucked him inside. Ash climbed in after him as Harvath picked up the two cell phones. Jambo was already pulling away as Harvath jumped in and slid the door closed.

He patted Hendrik down for weapons as Ash zip-tied his ankles. He found a Browning Hi-Power with two spare magazines as well as a folding knife in his pocket and a fixed blade in his boot. He carried cash as well as a blue United Nations Laissez-Passer also known as an UNLP. It acted like a travel document and was only supposed to be used for official United Nations travel.

Popping the covers off both of the phones, Harvath removed their batteries and put all of the pieces in his pocket. Hendrik was gasping, trying to get the air back into his lungs.

Neither Harvath nor Ash spoke. As he was a Special Forces operator, they were aware of the kind of SERE training Hendrik would have had. SERE stood for Survival, Evasion, Resistance, and Escape. Once his breath had fully returned, he was going to try to sort out what was going on. His mind would be calculating the odds of all different kinds of situations. Whatever situation he was most afraid of would weigh on him the heaviest. That's what Harvath wanted him focused on. The more unsettled and stressed out he was, the better. A man with Hendrik's background wasn't going to be easy to break.

They took a circuitous route, partly to make sure they weren't being followed, and partly to disorient Hendrik as much as possible. The less he knew, the better.

When the van came to a stop at the safe house on the outskirts of Bunia, Hendrik's body tensed. Harvath slid the door open and Asher nudged the South African to move forward. He refused. So pulling his arm back, Asher slammed his left elbow through the hood and into Hendrik's mouth. A stream of blood and saliva ran over his chin, down his neck, and stained the front of his shirt.

Harvath stepped out of the van and dragged Hendrik with him. Laying the man facedown in the dirt, he used his knife to slice through the restraints binding his ankles. He and Ash then lifted him to his feet and guided him to a shed at the rear of the property.

It was a stifling, unventilated space that smelled like gasoline and animal dung. It was not intended to be pleasant.

A metal chair had been placed in the middle of the shed. Hendrik was walked over to it and made to sit down. Ash zip-tied his left leg to the left leg of the chair and did the same on the right side. He then re-zip-tied his arms to the arms of the chair.

If Hendrik had resisted, or tried to lash out in any way, Asher had been prepared to punch him in a very sensitive part of his anatomy. Hendrik, though, had not resisted. He had not even spoken.

While Ash kept an eye on their prisoner, Harvath walked back to the house. Everything he had asked for was there. Stacking as much of it as he could in a metal washtub, he walked back out to the shed.

Mick and the Brute Squad had arrived. With all of the vehicles now inside the gate, Jambo locked it and then helped his relatives cover the van with a tarp. Simon and Eddie took guard duty while Mick helped carry the rest of the supplies out to the shed. He had already been told not to speak.

In his mind, Harvath walked through how best to choreograph the next step. The operation had come together so fast, and with so little actionable intelligence, it was difficult to decide what the right move was.

By now, Hendrik's men knew something had happened. They were well trained and would move quickly. They would start by canvassing the neighborhood. And while Harvath and his team had done all they could to minimize the potential risk of any witnesses, he had to assume that someone had seen something. Eventually Hendrik's men were going to begin piecing things together. The weakest link in Harvath's plan would then become the airport.

Once Hendrik's men figured out that his abductors had been white, and thereby likely foreigners, they would be all over it. At the very least, they would post a man there. And depending on their pull with MONUSCO, they might be able to ramp up security screening or even shut it down.

Harvath didn't want to find out. He needed to move fast, stay ahead of them. That was why Jan Hendrik would only get one opportunity to cooperate. If he refused, Harvath would have no choice but to crank things all the way up and rip off the knob.

CHAPTER 26

When time was on your side, interrogations could take as long as you wanted. They could play out over hours, days, or even weeks. With long-term detainees, interrogations could stretch months or even years. It all depended on how quickly you needed the information and what lengths you were willing to go to get it.

When time was a key factor, Harvath's definition of what was acceptable broadened dramatically. He nodded, and Asher flipped on the blinding halogen lights that had been set up on stands. Walking over to Hendrik, he pulled the bag from his head.

The man squinted and tried to get a good look at Harvath, but the lights were too bright. All he saw standing in front of him was a silhouette.

"Mr. Hendrik," Harvath began. "I am well aware of your background and your training, so I won't insult you by trying to build some sort of rapport. You have information I want, and I am in a hurry.

"If you cooperate, this'll be over fast. If you don't cooperate, this will still be over fast, but it'll be much more painful for you. I'll give you one chance to answer my questions. If you lie to me, or if I feel you are being evasive, all bets are off. Understand that I will go to any lengths necessary to extract from you the information I need. Is that clear?"

"Who are you?" Hendrik demanded.

Harvath gave the man an open-handed slap across the side of his face.

"That was for being evasive. You don't ask the questions. I do."

The South African spat a gob of blood onto the floor, squinted at him and replied, "You're American."

This time, Harvath hit him in the same spot, but with his fist. The blow was so hard, it rocked him to the point of almost tipping over in his chair.

"Fuck you," said Hendrik once he had recovered.

Harvath was done playing games.

Striking him again, he demanded, "Why were you at the Matumaini Clinic?"

"Fuck you," the man repeated.

Harvath put the bag back over his head and nodded to Ash and Mick. The two men circled around behind the South African's chair, grabbed hold of it and tipped it backward. As soon as they did, Harvath began pouring water through the fabric over his face.

Hendrik's body tensed, and he began to thrash wildly. Harvath stopped pouring the water and the Brits leaned him upright.

"Why were you at the Matumaini Clinic, Jan?"

Hendrik coughed and spat up water as he tried to catch his breath. Harvath gave him several more seconds and when he didn't answer, he nodded for the Brits to tip him over again, and he once more began pouring the water.

Exhausting his first pitcher, Harvath reached for a second. Hendrik thrashed even harder than before.

The tactic was inelegant but simple. He took no pleasure in it. It was simply a tool in the toolbox. All Hendrik had to do was cooperate, and it would be over.

"Why were you at the Matumaini Clinic?" Harvath asked as he eased up on the water.

The South African sputtered and hacked from beneath his hood, trying to clear the water from his airway.

"Whoever pays you, Jan, isn't paying you enough to go through this. Tell me why you were there, and I'll make it stop."

Hendrik managed a third, "Fuck you."

It went on and on. The floor was puddled with water and Harvath's shoes, as well as his trousers, were soaked. When pitcher number two was empty, he started in on number three.

The South African was one tough son of a bitch, but no one could hold out indefinitely. Everyone broke under waterboarding. It was only a matter of time. Hendrik was about to reach his breaking point.

"*Humanitarian*," he gurgled from beneath his drenched hood as he coughed and vomited up water.

Harvath motioned for the chair to be righted and waited for the man to catch his breath. Once he had, Harvath asked, "What did you say?"

Even when the hardest of men cracked, what they said had to be treated as suspect until independently confirmed. Sometimes things came pouring out in an obscure torrent. What they said could be true, could be the effect of psychological torment, or it could be complete and total bullshit.

Harvath motioned Ash and Mick back behind the lights. Once they were there, he pulled off Hendrik's hood.

"Listen to me," he said. "If you lie to me, you're going back under the water. Do you understand?"

Hendrik shook his head from side to side, confused. Harvath slapped him and reached for another pitcher.

"It was a humanitarian operation," he said feebly, trying to focus.

"A *humanitarian operation*?" Harvath said. "You wipe out a clinic and cremate an entire village and call that a humanitarian operation?"

"It needed to be contained. More would have died."

"What needed to be contained?"

"The infection."

"What infection?"

Hendrik didn't reply and so Harvath slapped him again.

"One of the patients got out," the South African stammered.

"From the Matumaini Clinic? What are you talking about?"

Hendrik failed to answer, so Harvath picked his hood back up and began to put it back over his head.

"Not Matumaini," he said as the hood came down. "*Ngoa*."

Harvath pulled it back up. "What's Ngoa?"

"A village. There's a WHO facility there. A lab."

"A World Health Organization lab?"

The man nodded.

"What were they working on?"

"I don't know," Hendrik replied.

The answer came a little too quickly for Harvath's liking. There was also the flash of a microexpression that told him the South African was lying.

Fixing his gaze on Hendrik, he said, "You're lying to me. What happens when you lie?"

"I am not lying," he pleaded as Harvath roughly pulled the hood down over his head and waved the Brits back over.

Harvath picked the pitcher back up as Ash and Mick tilted the chair backward.

"Hemorrhagic fever!" the man yelled. "They were experimenting with African Hemorrhagic Fever!"

"Like Ebola?"

"Worse."

"How much worse?" Harvath demanded.

Hendrik refused to respond, so Harvath started pouring water again over his nose and mouth.

"They found a way to weaponize it!"

Harvath poured again. "Tell me how."

"Airborne!" the South African confessed, shaking his head back and forth, trying to make the water stop. "They found a way to make it airborne!"

CHAPTER 27

Clifton—the luxury, four hundred and eleven acre estate and farm, an hour outside Washington, D.C.—had belonged to George Washington's cousin, Warner Washington. Pierre Damien loved it as much for its history as he did for its exquisite Classical Revival manor house and the panoramic views of the Blue Ridge Mountains.

George Washington had spent extensive time on the property and when Damien walked the grounds, he liked to imagine himself walking in the footsteps of history. Damien wondered, if Washington were alive today, would he see the world the same way. Would Washington realize that in a modern era such as this, certain viewpoints and philosophies of government had run their course? Wouldn't such a noble man realize that individual, selfish pursuits only served to harm mankind, not advance it? And as a farmer, a true man of the soil, certainly Washington would recognize the responsibilities that all human beings had to the planet.

Taking a deep breath of crisp fall air, Damien breathed in the scent of nature. The colors along the distant mountains were extraordinary. There was no better place to be in autumn. Of all the properties he owned, even his private Cay in the Bahamas, Clifton was his favorite. It was why he had wanted to bring Helena here. That, and there were final preparations to be made. Tonight would be the organization's last dinner for some time.

The tiny Thomas Malthus Society didn't have a web site or a mailing address. Its membership was one of most closely guarded secrets in D.C.

The society was based on the teachings of the eighteenth-century cleric and scholar, Reverend Thomas Robert Malthus—particularly his *An Essay on the Principle of Population*.

Influential in the fields of political economy and demography, Malthus believed that a Utopian society could never be achieved as long as the world's population was allowed to continue to grow unchecked. The only way to protect the earth and improve the existence of mankind was to have less of mankind—something he believed Mother Nature would eventually deliver in the form of widespread famine and disease.

The anticipated population reduction event was popularly, and rather dramatically, known as the "Malthusian catastrophe." It had yet to happen, but there were those who not only believed it necessary but who were eager to help usher it forward. They simply referred to it as "the event." Some of those people lived and worked in Washington, D.C.

By custom, the dinner's ingredients were locally sourced. Tonight, all of it came from Clifton. There would be fresh herbs, lettuce, radishes, sorrel, chives, and garlic, as well as farm-raised lamb shoulder and duck breast, foie gras emulsion, and goat's milk and sheep's milk cheeses.

The pièce de résistance was dessert. George Washington was an ice cream fanatic. In his honor, Damien served fresh, hand-cranked strawberry ice cream from an actual Washington family recipe.

There were organic wine pairings, an incredible vintage port, and the most delicious, fresh-roasted, certified free-trade coffee any of the guests had ever tasted.

The dinner party was a huge hit—as the guests had known it would be. Damien was a man of both astounding wealth and impeccable taste. It was the society's best dinner of the year.

The conversation, as usual, revolved around domestic and international affairs, but also included science, mathematics, literature, the arts, and culture. These were incredibly erudite men and women. The depth and breadth of their intelligence was equaled only by their power—and that's why Damien had selected them.

He knew a thing or two about power, small truths that others often failed to realize. Heads of agencies and their immediate underlings would come and go, subject to election cycles and political approval. The same was true of politicians. Their influence was only worth so much.

The truly powerful were those deepest inside the government. Like the Wizard of Oz, they were the ones behind the curtain. They were the ones who knew which ropes to pull. Their hands were on the very levers of power.

They could not only raise or lower the sets but also brighten or dim the house lights. They weren't just inside the machine as middle managers, they *were* the machine. They knew the game. They knew the system. They had been masters of it for years.

Theirs was a modern Rome, Rome on the Potomac—an empire in miniature—a land in and unto itself.

New Rome knew no economic vicissitudes. There were no vacant storefronts, no depressed housing prices, or reductions in take-home pay.

Taxes, fees, fines, and lines of credit that stretched to the stars and back made sure that the treasury was awash in coin. Things in New Rome were positively booming. The future was bright indeed.

That didn't mean, though, that the empire was secure. As its fortunes grew, it seemed to come under a more regular and more prolonged assault by the country class.

"Country class" had replaced "fly-over country" as the new contumelious term used to describe the great unwashed living outside D.C. or the nation's other Megalopoli.

Through social media, a handful of sympathetic news organizations, and grassroots activism, the country class waged incessant guerrilla warfare, demanding that the New Rome be put on a diet and scaled dramatically back.

As far as the New Romans were concerned, it was an odd, stupid little war waged by odd, stupid little people. They were most definitely in the minority. All of the polling showed it. Instead of shoving their faces full of McDonald's drive-thru and watching reality TV like the rest of the country-class Hobbits, they were strangely obsessed with what was happening in Washington and how things should be changed.

If they were so eager to dictate how it should be done in Washington, why were they sitting on their asses in Tennessee and Texas, Idaho and Indiana? Why weren't they trundling their fat little children onto buses and coming to D.C. to help lend a hand? The answer was simple— because it was beyond them.

They had no idea how government worked, much less how important government workers were to its continued function. Without Federal employees, it all stopped—all of it. Fees at National Parks didn't get collected, school lunch regulations didn't get enforced, borders were left unprotected, and that was only the beginning. The inmates wanted to run the asylum. There was no way that could ever be allowed to happen.

Anything that grows is, by definition, alive. Washington, D.C. was no exception.

As a living organism, the Federal Government's number one job was self-preservation. Any threat to its existence had to be dealt with.

When the country class came with its pathetic rhetorical torches and meddling electoral pitchforks, New Rome was ready.

It fought back with tools no one had ever seen coming. New Rome weaponized its own Federal agencies. The Internal Revenue Service, the Department of Justice, the Environmental Protection Agency, the Bureau of Alcohol, Tobacco, and Firearms—they all swatted away each and every attack.

The country class could storm the battlements over and over. They didn't stand a chance. Not only could you not fight City Hall, you couldn't survive a fight with the Federal Government. New Rome could take every single thing you have and put you in prison. It wasn't even a fair fight. (It wasn't supposed to be.)

New Rome would do what it took to win, and it would do so every single time. Its responsibility to its own survival was bigger than any responsibility to its clueless constituents. If they really cared about Washington, they'd be paying much closer attention. But they didn't, and so, New Rome proceeded accordingly.

The phenomenon was fascinating to Damien. Listening to the conversations around the table, he had been captivated. These were not evil people. They were actually incredibly compassionate, clear-eyed, and focused. In short, they *got* it.

They grasped not only what was at stake, but more importantly, what needed to be done. These were reasonable people.

Though not a religious man, Damien knew these people were meant to inherit the earth. It was why he had selected them.

It was a spectacular night. No one was feeling any pain, and no one wanted it to end. Breaking with their locally sourced tradition, Damien dispatched Jeffery to retrieve one of his best sauternes. It was a bottle of liquid gold, a 1934 Château d'Yquem. And he had been saving it for just this very night.

Its copper and orange hues reminded him of the magic bird the next phase of his operation celebrated. The seven-thousand-dollar dessert wine boasted rich crème brûlée, orange, caramel, flowers, spice, and butterscotch flavors, along with earthy whorls of cocoa, chocolate, and coffee.

It was delicious and the absolute best way imaginable to celebrate the rebirth of the world.

Of course, it was exquisitely painful not to be able to share any of this with Helena and be able to show her off. She wasn't a member of the society, though, and thereby wasn't allowed to attend the dinner. Instead, Damien had ordered in her favorite, Italian, and had set her up in the guesthouse. He would join her once his other guests had left.

He had Jeffery bring out a second bottle of Château d'Yquem. This one was a delicious yet much less expensive '66. Some partook, some did not.

Twenty minutes later, society members began to thank him and melt away into the night.

Once they were gone, the woman next to him reached out and put her hand on his arm.

"What a glorious evening, Pierre," she said.

Damien smiled in response. Linda Landon had been working for the Federal Government for over forty years and had seen it all. She was his lynchpin in everything that was about to happen.

Reaching into her shoulder bag, she pulled out a small box. "I brought you something."

"Linda, you shouldn't have gotten me a gift."

"No, no," she stated, looking down and shaking her head, "it's just a small token."

Damien lifted the lid. Inside was a pair of silver cuff links.

"Gordian Knots," she explained. "I thought you would appreciate them."

He did indeed. It was one of his favorite ancient myths. The knot was meant to symbolize an impossible problem solved with bold, outside-the-box thinking.

In the story, a man named Gordius celebrates becoming king by dedicating his chariot to Zeus and tying it to a pole with an impossible to unravel Gordian knot. An oracle predicts that a man will come and untie it, and that man will go on to become king of all Asia. Like the legend of the sword in the stone, many tried and failed to untie the knot. Then Alexander the Great visited the city.

He searched and searched for the loose ends of the knot so he could set to work. When he couldn't find them, he pulled out his sword and sliced right through it. Alexander then went on to conquer Asia.

"They are very handsome," he said. "Thank you."

"I'm glad you like them," Landon replied. "Now, I think you and I should talk about the—"

Damien held his finger up, suggesting she pause, as Jeffery entered the dining room to see if there was anything else they needed.

"Perhaps another coffee?" she said.

"Make it two," Damien stated. "We will take them in the library."

Jeffery nodded and walked back to the kitchen.

Damien stood and motioned his guest into the large main hall. It was hung with magnificent oil paintings in thick, gilded frames. They depicted bucolic scenes of hunting, fishing, and farm life. Landon could only imagine how much they had cost.

Beyond the grand staircase was an elegant paneled door. Damien paused just long enough to turn the handle and then step back so his guest could enter.

Landon barely made it two steps inside before coming to an abrupt stop. Curled up on a couch in front of the fireplace, reading, was an attractive young woman in jeans and a rather tight sweater.

"Helena," Damien said, taken off guard. "What are you doing here?"

"I came to find a book," she replied, laying aside the leather-bound copy of Edward Pollard's *The Lost Cause* and standing.

She walked over and extended her hand to Damien's guest. "My name is Helena. Helena Pestova."

"Pleased to meet you," the older woman replied coldly. "I'm Linda."

Helena waited, but the woman didn't give her last name.

Damien had not intended for the two to meet. In fact, he had not intended for Helena to meet any of the society members. The dinner was a boring philanthropic obligation, he had explained. No spouses. No significant others.

Helena had appeared to take it in stride, but entering the main house and establishing herself in the library communicated another message. She wanted his attention, and she would get it soon enough, plenty of it, but he needed to finish his business with Landon first.

"We have some business items to finish up," he said to her. "I'll find you afterward. Okay?"

"Okay," Helena replied as she picked up her book and cell phone, then walked over and kissed him on the cheek.

At the library door, she turned to the other woman and said, "It was nice meeting you."

Landon shot her a bitchy smile. "You too, dear."

As Helena exited, Jeffery entered with a tray and set up the coffee service on a small table near the fireplace.

Landon took a seat on the couch, removed her computer from her shoulder bag, and powered it up. Damien sat down at his antique desk.

"Will you be needing anything else?" Jeffery asked.

Damien looked everything over and replied, "I think we're fine. Thank you, Jeffery."

Clearing away the tray, Jeffery opened the door and stepped out into the hallway.

As he did, Damien noticed that Helena had left her cell phone charger behind. She always seemed to be forgetting it. She would forget her gorgeous head if it wasn't attached. She was always leaving that stupid charger somewhere.

He thought about having Jeffery unplug it and take it to her, but decided against it. The less that was said about her in front of Landon, the better.

Though married, Landon carried a torch for Damien. He knew it and had thoroughly manipulated it. Her loyalty to him was beyond question. It was also about to be put to the ultimate test.

Removing his laptop, he set it upon his desk and depressed the *power* button. Next to it, he placed the encrypted cell phone he had programmed for her.

With a smile, he said, "Let's get to work."

CHAPTER 28

Harvath had made the call to scrap the Bunia airport altogether. It was too dangerous. They were better off taking their chances on the road south to Goma.

The Hotel Ihusi on Lake Kivu near the Rwanda border crossing was the perfect place for them to hole up while they waited for their jet to arrive. It was filled with mercenaries, smugglers, hookers, NGO workers, and all sorts of other characters. It reminded Harvath of the cantina scene in *Star Wars*. The best part was that everyone minded their own business. If you didn't want to be social, no one bothered you.

It had taken Harvath all the cash he had left to organize their departure. But complicating matters was the fact that Decker had flat-out refused to cooperate.

She not only wouldn't help with Harvath's plan, but she also wanted to return to the Matumaini Clinic and begin to rebuild it. That, though, was absolutely out of the question. It was too dangerous. In addition to it being a crime scene, there was no telling if Hendrik's men, or the FRPI rebels for that matter, might show up there.

In only a handful of days, Harvath had blazed a trail the width of a twenty-lane highway through that part of Congo. It had pissed off a lot of people. The fallout was going to be intense.

Leaving the country as soon as possible was the right thing to do. He had tried to convince Decker of it too, but she wouldn't listen. Finally, he had to get Beaman on the sat phone to straighten her out.

Beaman made it perfectly clear that the Matumaini Clinic was off-limits. He suggested she come back to the United States until things cooled down. She refused and informed him that she intended to return to Kinshasa even though the CARE clinic there was still on hold. There was nothing Beaman could do to persuade her, and he told Harvath to let her go.

Harvath had no trouble letting her go, but he had no intention of doing it in Bunia. She could catch a plane to Kinshasa from Goma. It would be safer there.

Needless to say, Decker dug her heels in. She wanted to know where Harvath had been and why he had left her at the hotel for two days with Leonce and his son. He didn't owe her an explanation, but he gave her one anyway.

He told her that they had gotten a lead on who had been behind the attack on the clinic, as well as the village. When he refused to give her any further details, she went supernova on him. It was blistering, and much of it was uncalled for. He let her get it out of her system and then told her to pack her bag. He told her they were taking her to the airport. Technically, that was true. He just didn't tell her which one.

Once she had finished her next temper tantrum over not being taken to the airport in Bunia and had calmed down, he filled her in a little bit more on what had gone down.

He had a private MediJet flying in to Goma. Without telling her everything about Hendrik, he explained that he planned to smuggle him out of the country as an acute medical patient. To do that, he would need Decker's help as a doctor. She not only said no, she said *hell* no and lectured him about ethics.

Harvath had had just about as much as he could take from her. His bandwidth for her ideological bullshit was full.

When they arrived at the hotel, he helped carry her bag up to her room, and then zip-tied her in the bathroom. As soon as he had left the country, she would be released, taken to the airport, and put on a plane. Until then, Simon and Eddie would take shifts keeping an eye on her. The last thing he needed was her screwing up his departure.

With the rest of Harvath's money, Jambo scoured Goma to purchase the people and paperwork Harvath needed. Everything else would have to be "borrowed." Without even being asked, Ash and Mick volunteered.

As the men worked on their lists, Harvath unpacked Decker's gear. Over the phone, one of the Carlton Group's medical assets stepped him through preparation of the drugs he was going to give Hendrik.

Harvath had mixed feelings about leaving. With everything he had learned, he needed to get back to the United States. There were still several accounts, though, that needed to be settled in Congo.

While he wanted Hendrik's men placed on the front burner for the atrocities they had committed, the WHO lab in Ngoa was the U.S. Government's main focus.

Reed Carlton had conducted a very private briefing with the President, as well as the Director of the CIA. Based on Harvath's reporting, it was decided that a highly specialized, covert team from the U.S. Army's Medical Research Institute of Infectious Diseases at Fort Detrick, Maryland, would be sent in to investigate.

Known as a Scientific Tactical Assessment Response team, or STAR team for short, it was a hybrid of Special Operations and scientific personnel. Whatever threats they encountered, be they chemical, biological, or anthropological—i.e. human—the team members were equipped and trained to face them. If there was intelligence to be had at Ngoa, they would secure it, and bring it back to the United States.

Harvath's job was to get Hendrik out of Congo and deliver him to an interrogation team on the island of Malta. This was where Dr. Jessica Decker had refused to lend any assistance whatsoever.

Normally, Harvath wouldn't have cared, but Hendrik was of high intelligence value. If he coded during the flight, it would be left to Harvath to save him. The plane wasn't going to land anywhere else but Malta. If it did, and Hendrik came to and began talking, Harvath and the pilots would be thrown in the nearest prison.

The Carlton Group moved a lot of detainees via medical transport jets. The owner of Sentinel Medevac was a patriot who had been very generous to Harvath and the Old Man. There was no way they were going to allow two of his pilots to be incarcerated and one of his very expensive long-haul jets impounded. It was Malta or bust, which was why Harvath had spent so much time on the phone getting the dosing right.

Hendrik was going to be heavily sedated. So much so, he wouldn't talk, moan, or even move. Jambo's assignment was to take care of greasing the skids at the airport and buying the appropriate health ministry paperwork. Ash and Mick were in charge of sets and props. It all would come down to mounting an absolutely convincing show.

When his cell phone chimed, Harvath left Hendrik with one of the Brute Squad and walked down to the parking lot. He found Mick standing in front of the team's Land Cruisers with a smile.

United Nations vehicles were white with simple black lettering for a reason. It made them easy to spot and instantly recognizable. It also made them easy to counterfeit.

Both vehicles were already white, so all that they had needed was for the letters *U* and *N* to be stenciled in the right places. Mick, though, had gone a step further and had even matched the correct high-gloss black paint. Leave it to a team of Special Operations guys not only to get the job done but to get it done to precise detail.

Ash was standing behind LC2 and waved Harvath over. Because the vehicle was set up to carry cargo, it made the perfect makeshift ambulance. In fact, it was quite common in Congo to see them used that way.

Inside were all the things Harvath had asked for, plus a couple he hadn't. *Resourceful* didn't even come close to describing the two SAS men.

The health ministry documents Jambo acquired were the icing on the cake. Based on everything they had pulled together, Harvath had little doubt they were going to be able to smuggle Hendrik out without incident.

This was still Congo, though, and Harvath wouldn't rest completely assured of anything until the entire country was in his rearview mirror.

Back in his room, he thought about giving Decker a final opportunity to leave with him, but decided against it. She had made her decision. He couldn't risk her tanking this leg of the operation out of spite or misguided moralization. They would do fine without her. Harvath would monitor Hendrik's vitals throughout the flight and have a doctor on standby via sat phone. If anything happened, Harvath would handle it. Hendrik was going to Malta. End of story.

• • •

When the pilot contacted Harvath to let him know he was on the ground, the clock began ticking. The first thing they had to do was drug Hendrik.

The bound-and-gagged South African spun on the floor like a crocodile when he saw the syringe come out. It took Ash, Mick, *and* Jambo to hold him down so Harvath could inject him. Moments later, his eyes rolled up into his head, and he was out.

The men moved quickly. They changed Hendrik into a hospital gown, placed him on a stretcher, and Harvath started an IV.

When the second text came in from the pilot confirming that he had completed refueling and preflight, Harvath told the team it was time to roll.

They waited until things were clear at the side of the hotel and carried Hendrik out that way. After transferring him to the isolation stretcher in the back of LC2, they secured his arms and legs with zip-ties, and then disguised everything with hospital blankets. Harvath checked his vitals once more before closing the seams of the translucent tent.

Once Hendrik was ready for transport, the team donned goggles, facemasks, and disposable Tyvek coveralls. As it was just for show, they only put on one layer of gloves, but they taped them up just the same. Anyone who saw them now wouldn't want anything to do with them, much less get anywhere near them. Fear was the biggest thing Harvath was counting on.

Even by third world standards, Goma International Airport was a pit. It still hadn't fully recovered from the eruption of Mount Nyiragongo over a decade before. A lake of solidified lava two hundred meters wide by a thousand meters long had swallowed up a third of its main runway and cut off access to the terminal. All of the "temporary" work-arounds that airport authorities had come up with back then were still in place. This actually played right into Harvath's plan.

Nobody at Goma International wanted a contagious patient with a highly communicable disease passing through the commercial aviation area. Nor did they want them passing through the adjacent area that all of the military and relief flights used. The airport authority wanted the patient completely isolated and so Jambo had arranged for the team to be admitted via a gate at the far side of the airport.

When they rolled up in their UN-marked vehicles, Jambo—in full mask, goggles, and bunny suit—lowered his window and offered his paperwork and Hendrik's blue, UN Laissez-Passer passport for inspection.

The armed soldiers looked at him like he was crazy. They were all too familiar with disease in Congo. They weren't going to exit the safety of their booth and inspect anything. In fact, they immediately shut their own window, opened the security gates, and quickly waved the convoy through.

The jet's airstairs were already down as the Land Cruisers pulled up alongside. As instructed, the pilots remained in the cockpit and did not exit.

Knowing that they were under observation, Harvath waited until they had loaded Hendrik inside the aircraft to say thank you. He shook each man's hand and told them how much he appreciated what they had done.

While he would have loved to have bought them all beers and steak dinners to celebrate the completion of the assignment, his work wasn't done. They were professionals. They understood.

As they filed down the stairs, Asher was the last to leave the plane. He stopped in the aircraft's door and turned to Harvath.

"If you ever to come back to Africa," he said, "I'll be expecting a phone call. *And* that steak dinner."

"You got it," replied Harvath.

Asher stepped onto the top stair, gave the doorframe two quick taps and shouted "See ya, Superman," as he returned to the vehicles.

After retracting the airstairs and closing the aircraft door, Harvath checked to make sure Hendrik was secure and then informed the pilots that they were ready to take off.

As the plane began to taxi forward, Harvath took a seat, cinched his seat belt, and drew a deep breath. Goma International was known for its crashes—both on landing *and* on takeoff. He prayed Mr. Murphy had overlooked the airport today.

The plane had been given first position and had been cleared for takeoff. The engines whined as the pilot throttled up the power and turned onto the runway.

Harvath leaned back in his seat and looked out the window. Ash,

Mick, and Jambo had already cleared the gate and were headed back to the hotel. They were good men. Harvath had meant it when he said that he appreciated them. They had his back and had proven that he could trust them. That was everything in his book.

He could only imagine the new assholes Decker was going to tear them once they cut her loose. But no matter how arrogant or nasty she was, they would take it like pros and make sure she got on her flight, even if they had to carry her onto the plane.

As the jet raced down the runway and lifted off into the air, he watched Congo fall away beneath him. This was the point where he usually felt relieved. Not this time.

Throughout the flight, he monitored Hendrik and kept him pumped up with sedatives. When the jet touched down in Malta, it taxied into a private hangar where he handed over the prisoner to the interrogation team. The lead operative was a man named Vella. Harvath had never met him before, but he knew him by reputation. He was very good at what he did. He worked out of a facility masquerading as a rural Maltese farmhouse. It had been irreverently nicknamed the "Solarium" because most of it was deep below ground with no windows. If Hendrik was holding anything back, Vella was going to get it.

Waiting in the hangar for Harvath was a new jet and crew. The Gulfstream G650ER had been arranged by Beaman to get him back to the States as quickly as possible. It came fully catered along with a flight attendant. But the best feature as far as Harvath was concerned was the private bedroom.

He had a drink just after takeoff and another with his meal. By the time he took off his clothes and hit the bed, he was more than ready to close his eyes and fall asleep.

He woke up a couple of times in flight—just long enough to open his eyes, check his watch, and drift back asleep.

It was a godsend—a chunk of over eight hours of uninterrupted time. When he couldn't sleep any longer, he availed himself of the en suite bathroom and took a long, hot shower. He then shaved as he let the water pound against his body.

After drying off, he returned to the bedroom, where he found the bed made, his clothes hung up, the TV turned to a satellite news channel, and coffee waiting. Sitting on the bed was a menu offering a range of meals he could choose from before they landed.

This really was the way to fly. The only thing it was missing was some-one to share it with. He had no doubt Lara would love it. Who wouldn't?

Scanning the menu, he made his decision, and called up front to order. By the time he had dressed and walked out of the bedroom, the table had been set with new silver, new flowers, and a fresh linen tablecloth. A plate of fresh fruit was already waiting. *Lara would like this a lot.*

The flight attendant asked if he wanted a cocktail, and he politely de-clined. He knew he was going to have to hit the ground running when the plane landed.

After eating a double portion of bacon and eggs, he took a bottle of water back to the bedroom and closed the door. There wasn't much time before they touched down, and he wanted to use it to get his thoughts together.

He didn't know how secure the plane's WiFi was, so he had refrained from using his laptop. He didn't like going in to the office blind, but he didn't have any choice. Security always came first.

They would be landing at Dulles and Harvath assumed the Old Man would send someone to pick him up. If no one was there, he would just hop in a cab. The Carlton Group was not that far away. The building's proximity to Dulles had been one of the selling points for Carlton. Tak-ing in the crawl along the bottom of the screen, Harvath tried to get up to speed on what had transpired while he had been away. He also needed to make the mental shift from Congo mode to back home, CONUS mode—military speak for Continental United States.

Once the plane had landed and come to a stop, the flight attendant lowered the airstairs and a U.S. immigration agent boarded the plane. Harvath handed the man his passport, as well as the still blank declaration form the flight attendant had given him.

The agent looked at it and smiled. Harvath was on a very special VIP list.

"Nothing to declare then?" he asked.

"Only that I'm glad to be home."

"It's good to have you back, sir."

The man handed Harvath's passport back to him, and Harvath picked up his bag and stepped off the plane. The crew met him at the bottom of the airstairs and thanked him for flying with them. They were extremely professional and he thanked them in return before heading across the tarmac.

Though most of his travel was done out of D.C.'s Reagan International, he knew the private aviation routine at Dulles very well and walked toward the Signature Flight Support building.

When he stepped inside, he saw that Reed Carlton had sent someone to meet him. Standing with a garment bag over her shoulder was one of his colleagues from the Carlton Group, Sloane Ashby.

"You better not have been in my house," Harvath said as she held out the garment bag to him.

Only Reed Carlton had keys to Harvath's home, but on more than one occasion he had given them to Ashby for one reason or another.

Harvath didn't like it. Not only because he didn't want her looking around his house when he wasn't there but also because it was demeaning to an operator of Ashby's status to relegate her to errand-girl status.

That was the Old Man's style, though. No matter who you were or where you came from, you had to earn your way up in his organization.

The problem with sending Ashby to select clothes for Harvath was that every time she was sent to do it, she always pushed the envelope—picking combinations Harvath would never assemble for himself.

"I didn't pick these," she said, handing over the garment bag. "I wasn't in your house. I only drove up and popped the trunk."

Harvath unzipped the bag and looked inside. It wasn't the staid dark suit, white shirt, and dark tie he would have expected from the Old Man, but it wasn't the envelope-pushing ensemble he would have expected from Ashby. In fact, it fell tastefully right in the middle.

"Who gave this to you?" he asked.

"Lara."

"*Lara?*"

"Did you develop a hearing problem in Congo?" she joked. "Yeah, Lara."

"Why was she at my house?"

"You can ask the Old Man when you see him. Right now, you need to get changed into your party clothes, or he's going to chew my ass for being late. Let's go, pretty boy."

Harvath had a real soft spot for Ashby. She was a smartass, and he liked that. She could dish it out as well as she could take it. In fact, she probably dished it out too well, which was part of the reason the Army had agreed to let Carlton have her.

Ashby had killed so many of the enemy in Afghanistan that when a magazine back home did an unauthorized profile of her, a price was put on her head. She had taken out more bad guys than any other woman in combat, and more than even most male soldiers. The Army, though, couldn't risk the negative PR of a celebrity soldier, much less one who was killed or captured, so they pulled her from active duty.

To add insult to injury, they refused her request to be sent to Iraq. Instead, she was detailed to Fort Bragg where she helped train the top-secret, all female Delta Force detachment known as The Athena Project.

She couldn't believe her government had sidelined her for being good at what she had been trained to do—killing bad guys. While she may have been a good instructor, she was too talented and too young to be moth-balled. When Carlton offered to arrange for her to be released to his organization, she had jumped at the chance.

Everyone knew that Harvath was the Old Man's golden boy, but like any smart manager, he was always looking to add depth to his bench. At about the same time he hired Ashby, he had hired Chase Palmer. When Harvath stepped out of the Signature Flight Support building in his tailored Argentine blue suit, Palmer and Ashby were leaning against Palmer's car waiting for him.

"Did you go to Congo or a Day Spa?" Palmer asked when he saw him.

Being a smartass seemed to be part of the Old Man's corporate culture.

"It wasn't Congo," Harvath replied. "Your mom and I went to Turks and Caicos."

Palmer flipped him his middle finger as Harvath chucked his bag in the trunk and told his two colleagues to get in the car.

Their conversation grew more serious as they neared the office.

Ashby and Palmer were both privy to his operation, and he gave them a full recap of what had happened. It was good practice for what he would have to recount to the Old Man.

At the office building, they cleared security and pulled into the underground garage. Harvath retrieved his bag from the trunk and Ashby used her keycard to summon the elevator to take them upstairs.

Even though the Carlton Group was a private organization, they handled classified information, and so all of their systems were built to the strictest NSA specifications.

Every step had been taken to safeguard against "compromising emanations" or CE as they were known. CE was any electrical, mechanical, or acoustical signal from equipment that was transmitting, receiving, processing, analyzing, encrypting, or decrypting classified information. From preventing magnetic field radiation and line conduction, to actively vibrating the windows so that conversations and keyboard strokes couldn't be intercepted, nothing had been overlooked.

All of these measures, though, were largely invisible. To the untrained eye, the Carlton Group's offices resembled a successful, high-tech law firm.

Though Carlton believed in hiring the top people and staying out of their way so they could do their jobs, he ran a tight ship.

There were no casual dress Fridays. The Group's employees were the best. They were expected to dress and act like it. There were also strict rules about physical conditioning, grooming, and hygiene. The Old Man was old school.

As a smoker himself, Carlton allowed people to smoke, but they couldn't go outside to do it. Smokers had a habit of getting too chummy and chatty with strangers and other tenants in a building. That was dangerous in the intelligence business. They milled around outside and lingered over cigarettes, wasting productive time. They also made themselves vulnerable to surveillance and approach.

To cater to the smokers, he'd built what became known as "the coffin," a small glass booth barely big enough for two people at the far end of the office. It had an intense air purification system that roared so loudly you could barely hear yourself think.

It wasn't supposed to be comfortable. There wasn't even a place to sit down inside. You went in, got your fix, and got out.

Strangely enough, no one ever saw the Old Man using the coffin, and it was widely suspected he had an equally efficient though much quieter system placed in his office that allowed him to smoke whenever he wanted to.

When Harvath stepped off the elevator and entered the offices, he half expected to find the Old Man waiting for him up front in the main conference room. Instead, there was a medical team. Harvath recognized the doctor. It was the same one he had been on the phone with from Congo. The man waved him into the conference room.

Despite Harvath feeling perfectly fine, Carlton had ordered a full workup. They took his temperature and vitals, as well as several blood samples.

After the team was finished, the doc handed Harvath a digital thermometer. He told him to take his temperature twice daily and to text him the results.

Harvath tucked the device in his pocket, put his jacket on, and thanked the doctor. He then walked back toward the Old Man's office.

He and Jessica Decker had been wearing full protective gear when they explored the Matumaini Clinic, but only a respirator at the pit, and nothing at all in the village, nor in their encounter with the sick FRPI rebel commander.

From what he had gleaned from Hendrik, whatever the illness was that had been cooked up in Ngoa, it moved fast. The incubation period was days, not weeks. Oddly enough, Leonce and his son had been standing right there when the rebel commander had damaged one of the vials, but nothing had happened to them. They had been perfectly fine. If, and when, he started running a fever or had any other symptoms, then he'd raise his concern level. Right now, he tried not to think about it.

Reaching the Old Man's office, Harvath stuck his head inside, but it was empty.

As he had sent Ashby with a suit to pick him up at the airport, someone important had to be in the building, or on their way. Harvath figured it was Beaman. The Old Man probably wanted to give him an update.

But as he was a civilian, there was a lot that had happened in Congo that couldn't be shared with him. They would have to figure out what their story was and just how far they would read Beaman in.

Walking down the hall, Harvath breezed past the coffin, but still no sign of Carlton. Unless he had left the building, there was only one other place he could be.

CHAPTER 29

A Sensitive Compartmented Information Facility, commonly referred to in intelligence parlance as a "SCIF," was an enclosed space, fortified against all forms of eavesdropping and electronic surveillance, and used for processing sensitive information. The sign on the outside of the door read, DIGITAL OPS.

Harvath punched his code into the pad and stood still as biometric reader scanned his face. There was a hiss of air as the locks released, the light changed from red to green, and he was able to open the door.

Inside were three of the greatest players in the world of intelligence, and two enormous white dogs that looked like wolves on steroids.

The dogs belonged to Nicholas, the Carlton Group's digital guru. He was an amazingly talented little man who suffered from primordial dwarfism and stood less than three feet tall. Argos and Draco, as the dogs were named, were Russian Ovcharkas—the breed favored by the Russian Military and the former East German border patrol. They were highly intelligent, incredibly fast, and fiercely loyal. The dogs made excellent companions and even better protectors. That last part was especially important for a man who had spent his previous career buying, selling, and hacking black market intelligence used to blackmail some of the most powerful figures in the world.

In global intelligence circles, Nicholas was known only as "The Troll." Not much was known about his upbringing. Even less was known about where he was now, and whom he was working for. The fact that the

Deputy Director of the Central Intelligence Agency was sitting in a chair next to him, petting one of his dogs, said a lot about how far Nicholas had come. It also said a lot about how far Carlton and his relationship with the CIA had come.

The Old Man had worked at the Central Intelligence Agency for three decades. One of his proudest accomplishments during that time had been establishing its Counterterrorism Center.

But over the years, he had watched as the CIA had become more bloated and bureaucratic. Middle managers more concerned with protecting their own careers rather than the country they had sworn to serve fueled a risk-averse culture that was more focused on avoiding failure than securing success.

There were great men and women at the CIA, tons of them, but desk jockeys better suited to IBM than the world of international espionage were hamstringing them. When the Agency began paying foreign intelligence agencies to run ops for them, Carlton had had enough.

Tendering his resignation, he left and created his own company. Based on the CIA's precursor—the OSS, the Carlton Group hired the best intelligence and special operations people it could find. They broke all the rules with only one goal in mind—to keep America and her citizens safe, no matter what the cost.

Thanks to the frustration with the CIA's broken culture and the Agency's inability to conduct effective espionage, government contracts rolled in, especially from the Department of Defense.

But when a new President entered the White House, things at the CIA began to change. He named two highly respected operatives to take the number one and number two slots. Along with the Oval Office, they had begun to repair that broken culture and turn things around.

It was an amazing snapshot to see Nicholas, Reed Carlton, and Lydia Ryan all sitting there in the SCIF together.

Harvath liked Ryan. The product of an Irish father and a Greek mother, she was a tall, beautiful woman in her early thirties with dark hair and intense green eyes, but that wasn't why Harvath liked her. He liked her because she was smart; off-the-charts smart and a hell of a field operative.

The fact that she was good-looking didn't hurt, but Harvath had always found intelligence incredibly attractive. It was what drew him to Lara, and was part of what had created a spark with Decker. He could never be with a stupid woman. As a rule, though, he worked hard to keep his business and personal lives separate.

Stepping into the SCIF, the dogs leapt up to greet Harvath first, and he scratched both of them behind the ears. He had not only fought to get Nicholas his job, but he had also fought to get Carlton to allow him to bring the dogs to work. It was obvious from the start that Harvath had appointed himself the little man's guardian.

When the Old Man had resisted Argos and Draco coming to the office, Nicholas had threatened to sue him for violating the Americans with Disabilities Act, claiming they were "service animals." It was patently ridiculous, and they all got a good laugh out of it. In the end, Carlton relented and made a special exemption for Nicholas. The dogs quickly became unofficial mascots of the company.

That wasn't to say that Nicholas's transition into the Group had been without incident. Before Harvath had brought him in, Nicholas had been a full-on criminal. He had dealt in the theft and black market sale of highly sensitive, often classified information. From heads of corporations to heads of state, he had developed an impressive list of both clients and enemies.

The day after he started work at the Carlton Group, the sign identifying his SCIF as Digital Ops had been replaced with one that read THE LOLLIPOP GUILD, an insulting reference to the munchkins from *The Wizard of Oz*. When Harvath had heard about it, he went ballistic.

It had taken him less than fifteen minutes to track down the man who had done it. Harvath cornered him in the men's room, and it took every ounce of restraint he had not to beat him to a pulp right there.

The man was indignant and made it clear what a mistake he thought it was to bring a criminal like Nicholas into their midst.

Harvath didn't care and told him that if he ever got near Nicholas again, he would put a bullet in his head and dump his body where his family would never find it.

Immediately after Harvath had left the men's room, the man had bolted to his superior to register a complaint. A no-bullshit Iraq war vet, the superior director told him that if he didn't shut up and get back to work, he'd save Harvath the bullet and shoot him himself.

Word quickly got around that anybody who screwed with Nicholas would have to answer to Harvath, and that Harvath had carte blanche to do whatever he wanted.

"Look who's here," Nicholas exclaimed as Harvath coaxed the dogs back so he could shut the door.

"About time," remarked Carlton in his heavy New England accent. "What do we got, Nicky?"

Theirs was another relationship that had come a long way—a really long way. The Old Man had originally been dead set against hiring Nicholas. Now they sounded like bowling buddies.

"Why don't we start with the drone footage?" Nicholas replied.

"What drone footage?" asked Harvath as he grabbed a seat.

"Clifton Farm. Virginia. Northwest of D.C."

He looked at Lydia Ryan. "Whose drone? Yours or ours?"

"Yours," she replied. "The Central Intelligence Agency is forbidden from conducting domestic surveillance operations."

Harvath smiled and then looked back at Nicholas. "What were we doing with a drone there?"

"Paying a visit to Mr. Pierre Damien."

After Harvath had learned about the Ngoa lab, he had pressed Hendrik for information about who he was working for and where his Laissez-Passer had come from. It took a lot more water, but he eventually gave up a name—Pierre Damien.

Before leaving Bunia, Harvath filed his report and asked Carlton about Damien. The Old Man ran his name and came back with his dual Canadian/U.S. citizenship, his business background, the companies he was involved with, his current posting as Under-Secretary-General of the United Nations Population Fund, and then all of his anti-America, anti-Israel, save the planet stuff. There was nothing that pointed to an involvement with bioweapons or terrorism of any sort.

When Harvath had said as much, the Old Man had replied, "They don't normally take out ads in the paper."

He was right. It normally wasn't until after, but a man like Damien would never publically take credit for any sort of outbreak or attack.

"Have you seen this footage yet?" Harvath asked Ryan as it began playing on one of the large flat-panel monitors along the wall.

The Deputy CIA Director shook her head. "We were waiting for you."

From what he could see of it, Clifton was an amazing estate. Not only was there the manor house and the rolling manicured grounds, there appeared to be a fully functioning farm with lots of animals, pastures, and support buildings. The estate even had its own road system.

"Not bad," Harvath remarked.

Nicholas toggled a small joystick and sped the footage forward. There was a man standing outside the main house near its long infinity pool. Pulling up a file photo of Pierre Damien, he ran that piece of drone footage through their facial recognition system. A blue digital overlay appeared and announced "Match." Seconds later the words "Match ID" appeared, and columns of data pertaining to Pierre Damien unspooled.

"This is definitely our guy," stated Nicholas.

Harvath leaned forward and studied his face. "How did you know where to look for him?"

"As soon as you came up with his name, we started searching. He had flown in the day before and cleared passport control and customs via private aviation at Dulles International. We had a time stamp, so all I did was pull the surrounding CCTV footage."

Nicholas brought the footage up on another monitor as he continued speaking. "That also gave us the vehicles meeting him at the airport and their license plates. Traffic and other CCTV cameras got us as far as Berryville, Virginia, outside Leesburg. Then we lost him."

"How did you pinpoint him to Clifton Farm then?"

"*Architectural Digest*," the little man said with a smile. "Damien is a publicity hound. He posed for a spread six years ago. It came up in a generic web search. There was a satellite scheduled to be overhead about that time, so we requested some pictures and voila."

Nicholas punched a few keys on his keyboard and satellite images of the same SUVs that had picked up Damien and his party at the airport were shown parked at the manor house. Close-ups of the license plates confirmed it.

"Wait. Back up a second," said Ryan. "The woman travelling with Damien. Can you isolate her from the CCTV footage and run it against Passport Control and Customs?"

The little man nodded and got to work.

Moments later he popped several images up on the screen and replied, "Helena Pestova. Thirty-seven years old. Czech national."

Ryan studied the images and smiled. "She may be a Czech national, but she's technically an Israeli intelligence asset."

"You know her?" Harvath asked.

"We crossed paths multiple times in the sandbox. Amman, Beirut. The last time was in Doha. The Mossad uses her for their honey traps."

Nicholas brought up the drone footage of her and ran all the images through his facial recognition system. The blue overlay popped up instantly declaring "Match ID." Unlike Damien, there was no publically available information about her. As far as they could tell, she didn't even have a social media account.

"So the Mossad are looking at Damien as well," said Harvath. "Same reason? Or something else?"

"There's one way to find out," Ryan replied as she opened a new window on her laptop and hopped on the secure network back to Langley. After a few seconds, she had what she was searching for and turned her screen so the others could see it.

"Who's that?"

"Ben Zion Mordechai. Bentzi for short. He's part of the Metsada—the Mossad's Special Operations Division. According to our people, he's also Helena's handler."

"Do we know where he is?" said Harvath.

"Probably in Israel. Most likely Tel Aviv. Unless he's on assignment somewhere."

"Can you send his picture to my screen?" Nicholas asked.

Ryan nodded and sent it over.

"Do you have anything else? Date of birth? Military service? Aliases and known associates?"

Ryan scanned the file, copied what she felt comfortable sharing, and sent it to Nicholas who had received Mordechai's picture and now put it up on the screen.

Harvath looked at Ryan and asked, "Who do you have in Israel who can reach out to Mordechai to find out what's going on?"

"Knowing the Mossad," she replied, "they may not want to tell us."

"If they want to be that way," Carlton interjected, "tell them we're going to bounce her. And make sure they know that we're going to be very loud about it. If they don't want their op blown, they're going to have to share. We don't care if they like it or not."

"Okay. I'll have to make some phone calls. The first thing we need to do is find out if Mordechai is in Israel."

"He isn't," stated Nicholas who had been working furiously at his keyboard.

All eyes in the room turned and focused on him.

"What do you think?" he asked, popping up an image from a European airport's CCTV camera. "Is that him?"

Before anyone could answer, the blue overlay appeared with the words "Match."

"It looks like you'll get to ask Bentzi Mordechai your questions in person," Nicholas stated as he read the information on his screen. "He's inbound from Switzerland. His flight arrives at Dulles in two hours."

CHAPTER 30

In the world of intelligence, biometric technology was a blessing and a curse. Facial recognition made it easier to identify and locate terrorists, but it also made it very difficult for spies to slip in and out of different countries while using an assumed identity.

After the 9/11 attacks, the United States cracked down particularly hard, requiring biometric scanning of visitors at its ports of entry. Only U.S. citizens were allowed to bypass these requirements, which was exactly why Bentzi Mordechai had acquired an authentic American passport under the name Vincent Geller.

The real Geller was an American Jew from Miami who had wanted to do his part for Israel and had been recruited by the Mossad. In exchange for surrendering his legitimate identity, he was set up in a new life with a monthly stipend. The U.S. Government had never been the wiser.

"Excuse me, sir," said a pair of ICE agents at Dulles as they approached Mordechai. He was standing in the U.S. citizen lane, waiting for his passport to be inspected.

Mordechai acted as if they were addressing someone else, but it was obvious that they were speaking to him. "Me?"

"Yes, sir. Please step out of the line."

Mordechai showed them his passport. "I'm in the right spot."

Both agents put their hands on their weapons. "Right now, sir," the lead agent ordered.

The people standing near Mordechai nervously backed away from him.

"No problem," Bentzi said, making sure the officers could see his hands.

Once Mordechai had stepped out of the line, they closed on him. One agent covered him while the other put him in handcuffs.

Flying often exacerbated his arthritis. Despite having taken two pills, plus downing a handful of Scotches en route, his hands were still killing him. The force with which he had been cuffed, in addition to how tightly the cuffs had been applied, sent ripples of red-hot pain shooting through his entire body.

The agents walked him out of passport control and down a small corridor to a series of interrogation rooms. Unlocking one of the doors, the agents showed him inside. It wasn't very large, just fifteen by fifteen. It was all white, with bright fluorescent overhead lighting. There was no two-way glass. Just a boring Formica table and four plastic chairs. Mordechai was instructed to sit.

As he knew any innocent person would, he had protested the entire way, getting more indignant as he went. He railed about being a taxpayer and raised his Constitutional rights.

It was quite a convincing performance, but the ICE agents had been told to ignore everything he said, not to offer him anything, and not to speak to him.

Soon after he sat down, there was a knock on the door. He looked up as an attractive woman with dark hair and green eyes entered. She was accompanied by a well-dressed man who crossed to the other side of the room and leaned casually against the wall.

The woman instructed the agents to remove Mordechai's cuffs and then asked them to wait outside. Once they were gone, she sat down at the table and set a closed file folder in front of her.

"Mr. Mordechai," she said, "do you know who I am?"

"My name's not Mordechai," he replied. "It's Geller. Vincent Geller. I'm from Miami. *I am an American citizen.* You have no right to detain me like this. Those officers have my passport."

"Mr. Mordechai," she continued, "my name is Lydia Ryan. I'm Deputy Director of the Central Intelligence Agency. Now, you and I can play games, or we can work together. What's it going to be?"

"I wish I could help you, but I can't. My name's Geller, not Mordechai."

Harvath shifted his weight and moved a little closer.

"Who's he?" Mordechai asked.

"Never mind," Ryan replied, removing a photograph and sliding it over to him. "Let's talk about Helena."

"I'm sorry. I don't know who she is. You have the wrong guy."

Harvath moved so quickly, Mordechai didn't even see him coming. He was just about to strike him when Ryan held up her hand and stopped him.

"Mr. Mordechai, I'm treating you with respect out of professional courtesy," she stated. "But there's a limit to just how far that courtesy goes. I highly recommend you don't push it. Am I making myself clear?"

Mordechai remained silent.

"We know Helena is here. We know she is with Damien. We want to know why."

Mordechai opened his mouth to speak, but Ryan held up her hand to cut him off.

"If I hear the name Vincent Geller one more time, I'll have you rendered to a black site, and we can continue our conversation there. Is *that* clear?"

The Israeli sat perfectly still and said nothing, his face unreadable.

"At some point Mr. Mordechai, you are going to tell me what I want to know. The only question is when. And how difficult you want to make this for Helena.

"If you work with me, maybe I allow your operation to continue. If not, maybe we put a bag over Helena's head and render her to a black site as well. Maybe I'll give Pierre Damien everything I have in this file and let him decide what he wants to do with her.

"Part of me thinks it would be fun to get my matches out and watch all of you burn. And unless you give me a good reason not to, that's exactly what I might do."

Ryan then leaned back in her chair and said nothing further. Out of the corner of her eye, she could see Harvath ready to strike if Mordechai made one false move.

Slowly, he reached his gnarled hand out for the file. Ryan came forward and put her hand down on top of it.

"That belongs to me," she said. "Not you. You don't get to see what we have until you start cooperating."

"She's small time. If I cooperate, will you let her go?" Mordechai asked.

"I know exactly *what* she is, Mr. Mordechai. What I want to know is why you have put her next to Damien."

The Israeli smiled and shook his head. "Do you know what a pain in the ass Pierre Damien has been for Israel?"

"I've got a pretty good idea, but that doesn't answer my question."

"My government takes his efforts to undermine our nation very seriously."

"So seriously in fact," Ryan mocked, "that shortly after he and Helena arrived here you rushed to the airport, bought a plane ticket, and hightailed it to the United States." Standing, she picked up her file and said, "I hope you enjoy our rendition program Mr. Mordechai." She then looked at Harvath. "We're done here. Let's go."

Mordechai was in an impossible situation. He didn't want to work with the Americans. As soon as they knew what he knew, it would stop being about Israel and would be all about the United States. His mission would be subordinate to theirs.

He didn't have a choice, though. If he didn't cooperate, they'd throw him in a hole somewhere. By the time he got out, *if* he ever got out, the damage could already be done. It could be over for Israel. He was going to have to roll the dice. He was going to have to trust them.

Looking up at Ryan, he said, "What do you know about a United Nations body called the Secretary-General's Senior Management Group?"

CHAPTER 31

The Chesapeake and Ohio Canal National Historical Park stretched a hundred eighty-five miles from Georgetown to Cumberland, Maryland. Many of its thirteen hundred historical structures were open to the public. Six "lockhouses," or "canal quarters" as they were known, could be rented for overnight stays in order to experience what life was like along the once thriving canal that ran parallel to the Potomac.

Lockhouses 6, 10, 22, 25, 28, and 49 all came complete with kitchens, bedrooms, bathrooms, and showers. The "blue" lockhouse, so named for the color of its shutters and front door, was also historic, and equipped for overnight stays, but had never been opened to the public—and with good reason.

A short drive from D.C., the blue lockhouse was the property of the Central Intelligence Agency and had hosted debriefings of some of the most valuable Soviet defectors during the Cold War. The term "behind the blue door" became synonymous with interrogations at the highest level. Most agents who had used the phrase had no idea where the blue door was, much less that it was attached to a tiny C&O canal house. Many assumed the door simply existed somewhere deep within the bowels of the Central Intelligence Agency where only the Director and a handful of privileged others were ever allowed to go.

As they drove up to the canal house, Harvath couldn't help but notice the reds and golds of so many leaves that were already starting to turn color. Things had been so crazy that he hadn't had a chance to ask Carlton what Lara was doing down here from Boston and how she had connected with him to get the keys to his house. He hadn't even texted or called to let her know he was back, though he suspected she probably already knew. If the Old Man had given her the keys, he had probably also provided her with his itinerary. He wasn't looking forward to the showdown that was coming.

Inside the canal house, Harvath started a fire in the fireplace. Mordechai pulled up a chair to warm his hands. He kept kosher, and so Palmer was sent to a special deli near Dupont Circle. He came back with shopping bags full of food and bottled water.

He grabbed a sandwich for himself and one for Ashby, and then the pair sat outside, discreetly keeping watch. As far as they knew, no one was aware that Mordechai had fallen into their custody, but Dulles was a crowded airport, and there was no telling who saw what. It would be very foolish to underestimate the Israelis.

Two of Ryan's people had taken Mordechai's bag to his hotel, had checked him in, and placed it in the room. If anyone came looking for him, there would at least be some appearance that he had made it that far without incident.

Once they had eaten, Carlton conducted the Israeli intelligence operative's debriefing while Harvath and Ryan took notes. It was like watching a fencing match with clever *patinandos* and *passata-sottos* to spare.

Carlton scored points by asking the right questions. When he drifted too far afield or attempted to drill too deep into Mossad operations, the Israeli refused to answer. His duty was to the Mossad and to Israel. He had no intention of divulging any more than he had to. It was how any of those in the room would have acted if caught in a similar situation.

Mordechai described how Damien had landed on their radar, and he pulled no punches in expressing the Mossad's anger at American Intelligence for refusing to work with them on it.

Ryan listened with interest. She had no idea who had made that call, or why, but she intended to find out.

Carlton asked what Helena was doing with Damien.

Mordechai explained that they had copied his hard drive and one of his cell phones, but that no one at the Mossad had been able to crack the encryption.

"Can you describe the cell phone?"

When Mordechai was finished, Harvath pulled out his own phone and showed him pictures he had taken off Hendrik's phones, which had been turned over to the CIA for analysis.

"That one," the Israeli said, pointing. "Where'd you get it?"

"I took it from someone we believe has been working with Damien."

"Did he give you his password?"

"Not willingly."

"Did you find anything on it?" Mordechai asked.

"Nothing so far. Nothing was archived," said Ryan. "Whatever communications there had been were wiped clean."

"You're still a password ahead of us," he replied as he launched into explaining why Helena had been dangled and how Damien had taken the bait. Without his passwords, the mirrored phone and hard drive were useless. Everything was riding on Helena.

"I don't understand," Harvath said once he had finished. "Why has it taken her so long?"

Mordechai took a deep breath and briefly recounted who Helena was, as well as the incentive they had given her to speed her progress.

When he finished, the Old Man let out a long, low whistle.

Ryan looked at him and asked, "Whoever this *Enoch* is, do you even have him?"

"We do," Mordechai replied. "He doesn't work for us per se, but we know where he is and have used him from time to time."

He could sense the distaste in the room and added, "His is a horrible business, but he has value. Significant intelligence has been gleaned via his network."

Harvath shook his head. "I'm sure that's a comfort to all of the women he's forced into the sex trade."

Mordechai knew it was pointless to respond. Israel was at war. It did what it had to do to survive. He would never apologize for that.

"The Mossad has known about Enoch all along, but nothing has ever been said to Helena, correct?" asked Ryan.

The Israeli nodded solemnly. "Correct."

"And despite his alleged intelligence value, once Helena gives you what you want, the Mossad is just going to hand him over?"

The Israeli thought of his boss, Nava, and shook his head. "I think once they catch their fish, they will also want to keep their bait."

"In other words, they're not going to give Enoch to Helena."

Mordechai nodded.

Ryan figured as much. Theirs was a world of games, a world of half-truths and empty promises. It required lies, but some lies were beneath a nation—even when it believed its own survival hung in the balance. There was always another way. And one of the biggest problems with those lies was that they often created enemies, mortal enemies.

"She's going to blame you," said Harvath. "You're the one who made the promise."

"I'll make it up to her."

Harvath smiled. "That's what we all tell ourselves."

Mordechai fixed him with his gaze. "Except I actually mean it."

Harvath studied the man's eyes. There was something between him and the woman that went beyond asset and handler. It was written all over the Israeli's face.

Harvath resisted chalking it up to sex. Helena Pestova was indeed striking, and her beauty wouldn't have been lost on Mordechai, but he appeared to be above that. He struck Harvath as some sort of holy warrior, unwaveringly committed to the purity of his cause and the code that guided him.

Harvath could have been wrong. It could have been that the Israeli just wanted to bang her brains out, but he didn't think so. He sensed something better in him. It was rare to meet true believers anymore—and the Israeli struck him as a true believer—someone able to put a greater good, a higher purpose ahead of himself.

Maybe it gave Harvath hope, some small reassurance that there were others out there, that he wasn't alone in the world. Whatever it was, for the time being he was putting Mordechai in the true believer category.

Now that they knew why Helena was with Damien, Carlton wanted to know what Israel suspected he was up to and what they hoped to find on his laptop and cell phone.

In order to do that, Mordechai needed to describe how the laptop and cell came into the Mossad's possession in the first place.

Very few people had more than a basic understanding of how the UN worked, so Mordechai unpacked its power structure, likening it to a series of Russian nesting dolls. When he arrived at the Secretary-General's Senior Management Group and its secret retreat in the Austrian Alps, the only other sound in the room was the crackling of the fire.

Mordechai discussed the anonymous, seven-member "Plenary Panel," and then, saving the most disturbing information for last, launched into the chilling, ten-point "Outcome Conference" document he had uncovered in Pierre Damien's hotel room in Alpbach.

He didn't need notes. The entire, fetid manifesto was seared into his mind. He could recite each and every insane goal in his sleep: decrease human population below five hundred million, steer reproduction through eugenics, bind humanity with a brand-new language, redistribute wealth under the more acceptable term "global public goods," replace individual rights with the concept of "social duties," subvert faith and tradition with "reason," use technologies like the Internet and social media to end-run national governments in order to spread propaganda directly to citizens, convince people that global governance was not only inevitable, but that it was the fair, efficient, and logical next step, discredit and delegitimize the concept of national sovereignty, and finally—take out anyone or anything that got in the UN's way.

Mordechai explained that the biggest threats the Plenary Panel saw to achieving its goals were Israel and the United States. In order to remove the two democracies from the UN's path, some massive, mysterious event was mentioned.

He referenced Damien's handwritten notes, particularly those about the United States, and asked if the letters *MC* meant anything to anyone in the room.

Several possibilities ran through Harvath's mind. MC was the international country code for *Monaco*. It was the last two letters of *USMC*—United States Marine Corps. It was the abbreviation for *Mission Critical* and also the abbreviation for NATO's *Military Committee*, which helped guide NATO's defense measures.

But without more context, the letters could have represented anything. Carlton and Ryan were equally at a loss.

"Nothing? How about the letters *AHF* then?" Mordechai asked. "Damien wrote those followed by several other words, including *pathogenicity, absolute risk*, and *dose response*."

One by one, the color drained from the other three faces in the room.

CHAPTER 32

He looked to the Old Man, who nodded his assent, followed by Ryan. Turning to Mordechai, Harvath replied, "African Hemorrhagic Fever. A-H-F."

"Ebola?" the Israeli asked.

"Same family, worse disease. Much worse. It has a dramatically reduced incubation period—we're talking days, not weeks—and it has allegedly been modified so that it transmits easily from human to human through the air."

"That's not modification, it's *weaponization*. When did you discover this?"

"Only in the last several days. I just got back from Africa this morning."

"Does your President know?"

"We're not at liberty to discuss what the President knows or doesn't know," Carlton interjected.

Mordechai raised his hands in mock surrender. "All I'm trying to say is that if this is the event Damien and his Plenary Panel have planned, it's going to be aimed at Israel too. We need to get our governments working together."

"Agreed, but there's another problem," said Harvath. "Last night, Damien held a gathering at his estate."

"I know," Mordechai responded. "Helena sent me a report. It was something associated with his philanthropy. Some sort of charity board meeting."

Harvath looked back over at Ryan and the Old Man. When they nodded, he pulled up several images on his laptop and turned it so the Israeli could see.

"These are the vehicles that were parked in the driveway last night," he said. "And these are their owners."

"You had a drone overhead?"

Harvath nodded.

"Ironic," replied Mordechai.

"Why?"

"Because when Israel asks for your help, Mr. Damien's civil liberties are sacrosanct, but as soon as *you* suspect something is up, drones get launched. But I suppose to truly be ironic, your drone would have to have been christened *Liberty*, or something like that. Was it?"

Harvath bristled at the remark, as did Ryan. But before either of them could respond, Carlton jumped in. "Don't be an asshole, Mordechai. Israel has withheld information, slow-walked investigations, and refused to cooperate with us on numerous occasions, and you know it. Let's not pretend you guys are coming to this with your virginity intact."

It took a moment, but the man conceded the point. "Fair enough," he said.

"Good," Carlton replied. "Now, with the I-told-you-so's out of the way, do you recognize any of the people who were at Damien's last night?"

Mordechai pulled his chair closer and scrutinized the images. "No. Should I?"

"Not unless you like watching paint dry."

"Excuse me?"

"It's an American expression."

"I know what it means," Mordechai stated. "How does it apply here?"

Harvath pointed to each one on his screen. "They all work for the government. Department of Health and Human Services, Department of Transportation, Department of the Treasury, Federal Communications Commission, Office of Personnel Management, United States Agency for International Development, Department of Justice, Department of State, and last but not least, the Department of Homeland Security.

"Each one of them is mid- to upper-level management in their agencies. Even with a million-dollar prize, you'd be hard-pressed to find more than a handful of people in the entire country who could name any of them."

"In all fairness," Mordechai replied, "even with a million dollars, you'd be hard-pressed to find many Americans who can even name your Vice President."

He was right. Next to the self-preservation instinct of Washington's political establishment, that was one of Harvath's biggest hot-button issues.

American citizenship was an honor *and* a responsibility. Americans were stewards of their republic. The politicians weren't in charge, the citizens were. Yet there were Americans who not only didn't know a thing about how the government functioned, but there were staggering numbers who didn't even bother to vote.

Harvath had long since made peace with the fact that many of the people he risked everything to protect were self-absorbed and disengaged. There was no other way to put it. He wasn't a believer in political correctness. If you didn't know who the Vice President of the United States was, you weren't a "low-information voter," you were a *moron*. Worse than that, you were lazy.

He didn't expect the average citizen to know the head of every agency, but the second most important government official in the United States? That was by no means too much to ask.

While facts, in Harvath's opinion, rather than emotion, bore out which political ideas were healthiest for the country, he didn't begrudge anyone the right to vote for the candidate they believed was best for office. His only desire was for people to do their homework, develop an understanding of the issues, and marry that up to who and what they were voting for. In his heart, he knew every American was capable of leaping over that low bar. The fact that so many were unwilling, though, troubled him.

"So what's the connection? Why were they all there?" Mordechai asked, bringing Harvath's mind back to the matter at hand.

It was a question he had asked himself repeatedly since Nicholas had fast-forwarded through the drone footage before he and Ryan had raced off to Dulles to interdict Mordechai.

"We have run them through every database, and we can't find anything," said Harvath. "They all work for the U.S. Government, but we can't establish any ties between them, much less to Damien."

"He's one of the wealthiest men on the planet," Ryan added. "Everyone wants access to him. People want access to his money, to his power. Yet, one of the first things he does upon returning to the United States is invite this group of faceless bureaucrats to his estate. It doesn't make any sense."

"Maybe that's why he returned to the U.S.," said Mordechai.

"To meet with *them*?"

The Israeli nodded.

"Why?"

"Well, if you can't find something they all have in common, some philanthropic activity he was helping them with, then we have to assume that he needs something from them."

Harvath was skeptical. "Like what?"

Mordechai shrugged. "I don't know. If we throw African Hemorrhagic Fever into the mix, does it make the relationships more clear?"

"Department of Health and Human Services and Homeland Security? Sure. But an illness like that could conceivably impact *every* government agency. I can't say any one of them is necessarily special."

"But those two you just mentioned would be very involved with an outbreak of any sort, true?"

"So would the Centers for Disease Control and Prevention and the Federal Emergency Management Agency."

"Both of which," Ryan clarified, "are actually under Health and Human Services and DHS."

Mordechai looked at Harvath and raised an eyebrow.

"That still doesn't tell us why they were there," Harvath asserted. "They're not agency heads. They're management. They have limited power."

"I don't know about that," the Old Man intoned. "Hell hath no fury like a bureaucrat scorned."

"We're not talking about rejecting tax-exempt applications or overpaying for lavish conferences in Vegas," Harvath insisted. "We're talking about the subversion of the United States."

"You don't think they're connected?"

"*You* do?"

"I believe power corrupts and absolute power corrupts *absolutely*," Carlton replied. "At this point in history, there's no greater power than that of the American bureaucrat."

"That doesn't mean they're actively trying to subvert the country," said Harvath, stunned he had been forced to take their side.

"They don't have to be," the Old Man explained. "Do you think cancer knows it is killing its host? This is exactly why I left the CIA. The bureaucracy was eating it from the inside out, weakening it. It got to the point where we couldn't effectively do our jobs. Even so, I could give you a list of Agency bureaucrats a mile long who would each flat out deny their efforts had been harmful to the CIA or the country. And each one of them could pass a polygraph test while saying it. But the Agency was different."

"How?"

"Because as messed up as it was, our stakes were higher. The CIA's mission involved keeping people and secrets safe. When it screwed up, that screw-up made the front page of every newspaper and every major news broadcast. You couldn't run away from it. It couldn't be swept under the rug, not like the rest of the government. And I'm talking thirty years ago. It's only gotten worse since then.

"My point is that bureaucrats—like everyone else—have a mind-set. The longer they work for government, the more they believe government is the answer, and the less they trust the everyday citizen. In fact, they begin to believe that certain groups of citizens are the root of the nation's problems. They see them as a threat. If those citizens can be brought to heel, the bureaucracy sees itself as doing the citizenry at large a greater good, actually making their lives better."

"But bureaucrats *are* the government," Harvath insisted. "And the government has to remain impartial. It doesn't get to pick sides."

He regretted the words as soon as they were out of his mouth. Both Mordechai and Carlton chuckled. Ryan was the only one who didn't find it amusing.

"The tendency of bureaucrats to favor more bureaucracy notwithstanding," she said, "we're still a nation of laws, and they take an oath. They don't get to unilaterally decide what's best for the country and the rest of us."

"True," Carlton agreed, as the smile passed from his face. "What I'm trying to explain is that if your oar-pullers start pulling more in one direction, and nobody—i.e., the American citizens—is up on deck watching, your ship is going to be headed in another direction before you know it.

"Introduce someone belowdecks with charisma and personality and anything is possible. You could introduce the devil himself, and if the oar-pullers felt he was sympathetic to their wants and desires, and had their best interests at heart, there's no end to what he could achieve."

Harvath didn't want to believe it was possible, but to do that would be to ignore the story of history and every palace intrigue, coup, and revolution within it.

"Let's say you're right," Harvath offered. "Let's say there is some sort of connection between the people at Damien's house last night and the goals of this Plenary Panel. Do you think he would actually tell a bunch of middle management Federal workers what his grand plan was?"

"I suppose we would have to ask them."

"Are you serious?"

"Absolutely."

"Who would you start with?"

"Her," Carlton said, pointing to the image of Linda Landon from DHS. "The one who stayed after all the others had gone home."

"And as soon as she knows we're on to her, the first call she'll make is to Damien," said Harvath. "He'll flee or assert diplomatic immunity. Then he'll deny he knows Hendrik and claim the documents Mordechai found in his room were planted by the Mossad in order to impugn his integrity because he's pro-Palestine. That'll be it. Game over."

"What if we snatch and render him?" Ryan asked.

It wasn't a bad question. In fact, Carlton himself had already raised the issue with the President. But contrary to Mordechai's earlier quip, there were bright, Constitutional lines the President wouldn't agree to cross, not without a lot more actionable intelligence. For better or worse, Pierre Damien was an American citizen on American soil. They would have to find another way.

Harvath shook his head. "Nobody in our government is going to touch this. Not at this stage. We have to have enough to stop him cold."

"What do you propose then?"

"Everyone who was at Damien's house last night needs to be under around-the-clock surveillance. That includes phones, email accounts, all of it."

Ryan looked at him. "You're going to go to the Department of Justice and ask them to prepare the warrants?"

Harvath knew they couldn't do that, especially not when one of their members was on the list. Plus, the Attorney General would want to know how he got the information out of Hendrik and where the South African was now. And when you threw the Israelis in the mix and the fact that they were running an unsanctioned operation on U.S. soil, you were asking for everything to implode on the spot.

He knew, though, that the bad guys counted on America playing by the rules. It allowed them to keep the advantage and stay several steps ahead. Harvath was a big proponent of leveling the playing field by tossing out the rulebook. If the bad guys wouldn't fight fair, why should the United States?

He had heard countless arguments made about being no better than our enemies if we abandoned our laws and principles. There was merit to that argument. There was also merit to the argument made by Ben Franklin that those who would trade a little liberty for a little added security deserved neither and would lose both. That was why there needed to be a very dark, covert, third way.

Harvath understood that it was a slippery slope. If the United States was willing to color outside the lines when it came to foreign enemies, how long until it justified those tactics on its own citizens? In a sense, it had already happened.

U.S. citizens who had gone overseas to fight with Islamic terrorists had been killed in drone strikes without the benefit of trial. Harvath had no problem with that. If you were seen anywhere near those savages, on the battlefield or off, you deserved what was coming to you. Actively targeting Americans at home, on American soil, though, was where the slope got slipperier.

Over beers and lobster rolls on his dock, he could argue the finer points of national security policy all day long. As far as he was concerned, the government should be forbidden from looking in people's windows, recording their phone calls, and reading their emails without compelling probable cause. Government fishing expeditions, in his opinion, should result in the government getting its ass kicked in the parking lot before it can ever make it to the boat ramp.

Mass surveillance opened the door to incredible abuse. It also corroded the soul of a nation. People under constant surveillance ceased to be individuals with their own thoughts and ideas. They began to comport themselves in a manner which they believed was in accordance with what the "authorities" wanted. In a word, it was total bullshit.

The best kind of nation was one where the government feared the people. When the government feared the people there was liberty. When the people feared the government, there was tyranny. Harvath had vowed that he would obey his oath to protect and defend the Constitution and always side with the people.

What he was suggesting now, though, begged an important question: was he siding with the Constitution if he was taking it upon himself to circumvent the law? Was it "siding with the people" to decide that some people needed to be put under secret surveillance just because they had been seen at the home of someone who was under suspicion? If the shoe was on the other foot, how would Harvath feel about being surveilled himself?

They were all legitimate questions, none of which he had time for. Was he going to bend some laws? *Absolutely*. Was he likely to break a few? *Probably*. Was he going to feel guilty about any of it? *No*.

Harvath's attitude was: *If you break into my house in the middle of the night with a butcher knife, I'm not going to leave my shotgun under the bed out of "fairness." If you come at me, if you threaten my family, my home, or my country, I'm coming right back at you with everything I have. Don't want the horns? Stay the hell away from the bull.*

Looking at Lydia Ryan, he smiled and said, "We're going to hold off on the Department of Justice for the time being. It's just going to be us."

CHAPTER 33

Helena had never eaten farm-fresh eggs before. Even Jeffery, who never smiled, took pleasure in watching her eat.

"This is the way people were meant to eat," Damien said approvingly. "Fresh, local food."

She was embarrassed with how fast she had finished her omelet. The flavors from the eggs, the fresh spinach, the farm goat cheese—they were amazing.

Damien laughed. "Would you like another?"

"I shouldn't," Helena replied.

"Nonsense," he said. "Jeffery, make another please, and we'll split it."

The man nodded and disappeared back into the kitchen.

"I'm going to have to add an extra half hour on the treadmill this morning."

Damien reached out and pulled her chair closer. "You are absolutely perfect. Do you know that?"

Helena smiled and ran her fingers through his hair. "If I'm perfect, it's only because I'm honest about how long I need to be on the treadmill."

"I'm not talking about your body. I'm talking about *you*."

She had no idea what had gotten into him.

"You're in a good mood this morning."

"Aren't I always?" he asked.

She smiled. "Most days, yes, but you seem especially happy today."

He took a moment to compose his thoughts. "I look at you. I look at this farm. We have everything we could possibly need right here. The world could come to an end tomorrow and we'd be absolutely fine. In fact, we would be wonderful."

"Do you know something I don't?" she teased. "Is there a comet headed our way or something?"

Damien held her chin in his hand and kissed her. It was a long, slow, soft kiss. "What do you want to do today?"

"What are my choices?" she whispered, moving closer to him.

He smiled. "I meant here on the farm. I have to go out for a while. You have the horses, the ATVs, whatever you want. Just speak to Jeffery, and he'll take care of it."

Helena kissed him back. "I may want to ride later, I don't know. I have to finish my trafficking presentation for the UN."

"I wouldn't worry too much about that."

"Because the comet's coming."

It took Damien a moment to grasp her joke before he laughed.

"Pierre," she said. "Do you not take my work seriously?"

"Of course I do. It's just that it's going to be a beautiful day. Promise me you won't waste all of it inside."

"I promise," she replied. "As long as you promise that when you get back, we can swim naked."

He gave her another long kiss before breaking it off and standing up. "Should we go into town for lunch this afternoon, or would you prefer to stay here?"

She pretended to think about it and then said, "Can we bring our own wine?"

"Of course we can. Whatever you want."

"Wonderful. Let's go into town then."

"Okay. You choose the spot," he said. "Jeffery will make our reservations."

She smiled as she watched him walk out of the dining room. He picked up his coat in the front hall and exited the house.

There was the sound of his security team opening and closing car doors, engines starting, and then vehicles rolling away down the driveway. *One down*, she thought. Now all she had to do was wait for Jeffery to leave.

Damien had given him a list of errands he wanted him to run that morning. As soon as he was gone, she could get to work.

Changing into her running clothes, she walked to the outbuilding that held the gym. With its floor-to-ceiling windows, she had a perfect view of the driveway. After ten minutes of stretching, she popped her earbuds in and began running on the treadmill. Twenty minutes later, she saw Jeffery pull away in the farm's vintage Jeep Wagoneer with its wood-paneled sides. Hitting the *stop* button, she grabbed a towel and headed back up to the house.

After checking each room to make sure no one else was there, she made her way to the library. Damien had only taken his coat with him, which meant his laptop had to have been left behind. Setting her phone on the desk, she opened its lower right drawer. The safe, with its digital keypad, was identical to the one in Geneva.

Punching in the code, she waited for the light to turn green and then opened it. Inside was Damien's laptop. She quickly pulled it out and powered it up.

Thankfully, the keystroke reader differentiated between last night's entries on that bitch Linda's computer versus Damien's. Looking at her phone, into which she had inserted the reader's memory card, Helena made ready to enter the first string of letters, symbols, and numbers.

When the password screen came up, she plugged everything in and held her breath.

It felt like an eternity, but seconds later the main screen appeared, and she had access to Damien's machine.

As in his personal life, Damien's files were perfectly organized. Each one was labeled with a logical heading and subdivided into appropriate folders and documents.

Helena had six key words she was looking for. None of them were in any of the corresponding folder or document titles she was looking at.

Opening up the search function, she searched for the first word on her list. *Nothing*.

She then tried the second. *Nothing*.

Not allowing herself to become discouraged, she tried the third and fourth. The results were both the same. *Nothing*.

The fifth word also produced no results. Now, she was becoming nervous. Entering the sixth word on her list, she allowed her finger to hover over the *return* button for several seconds. If this didn't work, she didn't know what she was going to do. Finally, she pressed the button and waited for her search results.

Jackpot!

Smoothing her ponytailed hair, she began opening the documents. It was all there—all of it and more.

Picking up her phone, she switched it to camera mode and slowly scrolled through the documents, clicking picture after picture.

She had made it about halfway through when she heard a noise from outside the library. It sounded like it had come from the entry hall. Was it one of the farm staff? Had Damien come back already?

She rushed through the documents, taking picture after picture. There was the sound of heavy footsteps in the hallway. Whoever it was, it sounded like they were making their way right toward her. Helena took a deep breath and tried not to panic. She needed to photograph the rest of it.

She fired the camera repeatedly, capturing page after page.

The footsteps now sounded like they were right outside the door, but it was a long hallway and the echoes could be playing tricks on her ears. There was perspiration above her eyebrows, but she didn't dare waste a second wiping it away. She had to finish. It needed to be done.

Her heart was pounding in her chest. Her instincts were screaming for her to get the hell out of there.

Suddenly, there was a hand on the knob. Slowly, it began to turn. When it opened, Jeffery found Helena standing at Mr. Damien's desk, the local paper spread out across it.

"Jeffery," she said as he walked in. "Mr. Damien and I are going out to lunch this afternoon. I'm supposed to pick, but I can't decide. Which do you think? Violino or La Niçoise?"

Pointing at the paper, she added. "Violino has a ten percent off coupon, but La Niçoise has reduced corkage."

Jeffery seemed momentarily at a loss for words. Finally, he said, "I'm sure the finances won't be a problem. As to Mr. Damien's preferences, he enjoys them both, equally."

Even when caught off guard, he could be a smug son of a bitch. Helena smiled at him. "You're not much help. You know that right?"

"May I ask what you're doing in the library, miss?"

"Reading," she said, rattling the newspaper. "How about you?"

The direct approach seemed to confuse him. The man didn't have much of a sense of humor. She had only seen him smile once, and that was this morning.

"I'm looking for the list Mr. Damien gave me. I left without it," he said.

"Try the sideboard in the dining room. I saw you make a note on it there."

"Thank you," Jeffery replied as he backed out of the room and closed the door.

As soon as he was gone, Helena pulled Damien's laptop from under the newspaper, powered it down, and returned it to the safe.

CHAPTER 34

The second time his phone went off, Harvath gave up trying to sleep and got out of bed.

Walking downstairs to the kitchen, he put on some coffee, booted up his laptop, and turned on the TV. So far, there was nothing on the news.

Nicholas was tapped into the Centers for Disease Control and Prevention in Atlanta. He had hacked into the system and had been monitoring their Epi-X, or Epidemic Information Exchange. It was a password-protected area where local, county, state, and national public health officials could rapidly access and share disease outbreak surveillance information.

In the last twelve hours, two people—one in Chicago and one in Houston—had presented to their local emergency rooms with high fevers and flu-like symptoms. Each had rapidly deteriorated and bled out. They had bled from everywhere including their eyes, ears, nose, mouth, and gums. Any path the blood and liquefying organs could take to escape the body, it did. The ooze was so dark it was almost black. The ICU floors were covered with it and looked like something out of a horror movie.

Though the rapid test kits were not confirming it as Ebola, officials on Epi-X were already referring to it as "some form" of Hemorrhagic Fever. Samples had been dispatched to the CDC for analysis.

While Harvath wasn't a doctor, he already knew what they were looking at. Weaponized African Hemorrhagic Fever had been set loose.

Once Nicholas had the names of the two patients, he began working up backgrounds on them. The sample was too small to prove a pattern, but Harvath was worried. Both were male and both had Muslim names. His gut told him this was going to get much worse.

Looking at his watch, he debated calling Carlton, but decided against it. He already knew the questions he was going to ask. Until he and Nicholas had more information, it didn't make sense to wake him up.

Harvath also made a mental note to remember to thank him. It was Carlton who had invited Lara down from Boston so that she could be there when he got back from Congo. The Old Man knew Lara was special to him, and that she was someone he cared about.

While the blame wasn't his to take for spoiling their vacation, he took it anyway. Harvath wasn't quite sure what he had said to her, but it had gone a long way toward easing her disappointment over their trip.

Had she been upset? *Absolutely*. It was why she hadn't replied to his text. But by the time Harvath had arrived home, all she wanted to do was put her arms around him.

When he tried to speak, she wouldn't let him. They kissed and tumbled into bed.

Afterward, he drifted off to sleep exhausted. When he awoke, he opened his eyes and looked at her, hoping she was awake, but she wasn't.

That was okay. It would keep.

Now, as he poured his coffee, he heard the sound of bare feet crossing the worn, wooden planks of his kitchen floor. He smiled.

Lara wrapped her arms around him and kissed his back. "Jet lag?" she asked.

"There's a lot going on," he replied, hugging her back. Turning, he kissed her. "It's going to be a rough day."

"Anything I can do?"

He shook his head. "You already did it. You're here."

It felt so damn good holding her there in his kitchen. It was something he could get used to, something he could learn to look forward to.

Lowering his forehead until it touched hers, he interlaced his fingers in the small of her back and closed his eyes. In all the craziness, it was an exquisite moment of peace. *Maybe this was what it was all about.* Maybe life was about nothing more than moments.

"Not a bad way to start the day," she murmured.

"I know how we can make it even better," he replied, lowering his hands.

Pressing herself even tighter against him, she kissed her way over to his ear and whispered, "Tell me."

God, she was beautiful. *And so sexy.* He loved everything about her. She was tall, with amazing gold-flecked, green eyes and long brown hair that had kept its summer highlights. She was even still tan, something she attributed to the Brazilian DNA she received from her parents.

She so resembled one of the women from Victoria's Secret that his buddies jokingly referred to her as the "underwear model." It was a guy thing and actually an incredible compliment. They were jealous as hell of him. Not just because of how gorgeous Lara was, but also because of how happy the two of them were together—even if it was divided between Boston and D.C.

For Harvath, though, the way he felt about her went beyond her looks and how attracted he was to her. He loved how smart she was. She was off-the-charts brilliant. She also treated him better than anyone he had ever known.

Standing there in his kitchen, holding her, he realized that he loved her and wanted to tell her.

Gently, he pushed her back a step and looked into her eyes.

"What is it?" she asked.

He opened his lips to tell her, and his cell phone went off. He knew who it was by the ringtone.

The Old Man had been relegated to the classic ringing of an old school telephone, while Nicholas had chosen his own ringtone on Harvath's phone—"Atomic Dog" by George Clinton.

Their mutual love of funk music had been one of the first things they had learned about each other as their friendship evolved.

Glancing at his phone on the counter, he saw the wild picture of George Clinton that Nicholas used as his avatar. He hated breaking away from Lara, but he had to.

"It's okay," she said, reading his thoughts. "Answer it. I'll start breakfast."

He gave her a quick kiss as he reached over and picked up the phone.

"What's up?" he asked as he connected the call and lifted the phone to his ear.

"A third case has just been reported," Nicholas replied.

"Where?"

"Detroit."

"Same symptoms?" he asked.

"Unfortunately."

"Do we know anything about the patient?"

Nicholas clicked a couple of keys on his end and read the information. "Male. Thirty-seven years old."

"Name?"

"I was afraid you were going to ask that. Abdulraham Mafid Marzook."

That made three. "I'm guessing we can rule out Dutch Reformed again," said Harvath.

Nicholas let out a short laugh. Graveyard humor had always been part of their relationship. Without it, both men would have gone crazy a long time ago.

"Barring pictures of them riding bikes with wooden shoes, I'm going to say that's a safe bet. Even safer when you see what else I found. Are you near your computer?"

Lara poured a cup of coffee and handed it to him. Harvath mouthed "thank you" and walked over to the table where he sat down in front of his laptop.

"Okay, I'm at my computer. What did you find?"

"Check these out," Nicholas replied as he pressed *send* on the encrypted email. "Open them in order."

When the email arrived seconds later, Harvath did as instructed. The first attachment showed the passport applications and photos of the three deceased patients: Shukri Abu Odeh, Mousa Abulqader Elashi, and Abdulraham Mafid Marzook. The following attachments contained passenger flight manifests, U.S. Customs and Border Protection entry information, and three U.S. Customs Declaration Forms.

"What am I looking for?"

"I can't find anything connecting the three of them. No phone calls, no emails, no social media overlap, nothing. But in the last two weeks, all three of them travelled to the same place," Nicholas replied.

"Together or separately?"

"Separately."

Harvath scanned the Declaration forms and finally found it. "Saudi Arabia."

"Correct. And based on the flight manifests, they went in and out of King Abdulaziz International Airport in Jeddah."

Harvath went back through and looked at everything again.

As he did, Nicholas asked. "What do you think? Typhoid Moham-meds? Could the Saudis actually be part of this whole thing?"

The Saudis funded a lot of terrorism. Fifteen of the 9/11 hijackers had been from the Kingdom. They didn't have clean hands by any means, but the fact that Odeh, Elashi, and Marzook had done nothing to hide their travel bothered him. The Saudi Intelligence services wouldn't have left such an obvious trail. It had to be something else. Then it hit him.

"Jeddah wasn't their final destination," he said.

"Where do you think they went?"

Harvath pulled up a web site he used to help calculate dates in the Muslim calendar and said, "They, along with more than two million other people, went to Mecca for the Hajj."

CHAPTER 35

I t's referred to as the fifth pillar of Islam. Every Muslim who is physically and financially able is obligated to make at least one pilgrimage
to Mecca in their lifetime," said Harvath.

On his end, Nicholas was scrolling through the pictures of it he had
pulled up. "I don't think I have ever seen crowds this big."

"It's the largest gathering of people in the world. Last year, there were
two-point-one million people there."

"It's the ultimate petri dish."

Harvath agreed. "Especially when you have millions of hands trying
to touch or kiss the Ka'aba and drink from the sacred well of Zamzam."

"Is the Ka'aba that outdoor, box-shaped structure I see people walking
in circles around?

"That's it. When Muslims pray toward Mecca, technically it's toward
the Ka'aba, which is located in the center of Islam's most sacred mosque,
the Al-Masjid al-Haram. Muslims believe the Ka'aba was built by Abraham, and it's considered their holiest site."

"It looks like a crowd control nightmare," Nicholas stated.

"It is. In fact, thousands of people have died at the Hajj. There have
been fires, riots, bombings, stampedes, structural failures because of
overcrowding, you name it."

"What about disease?"

"Plenty of it, and none of it good," Harvath replied. "There have
been outbreaks of meningitis and cholera, as well as things like Middle

East Respiratory Syndrome, also known as MERS. It normally doesn't get caught until the Hajj participants return to their home countries, and then the illnesses flare there."

"Don't they screen them as they come into Saudi Arabia?"

"They try, but people can be asymptomatic when they arrive. They also require specific vaccinations as a condition of entry, but for many pilgrims forged immunization records are easier and cheaper to get than the actual vaccinations. It's a public health nightmare. The Saudis know it and so do we."

"Then what's being done about it?" Nicholas asked.

"I just told you."

"Global public health is based on the honor system, backed up by supposedly vigilant border guards and passport-stampers?"

"Pretty much."

"We're screwed."

Harvath agreed. "That's one of the problems of modern air travel. An infected person can get on a plane anywhere in the world and be anywhere else within twenty-four hours."

"Do you think that's what this is? Damien and his Plenary Panel cooked up this illness and somehow got it into Mecca? They spread it through the Hajj and then the infected get on planes back to their home countries to start a global pandemic?"

"It'd be a clever way to do it," said Harvath, as he clicked over to another site to look at something.

"If this is African Hemorrhagic Fever, how did they get it in to Saudi Arabia? You can't even get near Mecca unless you are Muslim."

"If I had the resources Damien does, and I was putting this operation together, I'd do it via Zakat."

"What's Zakat?" Nicholas replied.

"It's like an Islamic income tax, or a mandatory form of alms-giving. Allegedly, it's used in part to help poor Muslims and can even be applied to paying their costs for attending the Hajj.

"Because of how many people want to participate, Saudi Arabia sets quotas for each country. Not only is Congo extremely poor, but it has a very small Muslim population. If I were Damien, I would take advantage of both of those factors."

"Meaning, you'd fund a group of Muslims from Congo to go to Mecca?"

"Exactly," Harvath replied. "I would quietly work my diplomatic connections to get the amount of visas I needed and then put the word out in the Congolese Muslim community that a wealthy Muslim benefactor had established a fund to underwrite their pilgrimage to Mecca."

"Where does African Hemorrhagic Fever enter in?"

Harvath scrolled down on a web site with information about the Hajj. "The Saudi government publishes a list of required vaccines for pilgrims. Yellow fever, polio, things like that. Whether or not my Congolese Muslims had been vaccinated, I would send my own team in, tell them the list had been updated and that they needed an additional immunization.

"And after making sure their travel and medical documents were in order," Nicholas added, "all you would have to do is just send them on their way."

"You'd want to do more than that. I'd maximize the spread of the disease by breaking them up at different hotels and attaching them to different tour groups once they arrived in Mecca. But at that point, it would all come down to how communicable the disease was."

"Then what? Do the Congolese Muslims crash and bleed out in Saudi Arabia? Isn't that the kind of thing the Saudis would be on the lookout for?"

It was, and Harvath remembered what Leonce had told them about the sick man who had arrived at the Matumaini Clinic and how a nurse believed he could be Muslim because she thought she had overheard him moan the word "Allah."

No loose ends.

"You're right," Harvath replied. "Just because the fuse was lit, it doesn't mean Damien was off the hook. No bomb maker—even one who has cooked up a plague bomb—would want pieces of it traced to their source. If I were Damien, I'd want those pilgrims back before the Saudis knew what had happened."

"Which means you wouldn't leave their return up to commercial air travel. Too many things could go wrong. He probably would have chartered a flight for them."

"Good point. See what you can find—visas, all of it. And while you're at it, see what kind of CCTV footage you can get your hands on. The Saudis monitor everything, particularly during the Hajj."

"Anything else?"

"If Damien did take them back to Congo, I'm betting they were taken to the Ngoa facility. The staff would be able to quietly get rid of the bodies and public health authorities would be none the wiser."

"But wasn't the Matumaini Clinic in touch with the WHO representative in Kinshasa?" Nicholas asked.

"They were. Whoever that rep in Kinshasa is, he's a part of this. He either tipped Damien or the Ngoa lab about their missing patient. That's probably why he asked for a picture to be emailed. I assume somebody wanted confirmation before Damien sent Hendrik and his men in to kill everyone."

"If that's all he needed, why did he ask for blood and tissue samples?"

"Probably," said Harvath, "because that's what they normally do. He was smart enough to not break with protocol. If he ever gets called on the carpet, it looks like he followed every step to the letter."

That made him think of something, and he made a mental note.

While he was doing that, Nicholas brought up a new question, something that had been weighing on him as well.

"We know Damien wants to drastically reduce the earth's population," the little man said. "We also know that he's a eugenicist who believes that certain races and bloodlines are unfit and should be snuffed out."

"Correct."

"So if a guy like that launches a global pandemic, how does he control who gets it?"

It was an important question, especially now that the genie appeared to be out of the bottle, but it wasn't the right question.

When disease was used as a weapon, the intent was for it to go anywhere and everywhere. No place was to be off-limits or safe. The only people meant to survive were the ones who had launched it and whatever subgroup they felt was worthy of living.

To answer Nicholas's question, Harvath replied, "He doesn't control who gets it. What he controls is who *doesn't* get it."

"So there's some sort of an antidote?"

"Or a vaccine."

"But based on the 'Outcome Conference' document that Mordechai told you about," Nicholas said, pushing back, "the Plenary Panel's goal is to skin the earth's population from over seven point two billion down to five hundred million. That's a ninety-three percent drop. How do you do that?

"I mean, we've got a pretty good idea of how they want to get the six and a half billion–plus people infected, but how do you save the others? How do you not only give an antidote or a vaccine to five hundred million people, but the right five hundred million, the ones you want to see survive? And on top of that, how do you do that without them knowing what the hell is going on?"

They were terrifying questions, none of which Harvath had answers for. He couldn't even begin to fathom how the world wouldn't collapse with a die-off of over six point five billion people. There'd be nobody to bury the bodies, much less maintain civil order.

Even the Black Death, said to have been the most devastating pandemic in history and estimated to have claimed up to fifty percent of Europe's population, was no comparison to this. Weaponized African Hemorrhagic Fever would not only blow it away, it would take the lead for worst calamity ever on earth, second only to the extinction of the dinosaurs.

If there was one thing Harvath knew, it was that Mother Nature moved fast, while science moved very, very slowly. If they couldn't get out in front of this virus, billions of people were going to die.

Looking up from his computer, he wasn't thinking about himself. He was thinking about Lara and protecting her, as well as her little boy and her parents back up in Boston.

There was also his own mother out in California, as well as others he had always promised he would never let anything happen to.

The magnitude of the task pissed him off. Not because he had to figure how to take care of so many people so important to him, but because he had been put in this position in the first place by an insane, agenda-driven asshole like Pierre Damien.

Harvath knew that there was a special place in hell for a man like Damien; he just hoped the President would let him send him there.

As Nicholas went through the rest of his checklist, Harvath's mind was going in multiple directions. He had been taught to think in layers, to make plans for contingencies—if not that, then this. *What are my routes of attack and avenues of escape?*

He found himself needing not only to focus on his work, but also on the people he cared about. It was the very position he had always said he never wanted to be in. Yet, here he was.

While the SEAL mottos about perseverance and never giving up floated to the forefront of his mind, so did another saying. *You can't always choose the situation you find yourself in, but you can choose how you react to it.*

His mother had said it to him a million times growing up. She said it so often it drove him crazy to hear it. But he had never forgotten it, its wisdom timeless and invaluable.

"Scot?" Nicholas said, trying to regain Harvath's attention.

"I'm sorry, what did you say?"

"I asked how the hell Damien planned on immunizing five hundred million people. And then when you didn't answer, I said that if anyone could get it out of him, it'd be you."

"Only if the President sees this the way we do."

"How could he not?"

"He's the President. He operates at a completely different level of calculus. There are always other factors. I think he gets it, though."

"He'd better," replied Nicholas.

"Listen, one other thing. When we ran Damien, there were mentions about his involvement in pharmaceutical companies. See what you can find. If there is some sort of antidote or vaccine, there may be some connection there."

"Got it."

Harvath was about to reassure him when another call came in.

It was the Old Man.

CHAPTER 36

Harvath's plans for Lara were shelved as soon as Carlton called and told him he was wanted at the White House. In all fairness, the morning was actually already shot the moment he heard from Nicholas that there was a third likely case of African Hemorrhagic Fever in the United States.

He hated to leave her alone at his place, but she was a big girl, and it wasn't like he had any choice. Guests did not bring guests to the White House, and especially not under the circumstances by which he had been summoned.

He had barely gotten a sip of coffee before he had to dash upstairs and hop into the shower. Lara playfully offered to join him, and it took all he had to turn her down and ask for a rain check.

After a quick shampoo and running soap over his body in record time, he used his perpetually fogged "fogless" shower mirror to shave and then threw the water from hot to ice-cold and forced himself to stand there for thirty seconds. If he wasn't fully awake before, he definitely was now. It was like downing three rapid espressos.

When he stepped out of the shower, he found that Lara had picked out an outfit for him. All he had told her was that he had to go to the White House. That was all she needed to know. What she chose was perfect—dark suit, white shirt, dark tie.

"Is it like this every morning?" she asked as he moved through the kitchen and kissed her.

"That's the President for you," he said. "Can't live without me."

She knew he wasn't serious and grabbed his ass. "Tell him he needs to go through me from now on, or I'm not voting for him again."

Ever since he had come to the realization that he loved her, everything she did or said seemed to back it up.

"I'll tell him. Reed Carlton won't like being cut out of the loop, but he'll learn to live with it."

"Let him know he doesn't have a choice."

He smiled and kissed her again before grabbing his keys and heading for the door.

"Hey!" she shouted from behind him.

When he turned, he saw her holding up a roadie. "Black. Two shots of espresso."

Smiling, he crossed back over to her. "I love you. You know that?" he said, trying to take the cup from her.

"Wait. What did you just say?"

Shit. It had totally slipped out. He meant it, of course, but this wasn't the way he wanted to say it for the first time—not rushing out the door.

It was a watershed moment. He could make it better, or he could make it worse.

Setting down the mug, he took her face in his hands and said, "I love you."

Lara was speechless. She had only truly loved one other man, her husband, and had watched him drown right before her eyes. Now, here she was with this SEAL, whom she teasingly referred to as James Blond, and he had just told her that he loved her. For a moment, it felt like she couldn't even breathe.

"This sucks," he said.

"No, it doesn't," she replied. "This definitely *doesn't* suck."

"I thought we'd at least have the morning together. I didn't think I'd be saying this and running out the door."

She looked at him. "You were actually *planning* how you wanted to say that to me?"

He didn't know how to respond. Was "planning" to tell her a bad thing? Didn't women like when men planned?

He decided to explain how he had planned to do it and why, but all he could get out was, "Yes."

Lara put her arms around his neck, pulled his lips to hers, and gave him the longest kiss they had ever shared.

Then, she was the one who broke it off. "You'd better get going," she said. She was smiling from ear to ear. Slapping him on his backside as he picked up his coffee, she added, "Remember what I told you to tell the President."

All he could do was shake his head and laugh. It was another moment; another brief, wonderful moment where nothing else existed and nothing else mattered. Then he climbed into his SUV and the real world crowded in with him.

He did the time difference in his mind with his mother in California, as well as a former SEAL buddy of his who ran a remote fishing lodge in Alaska. It was too early to call either of them. He decided to put those phone calls on hold.

It was also too early to call Ben Beaman, but that call couldn't wait. There were some things about Congo that needing sorting out. He also needed a favor. A big one.

By the time Harvath rolled up to the White House security checkpoint at the West Gate, the biggest item on his personal list already had a check mark next to it. It was a good start and with that done, he could focus on work and why the President had called him in.

Pulling into one of the parking spaces near the West Wing entrance, he turned off the ignition and hung the badge he had been issued around his neck. It always felt weird coming back. He had practically lived at the White House at one point. He didn't miss the Secret Service, though. Leaving the SEALs hadn't been a mistake. He had learned a lot, met a lot of people, seen and heard some incredible things, but protecting a President had meant playing defense. That wasn't his strong suit.

Offense was what he did best—finding the bad guys and taking the fight to them before they could bring the fight to us. With the SEALs and the Secret Service, he had gone through the best training the United States had to offer. Then, the Old Man had shown him what else was out there and had taken his game to a level he never before could have imag-

ined. He had gone from being an Alpha dog to an Apex Predator—a spe-
cies that sat astride the top of the food chain with no competition.

He radiated a calm, effective confidence that had nothing to do with
arrogance, but rather an effective ability to handle anything that was
thrown at him, no matter how fast. It was a good thing too, because things
were about to speed up. Dramatically.

The Marine Guard outside the Situation Room waved him to the
blast-proof door, which was so well engineered that it opened without
any perceptible hiss of its locks releasing or any sound of its bolts sliding
back.

Reed Carlton was already inside, as was the President. At the long,
mahogany conference table were Lydia Ryan; her boss, CIA Director Bob
McGee; General Ian McCollum, the Chairman of the Joint Chiefs of
Staff; and Colonel Sheila White, MD, the Director of USAMRIID.

Absent were any other members of the President's national security
team. His own Chief of Staff wasn't even there. Per the Old Man's sug-
gestion, he had kept this meeting highly compartmentalized.

There was something in the wind, something he didn't like. Seeing
those government personnel assembled at Damien's Virginia estate troubled him. It had looked like a conclave of third-tier royal functionaries,
and, historically, when that many functionaries assembled outside a palace, it usually meant that they were up to no good.

The Old Man pulled out the chair next to him and waved Harvath
over. Their briefing was already in progress.

Sitting down next to Carlton, Harvath reached for the carafe of coffee in front of them, poured himself a cup, and listened as Colonel White
spoke.

"The STAR team's drone shows zero activity at the Ngoa facility. In
fact, it looks completely abandoned. We're getting the same thing from
the satellite.

"Normally, we'd conduct this kind of operation at night, but all things
considered, we decided to advance the timetable. With your permission,
Mr. President?"

President Paul Porter nodded. He had a glass of orange juice in front
of him and looked like he had been up all night.

General McCollum picked up his phone and gave the command to begin the operation. "This is Wedgewood," he said. "Raptor is a go."

The raid on the Ngoa facility, where the African Hemorrhagic Fever had allegedly been weaponized, would be coordinated by the United States Special Operations Command out of a highly secretive TOC, also known as a Tactical Operations Center, at a far corner of MacDill Air Force Base in Tampa. The large, acoustically protected, darkened, raised-floor room was packed with flat-panel monitors, electronics, and rows of desks. On the outside of its door, there was no name, no number. None of the personnel who worked there ever spoke of it. It was a black hole from which some of the countries' blackest operations were conducted. For all intents and purposes, the TOC and what happened within it didn't exist.

The Situation Room back at the White House was similarly adorned with flat screens. Synched with the TOC at MacDill, each of them show-cased a variety of images.

In addition to the satellite and drone footage, there were feeds from the helmet cams being worn by the STAR team.

A voice from the MacDill TOC came down through the Situation Room's overhead speakers. "Raptor Actual, this is Raptor Main. You are clear to commence."

"Roger that, Raptor Main," said a voice from the team in Congo. "Raptor is clear to commence."

Considering the distance it had travelled up the satellite and back down to the United States, the transmission was clear with almost no delay.

As the team emerged from the tree line and approached the facility, Harvath set his coffee down and leaned forward. It reminded him of his own approach of the Matumaini Clinic just six days ago.

The Ngoa facility was composed of similar one-story buildings clus-tered around a sizable clearing hacked out of the jungle. Unlike Matu-maini, though, Ngoa had layers of perimeter security. The first was a tall, chain-link fence capped with razor wire.

Harvath, the President, and everyone else watched from the safety of the Situation Room as a STAR team member cut through the fence. The rest of the team stood in the open clearing behind him, exposed.

Though they were armed, they were suited up in full biohazard gear, which meant that their ability to detect and react to threats was severely impaired. In other words, they were sitting ducks.

It put everyone on edge, but particularly Harvath, who knew exactly what it felt like to be in their boots at that moment. If they were spotted, it was game over.

The Team in the MacDill TOC seemed to be reading Harvath's thoughts and called for SITREPs from the two sniper teams that had been sent ahead to provide overwatch. Each team reported back that the coast was clear.

Once an opening had been cut into the fence, the operator with the cutters tucked them in his pack, transitioned back to his weapon, and held the curtain of chain-link open for everyone else to pass through.

The operator with the handheld mine detector got back on point and led the team forward.

As he had done when leading them out of the jungle, he swept the device back and forth, careful to keep his eyes peeled for trip wires or other improvised triggers. This was Congo, and Ngoa wouldn't be the first time they had encountered antipersonnel devices. The other members kept in tight formation behind.

The second ring of perimeter security was a concrete wall about ten feet high. Along the top, set into the cement, were shards of glass from broken wine and beer bottles. Though inelegant, the message was clear—this facility was not open to unauthorized visitors.

The team made their way to a set of large gates secured by a padlock and chain. The operator with the bolt cutters stepped forward and after another SITREP from the snipers, the team was authorized to make entry.

Once the chain was cut, the STAR team members swept into the compound in perfect coordination, their weapons up and at the ready.

With all of the video feeds coming into the Situation Room, it was like trying to drink from a fire hose. Harvath kept his attention focused on the satellite imagery, only occasionally glancing at one of the helmet cams when he needed a better idea of what the team was seeing.

Their primary target was the largest and most central building in the compound. Based on analysis of the reconnaissance imagery, it was deemed to be the most likely location of the laboratory.

Harvath checked his watch. The STAR team had to be burning up in those suits. They had covered much more ground than he and Decker had getting to their objective, plus the temperature was higher because it was broad daylight. They weren't going to be good for much longer.

Arriving at the main building, the bulk of the team formed a stack, or as it was sometimes called, a Conga line, while several other members took up defensive positions outside.

When everyone was in place, the team leader announced they were ready to make entry. Colonel White nodded to General McCollum who relayed permission to the MacDill TOC.

With a final sweep of the structure by satellite and the sniper teams once more radioing their all clear, a voice came over the speakers in the Situation Room.

"Raptor Actual," it said, "this is Raptor Main. You're good to go."

"Roger that, Raptor Main," the voice from Congo replied. "Raptor is good to go."

With that, the STAR team leader made sure his team was ready. Then, counting down from three, they breached the building and rushed inside.

CHAPTER 37

arvath had no idea how the patient who had escaped the Ngoa facility had gotten out. With a ten-foot-high wall and a razor-wire fence, it wouldn't have been easy. Did he stow away in a vehicle? Did he have help? Did he simply walk out the back gate when no one was looking? There was no way to know.

What Harvath did know was that as the crow flew, a healthy person could walk from the Ngoa facility to the Matumaini Clinic in a day. This guy, though, hadn't been healthy. He was on death's doorstep the minute he arrived at Matumaini. Did he steal a bicycle? Did a Good Samaritan come across him and help deliver him to the clinic?

That was probably an even more important question than how he got to the clinic. Anyone he came in contact with would have been exposed to the virus. Had Hendrik and his men reverse-engineered his route? They had murdered everyone at Matumaini as well as at the adjacent village to prevent the disease from spreading; what about anyone else he had come in contact with along the way?

Harvath made a mental note to make sure the question got transmitted to Vella and his interrogation team at the Solarium site in Malta.

Drawing his attention back to the video feeds, Harvath listened to a chorus of "Clear! Clear!" ringing out as the STAR team secured room after room of the Ngoa facility's main building. All of them were empty.

Not only were they devoid of people, but they had been stripped clean of furniture, equipment, computers, everything. The only things left were the paint and light fixtures.

Like Matumaini, Harvath figured it had been bleach bombed as well. In fact, as this was alleged to be ground zero for the new, highly communicable strain of African Hemorrhagic Fever, they had probably taken bleach bombing to a completely new level.

Based on the building's layout, there appeared to be two patient wings—likely one for men and one for women—communal bathrooms, showers, and a series of examination rooms. This wasn't where any actual experiments on the virus would have been conducted.

On the far side of the compound, they discovered the lab—or at least what was left of it. The structure had been burned to the ground. All that remained was the charred hulk of some sort of walk-in freezer.

"That can't be a Level 4 lab," Colonel White said. "It's too small."

Level 4 was the highest, CDC-spec'd biocontainment safety level possible. It was reserved for the most dangerous and severely lethal pathogens researchers might come in contact with.

Harvath saw something on one of the team member's helmet cams and asked McCollum to have MacDill back the man up and return to where he had just been.

"What do you see?" the General asked.

"Those depressions in the ground," he replied, before looking over at Colonel White and asking, "What if the lab was mobile?"

"As in a trailer? Like the Iraqis allegedly had?"

He nodded.

"I don't know how the hell you'd move one on the roads in Congo," she stated, putting the word *roads* in air quotes. "And God help you if it flipped over."

"But it could be done."

"Positive pressure suits, a segregated air supply, showers, a UV light room—building a mobile Level 4 would be a ton of work, not to mention a ton of money."

Something told Harvath expense wasn't something Damien and the Plenary Panel worried about. "But it could be done," he repeated.

"Seeing as how we've dropped some pretty high-tech shipping container expeditionary labs into war zones, anything is possible."

The STAR team was reaching the threshold of how long they could stay in the suits before heatstroke began to set in. They needed to break off and get to the decontamination showers they had set up back in the jungle.

Harvath had seen enough. The Ngoa facility was a bust. When Colonel White looked around the room and asked if anyone needed to see anything else, everyone shook their head. General McCollum notified the MacDill TOC that the STAR team could come off station and proceed to decon.

Once the team had exfiltrated the Ngoa facility and retreated into the jungle, President Porter opened the floor for discussion.

"Now what?" he asked, excusing himself for having to remove a handkerchief from his pocket and blow his nose. "Anyone have any ideas?"

Harvath cleared his throat and looked at Colonel White. "How much of my debrief from Congo did you read?"

"The whole thing."

He looked over at General McCollum, who nodded and said, "I did as well."

He knew Lydia Ryan and Bob McGee, as well as the President, had read theirs, so that meant everyone in the room was up to speed. He also knew that they had been made aware of the patients who had bled out in Chicago, Houston, and Detroit. It had been one of the reasons Colonel White had moved to push up the Ngoa operation.

Harvath filled them in on what they had learned about the patients and their travel histories. He then laid out his theory about the Hajj and how the virus might have been introduced.

"What kind of protocol do we even have for something like this?" President Porter asked, fishing his handkerchief back out.

"It's Federal, not military," McCollum responded.

"CDC, NIH, FEMA," White added, "all coordinated from DHS."

Out of an abundance of caution, White had not been told that right now, all of those organizations were suspect, and were being purposefully cut out of the loop by the White House.

"Let's say something happened," CIA Director McGee replied, fixing his eyes on White, "and DHS was unable to get spun up in time, how would you want to see things unfold?"

"Why wouldn't DHS, or more importantly FEMA or CDC or NIH be able to respond in a timely manner?" she asked.

"Just answer my question."

"Is this a drill?"

"No," the President replied. "This isn't a drill. Please answer."

"We'd want to know as much about this strain of African Hemorrhagic Fever as possible. We'd need samples. We'd need them from any newly diagnosed patients here, but if this thing did start in Congo, I'd like to get samples from there too.

"Ideally, I'd want the samples taken at the Matumaini Clinic from patient zero. I'd want anything you could get from that sick rebel commander, as well as samples from that Matumaini Clinic worker and his son who transported patient zero's samples and was there when the rebel commander was exposed. That's just for starters."

President Porter looked at Harvath. "On the Congo end of things, how doable is that list?"

"Provided the rebels are where we left them, I could give the STAR team coordinates and they could go in to get samples from the commander's corpse. We left him in the jungle, though, so his bones might be picked clean by now."

"We'll take that chance," said Colonel White.

"And the rest of it?" Porter asked.

"When we left Bunia with Dr. Decker, Leonce and Pepsy said they intended to stay there. There was nothing left for them in their village."

"Could we find them?"

"I have someone who could track them down," said Harvath, thinking of Jambo.

"Which just leaves us with recovering the patient zero samples from the WHO offices in Kinshasa," stated White. "Do you have somebody who could do that?"

Jessica Decker was back in Kinshasa, but he didn't believe for a minute that she would cooperate, much less that she could pull it off on her own.

Needless to say, he did know someone, and he nodded.

"We have an experienced team in-country we can use," Harvath replied.

"Extremis?" Carlton asked, referring to Ash and the three other SAS men.

He nodded once more.

"But do they know how to handle samples?" White inquired. "How to package them for transport? Will they even know how to locate them in the Kinshasa office?"

All good questions, the answers to which were *no*. Ash and his men, as far he knew, didn't have applicable experience in handling highly lethal pathogens. He shook his head.

"Colonel," Porter said. "How soon can you get someone from the STAR team to Kinshasa to supervise?"

"I can task one of them immediately, but it'll all come down to transport."

"And Extremis?" the President asked, looking at Harvath.

"Same answer."

"What about samples from the U.S. patients?" said Lydia Ryan.

"Normally, I'd say that wouldn't be a problem," White replied. "We have a good working relationship with the CDC. With something like this, they'd want as much help as they can get. But we began this discussion with Director McGee asking me what USAMRIID would do if the CDC couldn't respond."

McGee looked at the President, then at her. "Ask the CDC for the samples, just as you normally would in a situation like this. If you get any pushback, let us know and we'll take care of it."

"If this is some kind of terrorist attack," she stated, "why are we not telling them?"

"There are additional National Security issues involved," McCollum replied as he closed his briefing book. He had been read in on the full scope of the situation before White had arrived and that was all he said.

White was a highly skilled scientist, but she was also a soldier and a professional who respected the chain of command. "Understood," she responded.

After thanking General McCollum and Colonel White for their attendance, the President excused them from the Situation Room. He then turned to the remaining attendees and asked for a domestic update.

Carlton and McGee gave the President a quick rundown, hitting the high points and answering the handful of questions that were raised. The longer they sat in the Situation Room, the worse the Commander in Chief looked.

"Are you feeling okay, Mr. President?" Carlton finally asked.

"I'm fine," Porter replied, coughing briefly to clear his chest. "What about those letters *MC* that Damien wrote in relation to their plan for the United States? Have we figured that out yet?"

"No, sir," McGee said. "We're still working on that."

"Well, work faster. I want another update in two hours. And by *update*, I mean *progress*. Is that understood?"

Around the conference table, everyone nodded and replied, "Yes, Mr. President."

As the President stood, the rest of the room stood, and Harvath pressed his luck. "Mr. President, one last thing, if I may, sir?"

Porter didn't look happy, but he nodded.

"Sir," Harvath continued. "I know when it was originally presented, you tabled any talk of taking Damien into custody."

"You mean *rendering* him," the President clarified.

"Yes, sir."

"Do you know why I tabled it?"

"I think I have an idea, sir."

"Well allow me to clarify it for you," Porter retorted. "Pierre Damien is an American citizen currently on U.S. soil. He is also a citizen of Canada, which is an important American ally. Damien is also a diplomat, an Under-Secretary-General with the United Nations no less. He's a wealthy and powerful man with a lot of wealthy and powerful friends."

"I understand, sir, it's just—"

The President cut him off. "Don't interrupt me."

Never before had Harvath been chastised by Porter. He regretted interrupting him immediately.

"Any corners you may have to cut from time to time downrange, or things you may have do in the name of expediency, become considerably more complicated when the recipient of those measures is an American citizen. Place that citizen on U.S. soil, and the complication factor skyrockets so high that God himself couldn't even reach it."

Porter took a moment to catch his breath and look around the table before returning to Harvath. "Making a case is like laying bricks, and you don't have enough of them. You have the slaughter of workers at a medical clinic and a village in a part of Africa most Americans know nothing about. It's horrific, I'll give you that, but the only thing you have tying it to Pierre Damien is the word of some mercenary whom you subjected to waterboarding and then rendered to Malta without any authorization whatsoever.

"That's it. That's all you have. And that means that's all *I* have. That's all my Attorney General would have. It doesn't matter who was seen coming out of his house. He, like every other American, has a right to free association.

"Do I enjoy his anti-American rhetoric? No, but he also has a right to freedom of speech, along with a long list of other rights guaranteed to him in the Constitution, a document that I swore an oath to preserve, protect, and defend.

"So when you ask me if you can render an American citizen, from American soil, for a crime he allegedly orchestrated in the Democratic Republic of Congo, based upon a statement coerced from a non-U.S. citizen under unauthorized, harsh interrogation, my answer is not only no, it's *hell no*.

"Does that clarify my position for you?"

"Yes, Mr. President."

Paul Porter looked around the table one last time. Everyone else nodded, and with that, he exited the Situation Room.

Harvath, Carlton, Ryan, and McGee sat for a moment in stunned silence until McGee said, "That went well."

Carlton shook his head. "You never ask a question you don't already know the answer to."

Harvath didn't want to be disrespectful to the Old Man, but he couldn't hold his tongue. "It needed to be asked."

"No it didn't, at least not directly. You know better. He's the President of the United States. He doesn't mind a little coloring outside the lines, but there are certain things that you have to be very delicate about raising. And there are most definitely things that cannot be put to him point-blank."

Harvath glanced at Ryan. There were times where she seemed to understand him better than either of their bosses. "It all comes down to bricks, right?"

"What?"

"The President told you. You don't have enough bricks. He wants you to build the thickest, highest wall you can. Something Damien will never be able to scale. I didn't hear POTUS say stop. I just heard him say that for the time being, you can't choke any of your bricks out of Pierre Damien directly."

Was that it? Was that what the President was telegraphing? He hadn't shut them down. He had simply established a bright line. One that for now, they would all have to abide by.

Switching to strategy, they remained for a few more minutes to discuss roles and who was going to do what next.

After discussing the Israelis and Ben Mordechai, they agreed to talk again in an hour, and exited the Situation Room en masse.

Halfway up the stairs, Harvath's phone began to blow up, chiming with a string of texts—all of them from Nicholas, telling him to call in.

As he hit the exit for the West Wing, his phone sprang to life once more, this time with a call. "Atomic Dog" by George Clinton.

The Old Man looked at him.

"Nicholas," Harvath responded.

"Answer it."

CHAPTER 38

I t was a torrent of bad news. "Six more cases have been reported," said
Nicholas.

"Where?" Harvath replied.

"San Francisco, Cedar Rapids, Atlanta, Philadelphia, New York City,
and Washington, D.C."

Washington? Harvath shouldn't have been surprised. D.C. and Northern Virginia had large Muslim populations. He just hadn't expected this
thing to spread so quickly, much less wind up on his own doorstep overnight. But it was there, and they were going to have to deal with it.

"Has the media gotten ahold of this yet?" he asked.

"Yes," replied Nicholas. "And in the last two hours, health ministries
from eleven other countries have reached out to the CDC. They're trying to control the information flow in order to prevent a panic."

Good luck with that, Harvath thought. In his experience, life was predominantly made up of three distinct groups: sheep, sheepdogs, and
wolves. And if there was one thing he had learned from a lifetime of
hunting wolves and protecting sheep, it was that sheep had two speeds—
graze and stampede. Now that word was out that the virus was loose, all
bets were off. Very soon, chaos was going to ensue.

"What else do you have?" he asked, bracing himself for more bad
news.

"The pharmaceutical companies Damien's involved with appear
pretty benign. One focuses on dementia medication and the other on
birth control drugs."

Go figure.

"I think you were right about the Congolese Muslims, though," Nicholas continued. "There was a group of thirty. They arrived and departed Saudi Arabia via the same privately chartered aircraft."

Finally, some good news. "Any passport photos or CCTV footage?" he asked.

"All of it has been transmitted to the Solarium. Vella is personally going to go through it with Hendrik."

While it wouldn't move the ball down the field, at least it would confirm his theory. "Anything else?"

"Mordechai's asset made contact."

"The woman with Damien?"

"Yes," Nicholas replied. "She thinks she captured his password."

"That's even better news."

"And it keeps getting better. The keystroke logger captured activity from multiple devices in the room, one of which we were able to ID."

"Which was?"

"A laptop belonging to Linda Landon from the Department of Homeland Security."

"Have you reviewed all of the keystrokes they caught?"

"No one has seen them. Not even Mordechai. Without access to secure comms, his asset isn't transmitting the data. She and Damien are having lunch today at some place called La Niçoise in Winchester. She's going to pass the actual memory card to Mordechai there."

With all the tech the Israelis had, he was a little surprised they couldn't have equipped her with some way to encrypt and transmit the data. But by the same token, this was an incredibly important operation. They were risking a ton just sending her in with the keystroke logger. There was no telling what Damien or his people might have done if they had discovered any of it.

He also needed to keep in mind that Mordechai's operation had revolved around the City of Geneva, where it wouldn't have been a big deal to pass off the memory card on her way to work, or to a store, or something like that. Now that she was at Damien's rural Virginia estate, she was much more isolated.

There was no telling how secure his WiFi was and what possible digital eavesdropping measures he had in place. He was known to entertain wealthy and extremely powerful people. Did he eavesdrop on any of their communications?

The restaurant was a good play. The handoff would be low-tech, old-school Espionage 101. What he didn't like, though, was that they'd be burning hours in a battle where every second counted.

"Where's Mordechai now?" Harvath asked.

"Still at the canal house. The team that's on him is about to rotate off."

"Who's up next?"

"Sloane Ashby and Chase Palmer are back on."

Harvath put the phone on *mute*, spoke to the Old Man for a couple of seconds, and then returned to Nicholas. "How would you like to get out of the SCIF for a little bit?"

"That depends," the little man said. "What do you have in mind?"

"Lunch. I'll buy."

• • •

Nicholas's gray Sprinter cargo van was a rolling TOC. It had satellite communications equipment hidden in the roof and was packed with racks of electronics inside. Special hand-controls had been added that allowed him to drive the van himself.

They arrived in downtown Winchester well before the lunch rush and found parking half a block down from La Niçoise on the other side of the street. Its awning promised Mediterranean and French cuisine—two of Nicholas's favorites. Harvath exited the van and came back fifteen minutes later with Thai.

"What the hell is this?" the little man complained.

"Pad See Ew."

"I'm not eating this."

Harvath took the container back and set it on the dashboard.

"That's it?" Nicholas asked. "No Champignons Sauvages? No Pâté de Campagne? No Escargots Bourguignons?"

Harvath looked in his bag from Thai Winchester. "I guess they forgot."

He shook his head. "Less than fifty yards from a French restaurant and *you* stumble around until you find Thai food."

"Who doesn't like Thai?"

"Don't play stupid with me," Nicholas replied. "You're so much better at it."

Harvath laughed and reached inside the bag. "That's what I love about you. You never look down on anyone."

The little man fixed him with a stare. "Is that a short joke?"

"Maybe," he replied, handing him a styrofoam container. "Gourmet bison burger, rare, with caramelized onions and blue cheese."

Nicholas's stare softened into a smile.

"We good?" Harvath asked.

"It's not Gigot D'Agneau," he said, lifting the lid and admiring the sandwich, "but I'll take it. Did you bring back anything for the boys?"

Harvath looked into the back of the van at Argos and Draco, their noses in the air, taking in the smell of all the hot food. "Sorry, they only took cash and I came up a little—"

"Don't say it," Nicholas smiled.

Harvath smiled. "You're lucky I found someplace to get you a burger."

"Thanks."

In between bites of his food, Harvath said, "A TV was on in the Thai place. They broke from national news for a local report about another patient who had bled out at Georgetown University Hospital."

"They'll never contain this."

"The illness or the story?"

Nicholas took a bite of his burger and let his silence speak for itself.

Harvath had no doubt that reporters from coast to coast were scouring hospitals, working their sources, trying to uncover additional cases. The one thing the government had going for them, for the time being, was that all of the patients thus far had contracted the illness abroad.

Harvath reached for a bottle of water as Nicholas's phone chimed. The little man picked it up, plugged in his password, and read the message. He then opened the attachment and turned the phone so that Harvath could see the image.

"Here's your escapee from the Ngoa facility."

Harvath looked at the image. It appeared to be a scan of the man's passport made by the Saudis when he entered their country. His name was Yusuf Mukulu and he was twenty-seven years old.

"Who's that from?" he asked.

"Vella in Malta. Hendrik has confirmed that Mukulu is the man who escaped and ended up at the Matumaini Clinic."

It was surreal seeing the man's face—the person Colonel White had referred to as "Patient Zero." If only there were one Patient Zero and not thirty.

"What happened to the rest of the pilgrims he travelled to Mecca with?" Harvath asked.

Nicholas turned the phone back around and thumbed through the rest of the brief message. "According to Hendrik, the Ngoa staff watched them die, then dug a pit, burned the bodies, and covered it up."

"Literally and figuratively."

The little man returned his phone to the console and turned his attention back to his burger.

Harvath checked his own phone for an update from Ash and his team back in Congo. An aircraft had been chartered to get them to Kinshasa. Another was sent to Bunia to retrieve the STAR team member assigned to work with them. So far, there was nothing.

They ate in silence until Nicholas asked, "If we don't get a handle on this . . . if this whole thing spins out of control, what's your plan?"

"It's not going to."

The little man looked at him. "Right, but let's say it does. Let's say the wheels come completely off the bus. Do you have a plan? Where you would go, what you would do?"

Harvath nodded. "A friend of mine from the SEALs has a place in Alaska. It's cut off, remote, very tough to get to. But that's where I'd want to ride things out. He's a strategic guy. He's laid in a lot of supplies over the years, just in case."

"Doomsday prepper?"

"He's just a smart guy. He knows store shelves may not always be stocked. He also knows that if there's ever a major disaster, the government can't, and won't, take care of everyone. You've seen enough since you've been in D.C. There are some good people in government, but by and large the government looks out for itself.

"They've spent billions making sure that if the wheels come off the bus, they've got someplace safe to go with plenty of food to eat. They're protected. You and me? Not so much. We're on our own. So that's why Alaska is my plan."

"But you'd have to get there first," said Nicholas. "That's a pretty long way away."

"I've got that covered. What about you?"

The little man looked at his two dogs and then back at Harvath. "I don't know. I never really gave it much thought until now. I never felt like I had to. I guess it would depend on where the safest place was."

"And then what?"

"Then I would figure out how to get us all there."

"Meaning you, the dogs, and Nina," said Harvath, referring to the woman in Nicholas's life.

"Pretty much."

"Can I be honest with you?"

The little man nodded.

"That's a shitty plan."

"I know," he replied, "but it's the only plan I have."

"Well, we need to get you a new one."

"Until we do, Alaska sounds good."

"Don't worry," said Harvath. "It's not going to come to that."

"But if it does?"

"If it does, I'll take you with me, okay?"

Nicholas smiled. Harvath was a good man, one of the only real friends he had ever had. "Thank you."

Harvath was going to make a joke about stocking up on orange hair dye so they didn't lose Nicholas in any Alaskan snowdrifts, when his phone rang. It was Palmer.

Activating the call, he said, "What's up?"

"Look sharp. Damien and the woman are here."

CHAPTER 39

W hen the two black Suburbans pulled up in front of La
Niçoise, members of Damien's security team exited first.
They were hard men, fit, well-trained, and obviously experienced. After looking slowly up and down the block, they opened the
rear passenger door so Damien could exit, followed by Helena. He offered her his arm and the pair entered the restaurant together.

The owner rushed to greet him. They shook hands, Damien inquired after the man's family, and then handed him a leather wine tote
with two perfectly chilled bottles of 1978 Domaine de la Romanée-Conti
Montrachet.

It was fifty thousand dollars' worth of wine and the owner, also an
oenophile, knew it. Damien patted him on the shoulder. "When you
bring our glasses, bring one for yourself."

"My goodness," the man responded, thrilled. "Thank you, Mr. Damien.
That is very kind of you. Please, follow me this way. Let me show you to
your table."

Damien introduced Helena and once they were seated, the owner
shuttled off to fetch his own personal wineglasses for these guests.

The restaurant was housed in a tiny brick building. The tables were
covered with crisp linens, and the murals on the walls evoked the Mediterranean and the South of France. The music of Stéphane Grappelli
poured like a warm café au lait from speakers hidden somewhere nearby.

If she had closed her eyes, Helena could have almost imagined she was in France. There was just one thing preventing her—the sight of the extremely pretty young woman sitting at a table with Bentzi, on the other side of the restaurant.

Who was she? Helena wondered. *Was she a Mossad operative? Was she another one of his assets? What was she doing here? Was he trying to send her some sort of message? Had he replaced her already? But Bentzi doesn't even know yet that I am leaving him,* Helena thought to herself.

"Are you okay my dear?" Damien asked, snapping Helena out of her obsessive reverie.

She smiled at him. "The music, the smells from the kitchen, I guess I was daydreaming for a moment that we actually were in France."

"Wait until we add the Montrachet to the picture," he said with a wink.

"Two bottles, though, Pierre? You're going to have to carry me home."

The older man grinned. "I have always held that bottles of wine are like breasts. Three is too many and one is never enough."

"Pierre!" Helena exclaimed, blushing. "Shhhh. We're not the only ones here."

"I don't care," he replied reaching for her hand. His smile broadened when his fingers intertwined with hers. "You have become very special to me."

"I'm sure you tell that to all of the women you whisk away to America on your private jet."

"I'm serious."

"So am I."

"You're the first woman who didn't want anything from me."

"Are you sure about that?" she asked as she gently traced his palm with the tip of her finger.

"Besides that."

"I think that's the reason why you brought *two* bottles of wine. You want to get me drunk, so you can take advantage of me when we get home."

He gave her hand a gentle squeeze before releasing it. "Did you see what year the Montrachet is?"

She shook her head.

Damien looked up to signal the owner, but he was already on his way over. After setting down three glasses, the man presented the wine to Damien, and upon his approval, produced a corkscrew and carefully went to work opening the bottle.

After cellaring for so long, there were a million things that could go wrong with the wine. The cork, though, was perfect; not even a hint of taint. The owner placed the cork on the table so Damien could inspect it.

Once he had, he encouraged the owner to pour the first taste for himself.

The man took his time admiring the color and then savoring the aromas and bouquet. When he finally tasted it, his eyes remained closed for several moments. Upon opening them, he proclaimed, "Absolutely amazing," and poured glasses for Helena and Damien.

Laying his hand lightly on the bottle, he gauged its temperature. The great white wines from Burgundy drank more like reds. You didn't submerge them in a bucket of ice. Their flavors were best enjoyed between 60 and 65 degrees Fahrenheit. The Montrachet was right on the money and needed no additional assistance.

Damien encouraged the owner to pour himself a proper serving, instead of just a taste, which he did. After detailing the lunch specials, he excused himself, and went to check on his other customers.

Damien looked at Helena and turned the bottle so she could read the label. "Nineteen seventy-eight," he said.

"The year I was born."

"I know. That's why I chose it for our lunch today." Raising his glass, he proposed a toast. "To moderation in all things, except in love."

Helena touched her glass to his. She was dumbfounded. She didn't know what to say. Did Damien just tell her that he loved her?

She took a sip of her wine, buying time so she could collect her thoughts.

"I have something for you," he said.

Reaching down to the outer pocket of his wine tote, he removed a velvet jewelry box the size of a salad plate.

Lifting the lid, he presented it to her across the table.

It was the most exquisite diamond necklace she had ever seen. It had to be worth hundreds of thousands of dollars.

"May I?" Damien asked.

Helena was speechless. All she could do was nod.

Rising from his chair, Damien took the necklace from its case and walked over and stood behind her.

He laid the necklace against the soft cashmere of her turtleneck sweater, the heavy central diamond coming to rest right between her breasts.

She swept her hair up so he could fasten the clasp. When he was finished, he returned to his seat and once again smiled at her.

"I don't know what to say."

"You don't have to say anything," he replied.

Pressing the necklace against her sweater, she asked, "Is this where you went this morning? To get this for me?"

"Yes."

"I don't understand. Why?"

"Does there have to be a reason?"

"Pierre, look at this necklace. It's gorgeous. Men don't just give jewelry like this to anybody."

"You're not just anybody," he replied.

She smiled and looked at him lovingly. "Don't do this to me, Pierre."

"Do what?"

"This," she said with one hand still on her necklace, the other lifting her glass. "The trips. The necklace. The wine. I don't want to get used to this."

"But could you?"

"You have me, Pierre. You don't have to do all of this."

"I like doing it."

"And I like that you like doing it, but don't make it complicated. Please."

Damien stared at her for several moments. "When my wife died, it was a pain like nothing I had ever experienced. I swore that if I survived it, I would never allow it to happen again. And then I met you and everything changed."

"You're drunk already," she said, winking at him.

He smiled at her. "You have a perfect sense of humor, do you know that? Everything about you is perfect."

"You *are* drunk, because I am far from perfect."

"You are perfect to me. We are perfect for each other."

She looked at him. "Pierre, are you proposing to me?"

Damien laughed. "To tell you the truth, I don't know what I'm doing. All I know is that I cannot imagine being without you."

Helena reached across the table and took his hand.

He held her hand tightly. "Promise me you won't leave me."

It was an amazingly tender entreaty. She squeezed his hand right back and replied, "I'm not going anywhere."

They sat, like two lovesick teenagers, staring into each other's eyes and laughing. Damien refilled their glasses and ordered appetizers.

Between their salads and the main course, Helena said to him, "I have a confession to make."

Out of instinct, he braced. Suddenly, there was a flash of that pain that he hadn't known for decades—a taste of what he prayed wasn't to come.

"What is it?" he asked.

"When I told you I wasn't going anywhere?"

"Yes."

"I wasn't being completely honest with you."

"You weren't?"

"No. I have to go to the ladies' room."

It took a fraction of a second, but he got the joke and his look of concern evaporated into a smile.

Helena walked over to his chair, ran her fingers through his hair, and kissed him. "Thank you for this," she said. "For all of this. The necklace, everything."

He looked up and smiled at her and then watched as she walked away to the ladies' room. She was an incredible creature. He had made the right decision bringing her. He could feel it in the deepest recesses of his heart.

• • •

The security operatives followed her with their eyes only. They had no reason to accompany her to the restroom. Damien was their primary, not her.

The necklace was beyond incredible. She wanted to stare at it in the mirror, but there would be time for that later.

Locking the door, she pulled out her phone and took care of her business first. There were so many damn apps on her phone that it was hard to find the one she was looking for. But that was the point. If Damien or any of his people had ever picked it up, and someone probably had, there was nothing unusual about any of it. Not even the banking apps.

In fact, she had noticed a story in one of Damien's financial newspapers one morning and had made a throwaway comment about what she thought a certain Eastern European country might do if Russia cut off its natural gas supply. She finished with her opinion on how it might affect the markets.

It had impressed him. When he asked how she had come to such an erudite conclusion, she took the opportunity to tease him, explaining that she had dated a British investment banker for a while. The thought of her with another man drove him crazy and only made him want her more. All she had done was set the table. It was Damien who sat down and gorged himself on her.

Finding and opening the app she wanted, she placed her bets. This would turn out to either be the smartest thing she had ever done, or the most foolish. She would know soon enough, and she consoled herself with the knowledge that as bad as things might get, she had lived through worse, much worse, and it had only made her stronger.

Closing the app and tucking the phone back in her purse, she removed a tube of lipstick and a small travel pack of tissues.

Unscrewing the false bottom of her lipstick, she removed the tiny memory card from its hiding spot, and placed it between her teeth. Peeling off the sticker that held the tissue package closed, she placed the memory card in the center and then reached down and stuck it under the vanity, behind the sink.

Bentzi's little blonde was going to have to work to find it, but Helena couldn't have cared less. She had completed her assignment. The Mossad would have Damien's damn password. Once it was confirmed, they would give her their file on Enoch and she would simply disappear.

At some point she would take her revenge on the man who had been responsible for stealing her away from her family and subjecting her to so many unspeakable horrors. There was always the possibility that the

Mossad would try to double-cross her, but not Bentzi. She knew him well enough to know that he would honor his promise. He was a man of his word, if nothing else.

Standing in front of the mirror, she applied fresh lipstick and fixed her hair. The necklace was amazing. She would find a buyer for it somewhere in Central or South America at some point. There was no rush. She had nothing but time.

Smiling at her reflection, she decided to leave Bentzi a note and pressed her lips up against the mirror and left a lipstick kiss.

He was going to be upset at her leaving. No one left the service of the Mossad without being granted permission. But it would go deeper than that with Bentzi; he would take it personally. It would be an affront to him, like having a weekend guest who never sent a thank-you note.

His problem was that he had always seen himself as her savior. In the beginning, that's how she had seen him too. In fact, to such a degree that she had fallen in love with him. But as time wore on, and he sent her on assignment after assignment—making it perfectly clear the lengths he expected her to go for Israel—her feelings for him shifted.

She had traded one jailer for another. As a sex slave, she had been physically abused and threatened with death. As Bentzi's asset, she had been psychologically abused and threatened with prison.

Like her desperate hope that the pimps would eventually stop and let her go free, she had grown to begin hoping the same thing under Bentzi. And then she finally realized that she would have to facilitate her own escape.

Bentzi's anger at her leaving would be his own problem. He had more than gotten his money's worth out of her. She was ready to disappear. She had put all the pieces in place. He had taught her well, and now the student was preparing the final lesson. Trail after trail would end in dark alleys and dead-end streets. Bentzi and the Mossad could spend the next twenty years looking and they would never find her.

Considering all she had done for them and all that she knew, she hoped that they wouldn't come looking. They owed her that much. They owed it to her to leave her alone. There were other girls out there— younger, worse off. Replacing her wouldn't be a problem.

Adjusting her sweater, Helena opened the door and exited the ladies' room. She only had to keep Damien happy for a little while longer. As soon as she had everything she needed, her new life could begin. And once that new life began, the only thing that would matter would be what *she* needed.

CHAPTER 40

Ben Mordechai paid the check while Sloane Ashby was in the ladies' room. When she returned, they left the restaurant together.

It had pained him to see Helena with Damien like that. She really was in love with him, and he was head over heels in love with her. No one was that good of an actress.

Even from across the room, the necklace was amazing, and Mordechai questioned not only where he had lost control of this operation, but of her.

Making matters worse, there was a front moving in. Though it was bright and sunny outside, he could feel it in his hands. As they stepped outside, a cold burst of wind blew a rumble of fallen leaves down the sidewalk. Mordechai turned up the collar of his coat and kept pace with Ashby back to their car.

She didn't talk much, except during the meal where it had been important for them to appear as two colleagues out having lunch. When Damien's security men had clocked the room, their eyes had fallen on Mordechai and stayed there a beat longer than they had on anyone else. Then they had moved on.

He had assessed them too—the cut and fabric of their suits, the shoes, the haircuts—even their eyes, jawlines, and facial structures. They were good-sized men, all over six feet tall, and they appeared European. Western European, probably, definitely not Eastern European or Israeli. The world was changing so fast, though, that it was getting harder for Mordechai to tell anymore.

The takeaway was that the men were disciplined and carried themselves with military bearing. With the kind of money Damien had to spend, they were likely former soldiers who had seen combat in multiple war zones. Not men to be trifled with, or underestimated.

"She's quite lovely," Ashby said as they neared their vehicle.

"Who?" Mordechai replied, lost in his own thoughts.

"Helena."

He nodded, not sure how to reply. It was an uncomfortable situation he found himself in. He wasn't exactly their prisoner—Deputy CIA Director Ryan had made that clear—but he also wasn't free to go. He either cooperated fully, or they would eject him from the country, along with a handful of Israeli intelligence agents known to the CIA to be operating out of Israel's embassy. Mordechai had no choice but to comply.

Hopefully, he now had what he needed and would be able to part ways with the Americans. Per their agreement, though, the Americans would get to copy the memory card before turning it over to him.

When they got into the car, Ashby unlocked her phone and swiped to the picture she had taken of the lipstick kiss on the bathroom mirror. "I think she left this for you."

Handing him the phone, Ashby put the car in gear and pulled out into the street.

As they drove, Mordechai didn't speak. Their destination was an area several minutes north called Rutherford Crossing. It was a commercial shopping area with several big box retailers and plenty of parking.

Two surveillance teams had stayed behind to keep an eye on Damien. By the time Ashby pulled into the lot near the home improvement store, Nicholas and Harvath were already there. Chase Palmer arrived a couple of minutes later.

"Do you want us to join you?" Ashby asked.

"Just Mr. Mordechai," Harvath replied. "You and Chase stay out here."

She nodded and handed him the memory card she had recovered from beneath the sink of the ladies' room at La Niçoise.

Mordechai stepped out of the car and followed Harvath over to the van.

"Do you like dogs?" Harvath asked as he reached for the handle.

"I don't really have a problem with . . . *Jesus!*" he exclaimed upon seeing Argos and Draco sitting inside.

When he looked up and saw Nicholas, he added, "Son of a—"

But Nicholas cut him off. "Not two sentences you want to be putting together."

"You!"

The little man smiled. *"Me."*

"So this is why we haven't been able to find you," said Mordechai. "The Americans have been hiding you."

"First of all, I didn't know the Mossad was looking for me. Second of—"

"Like hell you didn't. It was you who tipped the Emiratis about the Mahmoud Al-Mabhouh operation."

Harvath looked at Nicholas. "You two know each other?"

"Only by reputation."

"Al-Mabhouh. Wasn't he the founder of Hamas's military wing? The one you guys got caught whacking in Dubai?"

"Cofounder," Mordechai asserted.

"Whatever," Harvath replied. "Get in the van."

Once the Israeli was inside, he climbed in behind him and shut the door.

Mordechai took one of the seats in front of the racks of electronic equipment.

Argos and Draco didn't care for him. Each of the enormous white dogs began to growl the moment he stepped inside.

Nicholas ordered them to be quiet, but they refused to obey, and the growling continued. Harvath had never seen that before.

Nicholas repeated the command, and the dogs finally fell silent.

"With or without assistance," the little man clarified, "Emirati intelligence would have figured out what happened."

"So you admit it came from you," Mordechai seethed.

"I had nothing to do with it. But considering what an embarrassment it was for the Mossad, I can understand your professional desire for a scapegoat."

Mordechai looked at Harvath while pointing his finger at Nicholas. "He is a global criminal wanted by more countries than I can count. America should not be giving this man safe haven."

"They gave me more than safe haven. I even received a Presidential pardon."

The Israeli couldn't even look at him. He continued to address his remarks to Harvath. "How could your country even consider bestowing the protections of its sovereignty on someone who blatantly traffics in stolen intelligence?"

"I don't know," Nicholas continued. "Why don't we ask the American intelligence analyst serving life in prison a hundred and fifty miles south of here for selling classified information to Israel? Remember him? He's the guy your government has made an official Israeli citizen. If I could only remember his name."

"Jonathan Pollard," Harvath replied.

"That's right, *Pollard*."

"Completely different," Mordechai snapped, turning to face Nicholas.

The dogs started growling again.

Harvath had had enough. "Listen, you two can meet at the bike rack after study hall. Right now, I want what's on this memory card."

Nicholas began to say something, but Harvath silenced him. The dogs seemed to sense his mood and fell quiet.

Harvath handed the card to him. "How long is this going to take?"

The little man responded, but did so while looking at Mordechai. "Piece of cake. This won't take long at all."

The pissing match notwithstanding, the reason Harvath had brought Nicholas and his rolling TOC to the exchange, was so that he could immediately go to work on the memory card.

Out of professional courtesy, Harvath had invited Mordechai into the van. He didn't have an axe to grind with him. He wanted him there when Nicholas examined the card. It was both a sign of respect and the right thing to do.

As Nicholas inserted the card into his Toughbook, Harvath reached into the cooler, withdrew a bottle of water, and offered it to Mordechai.

"You doing okay?" he asked.

The Israeli slowly curled and uncurled his hands. It was obvious he was in a tremendous amount of pain.

Harvath pulled the bottle back, twisted the cap off, and then offered it to him again.

"Thank you," Mordechai said.

"*Ein be'ad ma,*" he replied. *Don't mention it.*

The Israeli smiled. "You speak Hebrew."

"A little."

"Have you been to Israel?"

"Once or twice," Harvath lied. He had been there many times.

"Business or pleasure?"

"Are you interrogating me, Mr. Mordechai?"

"Please, call me Bentzi."

"So this is a recruitment then."

Mordechai winked at him. "That depends. Are you recruitable?"

"No, he's not," said Nicholas from behind his laptop.

Bentzi leaned in closer and whispered to Harvath, "It would drive me crazy working with him."

"He's changed."

The Israeli laughed. "Even the smallest of leopards do not change their spots."

"Trust me, this one has. And a word of advice? Don't make short jokes."

"He's that sensitive?"

Harvath gestured toward Argos and Draco. "And these two haven't eaten all day."

"I've heard stories about his dogs."

"All true."

Mordechai shook his head and kept his voice low. "Primordial dwarfism. He should be dead by now."

"So should we, yet here we are."

The Israeli nodded, conceding the point. After taking a long sip of water, he changed the subject. "What's going to happen to Damien?"

"That depends on what your colleagues back in Tel Aviv pull off the mirror of his hard drive."

Mordechai curled and uncurled his free hand.

"Arthritis?" Harvath asked.

He nodded. "Courtesy of Mahmoud Al-Mabhouh."

"What did you do? Break both of your hands against his head trying to help him get into a police car?"

Harvath expected a smile from the Israeli, but he didn't get one. Instead, Mordechai replied, "Many years ago, there was a member of the Knesset. He was popular in Israel, particularly when it came to his opinions on Gaza and the West Bank. He was a good man, a fair man. Even a majority of Palestinians liked him. He seemed poised not only to become Prime Minister, but to achieve something even more important—peace."

As peace had yet to come to Israel, Harvath knew the Knesset member's attempts had somehow been dashed and waited for Mordechai to explain.

"The man had two daughters," he said, taking another drink of water. "Beautiful girls. Young, stupid, *beautiful* girls. They liked going out to clubs and they liked doing drugs. They were Israeli royalty who could do no wrong. Their father was warned, repeatedly, about their behavior, but their celebrity fed his as much as his fed theirs. It was the dysfunctional epitome of a vicious cycle. Instead of throttling back, even a little, so that he could focus on his family, he admonished his daughters and turned his attention right back to his own career."

Harvath had seen the same thing in many American political families. In a culture obsessed with likes, shares, and number of followers, politics had become the ultimate social media contest where a man like Abraham Lincoln could never get off the ground without a Guy Fawkes mask.

"As is typical for children who have no boundaries, the girls were constantly in search of where the line was. How far could they actually go before their parents stepped in and lowered the proverbial boom?

"The mother, a popular Israeli television star with a fledgling pop music career, was worthless. She was the one who set the bad example for the girls—liquor, drugs, and rumors of an affair with not one, but *two* of her co-stars. The family was a disaster. And then things got really bad.

"As the father was focused on his upcoming campaign and the mother on her new album, the girls were left with zero supervision. They fell in with an even worse crowd and got involved with harder and harder drugs in search of higher and higher highs. One night, they wrapped their father's BMW around a tree. That should have been a wake-up call to everyone, right?"

Harvath nodded.

"Except it wasn't," Mordechai replied. "Their parents, Scotch-filled highballs in hand, hypocritically railed against the girls' exorbitant life-styles. As you might imagine, the brats returned fire. According to the put-upon neighbors, it was a battle of epic proportions.

"Desperate to find, as well as to exert, some vestige of his withering parental authority, the father opted to go nuclear. In a move that could only be appreciated by some feckless bureaucrat, he declared his daughters' finances *frozen*."

Harvath looked at him. "That was it? He didn't ground them? He didn't sign them up for forced labor at the world's worst kibbutz? He just took away their credit cards?"

Mordechai shook his head. "Didn't even take their car keys."

"So basically, his daughters still went out on the town; they were now just dependent upon other people to help provide their fun."

The Israeli nodded. "And guess who was right there ready to provide it?"

Harvath looked at the man flexing his hands and sensed the answer. "Hamas?"

Once again, Mordechai nodded. "The last thing they wanted was peace, and those drug-addled, self-important children provided them the perfect opportunity to knock it all off course.

"Inside the bowels of Hamas is a desk occupied by a little mouse of a man. We only have second- and third-hand accounts, but by all of them he is an effeminate Francophile who code-named his operation Colette. Are you familiar with Truffaut?"

"François Truffaut? The French filmmaker?" Harvath asked.

"That's him. Hamas's mouse named his operation after one of Truffaut's films, *Antoine and Colette*. It's an insipid French story about un-requited love between two attractive young teens in Paris. The mouse chose the name Colette for what is essentially a glorified Palestinian modeling agency.

"Unfortunately in Israel, there is no end to spoiled, privileged chil-dren looking to rebel against their parents. Our two Knesset princesses were no exception. When daddy cut up the credit cards, they turned to other means to fund their fun. Because they had developed such a dan-gerous appetite for getting high, they had also developed a dangerous tolerance for risk in the pursuit of reaching those highs. One night that pursuit led them out of Israel proper and into Gaza."

Harvath's expression must have said it all because Mordechai shared with him a heavy, sorrow-laden glance, and bowed his head and said, "The girls had been befriended by two extremely handsome boys, hand-picked by the little Palestinian Francophile.

"The boys provided a steady pipeline of drugs, and though they applied no pressure whatsoever, the girls fell into bed with them, eager to make sure the party train continued to roll.

"Then finally one night, with their trust and dependency secured, the boys informed them that they were zipping into Gaza to pick up more drugs and needed their help. Getting into Gaza wasn't the problem, getting back through the Israeli checkpoint was. With the girls' good looks, family name, and low-cut tops, it wouldn't be a problem at all."

It was amazing how many people in pursuit of the next high tossed all common sense aside and fell for this kind of bullshit ruse. It pissed Harvath off to no end, but the fact that the girls' father wasn't there to protect them from this pissed him off even more.

What kind of man doesn't protect his children from wolves? Harvath didn't care what the Knesset man's greater aspirations for Israel were. If he couldn't protect his own family, how the hell could he ever be expected to help protect his own nation?

For a moment, Harvath was thrust into the man's shoes. Wasn't this the exact thing he worried about? How could he ever protect a family of his own while he was a world away trying to protect his country from the next threat or terrorist attack?

"But when they arrived in Gaza," Mordechai continued, "there were no drugs waiting to be picked up. It was an ambush. Mahmoud Al-Mabhouh's men did unspeakable things to the girls, videotaping all of it and leaving their bloodied and defiled bodies on a road outside Nablus."

"The father must have been enraged."

"First he was in denial. Then he was in shock. Then came the rage, and it burned white-hot. Al-Mabhouh and Hamas had succeeded. The fighting would continue. The greatest instrument for peace either side had seen in a generation was now solely focused on revenge."

"Which is where you come in," said Harvath. "Correct?"

Mordechai nodded. "The atrocity committed by Hamas was unforgivable, and could only be repaid in blood. Even the doves of the Knesset wanted revenge.

"I was with Shin Bet at the time—the Special Operations Unit."

"Yamas," Harvath said.

"Correct. Our focus was to locate and eliminate terrorists inside Israel, Gaza, and the West Bank. We had a reputation for being able get to them anywhere, anytime. We even carried out strikes in broad daylight. No place was safe for them.

"It took us a year to track down all of the men responsible. Once we did, we spent another three months training and planning the missions to take them out. The only operation that failed was mine."

"You missed your target?"

"We got our target, but because of some bad intelligence my team zigged when it should have zagged. The three men with me were killed, I was captured. Al-Mabhouh personally oversaw my torture. As part of that torture, each one of my fingers was bent back until it snapped. Once the bones began to heal, they would repeat the process. The pain was unlike anything I have ever known.

"As if the torture were not bad enough, not being able to use my hands to feed myself or conduct other necessities was a demoralizing indignity."

Harvath had heard some sadistic POW stories in his time and this one ranked right up there. "How long were you in captivity?"

"It was seven months before I was rescued."

"That's a long time."

"At first, they weren't even sure I was alive. But once they figured out I was, they worked day and night to get me back. Israel never once gave up on me."

The Israelis were incredibly loyal to their warriors. It spoke to the character of their nation and was something Harvath had always admired. It was one of many reasons that explained the close kinship America and Israel enjoyed. As the only Democracy in the Middle East, Israel mirrored many of America's values.

Now that Harvath understood the barbarity of Mordechai's captivity and that it had been overseen by Al-Mabhouh, it was clear why the Israeli had been so angry with Nicholas.

Harvath was about to ask the little man what was taking so long with the memory card, when Nicholas looked up from his keyboard and said, "We may have a problem."

CHAPTER 41

W ait a second," Mordechai replied, leaning in to look at Nicholas's screen. "She erased everything?"

"How much information can you extract from it?" Harvath asked.

"Not much," the little man replied.

"How do I know I can believe you?" said Mordechai.

"You shouldn't," Nicholas said, removing the memory card and handing it to him. "Your IT people in Tel Aviv will tell you the same thing. She used a pretty sophisticated product to scrub the data, but they'll back up what I'm telling you."

"Why would she erase all of the earlier keystrokes she had captured and only give us the most recent?"

"You tell me. There's a lot of memory space available on that card. She could have stored keystrokes for years. It's not like she needed to continually free up space."

Harvath looked at Mordechai. "You said her op was taking longer than it should have, and you were concerned that she had fallen for Damien and didn't want to go through with it. That's why you offered up the sex-trafficking leader. But what if Helena had another agenda? What if she didn't want you to have all of the keystrokes she had captured?"

Mordechai was smart enough to know that you never *really* knew people, but he thought he knew Helena. The idea that she might be pursuing an alternate agenda had never entered into his mind. But it should have. Maybe she *was* that good of an actress. Maybe she had fooled everybody—even him.

It was a lot to process, but what mattered most at the moment, though, was transmitting the information from the memory card back to Israel.

"I'm going to need my laptop," said Mordechai.

Nicholas removed it from the cubby he was sitting next to and handed it over.

"I hope you didn't waste too much time going through it. There isn't anything on it."

"Didn't even power it up," the little man said, writing down the access code for the WiFi in his van and giving it to him.

Mordechai doubted that. "The laptop is a burner, as are the web sites and email addresses I am about to use."

"Best practices. I wouldn't expect anything less."

The man was a pro, and Nicholas had been telling the truth when he said he expected nothing less of him. While operatives like Mordechai can and did make mistakes, it was highly unlikely at his level. If there had been anything on his computer, it would have been highly suspicious, so much so that Nicholas would have considered it a trap, purposely meant to be uncovered.

What's more, Mordechai and the Mossad were smart enough to know that the United States had grown beyond unreasonable with personal electronics searches at points of entry, even demanding that returning American citizens hand over passwords to their encrypted data or be thrown in prison. It was out of control and something President Porter had vowed to fix.

Mordechai jumped through the digital hoops of preparing the data from Helena's memory card. It would be routed through a false front web site to a special cloud server that had been established by the Mossad's "Technology Department" in conjunction with Unit 8200—Israel's Ministry of Defense signal intelligence division akin to the NSA.

Once the data was ready, he began the transmission. If Damien's hard drive held what the Mossad hoped it held, then they would know the extent of his plans and be able to set the wheels in motion to stop him.

If it didn't, he had no idea what they were going to do next. There was no doubt in his mind that Damien's weaponized hemorrhagic fever was incredibly lethal. To meet his goal of slicing the world's population from over seven billion to under five hundred million, it would have to be the worst plague mankind had ever known.

And what bothered him the most was that as forthright as he had been with them, his American counterparts appeared to be holding back on him.

As if he needed any further proof, Nicholas motioned for Harvath— and only Harvath—to look at something on his screen. Once Harvath had seen it, he summoned Palmer and Ashby over to the van.

"How much money do you have on you?" he asked Palmer.

"Couple hundred bucks," he replied. "Why?"

"Any credit cards?"

Palmer nodded.

"I want you to max them out," he said, pulling up a web site on his phone and texting the link to his colleague. "Get as many things on this list as possible."

"SHTFPlan.com? The Top 100 Items That Disappear First in an Emergency? What's going on?"

"I'll explain later," Harvath replied. "Hit the home improvement store first and then go next door to Target. Make sure to top off your gas tank. Bring all of it to my place."

Mordechai looked at him. "What's happening?"

"The virus is spreading," he said. Turning to Ashby, he pointed at the PetSmart, "Nicholas will text you what he needs for the dogs. Get it, get gas, and then get Mr. Mordechai to my place and wait for me there."

"*Your* place? Are you sure about that?"

"Positive. Now get moving."

The Israeli held up his laptop. "I haven't heard anything back yet."

"We'll get you set up on my network when we get there," Harvath replied. "Now, let's go."

Exiting the van, they slid the door shut as Nicholas tapped out a quick list for Ashby and then climbed into the driver's seat and fired it up.

"How reliable are the numbers you just got?" Harvath asked as he slid into the passenger seat next to him.

"They're straight out of the CDC's Epi-X. It's the most current and up-to-date."

"Damn it."

The virus had now appeared in eleven more cities.

"There's something else," Nicholas said, as he put the vehicle in gear and navigated out to the road. "Those initials, *MC*—the ones Damien had scrawled on his Outcome Conference document—I know what they stand for."

"You do? How?"

"It was part of the keystroke data that Helena captured. While Linda Landon was in the room with Damien she accessed something. MC refers to a FEMA database called 'Main Core.' "

"I've never heard of it," replied Harvath. "Do you know what it is?"

"I've only heard rumors about it. It was supposedly developed in the 1980s as part of the United States Continuity of Government plan. It is a list classified above top secret with over ten million American names. These Americans have been classified as potential threats to national security. In the event of a national emergency, each person has been pre-ranked for surveillance, questioning, or even detention."

"What lands them on the list to begin with?"

"Usually, disagreeing with the government."

"Like being antiwar?" Harvath asked.

"Or you can be anti-universal health care. It is a completely nonpartisan list. It doesn't care how you vote. All that matters is that you are perceived as a threat to the government in some form or another."

"So just by attending a Code Pink or a Tea Party rally, you wind up on the list?"

"From what I have read, you have to do more than just attend the rally, although it wouldn't surprise me if they keep lists like that too. To land on Main Core, you'd have to have a more active role in a movement. The concept, as I understand it, is that the government would want to know where to find you in a time of national unrest in order to make sure that you weren't contributing to that unrest."

"And if I was?" Harvath asked indignantly.

"Then you'd be silenced."

"How?"

Nicholas shrugged. "I didn't write the plan, but I think you get the idea. Certain people are going to need more pressure applied than others. If you have a bad enough event take place, if something like martial law is imposed, then habeas corpus can be tossed out the window, and your rights don't mean anything. You get thrown in a cell and that's that."

"Except we wouldn't call it martial law. We'd use the term *state of national emergency*," Harvath replied.

"Correct. And under a state of national emergency, Congress can be bypassed and an incredible array of extraordinary powers get swept into the Oval Office. Just for starters, property and commodities could be seized, private sector businesses could be told what to do and how to do it, all means of transportation and communication could be taken over, the list goes on and on. It's quite remarkable how quickly a democratic republic could cease being democratic."

"But sometimes in an emergency, if it's bad enough, certain things are necessary. Kind of like the way blood in the body races to protect the internal organs."

"I'm not arguing," said Nicholas. "I'm just laying out the facts. That's a lot of power to concentrate in one location. And based upon what we know of Damien and who we saw leaving his estate, I think we've got more than a little reason for concern."

"Never let a good crisis go to waste," Harvath deadpanned, quoting a former White House Chief of Staff.

"Exactly. By all accounts, Main Core is nothing more than an enemies list. It incorporates people from across the ideological spectrum who are united by one thing, opposition to the Federal Government. The list exists only to identify and quash dissent. The First Amendment notwithstanding, what if that dissent is warranted? What if some of those voices are valuable, *particularly* at a time of national crisis?"

Harvath had heard the Federal Government likened to the *Star Wars* character Jabba the Hutt. It sat in Washington, D.C., gorging itself and increasing in size. If you suggested it go on a diet, or you threatened it in any way, it would send bounty hunters like Boba Fett after you in the form of multitudinous Federal agencies which no longer served the citizens, but were part and parcel of Jabba and only concerned about protecting themselves.

Nicholas's question about the value of certain dissenting voices concerned him. In the 1970s, a Senator named Frank Church had begun to ring the alarm bell about the incredible surveillance capabilities the United States was building. When focused outward on the rest of the world, America's giant listening ears were unbelievably valuable. But the Senator warned of a day that might come when those ears would be turned inward on the American people. That was exactly what had happened in the wake of the 9/11 attacks.

Church's biggest concern was that under the banner of "protecting" the American people, the Federal Government would pursue more and more invasive means of gathering, sifting, sorting, and storing personal information and private communications. He referred to it as crossing the Rubicon and warned that if—even generations hence—the U.S. Government ever began tilting toward tyranny, it would be impossible to mount any form of resistance whatsoever. Such was the government's ability to read everything, listen to everything, and know everything before it even happened.

"So how does Main Core help Damien?" Harvath asked.

"To understand that," Nicholas replied, "we're going to need to get a look at who's on the list."

CHAPTER 42

H arvath had called ahead to alert Lara that people were going to begin showing up at the house. By the time he and Nicholas arrived, the Old Man's vehicle was already parked in the drive.

Harvath's home, as well as the surrounding acreage, had been deeded to him as a thank-you by a prior U.S. President. In exchange for his one-dollar-per-annum rent, Harvath was expected to maintain the historical property in a manner befitting and contributing to its stature.

Overlooking the Potomac and just south of George Washington's Mount Vernon estate sat Bishop's Gate—a stubby, yet elegant stone church and rectory. During the Revolutionary War, it had been home to an outspoken Anglican priest and dedicated loyalist who had given aid and comfort to British spies. As a result, the church was attacked by the colonial army and left in ruins.

Bishop's Gate remained that way until the late 1800s when it was taken over by the United States Navy, renovated, and repurposed as a covert training center for the Office of Naval Intelligence.

Eventually, the ONI outgrew the facility, and after a short stint storing dead files, it was relegated to "mothball" status.

Although not as upscale as some of the other properties in the Navy's portfolio, its location was exceptional, as was its access to the water. The history of the estate, though, was what had won Harvath over.

On his very first exploration of the rectory attic, he had discovered a beautiful, hand-carved sign. Upon it, had been written the motto of the

Anglican missionaries: *TRANSIENS ADIUVANOS*. I GO OVERSEAS TO GIVE HELP. It was as if it had been carved expressly for him. The moment Harvath had seen it, he had known that he was home.

It had taken some doing, but he had gotten the place into great shape. He was good with his hands and knew his way around a toolbox. Fixing things was becoming a lost art. When Lara visited with her son, Marco, Harvath liked to find projects for the two of them to do together. He had even gotten him his own little boy–sized tool set. It gave him no end of joy to see the sense of pride and accomplishment in Marco when he successfully completed one of their tasks together. He was a good boy.

Entering the house, Harvath and Nicholas passed the Anglican missionary sign in the entry hall and walked toward the sound of voices in the kitchen. Argos and Draco trotted ahead. Nicholas spent a lot of time at Bishop's Gate, and the dogs knew their way around. It had become like a second home to them.

Carlton was seated at the kitchen table, a cup of coffee in front of him. Lara was leaning against the kitchen counter smiling, a cup of coffee in her hand and something simmering on the stove behind her.

"That smells good," he said, kissing her.

"Arroz Carreteiro. Your favorite."

Both of Lara's parents were amazing cooks and they had passed on their love of cooking to her. Arroz Carreteiro, which roughly translated into *Rice Wagoner* or *Cart Riders*, was a popular dish from southern Brazil. Meat, rice, tomato, onions, and spices—it was perfect for this time of year.

Grabbing a coffee cup, he looked at Nicholas, who nodded. After pouring coffee for each of them, he suggested to Carlton that they walk back to his study.

It was one of his favorite rooms in the house. Here he stored his vast library in floor-to-ceiling bookcases. There was an old desk, a large fireplace, a leather sofa, and two comfortable side chairs. He motioned for his guests to find a place to sit while he looked for his remote and powered on the television.

"Have you heard about the new cases?" Harvath asked.

Carlton nodded. "But that's not the worst part of it."

"Why? What's going on?"

"The dead ones, the ones who bled out, all of them travelled to Saudi Arabia for the Hajj. The bad news is that hospital emergency rooms, minute clinics, and family doctors across numerous cities are now reporting a surge in patients who haven't travelled outside the United States, but who are presenting with high fevers and other symptoms believed to be consistent with the initial stages of African Hemorrhagic Fever."

"Damn it," Harvath replied.

His instincts to send Palmer to stock up on supplies had been well founded. Though he always kept his pantry stocked and would be able to take care of a certain number of visitors for an extended period during an emergency, nobody in their right mind would pass up getting one last crack at the stores before they were overrun and stripped bare. All you had to do was ask anyone in a hurricane zone whether it was better to be two minutes early to the grocery store in advance of a storm, or two minutes late.

"There's something else," the Old Man added. "And it doesn't get repeated outside this room, but President Porter has developed a fever. Out of an abundance of caution, he has been transported to Bethesda Naval Hospital for observation."

"He said it was just a cold," Harvath replied. "Has he had contact with anyone who recently travelled to Mecca?"

"He's the President. He has contact with a lot of people."

"Including us."

The Old Man knew what he was suggesting—not that they had potentially infected Porter, but that he may have infected them.

"All the more reason we need to get moving," said Carlton. "We've got a lot of work to do. Let's start by you giving me an update on what happened in Winchester."

Harvath walked the Old Man through all of it, with Nicholas filling in where appropriate.

At one point, Carlton stopped him and asked, "What do you think this Helena woman was erasing from that memory card?"

"If I had to guess," said Nicholas, "I'd say passwords. Damien is a smart man. We should assume he changes his passwords often."

"But her assignment was to get his password. Period. Once she had done that, why didn't she send it to Mordechai and pull up stakes?"

"Again, if I had to guess, I'd say she had been accessing Damien's computer from early on in the operation. Whenever he changed his password, she'd have to recapture it in order to get back in."

"For what, though?" Carlton pushed. "All the Mossad wanted was the password. They didn't ask her to extract anything from the man's laptop."

Nicholas put up his hands. "I'm the zeros and ones guy. I don't attempt to assess or explain human motivations."

"Bullshit, Nick. Stop screwing around. Why do you think she kept hitting his hard drive?"

There was only one answer that came to his mind. "Money."

Slowly, Carlton nodded. He liked that answer. It was simple. More important, it made sense. "Okay, so let's say it was money. How does access to Damien's hard drive make her money?"

"Without seeing his hard drive, I can't tell you."

"As we don't have access to it, why don't you take a guess."

The little man shrugged. "I can think of a million ways to monetize what might be on the personal hard drive of a man like Pierre Damien. Was there anything that could be used to blackmail him or other powerful figures? Were there any soon-to-be-released reports about drugs Damien's pharmaceutical companies were working on? How about the status of pipeline or drilling agreements for his oil or natural gas companies?"

"Okay," said the Old Man, "but if you know, like Helena, that Damien has something massive planned, something he hopes is going to totally reshape the world, do you really care about some new Alzheimer's drug, some pipeline deal with Kurdistan, or some nude island frequented by some second-rate British royal?"

"No," Nicholas answered.

"Why?"

"First of all, if there was any blackmail material on the laptop, she should have been able to find it on her first pass through. That leaves financial material, and you're right. If Damien is going to crash the world as we know it, there's no value in knowing about some miracle Alzheimer's drug or pipeline deal before it happens."

"Unless," said Harvath.

Both Nicholas and Carlton looked at him.

"Unless what?" the Old Man asked.

"Unless her goal was to profit *from* the crash."

"How?"

"Suppose the Mossad was right," Harvath continued, "but only half right. Suppose Helena did want out, but that instead of Pierre Damien being her golden ticket, he unknowingly helped her pack her parachute?"

"Meaning what?" Carlton replied. "She was funneling cash from his accounts?"

"No, too easy to get caught. Let's assume she's smarter than that."

"If she was smarter than that, she would have stopped being a honey trap for the Mossad a long time ago."

Harvath held up his hand. "Damien is a lot of crazy things, but we all agree he isn't stupid. He's also a successful businessman—a businessman sitting on the biggest piece of insider information ever. He knows the exact date the world is going to end. Why in God's name wouldn't he play that?"

The Old Man's eyes widened. "Short the market?"

"There are lots of things he could be up to. Helena, though, would have to know where and when to place her bets. She'd need to get out before everything collapsed. That might be why she has been accessing Damien's laptop. She's trying to catch a falling knife."

"Good way to feather your nest if you were planning to leave the Mossad and disappear."

"Speaking of which," Harvath replied as his driveway alarm chimed and one of the outdoor camera feeds popped up on his TV. "Sloane's here with Mordechai."

"What should we do with him?"

"I think we should read him in on everything we've got," said Harvath.

"*Everything?*"

He nodded. "All of it."

CHAPTER 43

Mordechai accepted a cup of tea and moved a bit closer to the fire Harvath had started for him in the fireplace.

As the wood sizzled and popped, he listened to Harvath lay everything out. When he had finished, the first thing that came to mind to say was "Thank you."

"You're welcome," Harvath replied. "All we ask is that you don't broadcast to your people that President Porter has been taken to Bethesda. If that gets out, it will cause a panic."

"When it comes to causing a panic, I think there are one or two other things you should be more concerned about."

"And we are. We just don't want to contribute to a deteriorating situation."

"I understand," Mordechai said. "In the event the President is unable to execute his duties, who takes over? The Vice President, correct?"

"Correct."

"And if the Vice President happened to become ill?"

"Then the Speaker of the House followed by the President pro tempore of the Senate," Harvath replied.

"And then cabinet members," Carlton added. "Secretary of State, all the way down to the Secretary of Homeland Security."

"Which is where Linda Landon works," said Mordechai.

Harvath had his laptop open on his desk, and he pulled up the United States Presidential line of succession to show him.

"But if the Vice President is number one," he said, "Homeland Security is all the way down here at the bottom at number seventeen. And
that's for the current, acting secretary. Not only would he have to fall ill,
but so would several other people at DHS before she could ever hope to
ascend to the secretary position."

Mordechai shrugged. "If the virus moves fast enough."

It was almost too crazy to believe. Sickening everyone above you in
order to seize the Oval Office? But maybe there was something to it. Palace
coups had used poison throughout history, so why not disease? Was that
why Damien was rubbing elbows with all the backbencher bureaucrats?
Was it more than just securing the reins of power in the White House? Was
it a means by which to control the Federal Government from tip to tail?

It all came back to how Damien intended for the survivors of African
Hemorrhagic Fever to actually survive. If they could figure that out, then
maybe they could reverse engineer the plot.

Harvath looked at Carlton. "Who do we have at Homeland Security
that we can trust?"

"I can think of one or two people, but it depends on the task. Are you
looking for background on Linda Landon? Interoffice chatter, that kind
of thing?"

He shook his head. "No. Word might leak and like we said, she'll run
to Damien. Right now, I'm more concerned with the people above her.
Specifically, I want to know if any of them are sick."

The Old Man thought about it for a second and then said, "I have
someone I can call."

"Good. Do it," Harvath replied. Turning to Mordechai, he asked,
"What do you need?"

Tapping the laptop he had brought in with him, he said, "WiFi access."

"No problem. Anything else?"

"I'd also like my phone back so that I can call my people and bring
them up to speed."

Harvath looked at Carlton and the Old Man nodded. "Done."

He called to Sloane and asked her to bring Mordechai's cell phone in.
He then created a hotspot, firewalled off from all of his devices, and gave
the man a temporary password.

As Carlton stepped out of the room to call his contact at DHS, Nicholas asked, "What do you need from me?"

"How long would it take you to get inside that Main Core database and give me a thirty-thousand-foot view?"

The little man looked down at his chronograph, activated the stopwatch, and said, "Let's find out."

Sliding off the couch, he picked up his coffee, whistled for the dogs, and headed for the front door. He worked better without other people around, and the van had everything he needed.

Now, the only person without a designated assignment was Harvath. That didn't mean, though, that he didn't have something to do. He had a huge task in front of him—and it began in the kitchen.

He quietly asked Sloane to remain in the study with Mordechai. He also asked her to use her phone to covertly record any conversations the Israeli conducted over his cell phone. Harvath's Hebrew wasn't good enough to help translate them later, but Nicholas would have access to a program that could do it. With Sloane given her marching orders, Harvath went to speak with Lara.

She had the TV on. She was a news junkie like him. Even if she were not, today was the kind of day where everyone began turning on television sets, looking to pick up the latest information, wondering if the breaking news was going to impact them. Harvath knew that it was going to impact everyone.

"Not good," she said, nodding toward the TV.

"I know," he replied. "We need to talk."

Lara wiped her hands on a kitchen towel and poured herself a cup of coffee. Raising the pot, she looked to see if Harvath wanted some.

"Please," he said with a nod.

Lara brought it over to the kitchen table, warmed up his cup, and sat down next to him.

"How bad is it?" she asked.

"Bad."

"How the hell are you right in the middle of it?"

He smiled.

"I'm worried about Marco," she continued. "And my parents."

"So am I. That's what I want to talk with you about. I have made arrangements for you all to be taken someplace safe."

"Where?"

"Alaska."

"*Alaska?*" Lara repeated.

"Good friends of mine have a fishing lodge there. It's in the middle of nowhere. He's a SEAL and his wife is very squared away. They know what they're doing. You'll all be safe there."

"What about you?"

"Unfortunately, I have to stay behind. But I'm going to be okay. I'm going to put Nicholas in a backpack and stuff my pockets with bacon so the dogs don't leave my side."

Lara attempted a smile, her eyes cast toward the floor.

He raised her chin until she was looking at him. "It's going to be okay," he repeated.

"Does it have to be you?"

He nodded.

"Why?"

"You know why."

She turned away from him, but he gently turned her back. Her eyes were moist. He had never seen her cry.

"Everything is going to be okay," he said again.

"Come with us."

"I can't."

"Yes, you can. Porter has the whole government at his beck and call. Scientists, the military. Let's just go. Let's outrun it."

He pulled her to him and held her tighter than he had ever held her before.

They stayed like that for several minutes. It was long enough for their breathing to fall into synch. Finally, she pushed away from him.

As she did, she hit him right in the center of his chest as hard as she could and said, "Fuck you."

She was a cop, tough. She knew how to make it hurt, and it did.

"*Oof,*" Harvath groaned.

She stared at him, angry.

"Fuck you," he teased. "I haven't learned that one yet. Is it Brazilian Portuguese or *Portuguese* Portuguese?"

Lara smiled. This time, it was genuine.

"You need to understand that I'm doing this for you. For you and for Marco," he said. "And for your parents."

It had felt hollow as it took shape in his mind, but as soon as it touched his lips, he realized that he meant it.

"There isn't anybody else who can do this," he continued. "Not now. Nicholas, me, Reed, Sloane, Chase, we're it. Look," he said as he directed her attention back to the TV. "People are already dying, and it kills me that I couldn't help them. The only thing I can do right now is try to protect everyone else."

"But you can't protect everyone."

"I can try. I need to."

Stroking the side of his cheek, she leaned in and kissed him. "I love you too," she said.

Harvath pulled her into him and kissed her back. Closing his eyes, he drank her in—the way she felt, the way she kissed, the way she smelled. He tried to freeze everything about her; he tried to create a snapshot that would always be there whenever he needed her.

He didn't want the moment to end. But it did when Carlton sound-lessly slipped into the kitchen and cleared his throat.

Disentangling himself from Lara, Harvath looked up.

"I just got off the phone with my contact at Homeland Security," the Old Man said. "It's bad."

CHAPTER 44

"Y ou've got to be kidding me," said Harvath. "All the top tier management? The PASC through the SES?"

It was Washington-speak for Presidential Appointed Senate Confirmed staff through Senior Executive Service staff.

"They're not sure it's all of them yet, but it's enough. And it's not just at Homeland Security."

"Let me guess," Harvath replied. "HHS, OPM, DOT, USAID, Treasury, the FCC, DOJ. What am I missing?"

Carlton filled in several others. "Department of State. Department of Defense. Department of the Interior, Agriculture, Commerce, Labor, Housing and Urban Development, DOE, FBI, the VA . . . It's everywhere."

"All of them have lost their upper management?"

"No. Some have, some haven't, but all are starting to report attrition up and down the chains. I just asked Nick to work up a spreadsheet."

"A *spreadsheet*?" Harvath replied, separating himself from Lara and standing up from the table. "We need him focused on digging into Main Core. Have Sloane work up your spreadsheet."

He hated throwing Ashby under the bus like that, but there was no reason why she couldn't sit in Harvath's study with the Old Man, keeping one eye on Mordechai, and using her other to build a spreadsheet.

Looking at Lara, he said, "Tell your parents to get packed. Winter clothes. Have them put together a bag for you and for Marco too. I'm sending a plane to Logan to pick them up. Do you have somebody who can get them to the airport?"

Lara nodded. "I can call someone from Boston PD."

"Good."

She wanted to discuss it further, but before she could find the right words, Harvath had already left the kitchen and was headed back down the hall to his study.

The first person he locked eyes with when he walked in was Mordechai. "Anything?"

The Israeli shook his head. "The password Helena provided for the hard drive doesn't work. I think Nicholas was correct. Damien has probably changed it since we made our copy."

"So where does that leave us?"

"We obviously need to talk to Helena."

Obviously, thought Harvath, but she was over an hour's drive away. "What about the cell phone?"

"At least there, we have good news. When Damien met with Linda Landon, we believe he gave her her own, private cell phone. In the process of getting her set up, he turned his on and entered his password. The keystroke recorder caught it."

"So you were able to open the mirror you have back in Israel?"

Mordechai nodded. "Unlike his laptop, Damien hasn't changed the password on his mystery phone."

"What does it contain?"

The man turned his laptop around so everyone could see the screen. It showed a map of the world with throbbing red dots in a number of countries. "The phones are part of a small, highly-encrypted digital network."

"Can you zoom the map onto the U.S.?"

The Israeli obliged, hovering just above a red dot near Winchester, Virginia, and another in the District of Columbia.

"Damien and Linda Landon."

"Your people should be able to confirm," he said, "but yes, that's who we believe we are looking at."

"And the other dots?" Harvath asked.

"If I had to put money on it," replied Mordechai, "I would guess the other phones represent the other members of Damien's Plenary Panel."

Harvath looked at Carlton who had already been tumbling the technicalities and diplomatic consequences in his mind.

"The good news," Carlton slowly stated, "is that the Agency has operatives in each one of these countries. The bad news is that the countries are all American allies."

"So what?"

"So, this isn't like taking out some jihadist, or rolling up a terror financier. This is a different ballgame, a completely different set of rules. We're talking about citizens of allied nations who are diplomats, ranking members of the UN."

It was the President's Pierre Damien argument all over again.

Looking at the Old Man he said, "Let's pass this phone data to Ryan and let the Agency decide what they want to do. At least it should help them ID the Plenary Panel."

"We're going to want to be involved with that too," Mordechai responded.

Of course they would. And at this point, that was fine by Harvath. The more hands on deck the better.

His bigger issue, though, was what to do next. With the President at Bethesda and the virus taking off, they needed a break—a big one.

He was tempted to ignore Porter's orders and go snatch Damien right now. Landon too. They didn't have time to sit around and hope that something turned in their favor.

Just before pulling into his driveway, Harvath had received a text from Ash. He and his team were on the ground in Kinshasa and had hooked up with the STAR team member Colonel White had assigned to them. They were already prepping for how they were going to hit the WHO lab there and recover the samples of Yusuf Mukulu, the mysterious Muslim man who had shown up and collapsed at the Matumaini Clinic.

Other STAR team members, based on the map coordinates Harvath had provided, were searching for the corpse of the rebel commander, while still more had met up with Jambo back in Bunia, in an attempt to track down Leonce and his son to get blood and tissue samples from them to confirm that all the cases were connected.

Even once those had been secured, they would need to be flown back for analysis. There was no telling what condition things would be in by then. USAMRIID was already examining samples secured from the CDC. Unlike in the movies, it took a long time to produce a vaccine. Scientists had been studying some viruses forever and there still were no effective vaccines for them. Harvath, though normally optimistic, wasn't very hopeful that USAMRIID would come up with something in time.

"Can we speak about Main Core?" Mordechai asked, interrupting Harvath's train of thought. "We all agree that this is likely what the *MC* in Damien's handwritten notes referred to?"

Harvath nodded. "Based on what Linda Landon was typing, yes."

"Back in Tel Aviv, no one thought Main Core actually existed. They believed it was just a conspiracy theory."

"Well, they were wrong," Nicholas interrupted as he padded back into the study along with his laptop and his two gigantic dogs.

"You're already in?" Harvath asked.

"Guess who doesn't change her passwords as often as Damien?" the little man asked as he tossed his computer onto the couch and climbed up after it.

"Linda Landon."

Nicholas smiled and set the computer on his lap.

"I still don't understand the purpose of this list," said Mordechai. "The United States keeps a list of its own dissidents? Doesn't this contradict your vaunted Constitutional principles?"

Harvath couldn't tell if it was a veiled shot, or a sincere question. He decided to give him the benefit of the doubt when Nicholas jumped in and spoke up.

"The Constitution has always been meant as a check on government power. Proponents of larger government have lamented that it enshrines a set of negative liberties, specifically by detailing what the government can't do to you, rather than what the government should do for you.

"The Founders envisioned a limited government, particularly on the Federal level, but over time it has grown—essentially into its own living, breathing organism, whose prime directive, if you will, is its own continuing survival. That's where Main Core comes in.

"The name comes from the fact that it was a database designed to

bring together disparate pieces of data from across the commercial, judicial, and law enforcement spectrums and fuse them into a main file, or
main core of information if you will. Importance was placed on that information that would help the government immediately track you down
if it wanted you.

"The data has evolved from credit card receipts and utility bills in the
1980s to social media relationships and cell phone location data today.
The government, under the guise of 'we'd never use it, but it's better to
have it and not need it than to need it and not have it,' has created several
different database systems that very clearly violate the country's Constitutional principles. Of those, Main Core is one of the most insidious."

"How does it work?"

"If a state of national emergency is declared, the Main Core database
can be activated. Within the database, citizens are ranked as to the level of
threat they are deemed to pose. Recommendations ranging from covertly
monitoring communications to apprehension accompany each name.
Citizens marked for apprehension are color-coded based on the danger
they are expected to pose the arrest team."

Nicholas's eyes met Harvath's and remained.

"What?"

"Your name's on the list."

"For what?"

The little man shrugged. "It doesn't say why. But somebody sees you
as a serious threat to national security in a time of crisis."

"That's ridiculous."

"Is it? How many Senators have you pissed off? How many members of Congress? How many intelligence officials? I'm not saying you
weren't right, I'm just saying you have pissed off a lot of people over the
years. Apparently, somebody took it very personally."

"So take my name off the list."

"I tried."

"Try again."

"I can't," said Nicholas.

"Why not?"

"Because it flagged your file and locked me out."

Harvath looked at him. "What's that mean?"

"I don't know."

"What do you mean you *don't know*?"

Nicholas was exasperated and embarrassed at the same time. "I tripped something, and suddenly I was swarmed."

"Swarmed by what?"

"I don't know, but they knew what they were doing. They were all over me. They were doing things I had never seen before. Not only were they trying to capture my information, they were trying to trap me so that I couldn't get out."

"Out of a database?" Harvath replied. "Why didn't you just kick the cord out of the wall?"

"Seriously?"

"Of course not, but you understand what I'm saying."

"And *you're* not understanding what *I'm* saying. I have never seen anything this sophisticated. Not with a bank, not with a military, and definitely not with a government."

Nicholas was upset, and Harvath couldn't remember ever seeing him like this.

"Relax," he said. "It's all going to be okay."

"I hope so."

"Hope so?" said Harvath. "You peeled off your name tag before you wandered into their database, right?"

"I always do. In fact I put on somebody else's."

Now it was Carlton's turn to chime in. Nicholas had a bad habit of where he chose to make it look like his hacks had originated from. "Where this time?"

"Second Director's office, FSB in Moscow."

The Old Man thought about it, jutted his bottom lip out, and then nodded. "I don't have a problem with that."

"Just as long as it doesn't link back to you," Harvath stated.

Nicholas didn't say anything.

"It's not going to link back to you, is it?"

"Normally, I'd say no. But these guys weren't normal. I don't know what to say."

Harvath looked at his watch and wondered if it was too early for a drink. He was starting to get a headache. Which reminded him, he needed to take his temperature again and text it to the doctor. Of all the stupid things to have to remember to do, this one took the cake, but the Old Man had insisted and had been riding him like a jockey about it.

Excusing himself, he exited the study and jogged upstairs to his master bath. Removing the thermometer from the drawer where he'd left it that morning, he pulled the cover off and popped it in his mouth. When it beeped, he pulled it out.

He was up just a little over a degree from where he had been. *Interesting*. But as it was just a degree, he wasn't going to worry about it.

Pulling his phone from his pocket, he texted his temp to the doc and put the thermometer away. After trading texts with Ben Beaman, he returned to the study.

When he came in, Mordechai was on his phone, standing on the other side of the room speaking intensely in Hebrew. Harvath looked over at Sloane who nodded at her own phone sitting nearby. She was recording. *Good*. He liked Mordechai, but you learned quickly in their business not to trust anyone.

The Israeli pulled the phone away from his ear and said to Harvath, "It's in Israel. Seventy-five cases and counting. Nine people have bled out, and we're hearing there may be two to three times as many in the West Bank and Gaza."

The Old Man, who was seated next to Nicholas on the couch, looked up from his laptop and stated, "It's popping up everywhere now. Indonesia, Australia, and New Zealand. India, Pakistan, and Bangladesh. Brazil, Argentina, and Paraguay."

"They're talking about shutting down commercial air travel," Nicholas added.

Probably a little late for that, Harvath thought as he walked over and pulled up a chair next to the Old Man.

"Can you give us a minute?" he asked.

"Sure," Nicholas replied as he set his laptop down and slid off the couch.

When he had left the study, Harvath leaned in toward the Old Man and said, "I have a jet leaving from Reagan tonight. I'd like you to be on it."

"Me?" Carlton replied. "Why would I want to do that?"

Harvath loved Reed Carlton like he was his father. And because he loved him so much, often the line between employer and employee got blurred. "I've arranged for Lara and her family to be taken someplace safe. I want you to go with them and make sure they're okay."

The Old Man chortled. "So you need me for security?"

Harvath didn't respond.

"Where are you sending them? Up to that fishing lodge in Alaska?"

Harvath shouldn't have been surprised, but he was.

"It's okay," Carlton said. "Your secret destination is safe with me."

"Except that apparently, it's not so secret."

The Old Man smiled. "I've been there."

"When?"

"Before we hired you, we did a thorough background. Jon and Anya provided character references." He said, leaning in toward Harvath. "They never told you, did they? Good. Trustworthy family. I like them even more now."

Typical Old Man, thought Harvath. Always at least five steps ahead of everyone else. "Excellent, I'll make sure they have your favorite bourbon on the plane."

"Whoa," Carlton replied, holding his hand up. "I'm not going to Alaska. In fact, I'm not going anywhere."

"But, sir—"

"No buts. There's too much work to be done here."

"Agreed, but you can work from the plane as well as from Alaska. Jon's lodge is practically a full-on SCIF."

The Old Man smiled. "If you've got something to say, why don't you say it?"

Harvath worshipped Reed Carlton. And while he didn't dwell on it, he lamented the day the Old Man would eventually pass. Carlton was not only an American treasure, but he was the Babe Ruth of the espionage game. In a world of soft, unsophisticated men trapped in perpetual adolescence, he was not only a man's man, he was a patriot who always put his nation before himself.

Pulling no punches, Harvath gave it to him straight. "Babies and old people, that's who disease grabs first."

"Are you saying I'm old?"

"Of course not. I'd never say that. How about *other* than young?"

"*Other* than young." Carlton chuckled at how Harvath had used Arabic phrasing to soften his remark.

"All expenses paid. You can take Marco fishing for salmon. If any bears show up, they'll go running the minute they see you, so I know he'll be safe. Everyone wins."

"Anya does grill the world's best steak."

"There you go," Harvath replied, encouraged. "You don't even need to pack. Let me know what you need, and I'll shoot a list to Jon. Everything will be waiting for you."

"Everything," Carlton said, "except for Joey."

Immediately, Harvath felt terrible. It was like a knife had just been punched through his heart.

"Joey" was Reed Carlton's wife, Josephine. Ten years before Harvath had met Carlton, she had suffered a massive stroke, followed by very serious dementia. Everything had been downhill from there.

Joey now lived in a comfortable assisted living facility in northern Virginia not far from the Carltons' home.

The man wasn't going to leave his bride, and it made Harvath love him all the more.

"What if I got her on the plane?"

Carlton smiled. "I don't know if I ever told you this, Scot, but you're a good man. I wish I could go, but I can't. And as there's no way we're going to uproot Joey and transfer her all the way to Alaska, let's just let it lie. Okay?"

No, it wasn't okay. Harvath wanted him on that plane.

The Old Man put his hand on his arm. "This isn't my first rodeo. If God had wanted to take me, He has had more than ample opportunity."

Harvath didn't like it, but he understood it, and smiled back. Carlton was integrity personified. *For better or worse*, that was the promise he had made. He was a man of his word, a man of honor—and Harvath admired him to no end.

"There's something else we need to talk about," the Old Man said, pointing at the laptop. "Before Nick got caught tampering with your file, he was able to take a brief look around the Main Core database. He took some screen shots. Apparently, there was a new list, created just over a month ago. I think you need to see it."

"Why? Who's on it?"

"I'll let Nick show you," said Carlton as the little man came back into the study, his mug filled with hot coffee.

Balancing the mug on the end table, he climbed back up onto the couch.

"Show Scot that last screen grab you showed me," the Old Man said.

Nicholas keyed in his password and then tilted the screen so Harvath could see it.

Seeing the first name, Harvath exclaimed, "That's the Chief Justice of the United States Supreme Court."

"Keep reading," Carlton advised.

"The next four are United States Senators, followed by a handful of Congress people. What the hell are they all doing on the list?"

"That's what I was wondering."

"I thought Main Core was for civilians. Why would you add all these people, and why now?" Harvath asked.

"Somebody, maybe Damien or Linda Landon, sees them as a threat. They've been color-coded for detention, *Gold*, same as you."

"But out of nine SCOTUS justices, why just the Chief Justice? I agree he's outspoken when it comes to limiting the scope of government power, but what about the other justices who vote with him the majority of the time? Why aren't they on the list?"

"And why only those particular Senators and Congresspeople?" the Old Man replied, answering a question with a question. "They're also outspoken, I'll give you that, but there are others who are just as loud."

None of it made any sense. *What the hell were Damien and Landon up to?*

"We need to warn them," said Harvath. "They need to know about the list and the fact that they're on it."

"Then what?"

"Then they can decide what they want to do. But at least they'll know something may be coming."

"Who's going to call them?" Carlton asked. "You? Me? And assuming we could track them down, why would they listen to either of us?"

He had a point. What's more, none of them was going to like hearing they were on the list. They would take it as an incredible affront and be out for scalps and political blood. What would stop them from calling their own contacts at the Department of Homeland Security and elsewhere in order to get to the bottom of it? It was a dangerous gamble that could result in Damien accelerating whatever else he might have planned.

"What if McGee called them?"

"The CIA Director?"

Harvath nodded. "He'll tell them it's a matter of national security and that they can't breathe a word of it to anyone."

"Okay," the Old Man said after thinking about it for a moment. "Let's shoot this information to him."

"I'm on it," said Nicholas, as he closed his laptop and prepared to return to his van.

As he slid down from the couch, Harvath heard his driveway alarm chime. Looking up at the TV, he saw Palmer coming onto the property. He was going to have a lot of supplies to unload.

"Do you need any help?" Carlton asked as Harvath stood up.

"No thanks," Harvath replied. "Why don't you bring Mordechai up to speed when he gets off his call."

Stepping into the hall, he caught up with Nicholas and said, "Hold on a second."

The little man turned. "What's up?"

"I have a private jet coming in tonight. I think you should put Nina on it. If you want to get on too, I'll understand. You can take the dogs with you."

"Alaska?"

Harvath nodded.

"And if I say no?"

"Then you're stuck with me."

The little man smiled. "I like those odds."

Harvath smiled back. There was a time where Nicholas would have already fled, concerned only for himself. Regardless of what Mordechai or anyone else thought, Harvath knew a leopard could change its spots. He had seen it with his own eyes.

"Call Nina," he said. "Get her packed. We'll send somebody to pick her up."

Nicholas extended his small hand. "Thank you. I'll feel better knowing she's safe."

Watching the little man walk away, Harvath felt the weight of the world on his shoulders. Safe didn't exist anymore—not when it came to a virus. They could hole up in the middle of nowhere, but would they really be safe?

As far as Harvath was concerned, safe was a lie. All it did was make people feel better. He didn't want to be safe from the virus, he wanted to stop the virus.

Multiple plans of action had been pinging inside his brain, vying for attention. None of them were good. All of them were dangerous and outside the rule of law. They fell into only two categories—bad and worse—and the President would have said no to all of them.

The President, though, was in the hospital, and a tsunami was about to hit the beach. There was only one course of action Harvath could take.

CHAPTER 45

Pierre Damien stood at the edge of the pool in all of his naked glory. "Very handsome," Helena stated. "Can you turn for the judges, please? Let's see what fills out the back of those jeans."

Smiling, he dove into the illuminated water with a powerful splash.

His muscular arms rose like shark's fins as he raced toward the glorious, naked woman at the other end.

Stroke after stroke, he pulled himself toward her, getting more aroused the closer he came. He couldn't wait to ravish her.

She was lounging in the shallow end, and the water barely covered her breasts. Their time together was growing short. He was amazing, and she was going to miss him, but she vowed to think happy thoughts every time she reflected upon her bank balance.

Coming to a stop just in front of her, he stood.

For all of the crappy assignments the Mossad had ever given her, at least this last one had been halfway decent.

Reaching for him, she pulled him close and smiled. Pierre was in rare form. He hadn't had much to drink, yet. He was still tipsy from lunch, but not much. He wanted to make love, and they would. Probably twice.

He had been good to her, but he was also a monster. What he had planned for mankind was beyond horrible. She was beyond caring, though. She had lost that ability a long time ago. Life was cruel. If it ever gave you an opportunity, you took it. You made something of it or you didn't.

Once she had pieced together the extent of Damien's plans, she had made a personal decision. She would ride out the storm with him.

He not only knew what was coming, but how bad it was going to get, and had prepared accordingly. She had been trading her body for so long, what was a little longer? It was about survival, as it always had been. Damien cared for her and she would use that to her advantage.

Wrapping her in his arms, he crushed her against his chest as they kissed. She felt warm all over, even as he had lifted her halfway out of the pool, exposing her to the crisp, autumn air.

Momentarily, she broke from his kiss. "Pool house or guest house?" she asked, a naughty smile on her face.

"Right here," Damien said, placing her fully onto the edge of the pool. "Alfresco."

This was how she was going to remember him—passionate, powerful, tender. He had always treated her with kindness, with respect. He had treated her like a lady. There had been many bad men in her life, but Damien wasn't one of them. She would never forget that.

Wrapping her arms around him now, she tried to burn a snapshot in her mind—the pool, the house, the breeze on her damp skin, the sound of Wilhelmenia Fernandez singing *La Wally* from the terrace speakers.

She didn't want to forget any of it. She wanted to always remember both how well he had treated her, and how much she had actually enjoyed her assignment. How it hadn't even seemed like an assignment. How she had given herself freely to him.

Her only regret was that he would never know her—not the real her—and what her life had been. Not that it mattered. Without that life, without the Mossad, she and Damien never would have been drawn together.

All that mattered was that Bentzi and his people, his precious Israel, wanted him. That was what Bentzi cared about. It was all that he ever cared about. And Bentzi would do whatever he had to, including using her, to achieve Israel's goals.

It was why she had kept Damien's passwords for herself. She didn't care if the Mossad was ever able to access the hard drive they had back in Tel Aviv. That wasn't her fight. It had never been her fight.

Bentzi and Israel had used her, repeatedly. And in planning her exit, she had found a way to not only secure reparations for herself, but to stick it to the Mossad and everyone else in the process.

She had been an innocent, a good, young woman with her whole life in front of her. Israel could have done the right thing, it should have done the right thing. But it didn't. Instead of freeing her, returning her home, it kept her in bondage. All they did for her was upgrade her shackles.

They might come after her someday, if there was even an Israel left. It was a possibility. What was a certainty was that they would eventually come after Damien. Though Bentzi hadn't admitted it, she knew that they were thinking of killing him.

It was the biggest reason why she couldn't stay with him indefinitely. Men like Pierre Damien were incapable of disappearing.

She, on the other hand, *could* disappear. Like so many other things in life, it all came down to money.

Once she had captured the code to Damien's safe in Geneva, the password to his computer soon followed.

He kept everything on his laptop. A multitude of the files were also password protected, but patience proved to be its own reward. It was like having the keys to a palace in which locked doors and room after room contained some sort of secret or piles of treasure.

The most important thing she was able to ascertain was how to obtain immunity against the disease that was going to sweep the globe. As long as she survived the tumult and chaos in the immediate aftermath, the rest of her life would be hers to do with as she wished.

She quietly reached out to her parents and explained what they needed to do. Her father, always so stubborn and simpleminded, refused to believe her, instead calling it a grand conspiracy cooked up by the Jews. There was no circumventing his bigotry. She begged her mother to heed her advice and work on convincing her father. If he perished, it would be his fault, not Israel's.

With her health and that of her family addressed, she began to dig into the information on Damien's computer.

Knowing the financial markets were going to collapse, he had taken a series of positions in order to profit from the calamity. Some were so esoteric that she dismissed them out of hand. Others were quite simple, and those were the ones she focused on.

But like his passwords, many of Damien's financial bets kept changing. It made it very difficult to keep up.

She established a relationship with a Zurich-based trading firm with offices in Geneva. Upon setting up her account, they provided access to their proprietary app that would allow her to get real-time market info, establish trades, and conduct business with their banking division. It was like having a miniature Swiss banker in her purse or pocket at all times.

But the most interesting thing of all on Damien's laptop were his journals.

He had begun them shortly after his wife had passed away as a form of therapy, and had kept them going ever since. The insights deep into his mind and his soul were both fascinating and disturbing.

The transformation of a grief-stricken widower to a man determined to bring about the greatest holocaust in human history was riveting. And the closer the deadly event came, the more Damien's confidence grew.

In his most recent entries, it was as if he knew his diaries would be read and dissected by posterity. He was standing at a pivotal moment in time, calmly laying out his case, explaining what steps needed to be taken, and why. They were quite literally brilliant and mad at the same time.

If history had any sense of decency, it would see Damien through the lens of his macabre devotion to eugenics—his belief that if not for the "overkindness" of the Western world, entire strains of "inferior" lines would have been allowed to die off, releasing pressure upon the planet and its limited resources.

The journals stood in sharp contrast to the man whose bed she so often shared. She had never heard him say a disparaging word about any group or class of people. In fact, he had always seemed devoted to helping those in the greatest need. It was an unsettling dichotomy that made it feel as if a completely different person had written the journals. But there was one thing in particular about them that betrayed his hand—his love of birds.

From the golden faucet knobs shaped like swans on his jet, to the original Audubons hanging in the apartment in Geneva, she had not been surprised to see him reference birds in his journals, but it was the manner in which he had that was so unsettling.

Each phase in the plan he had created was named after a specific type of bird. The Congo phase was named after the Crow, while the American phase was named after the Hummingbird. It was the Hummingbird reference that she found the most disturbing of all.

While he professed a love for the bird, he also admitted—while intellectually patting himself on the back—a nod to a dark event that had taken place in 1934.

Known as the Night of the Long Knives, or the *Röhm-Putsch*, it was a political purge, a three-day killing spree where Adolf Hitler's SS and Gestapo were said to have killed hundreds and arrested thousands of his enemies in order to consolidate power. The code name they had adopted was Operation Hummingbird, the same name Damien would adopt almost a century later.

Helena knew that was why he had poured the 1934 sauternes for his dinner guests the other night. She had found the empty bottle in the kitchen trash. Dates mattered to Damien. It was why he had brought the bottles from 1978 to lunch. Wine was his portal to history, both good history and bad.

· · ·

After making love, they grabbed their thick white robes from where they had left them on the chairs. She took her phone from the pocket, wanting to capture a picture of him, but Damien was famished and hurried them inside.

A tray of charcuterie, his favorite snack, was already waiting for them in the TV room along with a decanted red wine.

Damien held up the bottle and showed it to her. "Romanée-Conti," he said. "Nineteen forty-five."

"The last year of World War II," she replied.

"And the founding of the United Nations. From fifty-one original member states to a hundred ninety-three today."

He poured glasses for both of them. After admiring the color, the aromas, and the bouquet, he lifted his glass and recited a UN motto, "To peace and security."

She met his glass with her own. "To peace and security."

It was another outstanding wine. After taking a sip, she set it down on the table and prepared two plates.

Jeffery had laid out a stunning array of pâtés, terrines, prosciutto, dry sausage, salami, and cheeses. There were three different kinds of breads, pickled vegetables, mustard, olive tapenade, nuts, and fruits.

While she worked on the plates, Damien turned on the TV. On almost every channel, there were scenes of reporters in front of various hospitals.

"What's going on?" she asked.

"I'm not sure," Damien responded. He was as good a liar as she was.

Handing him his plate, she sat down on the couch next to him and tucked her feet underneath her to keep them warm. Damien turned up the volume.

". . . a virus public health officials are likening to Ebola," the newscaster said. "Tonight we have team coverage across the country. We begin in the nation's capital."

The pair sat there watching as reporters at hospitals coast to coast tried to put together the breaking story from the pieces of information that were beginning to stream in.

After a while, Damien muted the TV and reached for more wine.

"So," Helena said. "Looks like it's not a meteor after all."

Damien smiled. "We'll be okay. Don't worry."

She was about to respond when Jeffery appeared in the doorway and asked to speak with Pierre. Damien waved him in, but Jeffery requested he step out into the hallway.

Damien excused himself as he stood up and walked across the room. As soon as he stepped into the hall, Jeffery began speaking and reached to pull the door closed, cutting her out of the conversation.

As he did, she noticed pieces of something in his other hand, and her heart leapt into her throat.

Jeffery not only had her cell phone charger, but he had completely disassembled it.

CHAPTER 46

There was a small substructure beneath the church that Harvath had retrofitted to securely hold his weapons and equipment. He and Palmer had already unloaded half of the new supplies into the house. The rest had taken several trips and were being hidden down there.

They were in the process of deciding what should go where, when they heard people descending the stairs.

Harvath looked out the door to see Ashby, followed by Mordechai.

"I think you're going to want to hear this," she said.

Stepping around her, Mordechai extended his cell phone.

Harvath took it, and, seeing that a video was cued up, pressed *play*.

There were sounds of a struggle. Then there was the sound of breaking glass, followed by a woman's voice screaming, "Pierre! Stop! I don't know what you're talking about!"

Harvath looked at Mordechai. "Helena?"

The Israeli nodded. "Her cell phone has a distress app. When it's activated, it records a few seconds of video, and then attaches it to an S.O.S. email along with a GPS location."

"There really wasn't any video. Only audio."

"The phone must have been in her purse or a pocket. The point is, she knows that distress app is only to be used in a life-or-death situation. She's been compromised. We have to get her out, *now*."

Harvath had already made up his mind about Damien, but there were other pieces he wanted to put in place before he moved. Helena's distress call, though, had just trumped all of that. As soon as Damien figured out who she was, and how badly he had been penetrated, he was going to take off. They needed to move, fast.

"I'm going to fill Carlton in," he said to Palmer. "Prep a platform for Mr. Mordechai and then stage everything in the driveway along with my kit." Looking at Ashby, he added, "Gather up whatever else you two need and add it to the pile. Night vision, suppressors, all of it. I want to be out of here in five minutes."

"Roger that," she replied, as Palmer flashed him the thumbs-up.

"We're driving?" Mordechai exclaimed as they moved quickly up the stairs. "It'll take us at least an hour to get there."

"Don't worry. We're not driving," Harvath said.

He knew how important time was. They needed to make every second count, and not just in order to grab Damien.

Only twice in his career had Harvath hit the panic button as it was sometimes called. Both times, he was reluctant to do it and waited too long. It meant your op was over, unrecoverable, and you needed immediate extraction. It was one of the hardest things in the world to admit.

The first time he had done it, help had arrived quickly, and he survived. The second time, though, he nearly lost his life. He knew what it was like not knowing if anyone would come—not knowing if you were going to live or die.

That said, there were a lot of questions about how loyal Mordechai's asset was, especially in light of the numerous deletions she had made on the memory card. For all he knew, they might be walking into some sort of a trap. It was an option they all needed to consider.

Hitting the top of the stairs, Harvath pulled out his cell phone and pressed the speed dial key for Lydia Ryan.

"We received the email from Nicholas and we're already working on it," she said as she picked up.

"That's not why I'm calling. I need a helicopter. Mordechai's asset has been blown. If Damien runs, we're going to lose him."

"Are you looking to extract Helena, or grab Damien?"

"Both."

"Does the President know?"

"Exigent circumstances. I'm making a command decision."

Ryan knew it was pointless to argue with him. "We don't have any helicopters available."

"What? Why not?"

"Everyone Director McGee has been able to contact from that Main Core VIP list has been offered protection. They and their families are being picked up and flown to The Farm. No one is getting on that base without the Director's say-so."

Moving them to The Farm—the CIA's clandestine training facility at Camp Peary—was a smart move. The fact that the Agency's helicopters were all tied up, though, presented a real problem.

"I need you to find me *something*," said Harvath. "I don't care what kind. Just call me when you have it."

"Who else can you call?" Mordechai asked as Harvath hung up.

"She'll find one for us. Don't worry."

"We have to get to Helena. We have to leave now."

"I understand," Harvath replied. "Go find Nicholas. Tell him what we're doing, and tell him we need the eagle."

"The *eagle*?"

"That's what we named our drone. We thought Liberty would be too ironic," he said. "Hurry up. Helo or no helo, we're out of here in five."

While Mordechai headed for the front door and the driveway, Harvath made a beeline for his study. It was empty, and so he headed for the kitchen.

He found Carlton, a fresh mug of coffee in his hand, staring at the TV.

"It's on every channel," the Old Man said. "They're beginning to link up all of the cases."

"We've got bigger problems. Mordechai's asset has been blown. She just hit the panic button."

"That means Damien is going to go to ground."

"Not if we can get to him first," Harvath replied. "I called Ryan for a helo, but they're tied up evacuating the Main Core VIPs and their families to The Farm. She's going to try to find us something else."

"And in the meantime?"

"In the meantime, I need you to stay here with Lara. If I'm not back in time, I need you to get her to the airport and get her on that plane. Beaman has all the details."

Carlton looked at his watch and then back at him. "Anything else?"

"I want you to take whatever you need from here, it doesn't matter what it is—food, water, fuel, whatever you want, and then get to Josephine."

"What are you going to do?"

"I don't know. Everything depends on Damien. Where's Lara?"

"Packing."

Harvath placed his hand on the Old Man's shoulder as he walked past and headed for the stairs. He found Lara in the master bedroom.

"I've got to go," he said from the doorway.

"Are you coming back?"

"I don't know. Reed is downstairs. He's going to make sure you get to the airport if I don't get back in time."

"So, is this goodbye?"

"For now," Harvath replied, stepping into the room.

Lara met him halfway and wrapped her arms around him. "Come back to me."

"I will," he replied. And then, giving her a quick kiss, he turned and left the room.

Outside, he found Palmer, Ashby, and Mordechai waiting for him with the gear. He did a fast inventory to make sure everything was there.

Because he was going to need to work the phone and plan the op, he said to Palmer, "I want you to drive. Let's load everything in your truck."

"Now we're driving?" Mordechai asked, the frustration evident in his voice.

"It's the best I can—"

"You've got Damien's estate under surveillance. Can't you send that team in?"

Harvath motioned for Palmer and Ashby to get to work and drew the Israeli aside. "The team at Damien's are not operators, Bentzi. They're surveillance personnel. If they try to go in there, they'll not only get themselves killed, they're going to get Helena killed too. Help me load the truck. We're wasting time."

Once the vehicle was loaded, he had Palmer drive so he could work

his phone and plan the operation. Ashby and Mordechai sat in the seats
behind them.

Traffic was a nightmare as panicked people rushed to get home. They
switched to the shoulder, but it soon became a de facto lane and their
progress slowed to a crawl.

"Get off," Harvath instructed.

"You want to use interior roads?" Palmer asked.

"I don't care what we use. Just get us the hell off this highway."

Harvath was pissed off and growing angrier by the moment. He didn't
need to turn around and look at Mordechai. He could only imagine what
he was going through.

As they finally got far enough over to take a ramp, Harvath's phone
rang. "Tell me you have good news," he said.

"Where are you?" Ryan replied.

Harvath looked at the GPS, confirmed with a mile marker, and relayed their position.

"I've got a bird for you. There's a helipad at the Reston Hospital Center. I can have him there in ten minutes."

"Do it," said Harvath, who then turned to Palmer and gave him their
new destination.

• • •

When they arrived at the Reston Hospital Center, the all-blue MD 600N
helicopter was already waiting, its rotors hot.

It looked like a stretch version of the military's Little Bird attack helicopter. It boasted a turbine-engine and an advanced anti-torque system
that allowed it to fly high, fast, and quiet, three features Harvath and his
team needed.

While the others quickly loaded their gear, Palmer parked the SUV
and ran back to the helipad. Once he was on board, the pilot took off.

Harvath sat second seat and scanned the electronic tablet the pilot had
handed him. It had a satellite link that allowed him to connect to several
different mapping services in order to select the best place to land. The
closer they were to Damien's home, the greater chance the helicopter's
approach would be overheard.

He selected a large pasture at a nearby farm and gave the pilot the co-ordinates. Over his headset, he asked Ashby to pull his satellite phone from his backpack and call the surveillance team on site. He wanted one of them to remain in position and keep eyes on the estate while the other used their vehicle to come pick them up when they landed.

Twenty minutes later, the pilot dropped down to the tree level before turning on his searchlight and scanning the landing area for any obstructions.

After touching down, he shut the engine off and then helped the team unload. Sitting on the grass a hundred yards away, their ride was already waiting. Palmer gave the driver two quick bursts from his flashlight and the black SUV rolled forward.

Harvath provided the helicopter pilot with a radio and, after conducting a quick comms check, grabbed his backpack and walked over to the SUV.

Palmer, Ashby, and Mordechai were already doing a final equipment check.

Harvath watched as the Israeli had a hard time with his hands racking the slide on his Glock.

"You going to be okay?" Harvath asked.

"I'll be fine," the man snapped, uncomfortable at having his abilities questioned.

Harvath extended his hand and Mordechai handed over the pistol. Racking the slide, Harvath then handed it back.

"*Toda*," the Israeli said. *Thank you*.

"*Ein be'ad ma.*"

As the team continued to prepare, Harvath asked the surveillance operative for any updates and they discussed the best way to approach.

According to the operative, nothing had changed since Damien and the woman had returned from lunch with their security detail. There were two men posted at the gatehouse at the bottom of the drive. And that was all they could see. Neither the main house nor any of the other buildings were visible from the street.

There was an access road that ran almost parallel up the adjoining property. Harvath had brought a pair of bolt cutters to get them through the gate.

As soon as Ashby had the drone assembled, he did one last check to make sure everyone was ready and then told her to launch it.

Stepping away from the SUV, she brought her arm back and then sent the drone sailing into the air.

"Eagle's away," she said over the bone microphone in her ear.

Via the drone's remote control unit, Palmer had it fly two wide circles above the pasture while he tested its responsiveness as well as the feed from its infrared camera.

"Moonracer," he then said, using Nicholas's call sign, "Eagle is ready when you are."

"Roger that," Nicholas replied from his van back at Harvath's. Clicking several keys, he then toggled the joystick in front of his monitor for several seconds. Once he was satisfied, he said, "Moonracer has the Eagle. You are good to go."

Harvath watched as the drone disappeared into the night sky toward Pierre Damien's estate. Once it was gone, he gave the command to mount up.

As they climbed into the vehicle, he said a silent prayer that they had made it on time.

Something told him, though, that not only had they not been fast enough, but that they were all going to pay for it.

CHAPTER 47

H arvath's trepidation grew with Nicholas's first SITREP.

Based on the drone's IR camera, Damien had drastically reduced his security footprint. The night of the dinner party, the drone had picked up at least twelve figures standing guard around the property. Now, all it was seeing was five. Maybe they had put on extra guards during the dinner. Either way, Harvath didn't like it. It seemed too light. There had to be more of them somewhere.

Rolling up the dirt road, they stopped only long enough to let Palmer bail out with his gear and head into the trees. There was a piece of high ground with an excellent view of the main house and surrounding buildings. If he could make it there, he'd be in a position to offer the team good protection.

The black SUV kept moving until it got to the top of the road and stopped once again. This was as far as it could take them. Harvath, Ashby, and Mordechai would go the rest of the way on foot.

Once out of the vehicle, Harvath radioed Nicholas for an additional SITREP. Nothing had changed. Stepping into the tree line, they moved toward the edge of the property and waited for Palmer to get into place. He had the harder trek because it required him to cross a wide expanse of terrain with no cover. If he got caught out in the open, he would be cut down.

Nicholas, though, was doing everything he could to make sure that didn't happen. The drone had become a game changer for all their operations. As it flew quietly overhead, you would have had to have known it was on station and be actively looking for it to have had any chance of ever finding it.

Once Palmer was tucked in behind Harvath's LaRue PredatOBR rifle with its HISS-XLR extended long-range thermal weapon sight and Surefire SOCOM suppressor, he radioed his status to the team. The operation was ready to go to the next phase.

Using hand signals, Harvath directed Ashby and Mordechai to follow him. They wore night vision goggles and carried suppressed H&K submachine guns—Harvath and Ashby the MP7A2, Mordechai the MP5SD.

They stayed in the trees, treading lightly upon the blanket of twigs, branches, and fallen leaves. Harvath moved slowly, purposefully. Part of it was his training; part of it was that he still had visions of the trip wire and crude rebel antipersonnel device he had almost triggered in Congo. He kept his eyes open and his senses alert.

When they arrived parallel to the farm buildings, they stopped and Harvath quietly radioed for another report. Nicholas replied that there was some sort of activity now at the rear of the main house. Two armed men appeared to be loading a truck. The ground in between, though, was all clear.

Once again, Harvath signaled his team to move forward.

It had been decided to cut onto the property at this point, in order to avoid the livestock pens. They didn't want to spook any of the animals and raise the alarm. Stepping out of the trees, they crossed the open ground quickly and pressed themselves up against the metal skin of an outbuilding. Two hundred yards away, they could see the manor house. None of its lights were on. The guesthouse just beyond it was also dark.

Harvath chose their next position of concealment and signaled for Ashby to head for it while he covered her. Then he sent Mordechai. When Ashby signaled that she was ready to cover him, he followed.

Structure by structure, they moved ever closer to the house until they could hear the sounds of men loading the truck in back.

According to Nicholas, two more armed men had just joined the party. They were loading supplies into the truck, utilizing a service entrance through the hillside beneath the house.

Thirty yards away was a stack of discarded pallets. They were halfway behind the house and would not only provide concealment, but looked like they would provide an excellent line of sight as well.

Harvath's only problem was that if bullets started flying, it would be like hiding behind a wall of toothpicks. Unfortunately, they didn't have any choice. After scanning the area, Harvath sent Ashby running toward it.

As soon as she was there, she took a moment to look around and then waved Mordechai over. Once he was in place, it was Harvath's turn.

Joining them behind the pallets, Harvath dropped to the prone position and tried to peer through the jumble of slats to see what was happening at the truck. All he could see were tires, a bit of the undercarriage, and light spilling from the entrance. As he prepared to roll over onto his left side and peek around the pile, they heard a woman's scream from somewhere inside the tunnel.

Mordechai tried to leap to his feet, but Ashby was faster. Grabbing hold of him, she yanked him back down.

"Let go of me," he whispered. "We have to move, *now*."

Placing her index finger against her lips, she warned him to be quiet.

Harvath waited until Mordechai had calmed down, and then rolled out from behind the pallets onto his left side.

Boxes had been stacked five high and three deep near the entrance. What was in them, though, he had no idea.

He was preparing to roll out a little bit more when he heard a voice from behind.

"Stop!" the man shouted.

Harvath looked over his shoulder just in time to see the man—one of Damien's security detail—take a round through his head courtesy of Chase Palmer.

There was a spray of blood, bone, and brain matter. It was one hell of a way to start a gunfight.

The man's shout immediately drew the attention of his colleagues back by the truck, who swung their weapons around on their slings and brought them up to fire. Harvath and Ashby, though, were faster.

Their shots happened in unison. There was a quick *pop*, followed by an even faster *pop, pop*. One shot to the head, two to the chest, and each man fell to the ground.

"Move, move, move," Harvath ordered as he jumped to his feet and the team advanced on the truck.

When another one of the security agents stuck his head out of the entrance, they showered him with rounds.

As soon as they got to the truck, Harvath and Ashby took cover, but Mordechai kept going. Harvath yelled for him to stop, but he didn't listen.

Charging the service entrance, he stepped off his line of attack, just in time to miss a hail of bullets that came whizzing past. When the same shooter as before peeked back out, Mordechai was ready for him and took him down with shots through his mouth and left eye. What he wasn't ready for was the man's colleague.

Mordechai was moving too fast. He couldn't keep his balance and bring his weapon to bear. He tried to pivot, but as he did, he stumbled and went down hard. It was all the advantage the shooter needed.

Sweeping his weapon down toward the fallen Israeli, the security operative began to apply pressure to his trigger. As he did, his head and chest exploded when Harvath stepped out from behind the truck and double-tapped him.

Ashby raced forward to guard the entrance as Harvath helped Mordechai off the ground.

"Are you okay? Can you fight?"

The Israeli nodded and got to his feet.

"Don't do that again," Harvath admonished. "Stick with the plan."

Before Mordechai could respond, they heard Nicholas's voice over the radio. "You're about to have company. The guards from the front gate are headed your way, fast. They're in an open-air side-by-side."

Harvath wasn't surprised. They had heard the gunfire or someone had called down for reinforcements.

Hailing Palmer, he asked, "Do you see them yet?"

"No, not yet. Stand by."

Seconds later, Palmer said, "I've got them."

"Take the shot."

Exhaling, he pressed his trigger and then acquiring his second target placed his TReMoR reticle on Number Two's head and pressed the trigger again.

As he watched the side-by-side career off the drive and slam into a tree, he said over the radio, "All clear. You're good to go."

"Let's move," said Harvath.

The tunnel had a vaulted ceiling and was paved with bricks in a herringbone pattern. Along the walls were sconces that resembled lanterns and which dimly lit the passage via natural gas.

Up ahead was a hand truck that had been abandoned, ostensibly by one of the two dead men at the entrance who had rushed to the fight. On it were three cases of military meals-ready-to-eat, atop two cases of French wine. Either Damien's people were cleaning him out, or packing him up. Regardless, someone had decided to bug out.

Harvath hated tunnels. They were death traps for a whole host of reasons, not the least of which was the lack of cover and the fact that they funneled bullets right at you. He moved Ashby and Mordechai forward as quickly as he could.

At the end of the passageway was a staircase with a door on either side. The door on the right had a heavy lock on it, but had been left ajar. Harvath signaled for Ashby to join him and for Mordechai to move to the side and watch their backs in case anyone came down the passage.

Pressed up against the brick wall, Harvath counted down from three and then used the toe of his boot to nudge the door the rest of the way open. With their weapons up and ready, they button-hooked into the room.

It was a long storeroom, stacked floor to ceiling with shelving. In addition to cases of wine and MREs, there were enormous cans of vegetables, fruit, soup, and stew. There was coffee, cleaning products, toilet paper, and soap. Batteries, lightbulbs, flashlights, and glow sticks took up shelf after shelf, while vitamins, medical supplies, sleeping bags, and bottled water took up still more. It was like walking into a wholesale warehouse club.

Carefully, they moved up and down the narrow aisles and then explored two walk-in freezers. There was a ton of food, but no people. Wherever the scream had come from, it hadn't been here.

Harvath was about to radio Mordechai that they were coming out, when he heard what sounded like a door being kicked in, followed by the sound of gunfire.

Shit, the Israeli had hit the other room by himself!

Retreating from the storeroom, Harvath and Ashby raced to join Mordechai, who had gone through the other door so hard, he had knocked it halfway off its hinges.

The sound of gunfire reverberating through the brick passageway was deafening.

When he leaned against the wall, only a sliver of the other room was visible through the doorway, but it was enough. Harvath could see that Mordechai had been shot and was pinned down behind a workbench of some sort.

The shots kept coming, one after another. Whoever it was, they weren't going to stop until they killed him.

Reaching for the grab tab on his vest, he pulled out a flashbang and held it so Ashby could see it and know what he was about to do. As soon as she nodded, he pulled the pin and tossed it into the room.

There was a brilliant white flash and a concussive *boom*!

Harvath and Ashby swept into the room. The instant he saw the shooter, he fired.

Two rounds hit center mass right around the man's sternum. Two additional rounds penetrated just beneath the man's nose and another at the bridge of his nose between his eyes. His weapon clattered to the floor along with his lifeless body.

Harvath and Ashby ignored Mordechai and kept moving through the room looking for threats.

It was a mechanical room with an old-fashioned boiler and plenty of pipes and other pieces of equipment to hide behind. Near the furnace, they found Helena.

She was naked and had been badly beaten. She was lying atop an old mattress, with both eyes swollen shut, and handcuffed to the wall. There was a soldering iron nearby and her body showed a myriad of burn marks.

After clearing the rest of the room, Ashby rushed to assist Helena while Harvath moved to help Mordechai.

"How bad?" he asked, as he moved him into a sitting position.

"Did you find Helena?"

"We found her. She's alive. Sloane's with her."

"I need to see her," the Israeli replied.

"In a minute. How bad are you hit?"

"I can't move my left arm."

Harvath radioed for Chase as he tore Mordechai's shirt open and examined his wounds. He had taken two rounds to his shoulder, one of them shattering his clavicle.

Opening a dressing, he laid it against his shoulder and placed Bentzi's right hand against it to help apply pressure. The man winced from the pain.

"You took two rounds," said Harvath. "Your collarbone is broken. I know it hurts, but we need to stop the bleeding."

When Chase appeared in the doorway, Harvath told him to swap his LaRue for Mordechai's smaller MP5. They needed to clear the rest of the house. If Damien was here, Harvath would find him.

After double-checking that Bentzi's Glock had a round in the chamber, Harvath set the pistol in the man's lap.

"If anyone other than us comes through that door," he said, "shoot them."

With that, he and Palmer headed for the stairs.

CHAPTER 48

Harvath and Palmer cleared the entire house. There was no one there. It was the same for the pool house, guesthouse, and other outbuildings. Damien and the rest of his security people had gone. But gone where?

They searched the bodies of the dead security operatives—all of whom were foreign nationals carrying blue, UN-issued Laissez-Passer passports. There was nothing on them, not even on their phones, indicating where Damien was. The truck was devoid of clues as well—no slip of paper with an address, no map with a circle on it, no preprogrammed GPS with a destination for the supplies.

Fetching a box of glow sticks from the storeroom, Harvath gave them to Palmer and sent him out to mark an LZ for the helicopter. After radioing the pilot, he then returned to the mechanical room.

Mordechai sat on the floor next to Helena, attempting to comfort her. They both looked terrible.

"Helicopter is on its way," said Harvath. "We're going to get you out of here."

Ashby had fashioned a sling for the Israeli, and after uncuffing Helena, had found a painter's cloth for her to cover herself with.

She pulled Harvath out of earshot and said, "Not only did they beat and torture her, but I'm pretty sure Damien's men raped her too."

Harvath shook his head. *Animals.* "Can she talk?"

"I haven't heard anything, but I think she's in shock. Her jaw may be broken as well."

"We need to know where Damien went."

"You can ask her, but I don't think you're going to get anything. You should give her a little time."

"I wish we had it," Harvath replied.

Gently, he approached Helena and Mordechai and explained that he needed to know what happened and where Damien went. Helena didn't reply. Mordechai tried some delicate coaxing, but she just closed her eyes. Harvath let it go.

Stepping outside, he helped Palmer collect the bodies. The side-by-side was still operable, and so they used that, stacking the corpses like cordwood and then hiding the vehicle in one of the outbuildings.

By the time they returned to the entrance of the passageway, they could already hear the helicopter approaching.

Palmer helped Mordechai and Harvath thought it better, given what had happened, that Ashby assist Helena. Though they moved slowly, they were at least both ambulatory.

Nicholas radioed that he wasn't picking up any additional heat signatures anywhere on the property, and that it looked safe to land. He made sure to keep the drone out of the helicopter's path.

When the helo touched down, Harvath stood guard until everyone was on board and then he joined them. The surveillance team would recover the drone.

The pilot lifted off fast, banking and taking several evasive maneuvers just in case there was a gunman, or worse, hidden somewhere out there in the darkness.

The torque was obviously painful for Helena and Mordechai, but neither of them complained.

As soon as they cleared Damien's estate, the pilot raced toward the Reston Hospital Center.

Looking down, Harvath could see that the traffic was still terrible. He had some decisions to make.

The first had to do with Mordechai and Helena. They couldn't go to a regular hospital. Not with his gunshot wounds and her trauma, and not with the virus spreading. There was only one option.

Asking Ashby to hand him the sat phone from his bag, Harvath called Lydia Ryan.

"Agreed," he said, after explaining the situation to her and listening to her response. "You'll have that relayed to the pilot?"

When Ryan said she would, Harvath thanked her, put his headset back on, and handed the phone back to Ashby.

"What's the plan?" she asked.

"We're dropping you and Chase in Reston to pick up his vehicle. The pilot will drop me at my place, and then he'll fly Helena and Mr. Mordechai to The Farm for medical treatment. Lydia Ryan is already there waiting for them."

"Once we have Chase's truck, what do you want us to do?"

"Since you'll be in Reston, you might as well go to the office," said Harvath. "Get a shower, get changed, and start figuring out how the hell we're going to find Damien."

"Roger that," she replied.

• • •

When the helicopter landed in his front yard, Harvath grabbed his gear and hopped out. He would have just enough time to toss everything inside, take a quick shower, and grab something to eat. He was worried about getting Lara safely to her plane, and wanted to do it himself.

He found Lara and the Old Man seated at the kitchen table watching the news. They both had plates of Arroz Carreteiro in front of them, but neither was eating.

"What's going on?" Harvath asked.

"Someone talked," Carlton replied. "The entire world now knows that the President is under observation at Bethesda."

"Are they saying he's sick? Have we gotten any classified updates?"

"Publically, they're downplaying it."

"And privately?"

The Old Man didn't respond.

Harvath looked at him. "He's got it? African Hemorrhagic Fever?"

Carlton nodded.

"My God. How long does he have?"

"They don't know. You know how fast this thing moves. It could be hours, it could be days."

"Or he could beat it."

"I think we better get ready for what happens if he doesn't," said Carlton.

"And the Vice President?"

"They've already invoked the Twenty-fifth Amendment. He's going to address the nation shortly."

"This is bad," Harvath replied.

"Any idea where Damien is?"

Harvath shook his head. "None. They worked Helena over real bad. Whatever information she gave up was enough to spook Damien into taking off. Speaking of which, we're watching his plane, correct?"

The Old Man nodded. "And I've put a team on his pilots as well."

"Good. I told our surveillance people at his estate to stay in place in case somebody comes back. He lost a lot of men. If it were me, I'd want to know what happened."

"If he was worried enough to flee, he'll chalk up their disappearance to whatever he's running from. He's not coming back. We need to let those surveillance people get home to their families."

"What about Damien's staff? The people who come in to maintain the grounds? The people who take care of the animals? If they show up, they might have an idea of where he went."

Gesturing toward the TV, the Old Man said, "That's a big *if*. I don't think anyone's going to be showing up for work for a while."

Harvath disagreed, especially when it came to whoever was responsible for taking care of the animals. They'd have a hard time staying away. In fact, it was probably someone local who did it, someone in town. He made a mental note to get Nicholas on it.

Lara offered to fix him a plate, and he thanked her as he sat down at the table and watched the crisis unfold.

Though the newscasters didn't have all of the information, they had enough.

He ate in silence as he listened to the reports. Then, once he had finished his meal, he ran upstairs to grab a shower and change.

After soaping up, he threw the temperature selector all the way to cold and stood there for as long as he could stand before climbing out and toweling off. The news that the President had contracted the virus had left a desperate pit in his stomach. It had been all he could do to get his food down.

Throwing on jeans and a shirt, he returned to the kitchen. Lara was waiting there with her bag. He looked around, but didn't see the Old Man.

"Where's Reed?"

"He said now that you're back, he needed to get going."

Harvath peered out the kitchen window. He saw Nicholas's van in the drive, but Carlton's vehicle was gone.

"He said you'd understand."

Harvath did understand. "Did he take any supplies with him?"

"No. He told me he'd figure everything out later."

That, Harvath didn't understand, but the Old Man was stubborn. He was also proud. Still, he should have taken something. Things were going to get much worse. Harvath could feel it. He was glad he was getting Lara and her family to safety.

"You ready to go?" he asked.

"Am I ready? *Yes*. Do I want to? *No*."

Harvath reached out and pulled her close to him. "You're going to be okay. Jon and Anya are going to take good care of you."

"We don't need taking care of."

He smiled. "I'll be out there as soon as I can."

She tried to smile back, but it came off looking as forced as it felt.

"Hey," he said, lifting her chin. "We're all going to be okay. I promise you."

He thought she was moving in to kiss him, but instead she buried her face in his shoulder.

They stood there like that for several moments, and he wondered if she was crying. When she finally pulled away, she turned so he couldn't see her face.

"I want to say goodbye to Nicholas," she stated, walking toward the front door.

"I'll put your bag in the Tahoe," he replied, watching her go.

Reaching the entry hall, he remembered that he had left something in his study and jogged down the hall to get it.

It was a children's woodworking kit, a present he had purchased for Marco. He had intended to give it to Lara on their fall colors trip.

Returning to the entry hall, he slipped it inside her suitcase and stepped outside.

Nicholas was standing outside his van, the dogs at his side, chatting with Lara. He watched as she bent down and gave him a long hug and then scratched each of the dogs behind their ears. He let them enjoy their moment before stepping out of the house and walking over to his SUV.

"All good?" he asked.

Lara turned and smiled, her eyes moist. "All good."

He looked at Nicholas. "How about Nina?"

"She just got picked up. She'll probably arrive at Reagan right about the same time you do."

"I'll give her a hug for you," Lara stated.

"Thank you," Nicholas replied. Then, jerking his thumb over his shoulder toward the inside of his van, he added, "I've got to get back to work."

The two hugged once more, and as Lara walked over to get in Harvath's SUV, Harvath added another item to Nicholas's to-do list—tracking down any of the staff that worked at Damien's estate.

Rolling out of his driveway, he activated the "avoid traffic" feature on his GPS and then tuned his radio to WMAL.

Iconic D.C. broadcaster Larry O'Connor was calmly breaking down the story, but he followed his analysis with one chilling question, "If the President of the United States couldn't be protected from the virus, how could anyone else hope to be?"

It was the right question to ask, and the answer was simple—no one was safe. A panic like nothing before was rapidly consuming the United States, and with it, the rest of the world.

CHAPTER 49

Once Harvath had said goodbye and knew Lara was safely on her way to the plane, he felt a sense of relief. It was just one last thing he had to worry about.

Stepping back inside the Signature Flight Support building, he looked at the text Nicholas had sent him out on the tarmac and tapped the icon to call him.

"Are you positive about this?" he asked when the little man answered.

"One hundred percent."

"How long do I have?"

"Could be hours. Could be days. What are you going to do?"

"What would you do?" Harvath asked.

"Get my affairs in order and hope it's painless."

Harvath chuckled at the idea of a DHS Team coming to forcibly take him into custody. "Very funny. I thought you said whoever is running the Main Core database was good. You even called them *sophisticated*. How do you know we're not being played?"

"Because as good as they are, I'm better."

"But they still caught you in their database," said Harvath, weaving his way through the crush of people.

"Something that will not happen again, believe me."

"And how do you know they didn't find your malware?"

"Because," replied Nicholas, "it would be like trying to pick up a water balloon, in the dark, with a pair of razor blades. It wasn't designed to turn on until they activated Main Core. Trust me, they didn't find my malware. The information we're getting from their servers is legit."

Harvath still found it hard to believe that they were going through with it. "Who authorized it? Linda Landon couldn't have ascended this fast. Could she?"

"Maybe she doesn't have to pull the trigger herself. All she has to do is convince someone else to."

That was a possibility Harvath hadn't considered.

"Is Nina on the plane?" Nicholas asked, changing the subject.

"I haven't seen her, but the parking lot is a mob scene. What about tracking down Damien's staff from Clifton? Any luck?"

"It took a lot of work, but I was able to speak to the vet they use, and he in turn put me in touch with Damien's farm manager who lives two towns over."

"What did you tell them?"

"I told them that I had a bunch of feedstock that Damien had ordered, and that I didn't know if he wanted it delivered to Clifton or to his other location."

"What other location?" asked Harvath.

"*Exactly,*" Nicholas replied. "Neither of them knew of any other location beyond his houses and apartments overseas."

"What about a housekeeper or landscaping service?"

"The farm manager said that his wife cleaned the house, and that his team maintained the grounds."

"So it's a dead end."

"Sure seems like it," Nicholas said, adding, "What's your plan? Do I wait around here for you, or should I get out before DHS shows up?"

It was a good question.

Harvath had no intention of letting the Department of Homeland Security take him into custody. He was going to have to go to ground. That meant he couldn't go home, he couldn't go to the office, and he would have to avoid any friends or known associates. He would also have to shed his ATM and credit cards, all of his electronics, and his vehicle. However long it lasted, it was going to be a very dangerous pain in the ass.

Part of him thought very seriously of just turning around and getting on the plane with Lara right now. It had already stopped in Boston and had picked up her parents and Marco. He could have Nicholas hightail it down here, and as soon as he and Nina had arrived, they could all take off for Alaska. Harvath's mother was already en route for Anchorage. They would connect there and disappear into the wild. It couldn't be any easier.

He was truly tempted to let it all burn to the ground. Maybe that's what this town needed—a massive reset. Maybe that was the only way to get things moving again, to clean all of the gunk out of the fuel lines.

Then he could come back after and help start over, help rebuild. Or maybe he wouldn't. They could all just stay in Alaska. He had never thought that far ahead. He had never actually thought things could get that bad.

But even if he had, he knew he would still have to be here—right in the fight. It was who he was. It was where he belonged. He cared too much to turn his back. When things were at their worst was when you knew who you were and who the people around you were. *The only easy day was yesterday.*

Harvath had made his decision. Now, he had to decide what he was going to do next.

Like it or not, DHS was going to come for him. And at this point, it didn't matter who had put him on the list—only that he was on it.

And while Nicholas had said it could be anywhere from days to hours, Harvath had to imagine they were going to move on him quickly. From the screen grabs Nicholas had taken, he had been coded for arrest and placed in the highest-risk category. When they took him down, they were going to take him down hard. There would be no reasoning with whoever it was. They would come prepared for him to resist and would therefore employ overwhelming force. But then what?

What happened once they had him? Would he be hidden away somewhere and left until he succumbed to the virus? Or did they have something worse than that planned? He didn't intend to find out.

"Lock up for me," Harvath said, "and get out of there."

"Will do. Where are we going?"

"Where DHS won't be able to touch us."

"Where's that?"

"Camp Peary."

• • •

On a good day, the drive from Reagan National to Camp Peary was two hours. Today wasn't a good day. Not by a long shot.

Leaving the Signature Flight Support building, Harvath had seen one of the Carlton Group's best operatives, Lee Gregory, shepherding Nina through the sea of cars and people in the parking lot. He was a big, tough guy with a lot of experience. The Old Man had sent the right person to pick her up. No matter what happened, nothing would stop him from getting Nina onto that plane.

They chatted briefly, before Harvath said goodbye to Nina and thanked Gregory for bringing her down. Lee had a family of his own and was probably anxious to get home to them.

Exiting the parking lot, Harvath walked up the road to his Tahoe and hopped in. There was a little diner on the Richmond Highway in Tappahannock, about halfway to Camp Peary. He and Nicholas would meet there and ditch his SUV near one of the docks on the river.

Before ending their call, he had asked Nicholas to tape a note to his front door that read MEET ME AT THE BOAT. He had no idea if it would throw DHS off his trail or not. But if it did, it would be worth it.

After abandoning Harvath's Tahoe, they would drive the rest of the way in Nicholas's van. It was too valuable and too useful a piece of equipment to leave behind.

When he turned WMAL back on, the Vice President's speech was already in progress.

"... your prayers for President Porter, and his family, who we trust will make a full and complete recovery. This evening, per Section 3 of the Twenty-fifth Amendment to the United States Constitution, President Porter transmitted a written declaration to the President pro tempore of the Senate and the Speaker of the House of Representatives that he is temporarily unable to discharge the powers and duties of the office of the Presidency.

"Until such time as President Porter is once again capable of executing his duties, I shall serve as Acting President of

the United States. In this capacity, and in order to better assist
state and Federal authorities, I am declaring a state of national
emergency.

"Together with the Department of Health and Human Services and the Centers for Disease Control and Prevention, I am
asking for the cooperation of all Americans over the next several
days. All public gatherings such as concerts, sporting events, and
conventions are hereby temporarily suspended. Schools will be
temporarily closed, and we are asking churches to also temporarily suspend services. If you don't have to leave your home, don't.
Only by slowing this virus can we hope to stop it.

"I have spoken with all of the country's governors who will be
mobilizing their National Guard forces to help maintain order and
deliver aid and assistance to those who need it.

"We have experts working around the clock and they are in
touch with their colleagues around the world. From Beijing to
Baltimore, the brightest scientific and medical minds on the planet
are doing all they can to find a way to halt this virus in its tracks.

"During this time, you can do your part by staying indoors
and cooperating with your local and state authorities. Please be
mindful of the burden on first responders, and do not call 911 or
approach your local hospital unless it is a life or death situation.
Every minute hospital or emergency response personnel spend on
non-life-threatening issues is a minute denied a heart attack or severely injured patient.

"These are trying times for America, but America has faced trying times before. We have always prevailed in the past and we will
prevail again. I know this because—"

The old school telephone ringtone belonging to the Old Man began
sounding and Harvath turned down the radio.

"I need you to turn around," Carlton said.

"Turn around?"

"Yeah, I need you to go back home."

Did Harvath hear that right? Home?

"Listen," Carlton continued, "this isn't a revolution. It's a goddamn coup."

"But the Vice President was just—"

"That was recorded hours ago. They've already activated the continuity of government plan and evacuated people out of D.C. to Mount Weather."

Harvath was familiar with the Mount Weather Emergency Operations Center. Located in the Blue Ridge Mountains about fifty miles from Washington, D.C., it was one of the bug-out locations for the United States Government in times of national emergency.

In the aftermath of the 9/11 attacks, key members of the administration and Congress had been relocated there in order to assure that the government continued to function.

It was also FEMA's base of operations and housed the control node for the nationwide, Federal Emergency Alert System, which allowed the government to interrupt television and radio broadcasts in order to transmit emergency messages.

Run by FEMA's parent agency, the Department of Homeland Security, the facility resembled a small college campus sitting on just over four hundred fenced-and-barbed-wired acres. Right underneath it was a sprawling six-hundred-thousand-square-foot, reinforced concrete complex designed to withstand multiple nuclear strikes. It was provisioned with air purifiers, water access, electricity, and enough food, medicine, and supplies to keep hundreds of people alive for years.

Most interesting of all, was that Mount Weather was less than fifteen miles from Pierre Damien's estate.

It would have been an incredible coincidence, if only Harvath believed in coincidences. People in his line of work who did usually ended up dead pretty fast.

"The Vice President spiked a fever on the helicopter on the way out," Carlton continued. "He threw up twice, a source tells me, before they even touched down."

"Where's is he now?" Harvath asked.

"The Mount Weather Infirmary under quarantine."

"Have they passed the baton to the Speaker of the House?"

"He's sick too, and so is the President pro tempore of the Senate. They're both in D.C. area hospitals, along with the goddamn Secretary of State."

Harvath was floored. He remembered Mordechai's comment about Presidential succession if the virus moved fast enough. "So who's in charge?"

"Unless he has magically taken ill in the last five minutes," Carlton replied, "Dennis Fleming, the Secretary of the Treasury."

"I can't believe it."

"And guess who's running things at Mount Weather?"

"Linda Landon," said Harvath, not wanting it to be true, but knowing it was.

"Correct."

"But what does any of this have to do with me turning around and going home?"

"Director McGee succeeded in persuading everyone on that Main Core VIP list to be transported to The Farm. Everyone that is, except for Chief Justice Leascht."

Harvath wasn't surprised that a man like Cameron Leascht had refused to hide out at Camp Peary. It was in keeping with the judge's personality to stand his ground and fight. But this wasn't a legal case. This was literally life and death. Harvath, though, still didn't understand what this had to do with him.

"Where is Chief Justice Leascht now?" he asked.

"DHS has him. They picked him up forty-five minutes ago."

"How do we know?"

"Mrs. Leascht called McGee. She said a team in hazmat suits showed up and took him. When he argued, they mentioned a journalist he had been interviewed by the day before, said he has the virus, and that they needed to bring Chief Justice Leascht in for mandatory observation. They claimed it was a public health emergency and showed him the declaration the Vice President had signed."

"They're not wasting any time, are they?"

"No," said the Old Man, "which is why I need you to get back home."

"And when they show up on my doorstep to grab me?" Harvath asked. "What then?"

"First, don't resist them. When they showed up at Judge Leascht's, they brought a lot of firepower."

"They'd need a lot more if they came to my house."

"Don't be stupid. They'll be prepared for you too. They know your background."

"But why would I surrender to them?"

"Because we have to get Judge Leascht out."

"With all due respect," Harvath replied, "he had his chance. Why risk it now?"

"Because symbolism is important," said Carlton. "As Chief Justice, Leascht is the highest judicial officer in the nation. People know him; they respect him, and he has more gravitas than the Secretary of the Treasury and all the Congressmen and Senators combined. He's someone the nation will rally behind."

"Are we still talking about a coup? Because it sounds to me like we're moving into the realm of a revolution?"

"If we can't stop this coup, we need to be thinking about what we do next, how we take back the country. No matter what happens, the nation needs Leascht."

Once again, the Old Man was demonstrating his penchant for thinking several steps ahead.

"So, I get detained," Harvath relented, "and then what? I have to concoct some sort of jailbreak?"

"No," said Carlton. "I have a better plan."

CHAPTER 50

W
hen the DHS team knocked on his door several hours later, it went down exactly as Chief Justice Leascht's wife, Virginia, had described their own encounter.

The team was polite but firm. In case there was any doubt as to the seriousness of their visit, they brought a lot of backup. They were extremely well armed and had brought along two armored personnel vehicles. And though he couldn't see them, he sensed at least two snipers out in the darkness.

It would have been a good fight. Hell, it would have been a great fight, but Carlton had been absolutely clear—no resistance.

Their ruse was very convincing. They even took his vitals and conducted a brief intake survey. It was designed, as best he could tell, for two reasons.

The first was to gain his cooperation—*we're from the government and we're here to help you.* The second was to put on a show for the neighbors—*he must be sick, that's why they came to take him.*

Using a public health crisis as cover for rounding up the people you wanted out of the way was clever. It certainly showed a lot more imagination than just pulling them out of their homes and shooting them in the head. If for no other reason, they got points for style. They even brought an ambulance and in doing so had answered one of his most pressing questions—was he immune? There was no reason to go to all of this trouble if he wasn't.

The same could be said for Chief Justice Leascht, as well as the members of Congress who had suddenly popped up on the new Main Core list. You didn't expend these kinds of resources on people likely to die in the worst global pandemic in history.

But if the people on the Main Core list were immune, how did that happen? Why them and not the President and so many others? He had raised that question with Carlton, as well the question of whether Pierre Damien had fled to Mount Weather. The Old Man was doing all he could to figure out both.

As if there was any doubt that the ambulance was only part of the charade, soon after leaving Bishop's Gate, their convoy pulled off Mount Vernon Memorial Highway into the parking lot for Grist Mill Park, where a DHS Astar helicopter sat waiting. He had wondered how they were going to maneuver through so much heavy traffic in order to get him to the transit point. Now he had his answer.

When they were taking his vitals, Harvath had asked one of the hazmat-suited men where they were planning on transporting him. "Fort A.P. Hill," he replied.

"Why?" Harvath had asked. "What's at Fort A.P. Hill?"

"The hospitals are being overwhelmed. A wellness center has been established there."

Wellness center, my ass, Harvath had thought. It was an internment camp.

While Carlton's contact inside DHS didn't know anything about Main Core, he did know that FEMA had identified a list of potentially infected citizens who were going to be sent to a supposed field hospital at Fort A.P. Hill, seventy-five miles south of D.C.

When asked how they were going to get there, his contact had explained that they would be going by train from Union Station once the first wave had been assembled.

Harvath was escorted out of the ambulance and handed over to another hazmat-suited crew sitting on board the helicopter.

As the helo lifted off, he looked down onto the phalanx of DHS vehicles already streaming out of the parking lot, onto the next name on their list. He wondered how many other teams there were at this very moment, doing the exact same thing in every state throughout the country. How many other "wellness centers" were out there?

The streets and highways leading in and out of D.C. were jammed-up rivers of red brake lights as people fled the city or fought to get home. From this elevation, Harvath could see that several fires had broken out. There were too many of them to be accidental. The thin veneer of civilization was stripping away. Looting had begun.

The helicopter landed in front of Union Station. Traffic had been blocked off and barricades erected. Thousands of angry people were attempting to push through. There were families with small children, the elderly. A group of young men had already breached one barricade and were helping lift a man in a wheelchair over it. D.C. and Amtrak Police were overwhelmed. It was a tinderbox and now matches were being struck.

Four uniformed DHS officers with heavy Kevlar vests, respirators, and latex gloves met the helicopter. As soon as they had cleared the rotors, Harvath was told to put his arms out so they could pat him down.

Yelling above the roar of the idling helicopter, one officer shouted to him, "Where's your paperwork?"

Harvath just looked at him.

"*Your paperwork,*" the man repeated. "Where are your papers?"

Realizing Harvath had no idea what he was talking about, the officer ran back to the helicopter and banged on the copilot's door before they could take off.

Returning with a sheaf of documents, the officer nodded to his colleagues, and they led Harvath inside.

A flow of civilians was being let in, but only if they already held a ticket or a train reservation. They were kept well away from DHS activities.

A long folding table had been set up. Sitting behind it were more DHS officers, masked and gloved.

"Harvath, Scot Thomas," said the lead DHS officer as he handed over the paperwork. "One *T* in *Scot.*"

The corpulent, ruddy-complexioned officer behind the table accepted the documents and then pointed a temperature gun at Harvath's head to get a reading.

"Ninety-eight point six," he said, not even making eye contact.

Harvath's temperature had dropped back down. Considering how much physical activity he had been engaged in earlier, he hadn't been surprised to see it slightly elevated previously.

"Any symptoms?" the man continued.

"Any symptoms of what?" Harvath replied.

"Muscle aches, headaches, chills, vomiting, or diarrhea?"

"No. There's nothing wrong with me. What's going on?"

"You had contact with a known infected. You're being transported to a FEMA wellness center for observation."

"What's a wellness center?"

"I don't know," said the officer.

"For how long?"

"I don't know."

"Do you at least know who I was exposed to?"

The officer leafed through the paperwork. "It looks like somebody at your office."

"Who?"

"I don't know."

"Well, if it's someone from my office, does that mean everybody I work with is going to this wellness center too?"

"I don't know," the man repeated. He then made a couple notes on the paperwork, reached into a box behind him, and removed an oversized campaign style button with a bright blue square in the middle. "Put this on."

"What is it? Wait, don't tell me, *you don't know*."

"You're a smartass, huh?" he asked, finally looking Harvath in the eye.

Smiling at him, Harvath replied, "I don't know."

"Get him out of here," the officer snapped, before shouting, "Next!"

Harvath and his entourage had made it only about twenty feet away from the table when the fat processing officer yelled for them to wait and came trundling up behind them. He was already out of breath.

"I gave you the wrong button," he said, pointing to the one on Harvath's chest. "Give that to me."

Harvath unpinned it and handed it over.

"This is yours," he said, slapping the new button into Harvath's hand and waddling away.

Harvath turned it over. In place of the blue square, he now had a gold star.

"What's this mean?" he asked one of the DHS officers standing next to him.

"Stop asking questions and put it on," the man replied.

Harvath did as he was told.

No sooner had he pinned on the new button than the DHS team made an abrupt left turn and took him toward a completely different part of the train station.

CHAPTER 51

Amtrak's ClubAcela lounge had been turned into a high-security, makeshift holding area. There were no windows, it had its own bathrooms, and its limited exits were all covered by heavily armed agents in black tactical gear like those who had shown up to collect him at his house. Harvath looked, but didn't recognize any of them.

DHS, like every other Federal agency, was a mixed bag of the good, the bad, and the indifferent. He was certain that these men had no idea what Main Core was and the unwitting role they were playing in its implementation. The fact that they were even still at their posts as the virus raged around them spoke volumes about their dedication and professionalism.

After being checked in at the front desk, Harvath was told to help himself to food, water, or coffee. When the train was ready, an announcement would be made. Harvath asked when that might be and of course, the response was "I don't know."

He poured himself a cup of coffee and slowly took in the room. Everyone else was wearing the same gold stars. There were a few women, but the crowd was predominantly male. Some were chatting and seemed to know each other. Others seemed to want to keep to themselves. There was a wide range of ages and colors. Harvath found Chief Justice Cameron Leascht toward the back, reading a newspaper, one of the ones trying to keep to himself.

"Judge Leascht?" Harvath asked as he approached.

The man folded the corner of his paper down long enough to examine the stranger, before returning to his article.

Harvath took the seat next to him. "Director McGee sent me."

Slowly, he turned his head and looked at Harvath.

"Mrs. Leascht called him as soon as you were taken away."

"Is that so?"

"Yes, sir."

"How do I know that you aren't part of all this?" Leascht asked, pointing at the room with his chin.

"You don't. You're going to have to trust me."

"And why should I trust you?"

"For two reasons," Harvath replied. "One, it's my people who discovered the Main Core list McGee warned you about. And two, Mrs. Leascht is waiting for you nearby, and I'm going to get you out of here."

He now had the judge's full attention. "Where are we going?"

"Where I wish you would have gone to begin with. Camp Peary."

The Chief Justice put his paper down. "What's the plan?"

Harvath was silent for a moment. "We're still working on it, but when I say it's time to go, stick close and do everything I tell you."

The judge began laughing.

"What?" Harvath asked.

"For the last several hours, I've been kicking myself for not listening to Bob McGee *and* praying for the Cavalry to come. But as I pictured them bursting through those doors, 'We're still working on the plan' wasn't what I thought they'd say."

Harvath instantly liked Leascht. "What would you want them to say?"

"I don't know," the judge replied. "Something from the movies like 'Navy SEALs, we're here to get you out.' "

Now it was Harvath's turn to laugh.

"What?" Leascht asked.

Harvath winked at him.

"You're a SEAL?"

"And I'm here to get you out. By the way, that movie was filled with inaccuracies."

"What was wrong with it?"

"For starters, SEALs are much better looking."

Leascht smiled and Harvath was glad that he had kept his sense of humor. Extracting a panic-stricken hostage was a nightmare. If the Chief Justice could continue to keep his spirits up and along with them, his wits, then that would help tilt the odds in their favor.

The judge hadn't eaten, so Harvath prepared a plate of sandwiches and returned with a couple bottles of water. As he ate, Harvath filled him in on everything they had learned so far.

"*Salus populi suprema lex esto,*" Leascht said. "Cicero. The good of the people should be the supreme law."

"*Inter arma enim silent leges,*" Harvath replied, reciting a familiar Latin phrase. "In times of violence, the law falls mute."

Leascht shook his head. "In times of violence, the law *remains* mute. Silence too often helps give rise to violence. As Dietrich Bonhoeffer said, 'Silence in the face of evil is itself evil. Not to speak is to speak. Not to act is to act.' "

Harvath was about to reply, when the overhead speaker crackled to life and the "Gold Stars" were alerted to the departure of their train.

Harvath looked at Judge Leascht. "It's time to act."

•　•　•

Moving down the platform, Harvath's head was on a swivel. He took in the position of every guard, every would-be passenger.

Some passengers seemed unconcerned about what might await them and continued to chat amiably. Others shuffled slowly, subconsciously resigned to what could lay ahead.

He counted the columns as they passed each one by. It was the correct platform, so it should be any moment now.

As he caught sight of the designated column, Harvath began to slow. He bent at the waist as if he was in pain.

"Are you okay?" Judge Leascht asked.

"Get ready," Harvath said. "Stay behind me. Move when I move."

Leascht nodded.

Nearing the column, Harvath made ready. Anywhere else, he would have felt like he had this under control. Headshots. Pop them and drop them. But not here, not DHS officers. They were not his enemy. These were good men and women just doing their job. Linda Landon, though, was another story. He would have no compunction about killing her. He'd kill her and Pierre Damien in a heartbeat, but none of these officers deserved to die. He hoped they felt the same way about him.

Reaching the designated column, Harvath paused, feigning nausea. He leaned against a garbage can, pushed back its flap, and prepared to get sick. The judge put a comforting hand on his back.

As soon as Harvath's fingers touched the inside of the lid, he swore. *Where was the rest of it?* He was supposed to exfil the Chief Justice of the United States Supreme Court with only two smoke grenades? *There had to be more.*

Dropping his hands, he realized the weapon he had requested was sitting right there, beneath a layer of newspaper. It was inside a styrofoam take-out container along with four loaded magazines.

He shoved the spare mags into his pocket and charged the weapon. He counted at least six uniformed DHS agents and four tactical officers along the platform.

Looking up at the judge, he said, "Ready?"

"Ready," Leascht replied.

Pulling the pins from the smoke grenades, Harvath tossed them in opposite directions and then leapt off the platform onto the tracks. Leascht was right behind him. He was much older than Harvath, but he moved fast enough.

They jumped onto the next platform and into a waiting train. Activating the emergency switch on the opposite doors, Harvath helped Leascht down onto the track area, and they kept moving.

Over the noise of the trains, he could hear men shouting. They were somewhere behind them and closing.

Harvath and Leascht crossed another platform and then another. When they came to the next train, they got on. But instead of opening up the opposite doors and jumping down again, they moved through the cars, parallel to the tracks.

Harvath removed his coat and had Leascht do the same, stuffing them down into a garbage can. He untucked his shirt to help hide his weapon.

Bursting into the next car, Harvath surprised two Amtrak cops who were doing a sweep. Their guns came out just as fast as his did.

"Drop your weapon!" one of them yelled. "Do it now! Drop your weapon!"

"U.S. Marshall," Harvath replied. "You lower *your* weapons."

"ID. Let's see it," the second cop said.

"I'm his ID," Leascht stated, as he leaned from behind Harvath. "I'm Cameron Leascht."

"The Supreme Court Justice?" the first cop asked.

"Yes."

"They didn't tell us that's who they're looking for," the cop replied as he lowered his weapon. "DHS only put out a description."

"That's because they don't want you to know," Harvath replied lowering his weapon.

As he did, cop number two lowered his as well and asked, "What the hell is going on?"

Harvath played it as honestly as he could. "Somebody in the government has targeted Chief Justice Leascht for assassination. I have to get him out of here, but DHS is standing in our way. Can you help us?"

The cops looked at each other and the first one said, "None of it has felt right. People being forced onto trains to take them to God-knows-where? I haven't liked any of this from the beginning. What do you want us to do?"

"Put out a call and draw them off. Someplace on the other side of the station."

"I can do that," said the cop.

"Thank you," Harvath replied as he moved the judge past the officers. "Give us thirty seconds to reach the end of the train."

The cop nodded and Harvath and Leascht picked up their pace. When they got to the final car, Harvath stopped for a moment to allow the judge to catch his breath.

"When we step off the train, just keep your head down and stick with me, okay?"

Leascht nodded and Harvath peered out one of the windows. The coast was as clear as it was going to be. They had caught a break with those two cops, but he didn't expect to get that lucky again. Only a fool would think that Murphy didn't ply his trade in D.C. as well.

"Let's go," Harvath said.

Stepping off the train, they saw two DHS officers running in the direction the Amtrak police had sent them. Leascht kept his head down as instructed and kept pace with Harvath as he moved.

Every time Harvath thought he had a clear path, though, he would catch sight of a DHS officer and be forced to change course. The last thing he wanted was an altercation, but it was beginning to look almost impossible to avoid. Then, they found an exit.

Facing Union Station Drive Northeast, and set into the stone arches of the building's façade, was a wall of two-story panes of glass. Pulling his pistol, he aimed high and began firing.

The sounds of gunshots and the shattering of glass sent the throngs of people outside into a panic. The barricades collapsed and the crowd began running in all directions.

Harvath grabbed Leascht, and they ran out of the building and onto the sidewalk.

They raced across the street and leapt over the stone railing onto the sidewalk that ran downhill toward F Street and the Securities and Exchange Commission.

Up ahead, he could see 2nd Street. That was where Chase Palmer would be waiting. He couldn't tell if the judge was going to make it. He was breathing heavily and appeared pained.

"Are you okay?"

"I'm fine," he replied. "Keep going."

Harvath slowed his pace.

"I told you," the judge repeated. "I'm fine."

"It's a long block."

"All the more reason to move faster," Leascht said, picking up the pace.

At 2nd Street they turned left and found Palmer exactly where he had said he would be, parked in the alley on the opposite side. They could hear sirens nearby. Palmer waved for them to hurry up.

They were less than fifteen yards away, moving down the middle of the street, when Palmer sprang from his truck with his rifle and seated the stock against his shoulder.

Harvath didn't need to look at what the man was going to shoot. He could hear the siren right behind him and see the reflection of the vehicle's blue strobes bouncing off the glass SEC building to their left.

"Move, move, move!" Harvath shouted, guiding Justice Leascht out of the street and up onto the sidewalk.

As soon as they were clear, Palmer began to press his trigger. The rounds pounded into the engine block and left front tire of the DHS Crown Victoria. Immediately, the officer threw the vehicle in reverse and backed up as fast as he could.

It had bought them some time, but not much. "Let's go!" Palmer shouted.

Harvath and the judge ran the rest of the way to Palmer and jumped in his SUV.

Palmer slammed his SUV into reverse and screamed down the alley. In a small parking area, he spun the vehicle around so he could continue forward and then headed for 3rd Street.

Exploding from the alley, he clipped two parked cars as he pulled a hard right turn and went south.

They blew through the intersection at E Street, headed toward D.

"Where are you going?" Harvath asked.

"They had to move to the alternate extraction point. Someone stumbled upon them."

Murphy, Harvath thought to himself. "We're going to need to get off this street then. It becomes one way, coming at us after D."

"Roger that," Palmer replied, pressing on the accelerator even harder.

At D, he slammed on his brakes and skidded into the intersection, pulling hard on the wheel to avoid a collision.

"I hear sirens, but I can't see where any of them are," he continued as he weaved through the traffic.

"Don't worry about that," said Harvath as they passed the Heritage Foundation and Massachusetts Avenue. "I'll watch for cops, you watch the road. Louisiana Avenue is coming up on your left. Take it."

Palmer did as Harvath instructed. When they crossed 1st Street NW, Harvath saw several blue light bars racing up Constitution Avenue in an attempt to cut them off.

"Now I see them," he said. "Eight o'clock."

"This is going to be close."

They hit Constitution and turned right with such speed that Palmer drifted into oncoming traffic and sideswiped three cars. DHS was now right on their tail.

"Make a left," Harvath ordered at the next intersection and Palmer swung onto 3rd Street.

They had barely made it a block before the traffic in both directions ground to a halt.

"Right turn! Right turn!" Harvath shouted. "Use the mall."

The National Mall was a park that stretched just under two miles from the Capitol steps to the Lincoln Memorial. With 3rd Street in their rearview mirror, there were five more thoroughfares that cut across the park in different places. Palmer didn't slow down for any of them.

They missed getting T-boned three times and left multiple accidents in their wake, dramatically slowing down the pursuit of DHS.

Harvath glanced at Palmer's speedometer as he reached for his radio. They were doing almost ninety miles an hour.

"We're coming in hot," Harvath relayed.

"Roger that," Sloane replied. "We're ready."

Blasting across 15th Street and then 17th, they passed the Washington Monument and the National World War II Memorial, and were now even with the Reflecting Pool. Up ahead, he could see the Lincoln Memorial. They were almost home free.

Palmer hung a hard left after the Reflecting Pool and headed for the Potomac.

Waiting under the Arlington Memorial Bridge was the high-speed, extreme weather Naval Special Warfare Rigid Hull Inflatable Boat, or RIB for short, that General McCollum had arranged. McCollum was one of the only people Reed Carlton fully trusted.

The RIB was powered by dual turbocharged, aftercooled Caterpillar diesels and crewed by three Special Warfare Combatant-Craft, or SWCC, crewmen.

Mrs. Leascht was already aboard, as was Sloane Ashby who had collected her from her house.

Bailing out of Palmer's truck near the John Ericsson National Memorial, they ran up the Rock Creek Park Trail toward the bridge. With their night vision goggles, the SWCC team picked up on them right away and brought the blacked-out boat forward.

Up on the mall, Harvath could hear the DHS sirens, but it was too late. Once they were all on board, the driver punched it, and they disappeared down the Potomac.

CHAPTER 52

The CIA was down two helicopter pilots due to the virus. They couldn't spare anyone to sit on a rooftop somewhere in D.C. not knowing when Harvath would show up with Justice Leascht. That was why the Old Man had turned to General McCollum.

McCollum had access to helos and pilots, but with a potential coup under way, he didn't want to send a military bird into metropolitan D.C. They were too easy to spot, and there was too much that could go wrong. And so, they had come up with a compromise.

The SWCC team with the RIB had provided the first part of the extraction. Once they were safely under way, McCollum got a helicopter aloft.

They rendezvoused at Joint Base Anacostia-Bolling, just across the Potomac from Reagan National Airport. The base's only aeronautical facility was a 100-by-100-foot helipad.

The RIB arrived just as a UH-60 Black Hawk helicopter was touching down. After the passengers had been transferred, it lifted off for Camp Peary.

When it landed at the CIA facility, Lydia Ryan was already waiting for Harvath.

"We got it!" she said, once they were far enough away from the noise of the helicopter. "Helena gave Mordechai all the passwords she had intercepted from Damien. She had them backed up in the cloud. As soon as the Mossad had access to them, they were able to crack their copy of

Damien's hard drive. They transmitted everything here just before the Internet went down."

Harvath stopped and looked at her. "The Internet went down? When? Why?"

Ryan nodded toward a waiting Suburban. "I'll fill you in on the way to the TOC."

• • •

Harvath let Ryan do all the talking, only interrupting her when he needed more specific detail on an issue.

In short, he was blown away by what they had uncovered. The fact that DHS had cited looting as being organized via social media in order to shut down the Internet didn't surprise him at all. And technically, they didn't shut it all the way down. They simply limited U.S.-based access to a key group of web sites like DHS.gov, CDC.gov, and NIH.gov, where they could control the flow of information. Blaming dangerous rumors that were contributing to panic and social unrest, they took over TV and radio as well.

The most stunning revelations, though, surrounded the virus— specifically who was protected and who was not.

Ryan explained how working with elements inside the United Nation's health organization—the WHO—Damien and his Plenary Panel were able to impact the flu vaccine.

"There's a global network of flu researchers. They all feed into the WHO. Every February in Geneva, the WHO makes its recommendation for the makeup of the next Northern Hemisphere seasonal flu vaccine," she said. "They also produce a substance called 'high-growth reassortants.' Basically, it's a mixture of the genes from different flu viruses that is given to private manufacturers from which they can grow their vaccines. But this time, it wasn't just flu viruses they were 'reassorting.' They found a way to sneak in African Hemorrhagic Fever genes too."

"So if you got the flu shot, you got immunity?" Harvath asked.

Ryan nodded. "But only if you got the special Northern Hemisphere version, which was limited to North America and Western Europe.

Damien was very specific about who he wanted to see survive. In the U.S., for example, where there's a population of over three hundred million, only about a hundred fifty to a hundred sixty million doses of flu vaccine get produced every year."

"But they ramped it up this year. If you recall, every doctor, every public health official was banging the drum about getting a flu shot. Even the morning shows were talking about how this year looked to be one of the worst ones on record."

"All of which was driven by the WHO."

"I guess the Carlton Group's 'Flu Fair' wasn't so stupid after all then," said Harvath. "I got my shot right at the office. But DHS wouldn't have known that."

"I have three words for you," Ryan countered. "Electronic medical records."

That made perfect sense. Anything was hackable.

"But the President, the Vice President, all of the people at the different agencies. None of them got the flu shot?" Harvath asked.

"They got last year's flu shot and therefore no immunity to African Hemorrhagic Fever."

"How, though? How do you control who gets what flu shot when you are dealing with that many people?"

"You said it already," Ryan replied. "A Flu Fair. Damien's person at the National Institutes for Health proposed a PR campaign that would showcase senior Federal leadership getting their flu shots early. They shot video of them rolling up their sleeves, took photographs of them smiling as they got their shots, and bombarded Federal employees with the images in the run-up to their Flu Fair where the real shots were given for free."

"What about you? And Director McGee?"

"We both had to travel, so we got our shots early from an in-house CIA doctor. McGee posed for pictures to do his part, but it was all staged. We're confident we're going to be fine.

"Everyone on that Main Core VIP list also saw a private doctor, including Chief Justice Leascht. He participated in the PR campaign, but only so far as allowing his picture to be used to encourage Judicial Branch employees to get their flu shot. By skirting the PR campaign and the actual Flu Fair, he and the others avoided their shot being substituted with last year's.

"Speaking of shots, Carlton reached out to Ben Beaman, who confirmed that everyone at the Matumaini Clinic, as well as the inhabitants of the adjacent village, had been vaccinated. CARE had arranged for the North American vaccine to be sent to them."

It explained why Leonce and Pepsy had survived exposure to the virus and the rebel commander hadn't.

"So, they would have survived the virus if Jan Hendrik and his men hadn't been sent in to slaughter them," said Harvath.

Ryan nodded again.

"So what do we do now?"

"Director McGee wants to take this directly to the Secretary of the Treasury," said Ryan. "I can't bring myself to call Dennis Fleming the President."

"Have you had any word on Porter?"

"He's a fighter. That's all we know."

"The Treasury Secretary is with everyone else at Mount Weather?" Harvath asked.

"He is. McGee is going to chopper up there, but he's coming here first. He wants you and Justice Leascht to join him. Mordechai too. They're going to patch the Israeli Prime Minister in on a phone call."

"My God," said Harvath. "Israel didn't get the good vaccine, did it?"

"No, they didn't."

"Has Colonel White at USAMRIID been brought up to speed on all of this? People who received the flu shot have to be informed that they're going to be okay. Those who didn't get it, if they stay indoors, maybe we can starve this thing of oxygen."

"McGee says first we take down Linda Landon, and put DHS back under competent authority," replied Ryan. "Then we tackle everything else."

"What about Damien? Do we know if he's at Mount Weather?"

"The Secret Service is covertly searching the facility right now."

"How long until McGee gets here?" Harvath asked.

"He's already in the air. He'll be here in twenty minutes. It's not much time, but I want you to see what the Israelis sent us."

CHAPTER 53

Ben Mordechai was in a lot of pain and didn't want to leave Helena, but he understood the importance of attending the meeting at Mount Weather. It would be much more powerful if he was there to answer questions and represent Israel's interests.

When CIA Director McGee's Sikorsky S-76 helicopter touched down, Harvath, Mordechai, and Justice Leascht were already assembled on the tarmac, waiting. The copilot helped everyone board and made sure they were buckled in before hopping back up front and confirming with the pilot that they were ready to go.

As the helicopter raced toward Mount Weather, McGee explained over his passenger's headsets how he wanted the meeting to go down. He wanted nothing short of complete discipline. They were going to get one crack at this and one crack only. The die had already been cast for the rest of the world. All McGee cared about at this point was rescuing the United States.

• • •

They were met at the Mount Weather Emergency Operations Center by the Secret Service and taken down to the subterranean complex via a secondary route. Acting President Fleming had been briefed that the CIA Director wanted as few people to know about his visit as possible.

The Secret Service had conducted a thorough search of the facility, but there had been no sign of Pierre Damien.

Showing the party into the makeshift Situation Room, the agents then stepped out. Minutes later, Dennis Fleming appeared on the large flat screen at the head of the conference table.

Everyone joined in a chorus of "Good evening, Mr. President."

"You can address me as Secretary Fleming," he said. "Paul Porter is still the President as far as I am concerned."

Fleming didn't look good. No one needed to ask him if he had been part of the Federal flu shot leadership campaign. The man was head of the Treasury Department. He had been a good leader and had set the example for the people working under him. For that, he had been rewarded with African Hemorrhagic Fever. It was incredibly unjust. There was no telling how long he had, but he had refused to quit working just because he was in isolation. Too much needed to be done.

McGee gave Fleming the thirty-thousand-foot view, hitting the high points and only going granular when the man asked.

When the CIA Director finished, he picked up a phone off-screen and said, "I want the full cabinet assembled, as well as the National Security Council, *now*. Find Linda Landon and have her standing by. I'll call for her when I'm ready."

It took less than five minutes for everyone to file into the room and take their places. All of the attendees knew Chief Justice Leascht and stopped to shake his hand. Those who knew Harvath nodded. No one knew Mordechai.

Fleming didn't want to waste any time and so immediately handed the meeting over to McGee. The CIA Director patched the Israeli Prime Minister in via videoconference on a split-screen and then gave the same briefing he had just given Secretary Fleming.

All of the attendees were shocked, doubly so those who had participated in the flu shot leadership program. Each of them had just been handed an almost certain death sentence.

Everyone wanted to know if there was a cure. If people took the correct flu shot now would the benefits be retroactive? They were questions that, sadly, had no answers at the moment.

The Acting Secretary of State, who had participated in the leadership program, but had yet to feel any ill effects from the virus, suggested the same thing Harvath had to Lydia Ryan. Israel was full of American and

Western European citizens who had been visiting Israel when the virus broke out. If they had been vaccinated, they could be instrumental in helping the Israelis.

The Israeli Prime Minister agreed and said something to someone off-camera about getting the word out via television and radio right away.

There was some back and forth with the Prime Minister about Pierre Damien and what the Israelis knew and when. McGee introduced Mordechai, who fielded a handful of questions before the CIA Director brought the conversation back to the United States and what needed to be done.

In particular, they focused on Linda Landon and the best way to deal with her. Once there was consensus, Fleming summoned her.

•   •   •

Harvath led the assault team through the pine and spruce, up the steep slope. McGee had choppered in Ashby, Palmer, and a small contingent of operators from the Carlton Group. No one knew yet how deep this plot went, and neither Fleming nor McGee wanted to draw in outside agencies.

What they did know was that Landon wasn't providing Damien sanctuary at Mount Weather. He was a man who understood contingencies, and he had established a redoubt. His fallback location was a log home at the end of an unpopulated road.

To his credit, Damien had not revealed a word of it to Landon. She had broken quickly, as Harvath had known she would. The look on her face when she walked into the room and saw Judge Leascht told everyone that she was guilty.

And while Damien had been smart enough not to reveal the existence of his bolt-hole, he had established windows during which he and Landon could communicate via the encrypted cell phone he had given her.

When he popped up, he didn't stay up for long. It wasn't until the third window that the NSA nailed his location.

Secretary Fleming knew Harvath only by his call sign and reputation.

He had been present in a briefing once where Harvath's exploits in Pakistan had been discussed. He knew President Porter thought very highly of him and so gave his blessing for Harvath to lead the team charged with going after Damien.

"How does this work?" he had asked. "Do I need to give you specific instructions? A list of dos and don'ts?"

"It is actually better if you just let me go and do what I have been trained to do."

"You know what I expect, correct?"

"Yes, sir."

"Go do it," Fleming had said. And with that, he had let Harvath off the chain.

It would be daylight in an hour. By then, everything would be over. Damien was the devil himself—worse than Stalin, worse than Hitler or Mao or Pol Pot. He was worse than all of them combined, and even then, the comparison failed to depict the horror of what he had done.

How many mothers and fathers were inconsolable with grief at this very moment, having had their children taken by the ghastly disease Damien had unleashed? How many children had lost parents, husbands their wives, and on and on?

The only thing that would come close to equaling the misery would be the guilt of the survivors. Though they had no knowledge of Damien's abhorrent plot, they had been the beneficiaries of his gruesome largess. Harvath couldn't wait to make him pay.

The first trip wire they encountered was a thousand yards out from the house. It was set at chest height so that most deer and other animals could pass beneath it. Harvath pointed it out to the team and kept moving.

They encountered two more trip wires before Harvath could begin to see the outline of the house through the trees. This was as close as he wanted to get for the moment. Damien's security detail would have night vision devices too. They needed to be careful.

After giving his team the signal to move into position, he unslung the suppressed rifle he was carrying, lay down on the ground, and crept slowly forward. There was no need to rush it. They had plenty of time.

It took him twenty minutes to move the last fifteen meters. But once he was in place, he had a perfect view through the last few trees of the back of the home.

There were no lights on. A guard, with night vision goggles, sat wrapped in a coat, his weapon across his lap. He sat so still, Harvath wondered if he was asleep.

Then, the man moved his head. He had heard something off to his right. Harvath wondered if he had picked up the sound of Ashby's portion of the team back in the trees.

"Just a raccoon," Harvath said to himself. "Don't get out of your chair."

But somehow the man sensed there was something lurking out there in the darkness, and he not only got out of his chair, he called it in on his radio. *Shit.*

Harvath watched as the man made a beeline right for where Ashby and her part of the assault team were dug in.

Congo, D.C., even the Blue Ridge Mountains—Murphy was everywhere.

As Harvath continued to watch, he willed the man to break it off, to pick up the radio and tell his colleagues that it was nothing.

Any hope of that happening, though, was dashed when the man neared the trees and definitely saw the operators beyond. His weapon came up so fast, Harvath barely had time to react. But he didn't need to. Ashby was ready for him and drilled a silenced round right through the guard's head.

Harvath leapt to his feet and gave the command to hit the house.

As the men appeared out of the woods like wraiths, Harvath had several meters' head start.

When one of the guards came around the back of the house, Harvath turned, fired, and dropped him.

There were muffled spits off to Harvath's right as Palmer took out another guard who had come to investigate. That was three down. Based on what Helena had told Mordechai, there were likely at least three more guards, plus Damien and his assistant cum valet, Jeffery.

Reaching the rear of the house, Harvath approached the sliding glass door. He gave the handle a tug, and it slid back. From further inside, he heard an alarm panel chime. *Murphy.*

He stepped over the threshold into a family room area. The house smelled musty and unused. There was the odor of stale coffee and a hint of a long-dead creature, probably a mouse, rotting somewhere behind one of the walls.

Harvath wanted Damien, and he moved quickly toward where he thought he would be. At the end of the hall was a door that looked like it belonged to a master bedroom. He headed right for it, stopping only to check two closets and a small powder room.

The carpeted floor creaked in spots beneath his boots. Pulling up short just before the door, he positioned himself off to the side and listened. He didn't hear anything and so reached for the handle.

But before he grabbed it, the door opened from the other side, and he was nose-to-nose with one of Damien's men.

Jamming his suppressor under the man's chin, he fired. The man, dressed only in his underwear and likely on his way to the bathroom, fell to the floor dead with half his head missing.

A second man who had been asleep now scrambled for his weapon. Harvath shot him too and exited the room.

Palmer and Ashby were making their way down the hallway toward him, and Harvath waved them off. Crossing back toward the kitchen, he located a staircase, and signaled for them to follow him upstairs.

The stairs creaked worse than the hallway floor. Undeterred, he kept moving.

When he reached the top, there was a door immediately to his right. Reaching for the knob, he twisted it, and pushed the door open. It was a small office of some sort stacked with Pelican Cases and electronic equipment. Standing back, he sent Palmer in to clear it.

Moving down a narrow hallway, the next door he encountered was on his left and opened onto a small walk-in closet. There were only two rooms left. One of them was bound to have Damien.

Pushing open the door to the first room, he could see that it was a guest room of some sort, and that the bed had been slept in. He was about to signal Ashby when suddenly his entire field of vision was obscured.

The man must have been pressed against the wall and had leapt out the minute he saw the door open. All Harvath could do was react. The man was literally on top of him. He couldn't get his weapon into a good enough angle to shoot, and so he snapped his head forward, driving his night vision goggles into his assailant's face.

The man staggered backward, blood pouring down his face. Instead of surrendering, though, he charged again. This time, Harvath had enough distance and dropped him with two shots to his head. That left one final door.

Harvath crossed over to it and listened. There was no sound. But there hadn't been in his other two encounters either.

Signaling the team, he twisted the doorknob. It was locked. Taking a step back, he kicked it open, and they poured in.

Like the other room, the bed was unmade, but there was no sign of its recent occupant. As Ashby quickly checked beneath it, Palmer checked the closet, and Harvath crossed to the bathroom.

It was secured by a sliding pocket door that hadn't been closed all the way. Through the crack, Harvath could see the man identified as Jeffery, Damien's valet, putting a shotgun in his mouth.

He took a step back and fired five shots in rapid succession through the door.

The valet screamed in agony as he dropped the shotgun onto the bathroom floor.

Harvath ripped open the door and kicked the weapon out of the way. This guy wasn't going to get the luxury of taking the coward's way out and committing suicide. All of his shots had been below the waist, including the valet's groin.

Leaning over he placed the hot suppressor against the wound, and the valet screamed even louder.

"That was from Helena," Harvath said. "Now tell me where Damien is."

CHAPTER 54

Harvath jumped from the ramp of a C-17 Globemaster transport plane, popped his chute, and glided through the warm night air toward the crystalline water below.

Undoing his chest strap and belly-band, he splashed down thirty-two nautical miles north-northwest of Nassau. As soon as his feet touched the water, he disconnected his leg straps and swam free of the main lift webs, leaving his rig to slowly sink. With his dry-bag bobbing in front of him, he paddled toward Pierre Damien's tropical two-hundred-fifty-acre Bahamian refuge.

Francis Francis—a British sportsman and heir to the Standard Oil fortune—had originally developed the private island in the 1940s. In addition to being an incredible amateur golfer and a member of both the English track and fencing teams, he had also been a renowned aviator who helped develop the ejector seat.

The island had played host to the rich and powerful of its day. Among Francis's many notable guests were Marlene Dietrich, Greta Garbo, Noël Coward, Rock Hudson, David Niven, the Duke of Windsor, and even King Leopold III of Belgium.

It was a tradition of hospitality that Pierre Damien had largely eschewed, preferring instead to keep his ownership of the island secret. Even the Mossad had been unaware of it.

Jeffery had given up its existence, but not without extreme coercion. There was something off about him. Though he had been in great pain as Harvath had interrogated him, he had seemed to enjoy parts of it. The man had problems, lots of them.

Those problems, though, created a psychological makeup that had complimented Damien's. Renfield-like, Jeffery was devoted both to him, and to his ultimate objective. They were a match made in hell.

Jeffery had not only conducted the torture of Helena, but had led her gang rape once Damien had fled. Like his employer, he was beyond evil.

He had been left behind at the Virginia redoubt to handle communications and to carry out any of Damien's dirty work should Linda Landon or any of the others fail to carry out their responsibilities. The men Harvath had encountered and killed at Clifton had been in the process of assembling supplies to augment what was already at the fallback location.

According to Jeffery, the only means of communicating with Damien was a highly encrypted email system that was sent via satellite burst.

None of that mattered to Harvath. He had no intention of communicating with Damien electronically. He wanted to chat with him face-to-face.

As he made landfall on the eastern side of the island, he picked his way across the rocks, careful not to leave any footprints in the sand. Once back in the brush, he unpacked his dry-bag and assembled his equipment.

Even though he didn't have to traverse much terrain, his plan had been to travel light. He had packed an H&K 45 Compact Tactical, a Knight's Armament Company suppressor, and a CRKT James Williams Shinbu knife. In and out. Cold, hard, and fast.

After lacing up his boots, he conducted one last comms check.

"Moonracer, this is Norseman. How do you read?"

"Reading you five by five," Nicholas replied.

"Current target locations?"

Nicholas relayed what he was seeing via satellite, and Harvath marked the men's positions on his map. He then signed off. It was time to move.

He followed the road from the beach until he reached a fork, and then headed west toward the clutch of whitewashed guest cottages on the other side of the narrow island. About half a kilometer from the main residence was where Damien would be housing the security team he had flown in. According to Nicholas, there was no activity. No one at that location was standing guard.

Stepping off the road as he approached, he examined a series of support buildings. There was a garage, a maintenance shed, and a storage building—all of which were devoid of people.

The next structure he came across appeared to be a caretaker's cottage and he slipped soundlessly inside via an unlocked screen door.

Clean dishes sat in a rack next to the sink, and the kitchen curtains fluttered in the ocean breeze of the open windows.

Attached to the refrigerator was a to-do list of groundskeeping items accompanied by a list entitled *Meal plans for Mr. Damien*. Raising his pistol Harvath crept toward the bedroom.

At the door, he took up the slack in his trigger and then eased it open. It slid quietly on well-oiled hinges. In the bed was an older couple fast asleep. They were not combatants.

Lowering his pistol, he retreated from the room, closing the door behind him and leaving their home.

Pushing on to the beach, he examined a large boathouse packed with all types of watercraft. An overhead winch system was used to place the selected toy onto a trailer. The trailer then rode on a narrow set of rails down into the water where the ski boat, sailboat, WaveRunner, and even a bright yellow mini-sub could be launched.

Confident that no one was inside the boathouse, Harvath moved on to the first guest cottage. The sound of the waves crashing along the beach masked his approach.

Like the caretaker's cottage, this cottage had its windows open and storm shutters pinned back to allow the breeze in. It was divided into two bedrooms, each with its own entrance facing the beach. Through the curtains, he could make out a figure sleeping in each room. Stepping around to the beach side, he silently entered the first cottage door.

Even though the man was asleep, Harvath recognized him instantly. He was one of Jan Hendrik's men who had helped butcher everyone in the Matumaini Clinic, as well as the village back in Congo.

With his pistol pointed at him, Harvath kicked the corner of the man's bedframe and waited for him to open his eyes.

When he did, Harvath raised his index finger to his lips and warned him to be quiet.

"I'm the one who kidnapped your boss in Bunia," he whispered.

"I wanted you to know that all of those people you murdered for Mr. Damien in Congo—the men, the women, and the children—they were all immune to the virus."

The man's look of shock quickly turned to something else. When he opened his mouth to yell for help, Harvath shot him twice in the head and quickly moved to the next room.

Here, another butcher lay sleeping, and Harvath repeated his drill, kicking the bedframe and making sure the man knew why he was there before shooting him in the face.

The next cottage was empty, as were the nearby toilet and shower facilities. The one after that, though, had two more of Hendrik's mercenaries, and Harvath rapidly dispatched them both.

He checked the final cottage only to find it empty. He knew where everyone else was.

Inserting a fresh magazine into his weapon, he stepped outside and headed toward the main house half a kilometer up the beach.

Halfway there, was another empty support building, which Harvath cleared before closing in on Damien's residence.

The large main house was at the tip of the island with stunning views of the ocean in three directions. It was shaped like a *U* with a two-story central structure and two, single-story wings jutting back off each end.

It had all been built of stone quarried right on Bird Cay and whitewashed like the cottages. There was also a dramatic walled pool and a paved courtyard surrounded by archways. The entire property was simple and elegant, a reminder of an era long gone.

The feature Harvath was interested in the most, though, was the external stone staircase that led to a terrace off the master bedroom and from there up onto the roof. But before he could get to Damien, he needed to get through the rest of his security team.

Two men were on a roving patrol around the outside of the house. That was where Harvath started.

His suppressor was exceptional, but he needed to make sure that absolutely no sound traversed the open air and gave him away. Securing his pistol, he drew the Shinbu.

It was 14.75 inches in length, 9.25 of which was its high-carbon steel, tapered-tip blade designed for slashing and deep penetration. It had been created for Special Forces Operatives to employ when their firearms couldn't be employed—like right now.

Using one of the archways of the open-air courtyard to conceal himself, Harvath waited for the first guard to pass, and then he sprang.

He clamped his left hand over the man's mouth and bent his head back as far as he could. Plunging the blade up and through his rib cage on an angle, he punctured both lungs and lacerated his heart.

He held on to the guard until he ceased struggling and then dragged his body off to the side where it wouldn't be seen.

Wiping his blade on the man's clothes, he returned behind the stone archway and waited for the next guard. Minutes later, he appeared. But then something went wrong. Instead of passing, he stopped—right on the other side of the arch. *Had he seen something? Did he know somehow that Harvath was there?* The only word that came to Harvath's mind was that one that rhymed with *truck*.

The man was so close, he could hear him breathing. And then he couldn't. But it wasn't because he had walked away—it was because he was about to attack.

Harvath charged to his left, but the man wasn't there. He had gone in the opposite direction.

Pivoting, Harvath sent the tip of his blade back in the direction he had come and followed it with his body.

The guard had indeed come around the other side of the wide column and Harvath's blade caught him in the lower abdomen.

He didn't waste any time. Pushing the knife the rest of the way in, he then jerked it upward, but the guard slammed his rifle down on top of it. He then swung the butt of his weapon as hard as he could toward Harvath's head.

Harvath jerked back, getting caught in the side of the face with a glancing but painful blow.

Bringing his rifle around, the guard prepared to fire. Harvath would get only one chance.

Pulling the blade from the man's stomach, he canted it forty-five degrees and sent it sailing upward.

It caught the guard beneath his right ear. With a quick twist, Harvath finished the job. *Two down, two to go.*

One guard was sitting outside the main entrance, the other was sitting near the French doors that opened onto the pool. At this point, Harvath didn't care if either of the men heard his suppressed pistol. By the time it happened, there would be no one they could call for backup. He decided to take the man at the main entrance first.

Hugging the south wing, he used the tall, ornamental grasses Damien had planted to his advantage.

When he was close enough to the front door and had a clean enough shot, Harvath took it. He depressed his trigger in rapid succession. The first two shots to the man's chest caused him to bend forward. The shot to his head snapped him backward and out of his chair. *Now, it was pool time.*

The final guard was right where Nicholas had said he would be. He was also committing a cardinal sin while on guard duty. He was smoking.

Harvath had been able to smell the smoke long before he saw the man. Sitting in the darkness, he waited until the man took another deep drag on his cigarette and then shot him twice through the head, splattering the French doors behind him. Now, only Damien remained.

While Harvath had originally considered the exterior staircase, he now decided against it. The master bedroom had too many windows, and if Damien was awake, there was too great a chance that he would see him coming. Instead, Harvath returned to the main entrance, rolled the dead guard out of the way, and let himself inside.

The home was just as he had imagined. From its marble entry floor and fixtures, to its sweeping staircase and green palm frond wallpaper, it looked frozen in the 1940s. All it was missing was Humphrey Bogart or Lauren Bacall passing through in search of more gin for another batch of martinis. Testing his weight on the stairs, Harvath carefully moved upward toward Damien's bedroom.

The second floor was decorated much the same as the first. There was a series of lesser bedrooms, all of which were empty. Arriving at the master, Harvath raised his suppressed pistol and pushed open the door.

Not only was the room empty, but the bed had not been slept in. *What the hell had Hendrik's men been guarding?*

After checking the master bath, Harvath retraced his steps and rechecked the rest of the rooms on the second floor. *Where the hell was he?*

Moving quietly back downstairs, Harvath checked the entire south wing. There was a library, a workout room, a billiards room and bar, and a sauna, but no Pierre Damien.

Coming back into the main structure, he checked the living and family rooms and then proceeded into the dining room. Just beyond it, he found him.

Damien was in a glass solarium, just before the kitchen. Several panels of glass had been retracted so he could smell and listen to the ocean. His back was to Harvath, but he knew he was there.

"Some of you Jews are more clever than I give you credit for. I have been wondering if you would come."

There was a newspaper in his lap, a glass of red wine and its bottle on a table to his right.

"Hands where I can see them," said Harvath, as he maneuvered around him.

"How many did the Mossad send? Just you?"

"Just me," Harvath replied, now face-to-face with Pierre Damien. "And I wasn't sent by the Mossad."

"No?"

Everything about the man was perfectly manicured—his hair, his nails, right down to his crisp, pressed robe and pajamas.

"You're an American citizen," said Harvath. "The United States has no intention of letting Israel have you."

"So America has sent you to kill me?"

"That depends."

"On what?"

"Whether you cooperate. We'll start by me telling you one last time to keep your hands where I can see them."

Damien returned his hands to the arms of his chair, but nodded toward his drink. "May I?"

"In a minute."

He looked at Harvath, trying to figure him out. Did he have a weakness, something he could exploit? He was very difficult to read. "What is it the United States wants?"

"An admission."

Damien smiled, and his smile then turned to laughter. "Now I know you're here to kill me."

"Why's that?"

"Because you don't know the first thing about negotiating."

Harvath adjusted his pistol, pressed the trigger, and shattered the 1947 bottle of Château Cheval Blanc next to him.

"As I was saying," he continued. "The United States wants your full and complete confession."

Discharging the weapon had startled Damien, but he tried not to show it. "In exchange for what?" he asked, slowly wiping bits of glass and red wine from his sleeve.

"That depends on how thoroughly you cooperate."

"You'll have to give me some sort of a hint."

"I don't have to give you anything," Harvath replied. "But I will tell you this, I am going to get a confession out of you one way or the other. It's up to you how painful it will be."

"And if I cooperate?"

"*If* you cooperate, then as an American citizen there are a number of things that the United States is prepared to do."

"None of which you'll tell me."

Harvath simply stared at him.

"Maybe you're a better negotiator than I thought," said Damien. "Where do we start?"

• • •

The man rambled on for over two hours, quite convinced of his clarity of vision and moral superiority.

He repeatedly attempted to explain to Harvath that there no longer would be any such thing as a United States, that the concept of the nation-state was finished.

Harvath's was a fool's errand, he stated, the wind in his sails the last breath of a dying empire. Within weeks, America as he knew it would cease to exist. And when it did, along with all of the other sovereign nations, the world's survivors would seek a new kind of leadership, a global leadership. The United Nations would then step forward and take up that mantle, and a new golden age of enlightenment, informed by a healthy respect and stewardship of the planet would begin.

Harvath remained inscrutable throughout, only speaking when he needed to nudge the man back on track.

When he had what he wanted, he returned the small digital video recording device to its weatherproof case and slid it back into his pocket. He now had everything he had come for.

"What now?" Damien demanded. "You have what you asked for. What about me?"

Harvath looked at him a long time before responding. "You have a choice. You return for a trial—"

The man scoffed at the idea, interrupting Harvath. "Where? At The Hague? Or maybe someplace more Nuremberg-esque? Perhaps the Jews could muster enough energy to have me extradited to Jerusalem or Tel Aviv. Maybe America would want me tried in front of its own Supreme Court? Better yet, let's have it in Congo or in front of the savages in Mecca. It can be televised around the world so that everyone can revel in my conviction, and then watch me swing from the gallows."

Harvath waited until the man had finished and said, "Or."

"*Or* what?"

"Or exile."

"*Exile?*" Damien laughed. "As in sending Napoleon to Elba?"

"Except you wouldn't be going to Elba."

The man laughed even louder. "Who cares?"

"I thought you'd feel that way," said Harvath as he raised his pistol and fired. "Don't worry, the rest of your colleagues will be joining you shortly."

CHAPTER 55

Secretary Fleming died shortly after Harvath transmitted the footage from Damien's interrogation on Bird Cay. The kill orders he had signed, though, remained open. When the Secretary of Defense ascended to the position of Acting President, he was unable to reach Harvath.

Moving like a cold wind through the capitals of Europe, Harvath was Death. Riding upon his pale horse, he struck with great fury and without mercy.

No matter where the members of the Plenary Panel hid, Harvath found them. And when he found them, he killed them.

When the last one was dead, he made his way from Lisbon to Malta, threw everyone out of the Solarium interrogation site, and killed Jan Hendrik. He then tracked down a case of Jack Daniel's and stayed drunk for three days.

He couldn't watch the news. He couldn't listen to the radio. He couldn't think about the future. There was no future. People around the world were dying so quickly and in such massive numbers that the bodies couldn't be buried fast enough.

When Vella came and tried to talk to him, Harvath took a shot at him. It was a warning. If he had wanted to kill him, he would have—even as drunk as he was. It was one of the lowest points in his life.

Thirty-six hours later, a priest showed up. It was as if he had appeared out of nowhere, somehow bypassing all of the Solarium's security systems and walking in.

"Jesus," Harvath exclaimed when he saw him.

"Far from it," the man replied.

"What are you doing here, Peio?"

"I've come to save you."

"From what?"

"From yourself."

Harvath began to lift his pistol, but set it back down and picked up his half-finished bottle of Jack instead.

"Do you want to talk?" Peio asked.

"Sure. How the hell did you find me?"

"A little bird told me."

Harvath began laughing. "Padre, you should be above short jokes."

Peio smiled, but it was a smile mixed with pity. He had been right where Harvath was now. Before he was a priest, he had been an intelligence officer in Madrid. He had lived through the horror of the Madrid train bombing and losing his wife. He had then hunted the men responsible, succumbing to his bloodlust. And when alcohol failed to assuage his pain and guilt, he had turned to drugs.

It was a spiral that lead him right to the very gates of hell. Death was extending its cold hand to him when a priest found and rescued him.

"Perhaps referring to Nicholas as a little bird is unfair. Let me try again. A friend told me you might need help."

"I'm fine," said Harvath.

Peio looked around at the disarray. "I can see that."

"You are wasting your time, Padre. There are others who need you more than me."

"Maybe, but I'm here now. Would you like to talk?" he asked again.

He was the most tenacious priest Harvath had ever met. "What's the death toll now?"

"On Malta?"

"Everywhere."

"It's not good," Peio conceded.

"I didn't think so."

"But there is a silver lining."

Harvath chuckled. "Really? What's that? Less traffic?"

"It's slowing."

That was something Harvath hadn't expected. Sitting up, he said, "*Slowing* how?"

"Some experts, not all, think it is burning itself out. Apparently, it was too lethal, killed too quickly. Getting the vaccinated out to help the unvaccinated appears to have made a huge difference. Nicholas tells me you thought of that."

"Somebody else thought of it."

"Modesty from a man in your condition is quite charming."

Harvath gave his friend the finger.

Padre Peio smiled. "This isn't you, Scot."

"You have no idea, Father."

"Maybe not. But I think I do."

Harvath didn't reply.

"You chose to shoulder a great burden, to do things that no one should ever be asked to do. But you did them, and if you hadn't, evil would be allowed to run unchecked."

Harvath still didn't reply.

Peio was about to say more, but decided to remain silent. He knew Harvath well enough to know that he wasn't a man to be pushed.

Reaching for the bottle of Jack Daniels, the priest poured himself a cup, sat down against the near wall, and said, "Salud" as he took a drink.

•   •   •

They sat in silence for at least an hour, passing the bottle back and forth while Harvath avoided Peio's gaze.

"These aren't the circumstances under which I usually hear confession, but if you'd like to confess, I'll hear yours," the priest said.

Harvath started to laugh, and it only built from there.

"What?" Peio asked.

"Someday, when it's all over and we're old men, maybe we'll sit together and I'll confess. Until then, keeping it inside is what keeps me going."

The priest knew the feeling all too well, and he nodded. "I understand."

"In the meantime," Harvath said, looking around and done wallowing. "I think I need to get back home."

Padre Peio smiled at him. "I can make that happen."

CHAPTER 56

T hank you," Reed Carlton said as he walked onto the nursing home veranda and handed Harvath a hot cup of coffee. "For everything."

The sun was slowly rising, chasing away the overnight cold. In the parking lot below was the truck Harvath had sent Palmer and Ashby to stuff full of supplies and bring back from Damien's Clifton Farm estate.

Carlton had promised the nursing home staff that if they stayed and saw to the patients, he would find a way to take care of them and their families. He began by going person-by-person, verifying who had been vaccinated. All of the nursing home staff had, as had most of their family members. Those who hadn't were made comfortable in their own protected wing.

With that out of the way, he had established a guard schedule. A nursing home with pharmaceuticals and a commercial kitchen was a prime target for looters.

By the time Harvath returned, the looting was still going on, but was much more sporadic. He had insisted on being added to guard duty. Their small group of battle-hardened operators continued to be more than enough to beat back the rabble that came sniffing around.

Twice a day, he spoke to Lara via sat phone and ended each call by telling her how much he loved her. He never spoke of his bloody path through Europe or his bottoming out in Malta. For now, some secrets would still remain a part of who he was.

"How is President Porter?" Harvath asked the Old Man.

"They think he's going to make it."

"How?"

"The virus has about a seventy percent lethality. They beat the hell out of it with antivirals, plus an experimental AIDS drug. It seems to be doing the trick."

"Have they shared that with the other countries?"

"Totally."

"What about Bentzi and Helena?" Harvath asked.

"They're both still recovering at Camp Peary. He didn't get the vaccine like she did, so they've also got him on antivirals and under observation. So far, so good."

"Any word from Jessica Decker?"

"Kinshasa, like the rest of Africa, looks like the Zombie Apocalypse. Very few got the good flu vaccine, but even there African Hemorrhagic Fever has quickly burned out. Your SAS team brought Jambo, Leonce, and Pepsy to Kinshasa and linked up with Decker. From what we hear, they're weathering the storm. They're doing okay."

Harvath was glad to hear that. And with everything else taken care of, it was time for him to go.

Taking a sip of his coffee, he prepared to speak, but the Old Man cut him off. "You need to get going. I've reached out to General McCollum. A plane has already been arranged for you."

•   •   •

As the Cessna Citation X jet raced toward Anchorage, Harvath tried to forget everything that had happened, and instead look forward to what was coming.

Pouring himself a large glass of Woodford Reserve, he put the cork back in the bottle and sat back down in his seat.

As he sipped his drink, he tried to let go. He had done his best. Whatever happened now was beyond his control. Like his mother had said over and over again to him, *you can't always control the situation you find yourself in, but you can control how you react to it*. It was a nice saying, though he doubted whether his mother had envisaged this kind of situation.

That said, the disease, by all accounts, was slowing. That was a good thing.

In the United States, the government had adopted a duck-and-cover posture. Every effort was being made to take care of the sick, while a quarantine remained in effect in the hopes that the virus would finally burn itself out. All Harvath cared about at this point, though, was getting to Lara.

He slept for a while, but not near enough to kill the time. After watching a movie, he tried to go back to sleep, but it was fitful.

When the jet finally landed in Anchorage, he couldn't wait to jump out of it and onto the floatplane that would fly him up to Lara and Marco.

Bag in hand, he thanked the pilots and charged down the airstairs, hurrying toward his next leg.

Halfway down, he was surprised to see her standing there, waiting for him. She had never looked more beautiful.

As he moved toward her, he was knocked out of the way by Nicholas's hounds, Argos and Draco, as they raced down the stairs toward Nina, who was also standing on the tarmac, waiting.

"Kids," the little man said as he brushed past Harvath. "They never listen."

Harvath smiled and walked down the last few stairs.

When he reached the bottom, Lara ran up to him and wrapped her arms around his neck. "I'm so glad you're back."

"Me too," he said, kissing her.

"Thank you," she said.

Harvath looked at her. "*Thank you* for what?"

"For doing what you do. As hard as it is, and as much as I may not like it, thank you."

He wanted to tell her how the dead weighed on his shoulders, how he wished there was some way he could save those who were still going to die, but he couldn't.

She "got" him, though not completely. No one really ever would. But she was better than anything he had ever known, and he loved her immeasurably.

"Come here," he said, pulling her closer and kissing her again. "Do you have any idea how much I love you?"

Lara was about to respond when his cell phone rang.

"Show me," she said.

Looking down at his phone, Harvath silenced the ringer and tucked it into his pocket.

"Good start," she said.

"Tell me what's next."

"There's a little boy who is extremely eager to see you and have you take him fishing."

"I can't wait," Harvath said as he put his arm around her and led everyone toward the waiting floatplane.

ACKNOWLEDGMENTS

My goal with each and every book is to stretch myself and, in so doing, become a better writer. That's what keeps this job so much fun—it's an incredibly rewarding challenge.

With this book, I tried to push the boundaries, and I hope you have enjoyed it. As I tell all the wonderful people I meet on the road, I work for you—the **readers**. Thank you for both your support and the incredible word of mouth you give my novels.

As an additional thank-you, and to add to your reading experience, I am always creating new material at BradThor.com. If you haven't yet stopped by, please do.

I also wish to thank all the fantastic **booksellers** around the world who turn new readers on to my novels every day. There is no more wonderful language than the language of books. When we draw each other's attention to great books, we are sharing something very special indeed.

Over a great bottle of whiskey, **Sean F.** shared a story that might have been amusing, had it not been so troubling. That story helped me better understand a certain mind-set in Washington, D.C. For that, and multiple other assists, I am very grateful. Thank you, Sean.

Rodney Cox has once again provided me with invaluable insights. Thank you, Rodney, for everything—but especially for your character, your integrity, and your selfless service to our great nation.

Every single time **James Ryan** helps me out, I thank God he is on our side. If I fully tried to explain the way his mind works, you wouldn't believe me. Suffice it to say, our nation needs more men like him. I was humbled by his early praise of the novel, and he continues to inspire me by his example. Thank you, JR.

I had been thinking about setting the novel in Sierra Leone before **J'ro** encouraged me to use Congo. The background he provided was fascinating. As J'ro is the epitome of the quiet professional, it has been an honor getting to know him over this past year. Thanks for all the help, J'ro.

Scott F. Hill, **PhD**, **Jon Sanchez**, **Peter Osyff**, **Jeff Boss**, **Pete Scobell**, **Steve Adelmann**, and **Robert O'Brien** all fielded questions from me at all hours, and they all came back with the answers I needed. They are amazing patriots from whom our nation has greatly benefited. Thank you, gentlemen, for your assistance with the book.

The characters of **Ian McCollum** (Chairman of the Joint Chiefs of Staff) and Colonel **Sheila White** (Director of USAMRIID) were so named in recognition of two very generous charitable donations. I thank everyone involved and look forward to seeing you again soon.

Code of Conduct is my fifteenth novel, and all my novels have been published by the extraordinary **team** at Simon & Schuster's Atria, Emily Bestler Books, and Pocket Books imprints. The marvelous **Carolyn Reidy**, the wonderful **Judith Curr**, and the spectacular **Louise Burke** continue to help take my books to brand-new heights. You are the best, and I cannot thank you enough.

The sun at the center of my publishing universe is my phenomenal editor and publisher, **Emily Bestler**. Time really does fly when you're having fun. We have done fifteen books together, and things only continue to grow and get more exciting. Thank you, Emily, for everything.

This year, I set the bar higher than ever before and said to my extraordinary publicist, **David Brown**, "Let's see you leap over that." You know what? He did—and he didn't even get his cape wrinkled. David, you rock. Thank you.

Cindi Berger, **Cara Masline**, and the **team** at PMK continue to amaze all of us each year. I couldn't imagine publishing without them. Thank you for each and every "get" along with all the great ideas.

I owe a big thanks to every astounding member of **Emily Bestler**

Books and **Pocket Books**, including **Michael Selleck**, **Megan Reid**, **Matthew Rossiter**, **Irene Lipsky**, **Lisa Keim**, **Hillary Tisman**, **Jin Yu**, **Emily Bamford**, the **Emily Bestler Books/Pocket Books sales team**—including **Gary Urda**, **John Hardy**, and **Colin Shields**; **Al Madocs** and the **Atria/Emily Bestler Books Production Department**; both the **Emily Bestler Books/Pocket Books Art Departments, including Albert Tang**; and I wish to thank **Chris Lynch, Tom Spain, Sarah Lieberman, Desiree Vecchio, Armand Schultz**, and the entire **Simon & Schuster audio division**.

If you found any mistakes in this novel, they are mine and mine alone. That said, copyeditor extraordinaire **Lisa Nicholas** made sure I made as few as possible. Welcome aboard, Lisa, and thank you.

This book is dedicated to my fabulous agent, **Heide Lange** of **Sanford J. Greenburger Associates**. Heide and I have been together from Book #1, and I look forward to many, many more to come. Thank you for all that you have done for me over the years, Heide. You are a superstar.

The incredibly dynamic duo of **Stephanie Delman** and **Rachel Mosner** are two wonderful players on the Sanford J. Greenburger Associates team who help me week in and week out throughout the year. Thank you, and everyone else at SJGA, for all that you do for me.

It has been a terrific year for us in Hollywood, and I want to thank my dear friend and magnificent entertainment attorney, **Scott Schwimer**. With everything we have going, I am looking forward to seeing much more of you.

Yvonne "Seabass" Ralsky helped to deliver an amazing year for our company (and even pulled in her husband, **Michael**, to help answer some D.C.—related questions for this novel). Thank you for your enthusiasm, your professionalism, your talent, and vision. Here's to some incredible "acceleration!"

I always save the best and most important acknowledgment for last. I couldn't do what I do without the love and support of my beautiful wife, **Trish**, and our wonderful **children**. The countless meals you prepared and brought to me while I was writing helped remind me of how much I am loved. It is nothing, though, in comparison to how much I love all of you. Thank you for your unfailing support and for making me the proudest husband and father on the planet.

It's time for me to get Scot Harvath and his team started on their next adventure. If you enjoyed this one, you won't believe what I have coming for you next.

Here endeth the acknowledgments. Go read more great books!